NO

WAY

BACK

NO WAY BACK

A NOVEL

MATTHEW KLEIN

PEGASUS CRIME

NEW YORK LONDON

No Way Back

Pegasus Crime is an Imprint of
Pegasus Books LLC
80 Broad Street, 5th Floor
New York, NY 10004

First Pegasus Books hardcover edition April 2014

ISBN: 978-1-60598-544-2

10 9 8 7 8 6 5 4 3 2 1

Printed in the United States of America
Distributed by W. W. Norton & Company, Inc.

For Mom

(Just skip over the sex scenes, please)

*I tell you a truth. No one can see the kingdom of God
unless he is born again.*
John 3:3

Things are not what they appear to be. Nor are they otherwise.
Surangama Sutra

PROLOGUE

How long could the victim last?

That was always the question, when he tortured someone. Over the years, he had developed some rough rules: women lasted longer than men, blacks longer than whites. Smart people lasted longer than dumb ones, rich longer than poor. He had long ago given up trying to find reasons for these apparent truths: did the rich fight longer because they had more to lose? Were blacks better physical specimens than whites, as the racists suggested? Were men cowards and women strong?

His tools varied. Knives were effective, particularly when used to amputate, rather than stab. Stabbing was messy, but more than that, it made people frantic, unable to concentrate on the question at hand. For him, torture was about getting answers. When a victim focused on the knife hilt in his gut, his answers were incomplete.

So he would chop a finger right away, to prove his seriousness, and then another while the victim still couldn't believe the first was gone. He'd leave the stubs on the floor, in front of the victim, little talismans of bone and skin, a testament to his power and their doom.

Even with his rough-hewn rules, he could be surprised. People he thought would break quickest often fought longest. The confident, muscular man – the former cop, the rival gang boss, the ex-Marine – might give up in minutes, after the loss of just one eye, or one testicle – and become a whimpering, snot-dripping mess. In contrast, the weak Jew, or the wispy Chinaman, or even the coked-up whore, might astound him, and last for hours, unafraid, stoic, dignified.

So how long would this one last? This victim was bound to a wooden chair, in the middle of a rude shack. Near him, a video camera stood on a tripod, recording the events with a dull unblinking eye. Black wool blankets – moth-eaten and horrid – were taped across the windows. In the corner, water dripped into a rusted sink. The victim's ankles were wrapped with electrical tape to chair legs, a sock stuffed in his mouth. His face was frantic, breathless – but not yet resigned. There was still more work to do.

The torturer held a finger to his own lips, and said, 'Shh.' He said it gently, the way a nurse comforts a patient. 'Now, shh. We can make this all stop. All of this can stop.'

The victim whimpered and nodded. He did want it to stop. He did indeed.

'I need to know certain things. I have questions. You must answer them honestly, yes?' The torturer spoke with an accent, which the victim knew was Russian.

The torturer reached out, grabbed the sock in the victim's mouth. 'I will take this out. Do not scream. No one can hear you. Yes?'

The victim nodded. Tears wet his cheeks.

The torturer removed the sock. The victim breathed hard through his mouth, in great gulping relief, as if – for the last hour – the problem had been the sock in his mouth, and not the fact that five of his fingers had been removed with a hunting knife.

'This is better, yes?' the torturer said.

'Yes,' the victim agreed, weakly.

'You know who I am, of course.'

More a statement than question. The victim had made a point not to look at the tormenter's face – in forlorn hope that this somehow might spare him – and even now he continued to look away. But the truth was that he did know. He knew his tormentor's name.

2

'You think,' the torturer said, 'that if you don't look at my face, I will let you live. That is what you think, yes?'

'No,' the victim said. But he was dismayed. How had the man known his thoughts?

From outside the log walls of the shack came the sound of lapping water – the gentle sound of ocean, of pebbles skittering into surf.

'Please,' the victim said. 'Please let me go.' But his voice was a whisper, without hope, because he knew now that no words would save him.

The victim was nearly ready, his tormentor knew. Hopelessness was key. Soon answers would pour forth, unbidden. A surfeit of facts, and details – so much information that it would be hard to capture it all. It would break over them both like long-awaited rain over hard-packed earth, flooding dry gullies; and the torturer would drink it down eagerly. He would tell his victim to slow down – slow down, please – go back to the beginning, and tell him again, and focus on just one moment. The first time the victim met his wife, for example, or that summer night they listened to music under the stars – please, go back to that time again, and tell me every fact you remember – every detail: what she wore, how she smelled, what her mouth tasted like when you kissed. He needed to know everything. No detail was too small, nothing that happened unimportant.

'Of course no one who sees my face, or hears my voice, lives to see the sun again. You've heard that about me? You've heard the stories they tell?'

The man in the chair whimpered and nodded.

'But there are other considerations. Family, wife, friends. Their children. Do you understand?'

'Yes.'

'I have so many questions,' the torturer said, taking a deep breath, as if steeling himself for new exertion. 'More questions than you have fingers left, I'm afraid.' He held up his knife, and laid the blade gently against the victim's cheek. 'Should I remove your eyes?'

3

'No—'

'Will you answer my questions?'

'Yes. Anything. Anything you want.'

'You must think carefully. I will ask you for so many facts! You will be tempted to ignore some details. You will think them unimportant. But details are what I care about. The smallest details. I love them, and I want to hear them. Every single one. Do you understand?'

'Yes.'

'Good.' He lifted the knife from the victim's cheek.

The victim exhaled, relieved at the apparent reprieve he was being granted.

When the next scream came, it was so loud that someone standing outside the shack would have heard it. Someone standing as far away as the edge of the beach would have heard it, muffled through the log walls – that long despairing wail of horror, rising and falling, that scream of pain and shock and disbelief.

But no one did hear that scream. No one was standing outside the shack. No one was walking on the beach. The torturer and his victim were alone.

When the screaming subsided, and turned into quiet whimpering, the torturer said, so gently that his words could have been a caress, 'Should I take your other eye too?'

'No, no, please,' the man whispered. 'I'll tell you everything. Everything you ask. Everything.'

'Every detail?'

'Every detail! I promise.'

There. Now he was ready, the torturer knew. Now the man would reveal everything.

The torturer would learn everything he needed to know. He would work slowly. He had all night.

He had all the time in the world.

PART ONE

CHAPTER 1

On Monday morning, at one minute past nine o'clock, I sit in a Florida parking lot, counting cars.

It's an old trick, the easiest way to take a company's pulse: arrive at the beginning of the business day – on the dot – and see how many employees have bothered to show up. You can tell a lot about a company from its parking lot.

This Monday morning, in this parking lot, at this company, there are twelve cars.

Twelve cars would be a healthy number for a company with fifteen employees.

Twelve cars would be an acceptable number for a company with thirty, or even forty, employees.

But Tao Software LLC – the company that I have been hired to rescue – has eighty-five employees. That's eighty-five *full-time* employees. That doesn't include contractors or part-timers – people like the masseuse who comes in twice a week to give back-rubs, or the guy who maintains the two cappuccino machines in the kitchen.

Twelve cars. Eighty-five employees.

Even before I've walked through the front door – before I've studied the Balance Sheet or the P&L – I have all the numbers that I need. They are: twelve and eighty-five. Investigation complete.

I'm conducting my inquiry from the front seat of a rental Ford, its air conditioner blasting. I study the cars around me. They differ in hue and upkeep, but what they share is the same relentless grinding economy: a Taurus, three low-end Hondas, a couple of Nissans, and a beat-up Chevy truck with dings in the door. Nothing showy, and, more importantly, nothing that indicates that the company's highly-paid executives have yet arrived.

I check my watch one last time, to make sure I haven't made a simple mistake, and perhaps arrived on a Saturday, or maybe an hour too early. I've done both those things, once even showing up for a Board of Directors meeting on a Sunday, and then proceeding to place outraged phone calls to the homes of the other board members who were so rudely late. But I was high on coke at the time, and everyone knew it, and so we all had a good laugh.

But no, today really *is* a Monday, and it really *is* nine o'clock. There really *are* only twelve cars in the lot. This really *is* the company I have been hired to save.

I kill the ignition and open the door. The Florida heat backhands my face. My suit wilts. What was once crisp wool pinstripe has been transformed, magically, into dark wet chamois, like a rag held aloft by a Mexican when he's done detailing a BMW at the car wash.

I trudge across the parking lot to a low-slung office. It is one of those nondescript buildings that dot industrial parks across America, an undistinguished shell behind which the actual dirty biological processes of capitalism take place, hidden from view. It is a building that reveals absolutely nothing about its occupant, save for the cheap plastic sign at the door that says: 'Tao Software LLC' with a swirled gust-of-air logo that, I suppose, is meant to indicate a majestic wind, sweeping aside all competition. Or it could just be a fart. Based on what I know about Tao Software LLC, I'm guessing more fart than wind.

But inside, everything changes. The reception area is chilled to the temperature of fine Chardonnay. The space is decorated like an interior design showroom. There is expensive grey felt wallpaper on the walls. Pinpoint spots highlight carefully selected furniture: a green Camden sofa; a high-gloss mahogany coffee table; a convex reception desk, chest high, gently curving across the open space like a relaxed letter *S*.

In my corporate travels, I have seen a lot of reception desks. I have developed a very general, but highly accurate, rule. The more money and attention lavished on the desk where the receptionist sits, the crappier the company, and the more incompetent the executives that hide behind it.

Behind this stylish and attractive reception desk sits a stylish and attractive woman. She wears a feather-weight telephone headset. She has long red hair pulled into an elaborate chignon. She wears far too much grey eye shadow, which makes her look like a very strung-out, but very chic, heroin addict. 'Good morning,' she says, with a voice indicating either exhaustion or severe ennui. 'Can I help you?'

From her look, she doubts very much that she can. Perhaps it is my crumpled suit, or the sweat glistening on my face. Or the bags under my eyes. Or the paunch I've been cultivating for the last five years – ever since I turned forty-two and decided that working out in the gym was a hobby for younger men.

I lean over her desk, try to get into her face. 'My name is Jim Thane.'

When the name doesn't register, I add: 'Your new CEO.'

She stiffens. '*Mr Thane*. I didn't know that was you.'

Meaning: You don't look like a CEO. Which is true. The image people conjure when they hear 'CEO' – a silver-haired gentleman with an imperious air and a steely gaze – surely doesn't fit me. I'm more of the cuddly teddy-bear type. The ex-alcoholic, ex-meth addict, ex-rehab cuddly teddy-bear type. Not the first thing that comes to mind, when you hear 'CEO', I bet.

I twinkle my fingers around my face, like Ethel Merman singing a show tune. 'Surprise,' I croon.

Suddenly Miss Strung-Out is all stutters and nervousness. 'Oh my Lord, *Mr Thane*. I didn't know you were coming *today*. I didn't get your office ready. Should I get your office ready? I can do that right now.'

She rolls her chair back and stands, forgetting the telephone cord still attached to her ear. When she rises, the phone yanks across her desk, skidding on rubber feet. The cord tugs her ear down sharply, as if she's being scolded by an invisible schoolmarm. 'Ouch,' she says. She leans down, fiddles with her ear, and extracts herself.

Finally, she looks up and smiles.

I say: 'And you are… '

'Embarrassed.'

'Hello, Embarrassed. I'm Jim.' I offer my hand.

'Amanda,' she says.

'Do you have an intercom, Amanda?'

She nods.

'Make an announcement. All-hands meeting. Where do those usually take place?'

'I'm not sure,' she says. Meaning the company never has meetings. Then again, how could they, when no one comes to work? She adds, helpfully: 'Maybe in the lunchroom?'

'That's fine,' I say. 'All-hands meeting in the lunchroom.'

'What time would you like it, Jim?'

'Now.'

'Now?' She's taken aback. 'Should we—' She peers past me, into the main office. The room is still dark, the desks mostly empty. 'Should we wait for more people to get here?'

'No.'

I walk through the building as if I'm a prospective buyer deciding how much to pay for a fixer-upper. Alas, this is just an act. I have already taken title, and there's no backing out now. And I have already determined – ten yards past the reception area – that the company now in my possession is steaming corporate turd.

But, of course, that's why I'm here. I'm a turnaround executive. A restart man. I get hired only at places that are falling apart. You won't see me at a well-run company minting money. But if you work at a company where management has taken a mental sabbatical, where the company is burning cash like coal in a Dickens novel, where customers are as scarce as July snow, then you might see a man like me walk through the front door. If you do, by the way, it's probably not a bad idea to start polishing your résumé.

Here's how it works. Imagine you are a venture capitalist who invests $20 million in a Florida software company. Months go by without any obvious success. The CEO telephones you breathlessly, and announces that a few huge sales deals are just weeks from closing. But those deals never seem to materialize. The new version of the company's software product is perpetually 'a month away'. The old version is buggy, virtually unsaleable. Meanwhile, the company's cash is dwindling. What do you do? Do you shut down the place, fire all the employees, eat the loss of everything you have invested so far? Do you shovel more money into the firm, and hope the incompetent CEO suddenly grows a brain?

No. You choose a third path. You call a man like me. I fly into the company, size it up, fire three-quarters of the staff, and try to salvage some value from what's left. It's called a restart. Perhaps I will figure out a way to sell the company to an acquirer. Or maybe I can knock a few of the engineers' heads together, and get a new version of the product out the door, and start making sales. From the venture capitalist's perspective, whatever I manage to do is better than calling the whole thing a total loss and writing it down to goose eggs.

Typically a restart assignment is brief – twelve months or less. I get paid a decent salary, but most of my compensation is what is euphemistically called 'upside'. Upside is another way of a venture capitalist saying, If I don't make money, there's no way in hell *you're* going to.

So that's the prize. If I can turn the place around, and restart it successfully, I make millions. If I can't, I make little. The job is half

Green Beret mission, half crapshoot. You have no idea what you're going to find until you walk through the door.

I hear Amanda's voice on the intercom. 'Attention Tao team members,' she says. She speaks languorously, as if the act of making a public announcement is exhausting. 'There will be an all-hands meeting in the lunchroom starting immediately. Repeat, all-hands in the lunchroom immediately.'

Despite the announcement, there's little movement – just a solitary chair squeaking somewhere behind me. Indeed, for a company haemorrhaging over a million dollars of cash each month, there's an obvious lack of brio on the floor. I see a Hispanic woman sitting in her cube, doing her nails. I pass another cube, where a young man – his back to me – is hunched over his desk with his phone at his ear, discussing what distinctly sounds like tonight's dinner plans with his girlfriend.

The office has an open floor plan – modern Steelcase cubicles and Herman Miller chairs. Around the perimeter are small private offices. Each has a window facing the building's exterior, and a glass wall facing the interior bullpen, presumably to allow management to keep tabs on the underlings, or maybe to allow the bigwigs to demonstrate good work habits to the rank-and-file. However, since all the private offices are dark and empty at five minutes past nine o'clock on a Monday morning, this inspirational message may be lost on employees at Tao.

From the entrance of the building, there's a commotion. Amanda is talking to an animated – and now rather disturbed – man. He carries a briefcase. He has just entered the lobby. I can't hear their words, but I see the man's eyebrows arch in surprise as he mouths the word '*Now?*' Amanda nods, says something, and points in my direction. The man takes a long look at me, then drops his conversation with Amanda without saying goodbye. He makes a beeline to me. Twenty feet away, he already has his hand outstretched, and a big smile planted on his face.

He rushes me. 'Hello. You must be Jim. I'm David Paris.' He says this without pause or breath, one long word: *HelloyoumustbeJim-I'mDavidParis*. He adds: 'VP of Marketing.'

I take his hand, shake it perfunctorily. David Paris is shorter than me, small-boned, with a wiry body that would look fine in spandex on a gym mat. Here in an office, wearing chinos and a shirt, he just looks peculiar. He has dark hair, ears the size of croissants, and eyelids pulled upward at the corners. His appearance is either the result of unfortunate genetics, or of a botched facelift. Either way, he reminds me of an elf.

'I'm Jim Thane,' I say.

He wags a long elven finger at me, as if I've been naughty. 'All-hands meeting? I like it! Trying to shake things up a little?'

'Exactly.'

'Good.' He lowers his voice to a stage whisper. 'I'm glad you're here. Jim. Really glad. It's time to get some competent management in this place.'

'I'll do my best, David.'

The lunchroom is twenty feet square, with three sets of tables and chairs. It's a typical corporate kitchen: stocked during a period of great corporate largess and ambition (microwave, dual cappuccino machines, cartons of Pop-Secret stacked along the wall), but depleted and worn down by tedious workday life. Several dirty, waterlogged laser-printed signs cajole the reader to behave properly: to clean the counter, wipe the microwave, empty old lunches from the fridge. There are many exclamation marks on each sign. From the look of the place, these pleas, despite the copious punctuation, have been ignored.

I go to the front of the room. The employees of Tao – the ones who have actually arrived for work – gather on the other side. There are now twenty of them. Each wears the official Software Company Uniform: slacks on the bottom, short sleeves on top. I'm the only person in the State of Florida apparently stupid enough to wear a suit and tie in August.

I clear my throat. 'Good morning!' I say loudly. I try to make my voice seem both authoritative and happy at the same time, but I realize, too late, that I sound like a drill sergeant getting a blow job. I lower my voice, try a more conversational tone. 'My name is Jim Thane. As you may have guessed, I'm the new CEO here at Tao Software.'

I peer into the audience. Not a single face looks glad to see me. The most common expression seems to be mild amusement: *Let's see how long the guy in the wool suit lasts.*

'I've been hired by the investors in Tao. My job is to help turn this company around.' I decide to leave out the part about how I was hired only after the previous CEO disappeared off the face of the earth, and how I was surely the last available choice to take the job, and how no one – including me – holds out much hope that I'll succeed.

Instead I say: 'From what I understand, there's a lot of terrific potential here at Tao. The investors in this company are very enthusiastic. They tell me there are fabulous people here, and that the company has created a very exciting technology.'

Which is half true. The investors *are* excited by the company's technology. It's the people they could do without. Indeed, if there were some kind of capitalist neutron bomb, a device that could make people disappear, but leave a company's intellectual property intact, the venture capitalists behind Tao would surely have deployed it, in this very lunchroom.

I continue: 'I know a lot of you are nervous. You see a new CEO. You don't know what to expect. You wonder if Tao will survive. You wonder if your job is safe.'

Finally, my words gain traction. People look at me expectantly. They *do* wonder. 'Well, I'm not going to lie to you. There *will* be changes. There have to be. We need to work harder. And we need to work smarter. We need to – let me be blunt – we need to make more money.'

I say these words slowly, and let them sink in. It's a simple point – that a business needs to make money – but you'd be surprised how often it's overlooked. After working in the same job for a couple of years, people tend to forget. They stop thinking about their company as a business, and see it more as adult daycare. It's the place they go to keep busy between weekends. They forget a business has only one purpose. Not to entertain them. Not to fulfil them. But to make money. For someone else. That's all.

'But there is good news,' I say. 'The fact that I'm here means that important people believe in Tao. If they didn't, the investors would not have hired me. They would have given up. They would have shut the place down and called it a day.'

Which is not exactly true. In fact, they almost did shut the place down. When Charles Adams, the previous CEO of Tao, failed to show up for work one morning, and then disappeared without leaving a forwarding address, the investors in Tao came *this* close to closing the company. It was only because I managed to run into Tad Billups at Il Fornaio, where he couldn't hide behind his secretary, and where I could relentlessly beg him for a job – *any* job – that I'm here. Tad is the Chairman of the Board at Tao, and a partner at Bedrock Ventures, the VC firm that owns most of the company's stock, and which supplies its capital. More importantly, Tad was my roommate at UC Berkley. We go back. Tad owes me.

But not that much, apparently. This job is bottom of the barrel: almost no chance of success, three thousand miles from my home in Silicon Valley, geographically undesirable, and, for any other man, a sure résumé killer.

I suppose Tad thought that, given my own colourful résumé – my alcohol and drug addictions, my gambling problem, my twenty-one-day stint in the Mountain Vista Recovery Centre – a gig at Tao might be a step up. He was right. I'm a bit of a restart project myself.

I say to the assembly: 'Does anyone have any questions?'

No one does.

'All right,' I say. 'I have a question for *you*.' I look at my watch. 'It's 9.15 on a Monday morning. I counted a dozen cars in the parking

14

lot. My question to you is: where the hell *is* everyone?'

No one volunteers an answer. I notice a familiar face in the crowd. It's the Hispanic woman whom I last observed giving herself a manicure at her desk. She's attractive, a bit overweight. I look to her and say: 'You. I'm sorry, I don't know your name.'

'Rosita.'

'Nice to meet you, Rosita. What do you do here at Tao?'

'Customer service.'

'OK, Rosita, please tell me. How many employees are there at Tao?'

'I don't know,' she says. 'Eighty, I think.'

I know the exact answer is eighty-five, but I don't correct her. Instead, I say, 'And how many people are in this room?'

She looks around, does a quick count. 'Maybe twenty?'

'Maybe twenty,' I repeat. 'So that means that even though the workday has started, sixty employees haven't bothered to show up. Maybe that's the reason we're having problems. What do you think, Rosita?'

She's noncommittal. 'Maybe.'

I lift my hand to my eyes and look around the room, like a man who has misplaced his car in the multiplex parking lot. 'Are there any VPs here? Tao has five Vice Presidents, if I remember correctly. How many of them are here?'

David Paris, the elfin Marketing Vice President, waves a bony finger. 'I'm here, Jim. David Paris, VP of Marketing—'

I cut him off. 'Yes, I know. David's here. Anyone else?'

A man pushes his way into the lunchroom. He's carrying a brown paper bag, neatly folded. He was on his way to the refrigerator to deposit it. He realizes that he's being talked about.

He says, 'I'm Randy Williams. VP of Engineering.' He's in his late thirties, with a round Midwestern face and a doughy gut. He has blond hair cut in a spiky style that's too young for him, and skin the colour of milk. He smiles, revealing a gap in his two front teeth, wide enough to ride a pony through.

15

I say: 'You're late.'

He bristles. He wasn't expecting a public reprimand. He stutters, 'Sorry, yes. Sorry. I know. I didn't think that—'

I cut him off mercilessly. This is where I establish that it's not business as usual any more. Time to light a few fires, burn the place down. I say: 'Randy, I expect everyone to arrive at nine o'clock. Not 9.01, not 9.02, and certainly not 9.15. If and when this company turns profitable, we can loosen things up. Until then, nine a.m. sharp. No exceptions.'

I pause. I look at Randy. 'Understand?'

He can't believe he's being publicly humiliated. His face turns cinnamon. 'Yes,' he says quietly.

'Now then,' I say. 'Where's our VP of Sales?'

I look around the room. At first no one answers. Then Rosita pipes up. She's smiling now, clearly enjoying this dressing down of the VPs. 'That's Dom Vanderbeek. He's not here.'

I hear laughter and gasps of pleasure from the edge of the room. People are looking forward to my tearing the VP of Sales a new asshole. I won't disappoint them.

Amanda is at the far side of the room, near the door. She says, 'Dom works from home on Mondays and Tuesdays.'

'Oh does he?' I say. 'Amanda, get him on the phone.' I point to a phone mounted on the nearby wall.

'That phone?' she asks.

'On speaker, please.'

She shrugs – couldn't give a shit – walks over to the phone, dials nimbly. In a moment, we hear ringing on the speaker. A voice answers. It's staccato, clipped. 'Yeah, this is Dom.' I've heard that voice a thousand times: the former athlete, the macho sales guy, the company blowhard.

'Dom,' I say into the phone. 'This is Jim Thane. I'm the new CEO at Tao.'

'Jim, how are you.' He says this like a statement of fact, not a question. The reason it doesn't *sound* like a question is because

16

it's not. He couldn't care less.

'I have you on speakerphone, Dom. We're all in the lunchroom, at the all-hands meeting, and we're wondering why you're not here. Since you probably have hands. And since you're the VP of Sales.'

Silence on the line. He's measuring me now, trying to figure out if this is a joke, or if I'm a lunatic. Finally, he decides on a course of action: he'll be friendly and patient, try to get the new guy up to speed.

'OK, Jim. Well on Mondays and Tuesdays, I usually work from home. It's easier to make sales calls from here.'

'The thing is, Dom, the sales team isn't exactly lighting the world on fire. So I want everyone working from the office. Every day. That includes you.'

Silence again. I look at the faces in the lunchroom. Most of the people here are low-level employees, and they've never heard executives argue. A girl titters nervously.

'All right,' Dom says, finally. 'I'll be there first thing tomorrow.'

I shake my head, for the benefit of my audience. I say: 'Now.'

'What?'

'Now, Dom.'

'Listen, at this hour, traffic is nuts. I wasn't planning on—'

'Start planning. I want you here. Now.'

More silence. The room is quiet. People are titillated. They know there's a chance that this conversation could spiral out of control, that Dom Vanderbeek could take my bait.

Everyone waits. There's a moment when I think Dom Vanderbeek might say something sharp to me, but instead he backs down. Now I have a sense of him: he's wily, knows not to fight when he's at a disadvantage. He'll wait until circumstances are in his favour.

'All right, Jim,' Dom says pleasantly. 'I'll be on the road in ten minutes.'

'Looking forward to meeting you, Dom,' I say.

'Me too,' he says, and hangs up.

CHAPTER 2

A corporate turnaround is like a murder investigation. The first thing you do is interview the suspects.

I ask Amanda where is the most convenient place to hold a series of private meetings. She points to the conference room right across from the reception area.

At first, I think the engraved plaque on the door – the one that proclaims 'Boardroom' – is an ironic joke, a small-company jibe at big-company pretension. But once I enter, I realize no irony was intended. Like every other space at Tao, the room is overwrought, designed to impress. There's a long black table, twelve Aeron chairs, a sideboard that may or may not hide a wet bar. Everything in the room is state of the art: two flat-panel video screens on opposite walls, remote-controlled halogen lighting, recessed audio speakers built into panelling, a huge whiteboard with coloured dry-erase markers.

I station myself at the centre of the table, on the long side of the oval. My message here – by not taking one of the two power seats at the ends – is that I'm just a regular guy who wants to shoot the breeze. Which isn't true, of course, but it's a CEO's job to be aware of appearances.

Each meeting lasts twenty minutes, and each follows roughly the same format. First, five minutes of pleasantries. A little friendly laughter on my part, to show that I am not an inhuman monster and that I have a heart, or at least that I can superficially simulate this fact.

Then, the important question, which I ask gently, as if afraid of causing offence: What, exactly, do you *do* here at Tao?

Perhaps not surprisingly, no one who works at this sinking ship can give me a simple and straightforward answer. Randy Williams, VP of Engineering, tells me his job is to make sure 'great software gets built'. Since Tao's new software version is nine months late, and nowhere near completion, I'm tempted to ask him if he has a second job somewhere else where he puts that skill to use.

Dmitri Sustev, VP of Quality Assurance, tells me through Coke-bottle glasses and a thick Bulgarian accent that his job is 'to make it all very very good, very very solid'.

Kathleen Rossi, the VP of Human Resources, tells me her job is to make sure Tao is a great place for people to come to work. I think, but do not say aloud, that her job will soon become making sure that Tao is a great place for people to leave work.

And David Paris, the elfin VP of Marketing, refuses to answer my question directly, but instead asks if he can take a moment to describe his 'strategic vision for Tao'. When I say indeed he can, he rises from his chair, circles the table, and approaches me. At first, I think he's coming to give me a hug, but at the last moment, he grabs a dry-erase marker from the whiteboard just behind my head and begins sketching a diagram. By the time he's done, fifteen minutes later, he has either laid out a startling strategic vision for our company, or he has sketched a nickel defense for the San Francisco 49ers. In either case, he has managed to convince me that he is worthless, and so I thank him, and shoo him from the room.

My most important meeting of the morning is with Joan Leggett. Joan is (according to the organizational chart I keep in front of me) 'Acting Controller' of Tao Software. Which means that Joan knows the one critical fact that I must now learn: how much cash is left in the bank.

Joan Leggett is a petite woman, dressed in one of those sharp Donna Karan outfits that you usually see on ambitious female go-getters on the rise. But the lines etched in her face, her once-blonde – now grey and mousy – hair, and the freckles that have melted into age spots betray her: the only thing Joan is going and getting is older.

Joan is the first person I've met at Tao who is competent and organized. She greets me crisply, sits down across the table, and slides a packet of information that she has prepared specifically for this meeting. She walks me through it.

It's a twenty-minute business presentation, but – as Joan catalogues the company's financial problems – it feels more like a two-hour horror movie. The kind of movie where you want to walk out in the middle and ask for your money back.

'Revenue growth over the past three quarters has been negligible,' Joan says. 'We hired a lot of people at the beginning of the year, to get ready for the new product launch. But the product is late. So now we have the people, and the burn rate, but no product. Which is expensive.'

'How expensive?'

'We're burning $1.4 million every month. We have $3 million in the bank. No other liquid assets.'

'So we have enough cash for two months,' I say.

'Seven weeks.'

The answer, then. Seven weeks of cash. I have seven weeks to turn around Tao. At the end of those seven weeks, I will either succeed, or I will slink back to Silicon Valley, a failure once again, having proven everyone's predictions – including my own – correct.

Joan says, 'Maybe you can convince our VCs to give us more time.'

She means I should ask Tad Billups and Bedrock Ventures for more money. I had the same thought, and it lasted approximately five seconds. I could barely convince Tad to pay for my coach flight on Air Trans. The chance of his sinking another five or ten mil into this shit hole is remote indeed. But I say: 'Yes, of course that's always a possibility.'

'Page eight,' she says. She waits for me to turn to the page. Now I see a pie chart. It's labelled: 'Expense by Department'.

Joan says: 'Speaking of burn rate, here's where all the cash goes. Four hundred thousand per month to Engineering. Two to Sales. Three to G&A. Four to Marketing. One to QA—'

'Wait,' I say. 'Back up. Four *hundred thousand dollars* each month for *marketing*?'

Joan looks at me coolly. If she disapproves of this spending, she doesn't show it. 'That's correct.'

'What the heck are we spending money on? Super Bowl ads?'

'David has very elaborate marketing plans,' Joan says. Her tone is without judgement. 'I assume he went over the details with you.'

'No,' I say. 'He discussed his... *strategic vision.*' I point to the diagram on the whiteboard behind me. Joan regards it thoughtfully. She has the sharp look of a museum curator trying to determine a new piece's provenance. Finally, she says: 'If you like, I can print an itemized transaction report. You can see where the money actually goes.'

'That would be very helpful.' I like Joan already. Super-competent, quiet, authoritative. I say, 'You're good, Joan.' What I want to ask is: How did you wind up in a place like this? But it's a question that could easily be thrown back at me. And one I'd rather not answer. So I say instead: 'Why only "Acting Controller"? Why not CFO? Or VP of Finance?'

She presses her thin freckled lips together and looks down. This is apparently a sore subject. She says, 'There was a CFO. Ellison Jeffries. He left a few months ago. It was all very sudden. I never found out why. Charles was going to hire a replacement, but he never got around to it. So I took over the CFO responsibilities, just not his title.'

'Well then,' I say. 'Congratulations. You're the new CFO of Tao Software.'

She studies me, trying to decide if I'm joking. When she realizes I'm not, her face brightens. 'Really?'

Sure, I think silently, why the hell not? Enjoy it while it lasts – seven weeks. But I say aloud: 'Absolutely. Congratulations. No pay raise, though. Not right now.'

'I understand. Thank you,' she says. She stands suddenly. She leans over the table, holds out her hand awkwardly. 'Thank you,' she says again.

I take her hand. 'Work hard,' I say, trying to sound dour and serious. I don't want anyone at the company to think I'm a softy.

'OK,' she says, and nods grimly, 'I will.'

She gathers her papers, stacks them into a neat pile, and turns to leave.

As she heads to the door, I say, 'Joan?'

She stops, with her hand on the knob, and turns to me.

I'm not sure what prompts my next question. Maybe it was Joan's remark about the Chief Financial Officer, whose role at Tao she assumed when he suddenly departed the company. Or maybe it's my sketchy knowledge about the CEO who preceded me, and his own sudden disappearance. That's a lot of mysterious departures, for one tiny company.

In fact, I know very little about the company I now run. I was so relieved to be given this job, I didn't ask many questions. A restart job in West Florida? Sure, why the hell not, I said.

What was my alternative? Running down the last six months of my and Libby's savings? Taking out a third mortgage on our Palo Alto house? Continuing my daily routine of flipping through old business cards, dialling lost friends and begging for second chances? No. They could have offered me a position in the seventh ring of hell, acting as chief bean counter for Satan, and I would have said yes.

But now that I'm here – and the job is mine, for better or worse – I might as well learn what I've gotten myself into. I say to Joan: 'What happened to Charles Adams?'

Joan's response is surprising. Her smile disappears. She looks down at the floor. Her face turns dark and troubled, as if I've brought up an uncomfortable topic, like masturbation or necrophilia.

I know almost nothing about Charles Adams, or about his disappearance. I know only the broad outlines, as related to me by

Tad Billups the day I signed my employment contract: one Wednesday morning, nine weeks ago, Charles Adams, CEO of Tao Software, vanished.

That's how Tad described it – he 'vanished'.

'Vanished?' I asked Tad.

Yes, vanished, Tad said. He left his car idling in his suburban driveway, its driver-side door open. He left his house unlocked. He never showed up for work. He left no note. He literally vanished from the face of the earth.

Now, back in the boardroom, whatever warmth I stoked in Joan when I promoted her to CFO thirty seconds earlier has dissipated, as if I've wrenched open a window to a gust of wintry December air. She looks at me warily. 'What do you mean?'

'Well,' I say. I think: Isn't my question clear enough? *What happened to Charles Adams?* I try to think of a different way to restate it. I come up with nothing better than: 'What do you think happened to Charles Adams?'

'He didn't show up for work.'

'Right,' I say. 'Got that part.'

'I don't know,' she says. She takes one step towards me, as if to sit once again. She decides against it, and instead remains halfway across the room, an awkward distance for an intimate conversation. Maybe that's the point.

She says: 'The police came around at first, interviewed everyone. I answered their questions. But they haven't been back in a while. I don't even know if they're still looking for Charles. Last I heard, they seemed to think he ran away.'

'Ran away?' I think to myself: Teenagers run away. Young girls who aren't allowed to date their boyfriends run away. High school students abused by stepfathers run away. Chief Executive Officers at technology firms do not run away. 'Ran away from what?'

'I don't know,' Joan says. But her expression indicates otherwise.

I try a different tack. 'Joan, I'm on your team. I just want to know what's going on. Any information you have could be really useful.' I add: 'Haven't I already shown you a little good faith?'

This last, not-so-subtle reminder of Joan's recent promotion does the trick. She sighs. 'Look,' she says, 'Charles Adams had... problems.'

'What kind of problems?'

She shakes her head and sighs. 'He was a weak man,' she says finally. 'A nice guy, deep down – heart of gold – but he was weak. He had a personal tragedy in his family, and then... ' She stops.

'And then... ?'

She looks thoughtfully at me, as if deciding whether she can trust me. At last she says: 'Things went downhill pretty fast. He got involved with bad people.'

My expression must be blank, because she adds, 'Not *software* people.'

'Ah,' I say.

'Tough men,' she continues. 'You know, out of place at a company like Tao. They'd come into reception, and wait for him to show up. They wore suits, but it was obvious they didn't fit. Like they were costumes. Charles would come out and greet them, and then he'd leave with them, into the parking lot. And they'd drive off somewhere. He'd come back hours later.'

A familiar-sounding story. Something I had the pleasure of experiencing first-hand, back in my gambling days. 'Did they hurt him?'

'Not that I could see. But when he came back, he was always very pale and very quiet. He'd lock himself into his office, and he wouldn't come out until the end of the day. Sometimes, when I'd leave the office at eight o'clock, he'd still be in there. I knocked once and asked if he was all right. He wouldn't open up. He just shouted through the door, and said he was fine. That he was working.'

'What did he get himself involved in?'

24

'I really don't know.'

She's telling the truth. I see that. 'Well,' I say. 'Thanks for telling me.'

She turns to the door. She stops again, with her hand on the knob, and looks at me. 'My turn to ask *you* a question?'

'Shoot.'

'What are the chances of turning this place around?'

I think about it. My first instinct is to play hero – to sit straight in my chair, puff my chest, and say forcefully, 'Excellent. We're going to do it!' That's what the restart executive needs to do: show confidence – everywhere, all the time, to everyone. To make them believe. To hypnotize them with his own will.

But I can't do that. Not to her. I say, more quietly than I mean to: 'Not very good. But we're going to try. I have a lot riding on this, personally. I really have to make it work. I don't have a choice.'

I'm thankful when she doesn't ask what I mean, but instead just nods and says, 'Yes,' as if what I told her were perfectly obvious.

CHAPTER 3

I spend the rest of the day walking around, getting a feel for the place. I introduce myself to people at random, catching them as they pass through the bullpen, or dropping by unexpectedly at their desks, or even – in one case – stopping them as they finish their business at the urinal. My introduction is always the same. 'Hi, I'm Jim,' I say, with a smile and an outstretched hand. (I neglect this last bit when I meet the kid at the urinal.) 'What's your name? What do you do here?' And then they tell me. And then I respond that I'm pleased to meet them, that I'm excited to be at Tao, and that together we're going to make the company succeed.

Despite my enthusiasm, their responses range from indifference to fear. The indifferent ones tend to be older – corporate veterans. They're outwardly friendly enough, but I can read their faces: they've seen turnaround attempts before, the parachuting CEO *du jour*, the grandiose announcements, the high hopes that never pan out. No doubt these are the ones surreptitiously crafting their résumés on Tao workstations, keeping an eye over their shoulder in case management should pass behind them. I don't resent this. As someone with a dim view of managerial competence myself, I'd probably be firing up the word processor too if I were in their shoes. It's my job to prove them wrong.

Around lunch time, I wander over to Randy Williams's cube. His desk is on the 'engineering side' of the building, near the foosball table and the Ms. Pac-Man arcade game. I ask him to arrange a product demonstration for me.

'A what?' Randy asks.

'A demonstration. Of our product.'

Randy looks at me, suspicious. Am I unaware of the company's plight, or am I cleverly testing him? He answers carefully. 'Jim,' he says, slowly, as if tiptoeing across a career minefield. 'The product isn't... *finished* yet.'

'I know it's not finished yet,' I say, affably. 'If it was finished, I wouldn't be here. Right?'

Randy smiles at this very reasonable answer, but then realizes that we're talking about his own incompetence, and so he shouldn't grin. His smiles fades. 'Right,' he says.

'But I would like to see what we *do* have. Even if it's not completely done.'

Randy sighs. He pushes back his chair, stands up. He calls to someone sitting in the next cubicle over. His lieutenant, no doubt. 'Darryl,' he says.

There's no answer. From my vantage point, I can't see into Darryl's cube. Frustration clouds Randy's face. He leans over the cube wall, plunks his hand down. When he lifts it, he's clutching an empty pair of headphones.

'Hey!' a disembodied voice shouts. 'What the fuck?'

Randy says into the cube: 'Jim wants to see a demo. Can you set something up?'

The voice snorts. 'A demo? Of our piece of shit product? That man is one stupid motherfucker!'

Randy's smile peels from his face like old paint. 'Jim's right here,' he says quietly.

'Oh.' Chair casters squeak, and a head pops over the cube like a prairie dog from a burrow. A kid – he can't be older than twenty-three, I guess – with long, stringy hair, and pale skin that indicates time spent mostly indoors, looks at me and smiles. 'You want a demo?'

'That would be nice,' I say.

'Give me ten.' With that, he's off, bounding across the cubicle farm with a merry step.

Randy looks at me. 'He's a good programmer,' he explains.

'I hope so,' I say.

Ten minutes later, Randy, Darryl, and I are crowded into a small room with no windows. There's a barnyard funk in the air, which I suspect emanates from Darryl.

We face a long wooden table pushed against the wall. At the centre is an old, unimpressive Dell computer, an LCD monitor, and a dusty keyboard.

The three of us stare at the screen, watching in silence as the computer chugs through the interminable Microsoft Windows start-up process.

'You ever think,' Darryl says, 'how much time we spend, watching computers boot? I mean, as a society.'

Randy shoots Darryl a look.

'Hundreds of man-years,' Darryl continues. 'Wasted. Watching the boot-up screen. We could have built a cathedral in the same amount of time. Or cured cancer. Or put a man on Mars.'

'I'm sure Jim doesn't want to hear your thoughts about this, Darryl.' From his tone, Randy has a clear idea whom he wants to volunteer for that first manned mission to Mars.

Darryl shrugs. 'Just saying.'

After what seems like eternity, the computer plays a friendly tone to indicate it is ready for use.

'All right,' Darryl says. 'May I?' He rubs his hands together, steps up to the keyboard, and cracks his knuckles like a concert pianist.

He types. A window appears on the screen. It's grey, undecorated, without the professional finish that adorns commercial software

programs. In plain block letters it says: 'TAO SOFTWARE –
GENERATION 2.0 – P-SCAN SERVICE – ALPHA RELEASE – SVN
BUILD 1262.'

Darryl explains, 'So this is it. At first, we called it Passive Image
Scanning Service. David spent like twenty grand on the brochures, but
then someone realized the acronym spelled P.I.S.S., so we had to throw
those out and reprint them. We changed the name, too.'

'Smart,' I say.

'We call it P-Scan now,' Darryl says. 'Want me to show you how it
works?'

Randy puts his hand on Darryl's shoulder and squeezes, in what
surely is an attempt to tell his protégé to pause, and to allow Randy to
take it from here. But Darryl is oblivious to subtlety. The younger man
almost shouts, 'Hey, dude, you're squeezing too tight!'

Randy ignores this. Still gripping Darryl, but looking straight at
me, Randy says: 'I just want to go on record and say this is a very early
alpha release. It's not fully functional, and it probably won't even work.'

'Understood, Randy,' I say.

Randy pauses, considering whether another round of ass-covering
and expectation-lowering is required. He decides not. He nods at
Darryl and says, 'Go ahead.'

'OK,' Darryl says. He speaks quickly, excitedly. 'Like I said, this is
generation two. Generation one was released two years ago, and it was
pretty good.' He stops, realizes something. He turns to me. 'Hey, Jim,
you know what the software does, right?'

Not really. It may surprise you to learn that a turnaround executive
seldom cares about the product his company makes. He's not a
technologist; he's not a programmer; he's not a salesperson. His
speciality – the products he cares about – are companies. By the time a
turnaround CEO arrives, the problem is larger than any single product,
or any software release, or any botched sales effort. The problem is
the company itself. It's like being a doctor for a patient whose body is

riddled by cancers. Concentrating on any single organ is useless. More important is to improve the remaining days, to try to make the whole last longer.

I lie: 'I know what the product does. But why don't you tell me, in your own words.'

Asking a programmer to describe software in his own words is like asking a salty old admiral to describe his favourite sea battle: surely, an account of the enemy's maritime manoeuvres, of the position of the sun in the sky, of the wind in the rigging, is fascinating only to one person in the room.

So allow me to summarize Darryl's speech.

Tao's product belongs to a software category called 'passive image recognition'. That's a fancy way of saying what it really does, which is quite simple. It recognizes faces. The idea is: you show it a photograph, and it tells you who is in it.

Simple enough. Tao Software, and its venture capital sugar daddies, have spent over twenty-two million dollars to build P-Scan. Even after this vast amount of money, the product still suffers from two main problems.

The first is technical. It doesn't work. Well, to be more exact, it *kind of* works... *sometimes*. At least, that's how Darryl describes it. He doesn't go into detail about what 'sometimes' means, or how software can 'kind of' work, but I take the general gist to be that P-Scan's accuracy depends a lot on the quality of the photograph fed into it. Give it a good photo, clear and in-focus, and it will return accurate results. But blurry photographs, or photos taken at anything other than a head-on angle, or with a shaky hand, and poor lighting, will be less accurately identified. In other words, the vast majority of photos taken by actual human beings on planet Earth will not be processed correctly. This, Darryl concedes, might possibly be a flaw.

The second problem with P-Scan – and this one is non-technical – is equally serious in my mind, particularly since I'm supposed to be the 'business person' in the room. No one has any idea how to make money with it. The product was born in the burst of enthusiasm that accompanied the rise of social networks like Friendster and Facebook. Everyone in the world was putting their private photographs online, on the Internet, thereby making them public. Wouldn't it be interesting (or so the thinking apparently went in the Tao Software boardroom, perhaps as cannabis smoke wafted under the door) if a computer program could automatically identify everyone in a photograph? That way, you could search for photos of yourself, or for friends, or for family – no matter whose camera took them, and no matter who put them online. A good idea, and interesting... except for that small, nagging problem that no one is willing to pay for such a service.

These are the main points I glean from Darryl's lengthy description of the product that he and the Tao engineers have built. After Darryl continues for some time about the beauty of Tao's latest algorithm, about how it translates photographic pixels into a 1024-bit hash, and not a 128-bit hash; about how Tao's algorithm can 'gridify' a scan at 1/10th of a millimetre resolution – after he tells me all this, and drones on for what seems like eternity, he finally turns to me and says: 'So let me show you.'

Even if the software doesn't work, at this point I feel an enormous relief, simply that Darryl has stopped talking. Randy must feel it, too, because he nods vigorously, like one of those bobble head dolls on the dashboard of an old Dodge El Camino.

Darryl taps his keyboard. Rows of small colour photographs appear on-screen, like a high-school yearbook. I recognize most of the faces as Tao Software employees.

'Choose one,' Darryl says.

'All right,' I say, and point to the screen. 'That one.'

I have pointed to Rosita, the heavy-set trouble-maker from the lunchroom this morning.

'Good choice,' Darryl says. 'Lovely Rosita.'

He presses a key. A yellow square appears around Rosita's head. The image is progressively enlarged until her face fills the screen. It's blurry, not particularly well-photographed. Blown up to this size, the image is barely recognizable as Rosita at all.

Darryl clicks another key. The image is transformed into boxy pixels, various shades of grey. As if the P-Scan software is trying to distil the most important aspects of the picture – the essence of what makes Rosita look like Rosita – it selects some of the blocks, and highlights these in yellow. These yellow blocks mostly come from her cheek and jowl, and from a series of blocks stretching across her shoulder, as if the P-Scan software has determined that Rosita's weight and width are the singular aspects of what makes her who she is. I think silently to myself that we must be very careful about how we demonstrate this product in public, particularly to women.

The remainder of the photograph fades, leaving behind only the series of yellow blocks, like a photographic signature.

The word, 'Scanning… ' appears on the screen, and then, below it, come quick bursts of text: 'DMV:Alabama… DMV:Alaska… DMV:American Samoa… DMV:Arizona… ' and so on – through the US states and territories.

It's probably at this point that I should mention what makes Tao's software unique. Facial recognition is, in itself, an old art. Programmers have been doing it for years. You can generally match any two photographs of the same person, assuming that you first tell the computer who is who. But Tao's P-Scan does not require any sort of 'who-is-who' directory. Instead, P-Scan uses the entire Internet as its directory.

So, when you ask P-Scan to identify a person in a photo, it sifts through millions of images on the Internet – from both formal sources (government driver's licences and passport photos), and informal sources (wedding announcements in the *New York Times*, magazine photos, or even private personal Web sites).

The idea behind P-Scan – and it is audacious, I have to give them that – is that any person, in any photograph, should be identifiable. Point to a photo, and say, 'Who is this?' and let the software search the Internet to figure out the answer.

On-screen, the cursor flickers as the various databases are scanned. During the search of 'DMV:Maryland', the computer pauses, and dings a soft musical chime, and displays: 'Possible Match': along with a photograph. It's a driver's licence photo of a Maryland woman, with the same wide face and Hispanic complexion as Rosita. But it's clearly not the customer service person who works at Tao, and the computer seems to realize this, because it immediately appends: 'Match probability: 48%' and resumes scanning.

This process continues through the various state Department of Motor Vehicles databases. Simultaneously, I notice, P-Scan sifts through other databases, in parallel: 'Flickr.com photos... NBC network news... Facebook.com... Poughkeepsie Register...'

It's an amazing demonstration, really – hundreds of image sources, possibly millions of images – zipping through the computer's memory, being compared to a mathematical representation of Rosita.

I'm about to comment on this, and ask Darryl something like, 'How many images can it process per hour? How many per day?' – because those are the units of time I think are applicable here – hours or days – and I am sure that it will take at least an entire day to process Rosita's image and to find her needle in the haystack of the world Internet.

But before the words can form on my lips, the screen goes black, and then two images appear, side by side. On the left, the grainy image from Tao's employee photo of Rosita; and on the right, an enlarged colour photograph from a high-school yearbook. It says: 'Rosita Morales, St. Cloud High School, Class of 2003'. It's a picture of Rosita – much younger and thinner than I know her – with neatly coiffed hair, sitting primly with clasped hands, in front of a fake sky-blue background.

'Ta da!' Darryl says triumphantly. 'It worked!' He sounds quite surprised that it did.

'Holy shit,' I say, softly. I'm not much of a technologist – can barely use a spreadsheet, I admit – but this is one of the most amazing software demonstrations I've ever seen. 'How did it—' I start.

Darryl launches into yet another description of his software, beaming like a proud father. 'Brilliant, right? Well, that was pretty lucky, to be honest, because we happen to have a lot of Florida high-school yearbooks in the database. But if you chose an employee from Oregon – you know, like David Paris? – we would have been S.O.L., because that state is insane, I mean really insane – they won't give us DMV access. They won't give *anyone* DMV access. So we're really at the mercy of the data sources. And then there's the CPU problem. The more data, the more CPUs you need. That's why you gotta run this as SAAS from a data centre.'

'But still,' I say, not quite sure what he's talking about, and also knowing it doesn't really matter. This is a good demo. Lots of sizzle. Even if there's not much steak. Sizzle sells. Sizzle gets contracts signed.

Randy looks to me. 'Jim, I just want to say, one more time for the record, that it's a very early alpha release. We only get 80% accuracy. That's it.'

I make a snap decision. 'I don't care. Let's do it.'

Randy looks wary. 'Do what?'

'We're going to show this. We need to get cash in the door. And the only way to make people sign cheques is to show them something they can touch.' I indicate the computer. 'Can we bring this thing to a meeting?'

'It'll run anywhere,' Darryl says. 'We just need an Internet connection.'

'Jim—' Randy starts, sounding as if he's about to protest.

I turn to him. Something in my face tells him not to.

'What?' I ask.

'Nothing.'

Darryl says, 'I can have it ready for tomorrow.'

'Do it,' I say.

When I find David Paris, he's in the kitchen, making popcorn. He's bent over the counter, with his nose pressed against the microwave glass, staring into the oven with the concentration of a warden counting prisoners.

'David?'

He turns. 'Yes?' He looks guilty. 'I was just making popcorn. Do you like popcorn, Jim?'

'No,' I say. 'Tell me how you plan to make money.'

'Money?'

'With our product. You're the marketing person here. What's the marketing plan? How do we actually make money?'

'Oh, Jim,' he says, with a strained uncomfortable look, as if I am a simpleton and he doesn't want to embarrass me, not here in public. 'We won't be making money for quite some time. Quite some time.'

'How long, about?'

'Well... ' His voice trails off. He shrugs. 'It's hard to say.'

Ding, says the microwave. Time is up. David reaches in, takes out the popcorn, and carefully opens the bag, mindful of the scalding steam that puffs out when he prises the paper apart. He turns to me. 'Why do you ask?'

'Why do I ask... how we're going to make money? I don't know. Just a passing fancy.'

'Jim, you're not from this industry, are you?'

'What industry?'

'Social, Jim,' he says. 'Social. Everything is social right now. It's the new thing. Facebook. You use Facebook, don't you?'

'No.'

'Well, there, you see,' he says, as if he's just proven his point. He reaches into the popcorn bag, munches on a handful, licks his fingers, reaches back into the bag, then remembers to offer me some. 'Want?' he says, holding it out.

'No,' I say. 'Maybe I'm not making myself clear. Who is going to pay us money for our product?'

'Oh,' he says, 'I don't think anyone. Not right away. But if you build it, they will come.'

'Who will come?'

'*They*,' he says, looking around the room, as if *they* might be in the kitchen.

'I don't think anyone is going to come,' I say. 'And if they do come, *they* is going to be a bunch of kids who don't have any money. You can't run a company if you don't make money. You are aware of that fact, aren't you, David?'

'That's very old-school,' he says, smiling. 'That's not the way people think nowadays.'

'It's the way I think nowadays.'

The tone of my voice registers somewhere in the deep recesses of his elfin brain. He becomes meek and obsequious. 'Very good, Jim. Very good. Tell me what you have in mind, and I will implement it.'

'Nothing,' I say. 'I don't have anything in mind. Not yet. But we need to figure out a way to make money with the product that we built.'

'Very good,' he says, nodding. 'Very good.' A little kernel of popcorn is stuck at the corner of his lips. 'I'll start thinking about that. How to make money.' He points to his head, squinting and nodding. 'How to make money... How to make money.'

He continues to mumble the phrase, and I leave him there, with his popcorn, to consider his new mantra in peace.

CHAPTER 4

I stay until six.

When I call it a day, and step into the parking lot, with my suit jacket slung over my shoulder, I'm struck again by the Florida heat. Three steps to my car, and I've broken a sweat. Four steps and I'm soaked. By the time I climb into the seat of the Ford, my hair is plastered to my forehead, and my skin is red and blotchy, as if I've spent the day working at a smelter and not a software shop.

I crank the air, and drive home.

I call it home, but I've never seen it before. When I won the job at Tao, Libby and I agreed that I would take a one-week vacation without her. I flew from Palo Alto, where we live, to our cabin in Orcas Island, just off the coast of Seattle. I spent the week fishing and thinking, in solitude. While I was there, Libby preceded me to Florida. She found us a house to rent, and prepared it for my arrival.

It doesn't sound very romantic, or very fair, and it's probably not. But turnaround jobs can stretch for twelve months, without vacation or weekends. The days last fourteen hours. The pressure is non-stop. You need to arrive at the company ready for work. It helps to have a few days of quiet under your belt before you start. Libby and I are a team, and she did her part so that I could do mine.

So I flew in on the red-eye last night, from Seattle to Atlanta, and then to Fort Myers, and went straight to the office this morning. I haven't seen the new house. I haven't seen Libby. The last time I saw my wife was seven days ago, when she dropped me off kerbside at SFO, kissed me, and told me to have a good time on my private vacation without her. I don't think, by the way, that she really meant it.

While I was on that vacation, Libby found us a house. Not a particularly nice house, she warned me – not really our style – but a house that would suffice for a temporary assignment. And a house that happened to be ridiculously convenient – just ten minutes from my office at Tao.

I follow the directions on my GPS to the house. Minutes later, I turn into a deserted cul-de-sac, and pull the Ford into a gravel driveway. I see my wife right away. She is in the front garden, on her haunches, digging with a trowel in dark earth.

When Libby hears my tyres pop the gravel, she looks up. She's wearing a wide-brimmed linen hat, a yellow sundress, rubber clogs on bare feet. I climb out of the car, stretch my legs, slam the door with the bottom of my shoe. I walk to her.

Every time I see my wife after an absence – even if only a day – I think to myself: How did *I* manage to get a woman like that? She is fifteen years younger than me, which makes her thirty-something – just old enough not to be embarrassing when we show up together at a dinner party. She has chestnut hair to her shoulders, pale eyes, a pretty face, and a tall, lanky body forged by regular gym workouts and a relentless discipline that I used to find charming but now think just a bit ruthless and scary.

I don't know what I'm expecting Libby to do when she sees me – maybe throw down the trowel, jump up, and hug me with mud-caked gardening gloves? – or, at a minimum, smile that awkward, toothy smile I fell in love with so many years ago? – but she does neither. Instead, this is what she does. She remains kneeling in the vegetable patch, and regards me curiously, as if I've returned from a ten-minute trip to the grocery store, and not a seven-day absence.

38

When I'm close enough to her that she can't ignore me any longer, she rises, finally, brushes mud from her gloves, cocks her head. I step into soft loamy soil – brown earth and manure and peat – and walk through the vegetable garden. There are neatly-staked tomatoes tied to bamboo poles with green string, orderly rows of lettuce, sprigs of herbs.

I say: 'Still mad at me?'

'For what?' she asks.

My wife's question is a good one. There is so much to choose from. I shrug.

'Of course not,' she says.

'How about a kiss then?'

She hugs me awkwardly. She tilts her face up, and I kiss her. She wraps leather gardening gloves around my head, and I feel brittle dead animal skin on my neck, and pieces of dirt dropping into my collar.

We break the kiss.

'You're sweaty,' she says.

'I love you too.'

'Want to see the house?'

The house is faux Southern Genteel, an old white colonial, with a shaded portico and two wicker rocking chairs out front. There's a big live oak shading the north side.

Inside it is tastefully decorated the way rentals usually are, with furniture chosen for sturdiness, not style. Colours are muted, designed not to offend. There's a tall foyer in the front, and a semicircular staircase leading up to the upper floor and, presumably, the bedrooms. The living room is off to the side, the kitchen in back. In the rear of the living room is a sliding glass door leading to a patio, where I see a swimming pool among a grove of spiky palmettos.

'What do you think?' Libby asks.

'Nice.'

'I didn't have much time to look, you know – just a week. There weren't a lot of options.' She sounds nervous, defensive.

'It's OK, Libby,' I say. I squeeze her shoulder. 'You done good.'

She laughs. She sounds oddly anxious. 'I didn't think you'd like it. It seems a bit… ' she searches for the word. '*Fake.*'

I peer into the living room. The couch is canvas, dark brown, the colour of chocolate that has been left in a cupboard too long. A grandfather clock stands in the corner, encased in glass and walnut. It ticks loudly. I don't disagree with her *fake* comment, but I say: 'We're only here for twelve months. It'll be our little adventure. Right?'

'Right,' Libby says, not sounding particularly adventurous.

I met Libby eleven years ago, when I was Director of Sales at Lantek, the now-defunct Ethernet networking company. Those were the days when Lantek could sell as much gear as it could manufacture, and I was pulling down more money in commissions than I ever imagined earning as the son of a San Jose cop. I was just one more idiotic sales executive speeding around the Valley in his Porsche, attributing my success to talent rather than luck, hitting on waitresses, and generally enjoying life far too much.

Libby was one of those waitresses. She worked at The Goose, a Lantek watering hole. Most of The Goose's customers hit on her – often giving new meaning to the establishment's name – and so my own advances, which consisted merely of words, didn't seem particularly egregious.

But they were persistent. Relentlessly persistent.

I asked out the woman who would become my wife four times before she finally agreed to be alone in a room with me.

The first time I asked Libby out, she told me very calmly to go to hell. I still remember the way she said those words, *Go to hell*. Even today, I remember. They weren't angry words, which is what surprised me. They were gentle. She said *Go to hell*, and she pointed her finger, as if to indicate helpfully which way to start walking.

40

The second time I asked Libby out, two days later, she threw her head back, and laughed, as if I had said something hilarious. 'Very funny, Jimmy!' she told me, when she recovered. 'Me and you on a date!' Then she walked off, laughing still.

That took a little wind out of my sails, I have to admit, and so I didn't dare a third attempt until a few months later. It happened during one of those lulls that sometimes hit downtown bars – right after the post-work Happy Hour crowd goes home to their families, leaving behind only the incorrigible drunks. This time, the waitress named Libby Granville ignored my question entirely. She had just brought my fourth scotch of the evening, and had put it on the bar in front of me; and when she leaned over, to lay down the glass, I asked her softly – so softly that no one else could hear – if I could take her away from this place and buy her dinner. She froze in that position, leaning over the bar, wisps of brown hair in her eyes, and she didn't look up. I still remember that – the way she stood there, motionless – the graceful lithe posture, the tendons in her outstretched arm, the hair in her eyes. There was a moment of frozen indecision. And then, her uncertainty vanished, and she stood up, and walked off, shaking her head, as if reprimanding herself for coming so close to making a terrible choice.

Finally, on the fourth try – six months after the first attempt – she relented – 'so that you would finally leave me alone', she told me later. I ran into her not at the bar, but at the supermarket. She was in the checkout line ahead of me. There's something sad about a grocery-store express line at eight p.m.; only the loners and the heartbroken use it. We stood there, smiling and embarrassed, clandestinely comparing each other's purchases, scattered on the neoprene conveyor belt in front of us – for myself, a rotisserie chicken; for her, a pre-made salad – and it was then that we decided to join forces and have the dinner together.

We were married one year later.

That was the end of the romance. I worked insane hours, giving myself entirely to my career. I had little time left for Libby. When we had our first child, I had little time left for him. I was always grasping for that next rung on the corporate ladder. From VP of Sales, I jumped to Chief Operating Officer at NetGuard. From there, it was just one more leap to Chief Executive Officer. I got my first CEO job when I was only thirty-eight years old. It was the peak of my career.

As my career ascended, the rest of my life fell apart. I had always drunk, but somehow managed to control how and when I did it. I was what is referred to as a 'highly functional drunk' – which is a term used by people who can't admit they have a problem. I'd show up to work sober and perform competently – even brilliantly – but as soon as the hands on my Rolex said six o'clock, I knew it was time to leave work and drink. '*My* time,' I called it, possessively, as if my employer could control me from eight to six, but, after that, it was my right to claim my body and destroy it however I damn pleased. I stayed drunk most nights, sometimes blacking out, which I suppose was a mercy, since at least I forgot most of the sins I committed while loaded.

Over the years drinking turned into snorting, and snorting into whoring, and whoring into crystal meth. Oh, and there was gambling, too. How *that* started, I still do not know. My father never gambled, and – until I started using – neither did I. But one day, with a straw in my nose, a whore in my bed, and a *Racing Form* on my lap, I looked up and realized that the thrill of a new bet made me almost as high as the thrill of a new woman. When you find yourself calling your bookie at two in the morning, laying ten g's on the coin toss at Ball State, you know you have a problem.

By the time I made it to CEO, I was out of control – fighting in bars, screwing strangers, gambling everything I earned, losing it and winning it back, owing money to scary men, arriving home high or drunk, hurting Libby in every way I could, short of violence.

The end came when my son died. Cole was three years old the night he drowned.

Even after the DA cleared me of his death, Libby did not leave me. To this day, I have no idea why she stayed. Maybe it was because she knew no one else but me. Maybe it was because her father was a drunk, too, and – like so many other people – she could only repeat her past. Or maybe it was exactly what she claims: that she loves me, despite what I did that night.

After the death of my son, I got clean. I tried turning my life around. I tried rebuilding my career. It took a long time. I made a lot of phone calls in those dark days, begged a lot of people for second chances. I started small, with one-off gigs: consulting for cash-strapped start-ups; rescuing a software company that had fired its VP; serving as an interim CEO for a company whose founder had a heart attack. I worked for stock options – pieces of paper – usually worthless. No one paid me cash. But once I had a little momentum, I starting offering myself as a rent-a-CEO – a 'turnaround guy' is what I called myself – and had some success. The farther away from Palo Alto I went, the fewer people knew about my past. My jobs stayed low-profile, my compensation meagre, my progress incremental. But it was progress. A little at a time, I worked my way back.

Now, standing in the middle of Florida, three thousand miles from our home, our real home, I think I understand why Libby is treating me like a stranger. She started with me when I was high, in every sense of the word, and stuck with me when I was low. She forgave me for the things I did. She nursed me to health. And now, finally, we're back to where we began. I have a chance to turn around a real company, with real venture-capital investors. This is the biggest opportunity we've had in five years. Maybe ever. I can earn ten or eleven million dollars if I succeed.

Libby probably wonders if I'll ruin this chance too – the way I've ruined everything else in our life.

'Hey,' I say. I reach out, take her fingers in mine. They stay limp in my hand. 'Everything is going to be fine. No more mistakes. I promise.'

She nods. She doesn't return my stare. Doesn't look at me.

She doesn't believe me, I know.

Doesn't believe a fucking word I say.

She leads me upstairs to the bedroom.

The bed is neatly made, with a brown duvet pulled tight as a drum head. Libby has always been fastidious – fussing with beds, stacking pantries, scrubbing toilets. Her obsession with neatness and order developed around the same time that I began to spiral so desperately out of control. You don't have to be Freud to figure that one out.

The ceiling of the bedroom is high and vaulted. Above the bed is a ceiling fan with oversized teak blades, like something out of post-war Havana. It twirls slowly, squeaking on each turn. Near the bed is a window, and just beyond it, outside, the giant live oak, its branches touching the glass. There's a sliding door that leads out to a little veranda overlooking the backyard pool.

'What do you think?' she asks.

'Little bit Cuba, little bit Shangri-La.'

I go to the bureau and pull a drawer at random. Libby has unpacked for me. Undershirts and socks sit in neat square piles, exactly fourteen days' worth. Before we left Palo Alto, we agreed to bring only the barest minimum with us to Florida, just a few clothes and knick-knacks. We would leave the rest of our lives behind, in our real house, awaiting our return. Our *triumphant* return, we hoped.

On top of the bureau, Libby has arranged three photographs in metal frames. One is of me, much younger, standing on a boardwalk, my hands in my pockets, staring at the photographer with a surly sneer. Like James Dean on crystal meth.

The second photo is of Libby, sunlight dappling her face, standing alone in a forest.

The final photo shows the two of us together, sitting on a couch. Neither of us smiles.

The paltry selection makes me sad. Libby must have made an effort to choose 'highlights' from our years together – but so much of our past is off limits now, so much forbidden – that this is the best she can do: three desultory shots – all out of focus, and all with that queer Beirut-hostage quality of pictures snapped against the subjects' will. What does it say about a marriage, when, after a decade, there is only one photo of husband and wife in the same frame?

I stare at that one, that photo of me and Libby on the couch together. We're in a stylish loft, in front of an exposed brick wall. Behind us hangs an art deco poster – a wine advertisement, from 1920s Italy. It says 'Vini di Lusso' and shows a grotesque red satyr, with curved horns and a hooked nose, hungrily gobbling a bunch of grapes. In the photograph, Libby and I stare at the camera, creepily oblivious to the creature behind us. My arm is wrapped around Libby, but now – in hindsight – it looks as if she's shrinking from my touch.

I remember the night that photo was taken. It was seven years ago. We were in San Francisco. The condo was owned by my friend, Bob Parker, and it was his New Year's Eve party. Bob was a buddy from Lantek, one of my best friends at the time – but also one of the friends who disappeared after the death of my son, either too embarrassed to know me, or too suspicious of what happened that night.

The evening the picture was taken, I was a walking disaster: aware, hazily, that I had a problem; but still drinking, still gambling, still getting high. At the end of the night, Libby dutifully escorted me home, but not before I had made a drunken pass at Bob Parker's wife while she leaned over and served me canapés.

Now, in our bedroom, Libby comes up behind me, takes the photograph from my hand, and lays it back on the dresser. 'I wanted one of us together,' she says, as if to explain why she chose one that brings back bad memories.

I turn. She's standing very close to me. I feel her breasts against my chest. She smells of sweat, and peat, and talcum powder. A line of dirt is smudged on her face. I lick my finger and wipe it across her cheek. The smudge disappears. I feel the stir of an erection.

'How's the bed?' I ask.

'Soft.'

'Want to break it in?'

I look past her, out of the window, past the oak tree, and I'm surprised that the sky is dark. The first drops of rain fall.

We make love. Until we start, I think it's going to be quick and animal – tearing off her clothes, throwing her down, pounding into each other after seven days of abstinence. But it's not like that at all. We stand at the foot of the bed. She undresses me slowly, one shirt button at a time. She unzips my pants, unfastens my belt. She drops my clothes to the floor. I slide the straps of her sundress from her shoulders, let the fabric fall. We remove our underwear, stand naked in front of each other, in the chill of the air-conditioned room. Without words, we step to the bed.

We lie on our sides, face each other. We stroke each other's skin. I run the back of my hand over her abdomen, her nipples, her pubic hair.

She pulls my fingers to her face. She kisses each finger, starting at my thumb. When she gets to the pinky, she puts it in her mouth, sucks on it. She takes it from her lips, stares at it.

Now might be a good time to mention that, on my left hand, I'm missing the first two segments of my pinky. It happened eight years ago, due either to a slammed car door one drunken night, or an angry bookie named Hector Gonzales. In either case, I blacked out, and don't remember exactly what happened. Libby tells the story this way: that I arrived home one morning at three o'clock, with a dish towel wrapped around the stump of my finger. But rather than remark upon my curiously missing digit, I complained that I was starving, and needed to find a good hamburger. To lure me into the car, she lied and

46

told me she would take me to Jack in the Box, but she took me to the emergency room, instead.

Now, she grabs my half-pinky, brings it down between her legs, strokes her pussy with it. She closes her eyes, shivers.

I leave my mangled hand limp, let her manipulate it. She moves it faster, finds a rhythm that's familiar to me. In another minute her body shudders. She gasps. Her orgasm sounds like a surprise – the noise a woman makes when she's been told someone has died.

After she comes, she closes her eyes. She keeps my half-pinky inside her. Another minute, and I climb on top of her, slide inside. We fuck slowly. She keeps her eyes shut.

Outside, the rain falls. A crack of thunder rolls off the ocean.

I pump faster, keeping rhythm with the rain tapping the window. Libby is barely moving, I realize, too late. Probably wants me to come already, and climb off.

I do. I give a little grunt, let her know I'm done.

I stay on top of her for a moment, because it's unseemly to dismount too fast, like a gymnast from a pommel horse. After a ten-count, I roll off. Libby is staring up at the teak ceiling fan, which is rotating slowly, squeaking.

'I missed you, Libby,' I say.

'Now you have me,' she says.

I cannot tell if these words are plain and sweet, or if there is bitterness underneath. I kiss her lips, roll off the bed, and pad to the bathroom.

When I return, she's under the covers, with her back to me. Outside the rain has slowed. Thunder sounds – muffled, distant. The storm is leaving.

I look at Libby's shape under the covers. It's moving strangely, shaking.

'Libby?' I say. 'Are you crying?'

'No.'

47

But she is. I walk to the foot of the bed. I reach down, touch her calf through the sheet. She turns with a start. Her eyes are tear-streaked.

'What's wrong, baby?' I say.

She shakes her head. 'Nothing. I'm sorry.'

'Tell me.'

'I'm so sorry,' she says again.

'You're not happy we came here.'

'I am happy,' she says dully. She sniffles.

'I'll make it worth your while,' I say, but immediately regret it. It sounds like something you say to a whore. I try again. 'What I mean to say is... ' I take a breath. What *do* I mean to say? 'Libby, this is a big deal for me. This is my chance.'

'I know it is.'

'It's not easy for you. I understand that. I'm grateful you came with me. I'm grateful you're still here, after everything that I've... ' I stop. 'Everything that happened.'

She says: 'I love you, Jimmy.'

Those are the right words. I'm glad she says them. But there is something odd about her tone. Her words don't sound like love at all; they sound like lines from a script that she is being forced to read.

My cellphone rings.

I'm relieved by the jarring sound. It gives me a chance to leave her, a chance to walk away without speaking any more, without hurting her, without being forced to remember the things that I've done.

CHAPTER 5

I retrieve my cellphone from my pants, which are crumpled in a ball on the floor. I answer on the third ring. I leave the room, pressing the phone to my ear.

'This is Jim,' I say.

'How's it going, hotshot?'

It's Tad Billups. He's my oldest friend. Probably my *only* friend, come to think of it. The rest gave up on me. Somehow, preposterously, Tad not only stuck with me; he also gave me this job at Tao. Which makes him more than my friend. He's also my boss.

With the phone under my chin, I pull the door closed behind me, so that I don't disturb Libby. I walk down the hall. 'How's it *going*?' I repeat. 'It's going to hell, Tad. It's a crappy company, with crappy people, and a crappy product that no one wants to buy. And it's burning a million dollars a month. And there's only seven weeks of cash left.'

'Yeah,' he says. 'I probably should have mentioned all that, before offering you the job. Any good restaurants down there?'

'Restaurants? How would I know?' I pad down the stairs. 'Remind me again. How did you convince me to come here?'

'I didn't convince *you*. You convinced *me*. You begged. You were desperate.'

'Hardly,' I say. But his banter, meant in fun, cuts close to the bone. The afternoon that I tracked him down in Il Fornaio, I was a bit desperate.

No.

Desperate suggests more dignity than I actually had. *Pathetic* might be a better word.

He changes the subject. 'How's Libby?'

I lower my voice. 'Sullen, angry.'

'Well,' he says brightly. 'Sounds like everything's coming up roses.'

'Oh, and also, it's one hundred degrees.'

'Yeah, I should have warned you about that, too. Florida gets kind of… what's the word they use down there? *Muggy.*'

'Thanks for the warning.'

'Let me guess. You wore a suit to the office today, didn't you?'

'No,' I lie.

'No one in Florida wears a suit, Jimmy. How many of them did you pack?'

'I didn't bring any suits, Tad.'

'How many?'

'Three. All wool.'

Tad makes a *tsk-tsk* sound. 'Is there any hope whatsoever?'

'They say it cools down in December.'

'I mean for the company, Jimmy.'

'I don't know,' I say. 'Give me a couple of days to poke around, see what I can find.' I work my way into the living room, go to the sliding glass door. I peer outside, to the patio. The rain has stopped. The swimming pool is placid and clear.

Tad says: 'What do you mean: "Poke around"?'

'I just mean—'

Tad interrupts, 'Remember what I told you, when I hired you?'

'That you were going to make me rich?'

'No, that part was a lie. Remember the *other* part?' Tad's voice fades in and out, and I distinctly hear the sound of wind sputtering against his microphone. I picture him driving in his BMW convertible, top down, in sunny, temperate Palo Alto, with his Bluetooth headset clipped to his ear.

'What other part?'

'I said: Protect my investment and protect *me*.'

Now that he mentions it, I do remember that. Those words struck me as odd even then: *Protect my investment and protect me.* 'What does that mean, exactly?'

'Just what it sounds like. Your first priority is to save the company... if you can.'

'And my second priority?'

'Nothing. That's it.' After a pause, he adds: 'Just make sure my generosity doesn't come back to bite me in the ass.'

'Meaning what, Tad?'

'Meaning,' he says, talking slowly now, as if I'm an idiot, 'I hired you because you're my friend. I'm taking a chance on you. Just make me proud. That's all.'

'I understand.' Actually, I don't. It's hard to believe that Tad Billups is concerned about the fate of Tao Software LLC – a tiny third-rate start-up he convinced his partners to invest in nearly four years ago – and a company that's only one of dozens in his portfolio. Tad's reputation won't be ruined if Tao fails. Ninety per cent of venture-capital-funded companies fail. That's the nature of his business. A venture capitalist is considered a success if one out of ten companies is a home run. So what does Tad mean when he tells me to 'protect him'? Protect him from *what*?

But now suddenly, Tad's ready to scram. 'All right,' he says. 'Anything else to report, before I go?'

'Listen, Tad,' I say. 'I know the answer to my next question, even before I ask, but I *do* have to ask. 'We need more money. At least another five or ten million. You didn't tell me what a mess it was down here.'

'Not going to happen, hotshot.'

'Make it a down round. Dilute me. Otherwise, it's not going to work—'

'Make it work!' he yells. I'm surprised by the harshness of his words. I've known Tad Billups a long time, and never once has he raised his voice to me. He's the kind of man who doesn't think twice about stabbing a guy in the back, but he'll do it quietly, with a friendly smile. His voice grows soft again. 'Really, Jimmy. Make it work.' He's so quiet, in fact, that I think I must have imagined his yell. Maybe it was a trick of his Bluetooth headset. Tad continues: 'I don't know what else to tell you. My partners won't put another dime into that dog. *Comprende*?'

'Yeah,' I say. '*Comprendo*.'

'Anything else I can do for you?' Tad asks.

'Anything *else*?' I repeat, and laugh. 'What have you done for me so far?'

'Well, I gave you a great job, and I'm going to make you rich.'

'You said that part was a lie.'

'Did I? Ah well, you caught me. Anyway, do what you can.'

'I'll do my best.'

'I know you will, buddy. That's why I hired you. Ta ta.'

He hangs up, leaving me holding a dead phone to my ear.

CHAPTER 6

When I wake from my nightmares, I never shout.

I wake the same way, every morning, having dreamed the same dream. My son in a bathtub. His body floating just below the water's surface. His face blue, his mouth open in a silent scream. That yellow hair, spread thin on the water, like gossamer, hair too long for a boy's. And that stare – the way his dead eyes look into mine. The way they ask, 'Why did you do this to me?' Terrified eyes.

I sit bolt upright in bed, the sheets bunched around me in a wet tangle, my pyjama top soaked with sweat, the scream still-born on my lips. I never shout. Not out loud. Not ever.

I allow the dread to fade. The same way that other people wake, and allow circulation to return to an arm, after having slept on it. This is my morning ritual. I sit in bed, and breath slowly, and let terror fade.

I look at the clock. Not quite seven o'clock. Libby is snoring beside me.

I climb from the bed, quietly. I take a cold shower, and dress.

Today I leave my wool suit on a hanger in the closet, and instead put on chinos and a short-sleeved polo. I walk to Libby's side of the bed, lean over. Still asleep.

'Libby?'

She grunts, pulls the blanket over her shoulder, turns away from me.

'Libby, baby, I'm leaving now, OK?'

'Mmm,' she says.

'So we'll talk when I get back. You know, about last night. OK?'

About you sobbing hysterically after we made love.

Libby says, 'Mmm.'

I was hoping for more of a response. *Any* response.

'OK?' I ask again.

She sighs. She turns to face me. Her eyes open wide. 'OK,' she says.

'Things will get better,' I say, because I think she needs to hear it. I realize, after I say it, that maybe it's me that needs to hear it. 'They will. You'll see.'

She pulls the blanket to her chin, and nods.

I take my briefcase. On the way out of the room, I stop at the bureau. I lift the photograph of Libby and me sitting on the couch that New Year's Eve long ago, when the red-skinned, horned satyr loomed behind us. Even in the half-light of the room, I'm struck by that image: my arm around Libby, Libby pulling away. It's not a photograph of a husband and wife enjoying a night of revelry; it's a photograph of a kidnapping in progress.

I lay it back on the bureau. I'd like to take a photo to work with me, but not that one. I wish there was a photo of Cole. But Libby hid them all, after the night he died.

From the bed, Libby says: 'Take the one of us together.'

I turn to her. She's been watching. Even though I heard what she said, I ask, 'What?'

'If you're going to bring one, bring the one of us together. Please.'

I shrug. Again I lift the photo of the two of us in the San Francisco loft. I examine it. 'It's just... weird-looking,' I say finally.

'It has both of us,' she explains.

I'm not sure what she means, or why she cares, but at least she cares about something. So I say, 'All right, baby.'

I heft the photograph in one hand. The frame is strangely heavy. I pop my briefcase, lay the metal frame inside. I walk to the bedroom door. 'Wish me luck,' I say.

'Knock them dead.'

'I always do,' I say, and shut the door behind me.

I go downstairs and head out to the porch. It's already seventy degrees. The sky is cloudless. The air smells like honeysuckle and hot gravel. I'm suddenly very glad about my decision to ditch the suit.

Across the street, a blue Pontiac pulls into my neighbour's driveway. It's the only other house on the cul-de-sac – a mirror image of the house that Libby and I rent.

The Pontiac cuts its motor. From the car steps a large, muscled man in expensive jeans and a tight silk T-shirt. He wears leather work boots.

He stares at me from across the street. He has black deep-set eyes, a protruding forehead, and a small mouth and chin. The bulbous head and little lips make him look lizard-like, feral, carnivorous – like a velociraptor.

I wave. I'm about to call hello, too, perhaps even walk across the street to introduce myself, but before I can, he turns and, without acknowledging me, lopes up his driveway and onto the porch. He doesn't bother inserting a key into the door. He just turns the knob and walks inside. He's gone.

Something about what I just saw is odd. It's not only the man's physical appearance, although that is peculiar. There's something about the way he's dressed, too – those expensive tight-fitting clothes that don't belong in a white-collar office. It's an outfit you might see on a bouncer at a downtown nightclub – the clothes cost money, but you can't hide the fact that, underneath, there's a brute.

And another thing. I look at my watch. Only a few minutes past eight o'clock. Why is my neighbour pulling *into* his driveway and coming home, when the rest of the world is going out towards work? I wonder what kind of job he has.

I try to peer into his house, but the shades are closed tight, the windows dark. Everything about his house is uninviting.

Welcome to the neighbourhood, I think to myself, as I get into my car and drive to work.

CHAPTER 7

Not *directly* to work, mind you.

There's that little matter of breakfast. You can't turn a company around on an empty stomach. Indeed, there's not much you *can* do on an empty stomach, except lose weight, and so I swing through the McDonald's drive-thru for my daily Egg McMuffin.

The Egg McMuffin is my morning ritual, having replaced cigarettes and booze a few years back. Not many people can feel virtuous eating an Egg McMuffin in the morning, but I can.

Having driven through the drive-thru, I plop the car into park, and I eat the muffin at the side of the restaurant, with the engine running and the air blasting in my face. Twenty seconds later, I crumple the paper wrapper into a little ball, put the car into drive, dart out of the exit, then screech two quick lefts – *Rockford Files* style – and drive back through the drive-thru yet again, for a second McMuffin.

Somewhere in the back of my mind, gulping down that second muffin, I sense there may be a tenuous link between my morning breakfast ritual and my ever-expanding abdomen. But that link, whatever it is, is shrouded in uncertainty, and requires further scientific study.

I stop next at the bank, pull $200 out of the ATM, and finally arrive at the Tao office at 8.30. Apparently my ball-busting speech at the meeting yesterday had an effect: I'm not the first to have arrived. There are more than a few cars in the lot.

Inside, Amanda is at the front reception desk, reading a book intently and underlining a passage with her pen. She's so engrossed – staring at the text, biting her lower lip, concentrating – that she doesn't notice me until I'm upon her. She looks up, surprised, and shuts the book.

'Good morning, Jim,' she says.

'Morning, Amanda. Whatcha reading?'

She smiles. 'It's a good book. Have you ever read it?'

She holds it up for my inspection. It's small, dog-eared, so old and worn from use that the gold foil stamp on the cover says only 'Holy Bib' – with the le just a faint embossment.

'Not lately,' I admit. But I'm not thrown by this. In my line of work – drug-induced self-destruction, that is – I've met more than a few super-hot women who turn out to be religious kooks. It's no coincidence, either. Being attractive tends to get you into trouble, and loose women always think Jesus can get them out. Who am I to say they're wrong?

'All right,' I say, nodding. 'Rock on.' I give a little fist pump to show I'm OK with Bible-reading at work. Better than porn, less good than the Employee Manual. Somewhere in between.

I continue past, but she calls, 'Jim.' She lowers her voice, glances to the back of the bullpen. Her eyes convey warning. 'Dom Vanderbeek is here. He's been waiting for you.'

Yesterday morning, I humiliated Dom Vanderbeek, our Vice President of Sales, by summoning him imperiously to the office at a moment's notice. Once he arrived, I ignored him for the rest of the day, letting him seethe and glare at me across the tops of the cubicles in the bullpen. When he seemed unable to bear it any longer, I had Amanda send him a terse email inviting him to a 'one-on-one' meeting with me the following morning. It's a little trick I've learned over the years: if you want to establish dominance in a corporate hierarchy, you have to be brutal. There must never be doubt about who is in charge.

Now our meeting has begun, and I'm sitting in the high-tech boardroom, listening to Dom Vanderbeek. Rather than acting like a beaten man, humbly begging my approval, Dom has spent the past five minutes telling me why he's the most important person in my world.

These reasons include, in no particular order: Without Dom Vanderbeek, sales at Tao would plummet; Dom Vanderbeek's mere presence boosts company morale; and Dom Vanderbeek can help me – a novice CEO – navigate insoluble management problems.

Dom Vanderbeek looks exactly the way I expected him to. He's in his early forties, tall and trim, with the build of a tri-athlete. He has a handsome face; short dark hair cut in a Caesar, greying at the temples; and a bright smile that is the result, I am sure, of expensive bleaching treatments. He wears a big masculine watch, which he makes a point of showing off by wearing his sleeves rolled. A Rolex Submariner, I note. The watch of choice for Sales VPs.

When Dom finishes telling me why he is important to me, I nod thoughtfully, sit back in my chair, and say, 'I understand what you're saying.'

'Do you, Jim?' He leans forward, drills me with his gaze. 'Do you really? Because yesterday you treated me very shabbily. I felt very bad about it.'

I've met Dom's type before. In his effort to move up the corporate ranks, Dom has taken several weekend seminars where they teach you effective 'interpersonal skills'. Invariably these seminars advise you to confront co-workers, bosses, and subordinates openly and honestly, rather than stewing about perceived slights. In theory, it's a good idea, but in practice it has the opposite effect of what you're trying to achieve. Rather than making you seem open and honest, your co-workers perceive you as abrasive and confrontational. After all, you're always telling them what's bothering you.

Dom says, 'Do you know what I'm referring to, Jim?'

I do. He's referring to yesterday's phone call where I put him on speakerphone and humiliated him in front of the rest of Tao's employees. Actually, I do feel bad about that. But it's one of those things you need to do when you arrive at a company that's going down the shitter. There is no time for social niceties. You need to establish your authority. It's immaterial who your target is. You need to pick *someone*. All that matters is that you let everyone at the company know that you are the alpha male, that you are in charge. In that way, the executive suite isn't much different from prison. In both places, the leader needs to pick a bitch. I guess that makes Dom my bitch.

'Listen, Dom,' I say. 'I'm sorry I was rude to you yesterday. Really I am. The truth is, I need you on my side.'

'That's good to hear.'

'Every company needs a sales king. And I want you to be mine.'

He nods. 'All right, then.'

'So tell me about sales.'

'Sales?'

'Since you are my sales king. Maybe you can let me know what's in the sales pipeline.'

'The pipeline is good,' Dom says. 'The pipeline is strong.'

'OK.' I nod. I wait for more. But he's silent. So I say: 'Can you give me a *hint* what's in it?'

'Well,' he says, and sighs, as if the thought of having to run through the massive sales pipeline is frankly exhausting. 'We're talking to Facebook, of course. They're the big player now. And MySpace. And Yahoo. And Google.'

'You're talking to them?'

'And lots of smaller players, too.'

'Great.'

'So, my message is' – he points his index finger at me – 'I'm on top of it.'

'Great,' I say again. 'But when you say that you're *talking* to them, what does that mean? Talking like: "Hello, nice to meet you"? Or talking like: "Here's the contract. Sign on the dotted line"?'

'More like the second. The dotted line.'

'OK,' I say. 'So do you have a pipeline report I can look at?'

'A what?'

'It's a report that sales executives usually prepare. It describes what's in the sales pipeline, and where we stand with every prospect—'

'I know what a pipeline report is, Jim. I'm asking why you want one.'

'Well,' I say patiently, 'I'm curious whether our company will still exist in September. I'm curious if you and I will still have jobs. I'm hoping you can enlighten me.'

'I see.'

'So will you prepare one for me? A pipeline report?'

Dom looks at me as if I've asked him to change a dirty diaper.

'Jim,' he says. 'Let me ask you something.' He swivels in his chair, leans back, looks down his nose at me. 'You seem to know all about me. Maybe I can ask about you. What's *your* background?'

'Fair question, Dom,' I say, pleasantly, even though, at this instant, I make the decision that I will need to fire him. 'Let's see. I grew up in California. I graduated from Berkley undergrad. I worked twenty-five years in Silicon Valley. I've held sales and management jobs at several companies, including SGI, Lantek, NetGuard. A few others, too.'

If my résumé impresses Dom, he doesn't show it. 'The reason I ask,' Dom says, 'is that I'm just wondering.'

'Wondering what?'

'Wondering why they appointed you CEO.' He cocks his head and speaks in a gentle, quiet voice – as if he's a child asking me to retell a particularly charming fairytale: the one where the village idiot wanders into the castle and is mistaken for king.

'I suppose,' I say, 'because I have a track record.' But it is a good question. I'm not exactly the most likely candidate for this job – or *any*

60

turnaround job – with a résumé that includes two addictions, three arrests, and more than my share of day-long blackouts.

'*Do* you have a track record?' he asks. Again, it's a friendly, encouraging tone of voice. There's no malice, no hint of challenge.

'Are you disappointed that they didn't ask you to be CEO, Dom?'

Dom nods. 'I am. Yes, I am, Jim.' Again, the in-your-face honesty. He must have passed that Interpersonal Skills Seminar with flying colours.

The funny thing about Sales VPs is that they always think *they* should be CEO. In every company I've ever worked for, every sales guy guns for the top job, but doesn't get it; and he winds up bitter and disappointed. It's the nature of being good at sales. To be good at sales, you need to be completely unaware of what a tool you are. After all, what kind of man can talk his way into a corporate executive suite at some media company, and blow smoke about Tao's half-assed software – software that doesn't always work – and then ask for a fifty-thousand-dollar cheque? The kind of man who isn't easily embarrassed. The kind of man who doesn't know how ridiculous he appears to others. The kind of man who thinks that he, above all other candidates, should be CEO. In other words: the Sales VP.

As much as I'd like to cut Dom loose – to fire him right now, as he sits across the table from me, smiling with those bleached white teeth of his – such a move would be impossible. With only seven weeks of cash left, we need to make sales. *Now.* Without Dom, we start from zero. I say gently, 'I sympathize, Dom. I really do. Probably, you *should* be CEO of this company.'

He smiles. He likes that idea.

I continue. 'Here's the good news. I'm only temporary. If we can turn this thing around, then I can leave. Which means the CEO job will be open. And of course I'll put in a good word for anyone who helps me. That could be you.' *It could be,* I think, *but it's pretty unlikely.*

I look at Dom, see if my words have had a soothing effect. Dom says, 'I appreciate what you're saying, Jim. What you're saying is: If I help you turn around Tao, you'll help me get the CEO job.' He adds, 'When you leave.'

Sales 101: Repeat the pitch, and encourage the customer to say it out loud, too. I play along. 'That's exactly what I'm saying, Dom. When I leave, I'll help you get the job.'

He nods and smiles. 'I like what I'm hearing.'

'But here's the problem. You want to be CEO? We need to have a company for you to be the CEO of. And that means we need to keep Tao Software alive. Which means we need to get cash in the door.'

'Which I'm working on.'

'You don't understand,' I say. 'More of the same ain't gonna cut it.' I lean over the table and lower my voice, as if sharing a great confidence. 'We're running out of cash, Dom. We have seven weeks left.'

'Seven weeks?' He raises an eyebrow. Normally, it's not good policy to tell employees how dire the situation really is. Honesty is never, despite the old maxim, the best policy. Honesty makes people look for new jobs. But Dom, I wager, isn't going anywhere. Not if he has a shot at the top spot at Tao. He'll stick around long enough to give it a try.

'That is why,' I say, 'we need to sell something. This week.'

Dom smiles, the way you smile at your pudgy nephew, when he says something cute. 'Sell something this week? Sure. Why the hell not?' He shrugs. 'Except that we don't have a fucking product to sell, Jim. If those idiots in engineering would give me something, something that actually worked, maybe I could help you, but—'

'We have a demo,' I say. 'I saw it yesterday. It works.' I think about Randy's warnings. I add quickly, 'Most of the time, anyway. But we can sell it.'

'Aw, shit,' Dom says.

'I've been doing some thinking,' I say.

'Five dangerous words from a CEO,' he mutters.

'We're selling to the wrong people. We're selling the wrong product.'

'Oh, OK,' Dom says agreeably. 'Let's just build a new product, you and me. We won't tell any of the Computer Science PhDs who work here until we're all done.'

'Think about it. We're trying to make money by selling software to teenagers who use Facebook. They're fifteen-year-old girls with braces and crushes. They get an allowance from Mommy and Daddy. Is it any surprise we don't have any revenue?'

'That's the business plan, Jim. We build technology, and we licence it to social networks. That's always been our plan.'

'Well it's a crappy plan.'

'You have a better one?'

'I do. It came to me this morning.'

'It came to you?'

'You know what I did this morning, before I drove to work?' I decide to leave out the part about the Egg McMuffin. Or the second Egg McMuffin. 'I stopped by the bank. I took out money.' I pause. 'The *bank*, Dom. The bank.'

He looks confused.

'You know the old Willie Sutton line?' I say. '"Why do you rob banks, Willie?": "Because that's where the money is."'

Still, Dom has no idea what I'm talking about. Subtlety and intellectual nimbleness are not his strong suit. I say: 'Listen, you know the problem that banks have? People are always demanding their money. Banks need to make sure they give money to the right person. That's why we're always typing in PINs and passwords and secret codes. You have to prove who you are. What if you didn't have to do that? What if banks could know with complete certainty who you were, by just looking at you?'

Something registers on his face. His brows unknit. He's beginning to understand.

I go on. 'From now on, we sell our product to banks. That's where the money is. We're not a consumer software company any more. We're corporate. Starting today, we market ourselves as a security solution.

Corporations love security. We'll just call our technology something different. We can make up a fancy name for it. Identity Management Technology. Some crap like that.'

'Hmm,' he says. He wants very much to disagree with me, but even he recognizes there's value in what I say.

I continue. 'And here's the beauty of it. We don't need to build a new product. We just need to change the way we market what we have. We simply re-invent ourselves. We become someone else. From now on, we are the leader in Identity Management Technology. IMT. You're the sales guy, Dom. Make up some cockamamie story about how our technology works – how we can help banks. We identify customers when they walk in the door. We eliminate identity theft. That sort of thing.'

Vanderbeek thinks about this. 'Actually, it's a pretty good idea,' he admits, finally. 'IMT. I like it.'

'So... do you have any contacts?'

'Contacts?'

'At retail banks. We need to get a meeting. As soon as possible. Can you set something up? A sales meeting with C-levels?'

'Maybe.' He thinks about it. 'Yes. I think I can.'

'Good. I'll come to the meeting. You arrange it. This week. I don't care who with. Anyone who can sign a cheque for a half-million dollars.'

Dom throws back his head and lets out a joyous laugh, as if I am the most amusing person he has ever met – a delightful companion!

Having been VP of Sales myself, long ago, I know how he feels. I have sat in his chair: trying to sell a product that doesn't exist, coping with a meddlesome boss who wants to tag along on the next sales call, and being instructed to have someone 'write a cheque for a half-million dollars'. As if it were that easy.

I wait for Dom's laughter to subside. Finally, he lowers his gaze, looks at me. It's a friendly gaze, and a friendly smile. But I can read his thoughts: He'll put up with me for seven more weeks. If we're lucky, then he'll take credit for the success; and if we're not, he'll blame me for the failure.

Which is probably Tad Billups's strategy, too, come to think of it. Put an ex-addict at the helm of a failing company, see what happens.

Dom waves his hand magnanimously. 'Whatever you say, boss.'

'So you'll set up a sales call?'

'Tomorrow.'

'Thanks.' I stand and offer him my hand. He shakes.

He's on my side. For now.

I ask Amanda to help me find a permanent desk. She leads me around the bullpen. At first she suggests I take the spacious corner office where the former CEO, Charles Adams, used to preside. But I demur. It's not merely because I'm superstitious and his fate gives me the heebie-jeebies – although to be honest, that's part of it. It's because big corner offices tend to send the wrong message to employees.

I ask Amanda if there is anything a little less showy. We settle on a nondescript closet-sized office, without any exterior windows at all, beside the bathroom. It's the least desirable location in the building, which makes it perfect for my purpose.

With Amanda watching, I set up my desk. Which means: I open my briefcase, take out a spiral notebook, and lay two Ticonderoga Number 2 Soft pencils at an angle across the first blank page. Next to it I place a battery-powered pencil sharpener. Finally, I take from my briefcase the photograph of me and my wife. I place it at the far corner of my desk.

Amanda leans over and studies the photo with great interest. She says: 'Wow. Nice picture,' in a way that suggests it is not.

'Yeah,' I say. Still, I feel the need to explain, to apologize for the photo. 'Actually, we didn't bring a lot of photographs with us. We packed light.'

'Is that your wife?' she asks.

'Libby.'

Deadpan: 'She seems so happy.'

For the first time I realize that Amanda may actually have a sense of humour.

'And why is Satan in the background?' she continues.

'That's not Satan,' I say, evenly. 'He's a satyr. Half-man, half-beast. From Greek mythology. You know Greek mythology, don't you Amanda?'

'No.'

'They love wine.'

'Do they?'

'And dancing in the woods naked. And music.'

'Hmm,' she says.

'Amanda,' I say, 'don't you have a reception desk to monitor?'

She curtsies primly, and without a word leaves my office.

I sit at my new desk. Spread before me is Tao's old marketing material – nearly a half-million dollars' worth of glossy folders, three-colour inserts, and slick brochures – offset-printed chum on the water. It explains how Tao's P-Scan can identify the faces in any photograph. It goes on to describe how, by using Tao technology, online media companies can enliven social networks, increase user 'stickiness', reduce account churn, and increase customer eyeballs. I was hoping we might be able to save a few bucks and re-use this marketing material for our new customers – multi-national banks – but all the talk about stickiness and eyeballs nauseates me, and I think it unlikely.

My cellphone rings. I look at the Caller ID. The number is unfamiliar. 'Jim Thane,' I say.

'Jimmy Thane,' a loud, raspy voice shoots back, 'how're you holding up?'

It's Gordon Kramer. Gordon's my sponsor. Which means he's somewhere between dear friend and parole officer.

'Gordon,' I say. 'It's great to hear your voice.'

I've known Gordon for seven years. He was at my first meeting, in the YMCA basement in San Jose, which I attended two weeks after Cole died, when I realized how low I had fallen. Somehow Gordon stuck with me, despite my best efforts to shake him loose. Over the years, we've grown close. Maybe it's because he's an ex-cop, like my father. There's something familiar and comforting about his presence – his bulk, his silver hair, his tired eyes and seen-it-all-before expression.

'I'm calling to check up on you,' Gordon says.

'I'm doing great.'

'Anything to report?'

He's asking if I've had a drink, or smoked crank, or placed a bet, or cheated on Libby – or even come close to any of those things.

'I've been fine,' I say.

'Good. Good.' He thinks about it. 'Work stressful?'

'A little.'

'Because, you know, that's when it happens.'

'I do know.'

'You're a superman in the office, and the pressure builds up, and you need a little help, need to take the edge off.'

'Right,' I say. It's hard to have a frank conversation with Gordon about meth addiction while I'm sitting in an office with my door wide open. People listen to the CEO's phone calls. So it's probably best that I don't insist loudly that my drug problem is under control.

'Can't talk, can you?' Gordon says. Still the ex-cop.

'Right,' I say again.

'Fine. We'll talk later. In the meantime, I got that phone number for you.'

'What phone number?'

'Don't pretend you don't know what the hell I'm talking about,' he roars.

Damn. I promised Gordon I would see a new shrink once I got to Florida, if he found one that he approved of.

Gordon is not your typical twelve-step sponsor. He doesn't buy into all that crap about the power of God to cure an addict. He wants science, and doctors, and white lab coats. He wants shrinks and therapy. After Cole's death, it was Gordon's idea for me to visit Doc Curtis, the matronly dyke with the husky cigarette voice. After a few sessions spilling my guts to her, crying, with snot dripping down my nose, I relented and agreed to undergo hypnotherapy. The therapy has helped. At least, I think it has. At least now the nightmares mostly happen at night. During the day, I can forget.

'I know what you're talking about, Gordon,' I say, and sigh.

Doc Curtis was helpful, but the prospect of starting again with someone new is daunting. And besides – how can I afford the time to visit a doctor? There is a magic number seared into the back of my eyelids, and, right now, it's all that I can see. The number is seven. As in: Seven Weeks Of Cash Left.

'Here's the phone number,' Gordon says. 'Write it down.' He rattles off a phone number. I pretend to write it down.

'Got it?' he asks.

'Yeah, I got it.'

'Read it back to me.'

Whoops. 'OK,' I say, sheepishly. 'Repeat it one more time.'

He does. This time I write it on my pad and successfully repeat it aloud.

'His name is Liago,' Gordon continues. 'Dr George Liago. He comes highly recommended. He's successful at treating people like you.' He means addicts who have done shameful things, inhuman things, dreadful things. 'He knows the programme.'

'All right, Gordon,' I say. 'I'll try to make some time".'

'You won't "try to make some time".' He mimics me as if I'm a sissy complaining about the hem line of my dress. 'You *will* go see him. Today. He's expecting your call.'

I sigh. 'All right, Gordon.' I know he loves me, in his weird Roman Centurion way, but boy can he be a pain in the ass.

Gordon says: 'I'm calling Liago tomorrow. If you haven't shown up by then, I'm flying down there and personally dragging your ass onto his couch.'

This is no idle threat. Five years ago, when I was still drowning in the shit, I missed one of my first appointments with Doc Curtis. Gordon Kramer called my cell, tracked me down, and somehow found me in the St Regis Hotel in San Francisco, binging on minibar vodkas, and going through hookers like packs of chewing gum. He showed up, punched me, cuffed me, dragged me down into the hotel's subterranean parking garage, and re-cuffed me against a sprinkler pipe. He left me alone, to air out for three hours in Parking Area 4C, which I try to avoid to this very day, any time I find myself in the St Regis. Then he returned, stuffed me into his car, and personally chauffeured me to Dr Curtis's office. He waited in the reception room until I was done, then dropped me off into Libby's care.

'I know you will,' I say. The last thing I want is Gordon Kramer showing up at Tao and cuffing me to his wrist in front of my software engineers.

'You promise you'll call? He's waiting.'

'I promise. I'll go today, if he has any time available.'

'He has time available,' Gordon says, simply. Which makes me wonder if he threatened to handcuff Dr Liago, too.

'I'll go.'

'That's my boy.'

'You're one hard motherfucker, Gordon Kramer.'

'It's called tough love, kid. If either of us had it growing up, we wouldn't be having this conversation. We wouldn't even know each other.'

It's twelve noon and I'm slinking out of the office, to visit Dr Liago. Gordon was right: the doctor knew I'd be calling – was expecting it – and, lo and behold, he had an appointment open this very day. That Gordon managed to pull off this feat, controlling the schedules of two very busy, very expensive people while three thousand miles away from both, is a testament to his power and authority.

I pass Amanda at the reception desk. I hoped to escape before she noticed my leaving. But she looks up and asks, 'Lunch time?'

'Appointment,' I say.

'OK.' Just two syllables, but I hear it in her voice: twenty-four hours after the new CEO reprimanded people for showing up late, he's off to a leisurely lunch.

I say: 'I'll be back in exactly one hour.'

'OK, Jim.'

'It's not a lunch,' I say. 'It's medical.'

'OK, Jim.' She keeps a straight face, but looks at me with those droopy, slacker eyelids. It's the kind of look that makes you question yourself.

I head for the door.

She calls after me, 'Enjoy your lunch.'

I turn, am about to protest once again that it's not a lunch. She winks and smiles. The PBX rings, a soft warm tone, and she looks down, presses a button, answers it. 'Tao Software,' she says. 'How may I direct your call?' She waves goodbye to me, and looks away before I can argue.

CHAPTER 8

Highway 876 is a rural four-lane road that cuts across the middle of nowhere. The land is flat, the view goes on for ever – brush and cypress, sinkholes and swamp. I pass a billboard rising above the brush. As if its only purpose is to remind me exactly how far I have travelled from Silicon Valley, it is an advertisement for a Baptist church. It shows an image of flames licking at big block letters that say, 'HELL IS REAL'. As if I don't know.

It's a long fifteen miles, and finally I leave the big road and find myself in a sparse residential neighbourhood – split-rail fences, Florida bungalows, old Victorians not well kept. I find 23 Churchill Street – which is the address I've written down – and I pull up in front of a yellow Queen Anne Victorian that – if it were in a town that attracted tourists – might actually make a charming bed and breakfast. Since it's in a town that does not attract tourists, it is instead merely a spooky oversized home-office.

I park at the base of a gravel driveway. There's a post-mounted mailbox with a small placard that says: 'Dr George Liago, PhD, MD'. A vigorous growth of purple clematis climbs up the post, and the flowery vines nearly hide the portion of the sign that says: 'PhD, MD'. I think to myself that, if I had spent all that money on school, I'd be out front every morning with a pair of clippers.

I trudge up the gravel. There's a single Crown Victoria parked beside the house, presumably Dr Liago's.

71

I ring the bell. After a moment the door is opened by a man in a suit and tie. He's tall, balding, with grey feathery hair and a neatly-trimmed white beard. His eyes are opened preternaturally wide, which gives him the look of someone who is quite surprised to see me.

'Mr Thane?' he says.

'Dr Liago.'

'Please, come in.'

He leads me through the foyer, past a sitting room, into a study. There is no carpeting; our shoes stamp and echo on bare oak. Inside the study, the walls are lined with wooden bookcases containing leather-bound medical books and matching sets of classics. There's a large oak desk, a calf-skin couch, and two comfortable-looking high-backed chairs facing each other. Dr Liago sweeps his hand across the quadrant of the room that contains the chairs and the couch. That means I should choose whichever makes me comfortable – chair or couch.

I choose chair. I sink back into one. I'm surprised by how soft it is.

Dr Liago sits down across from me.

'So,' he says, and smiles. 'Welcome.' He has a soothing voice. It's the kind of quiet, breathy voice they teach you in medical school. I think they devote at least one semester to it. There is a tenured professor somewhere who has conducted extensive peer-reviewed research and concluded that the softer you speak – the closer to a whisper – the more carefully your words will be regarded, and the more money you can charge to speak them.

Liago says, 'Gordon Kramer filled me in about your background. But I think it's best if you tell me, in your own words, why you're here.'

I look around the room. On the wall facing me hangs a diploma proclaiming in cursive, Latin writing that George Liago graduated from Cornell Medical School. In the corner furthest away is a gunmetal grey filing cabinet with a serious-looking lock. Nearby is a desk. There's an electric clock on the desk with a sweeping seconds hand,

and a face that glows a comforting orange. All shrinks have big clocks turned discreetly towards the patient, so that the patient knows when he has only a few minutes remaining in the session – just enough time, for example, to describe the soul-crushing emotion that comes from letting your son drown in a bathtub. Just for example.

Liago's office is dark. The effect is achieved with heavy wood shutters blocking all windows. The room is very quiet, very restful. You can't help but feel protected and safe here.

And yet.

Yet there is something peculiar about it.

It takes a moment to figure out.

It's too tidy. There are no papers on the doctor's desk – not even a neat pile of folders. Other than the clock, the desk is bare. There are no photographs, no knick-knacks, no mementos anywhere in the room. Every doctor I've ever been to – internist, gastroenterologist, shrink – makes at least a minimal effort to decorate his workspace and make it his own, even if only to display a small keepsake – a trophy, a sea shell, a drawing by a child. But here, there's nothing. What makes this fact even stranger is that this is apparently a home-office. The house seems provisional, unlived in. Like a movie set.

'You live here?' I ask.

A simple question, but Dr Liago treats it gingerly. He does not immediately answer. He looks at me for a long moment. Finally, he says: 'Why do you ask? Would it comfort you to know that I do live here?'

I laugh. 'No, Doc. Just making small talk.'

'I do,' he says. 'I do live here.' He tries to join my laughter and gives a weak smile.

'Now then,' he says.

'Now then,' I agree. 'You want to know why I'm here. In my own words.' I take a deep breath. I feel myself sink further into my chair. I might get lost in it. Suffocate. 'The *Reader's Digest* version?'

'That'll be fine.'

'Here goes. I'm an addict. I'm sure Gordon told you that.'

His voice is soft, like an angel: 'He did.' He lays a yellow legal pad on his lap, scribbles something.

'My vices vary. I started with drinking and gambling. Amateur stuff. Eventually I turned pro – worked my way up to crystal meth and whores. You know what they say about practise, practise, practise.'

My attempt at humour – if you can call it that – falls flat. Dr Liago stares at me, stone faced. He looks down and jots something on his pad. I try to peer at the scribbles, to see if he actually wrote the word 'whores', but my chair is too far, his writing too small.

'Anyway,' I say, 'I've been sober for two years. Two years, nine months, and twenty-two days, to be exact. I started a new job yesterday. I'm the CEO of a software company.'

'CEO,' he says. 'That sounds like an impressive job.'

'It's not. The company's a piece of shit. That's why I was hired. It's called a "restart". When a bunch of the investors get together and decide a company is failing. They bring in someone new to turn it around. That's my speciality, restarts.'

'That's ironic.'

'What is?'

'You're a bit of a restart yourself. Aren't you?'

'I hope not. Most restarts don't actually work. That's the dirty little secret. They sound like good ideas, but usually they happen way too late. They're like a Hail Mary pass at the end of a football game.'

'I see.' He nods significantly, as if I have just revealed something very significant about myself. His pen flies across his pad, scratching. God, I'd love to see that pad.

'And so that's why I came to see you,' I conclude, lamely. 'Gordon Kramer is my sponsor. He recommended you. Gordon is very – how do I say it? – he's very persuasive. I've done hypnotherapy before, at Gordon's insistence. It worked for him – for his recovery – and so he wanted me to try it for myself.'

'Has it worked for you?'

'You tell me. I've been sober for two years, nine months, twenty-two days… and twenty seconds.'

'Are you married, Mr Thane?'

'Almost ten years.'

'And your wife came to Florida with you?'

'That's right.'

'But she's not happy about it?'

'How did you know that?'

He doesn't answer the question. Instead, he says: 'So you have a lot of stress in your life, don't you? A new job. A lot of people counting on you. Plus one unhappy wife.'

'Hey, you're right. I *am* stressed out. You have any scotch?'

'I see you use humour to deflect your stress.'

'I wasn't aware that I did that.'

'It's a good strategy,' he says, nodding. 'Would you like to begin?'

'Begin what?'

'Our therapy.'

'I thought we already did.'

'The hypnotherapy part, Mr Thane.'

'Oh,' I say. 'Sure.'

'Good. Let's begin.'

Forty minutes later, I leave Dr Liago's office. I feel calm, relaxed, in control. The session flew by. Hypnosis is not like what you see in the movies, where you go into a deep sleep and start clucking like a chicken. It's more like a nap – one of those long afternoon naps you take on a weekend, when you have nowhere in particular to be, when you open a window and it's autumn cool outside, and you lie under a warm blanket. You rest, you listen to your own breathing, you repeat statements about how you won't drink or gamble. (Fill in your own devastating personal weakness here.)

75

At the end of the session, Dr Liago – quietly, without pressure – asked if I would like to return next week. My own answer surprised me.

Yes, I have a company to run. Yes, I have a busy schedule. But I can afford one hour each week, in the middle of the workday, to drive to Parkdale, Florida, and have my brain rejiggered. I'll put up with a lot worse, if it means not going back to where I came from.

CHAPTER 9

When I return to the office, I find on my new desk a stack of impersonal junk mail addressed to 'CEO, Tao Software'. Beside it is a Manila envelope with a Post-it that says: 'Jim – The itemized transactions you requested – Joan.'

I open Joan's envelope, pull out a stack of laser-printed accounting reports. Yesterday, Joan revealed to me that Tao, desperately short of cash, burning its precious supply, is somehow – preposterously – spending $400,000 each month on 'marketing'. How do you spend that much money marketing a product that isn't even finished? It doesn't take a highly-trained CEO to smell something fishy. So, even before I examine Joan's report, my corporate-embezzlement antenna is twitching.

It takes me exactly thirteen seconds to find the smoking gun. It's right there on the first page: a list of the vendors that have been paid recently by Tao Software, and the amounts paid. Nothing unusual in the first few lines: $327 to Staples for 'office supplies', $267 to BetaGraphics for 'copying and reproduction', $847 to Federal Express for 'postage and delivery'.

But then, fourth item on the list, there it is, staring me in the face: 'International Tradeshow Services – $48,000'.

And that's not all. Five days earlier, there was another payment to International Tradeshow Services, for $26,500. Two weeks before that, a payment for $52,756. All of the transactions are labelled 'Marketing (Tradeshows & Exhibits)'.

I pore over Joan's report. In all, over three million dollars has been spent. And Joan's report only goes back a year. Was even more spent on International Tradeshow Services before then?

I toss the pile of paper onto my desk, pick up my phone. I dial David Paris's extension.

He must see my name on his Caller ID, for he answers with a delighted tone. 'Hello, Jim!' he says. He sounds like a pining teenage boy who is finally called by the girl he longs for. 'What can I do for you?'

'You can come to my office,' I say, all trace of civility drained from my voice. 'Now.'

He appears at the entrance to my office mere seconds after I hang up the phone. He must have bounded over desks and cubicles, like some sort of office Superman, to reach me so quickly. I swivel in my seat and glare at him.

'Yes, Jim?' David says.

'International Tradeshow Services,' I say.

He looks at me blankly.

I drill him with my gaze, remaining silent.

'I'm sorry?' he says.

I repeat: 'International Tradeshow Services.' I try to keep my voice flat, emotionless. But I can feel it: a rush of triumph. Could it really be this easy? Could Tao's problems really boil down to one rogue VP of Marketing who is embezzling corporate funds?

It's called a sham vendor. I have found one in nearly every company I've ever been hired to turn around. Here's how it works. A criminal rents a post office box, prints up a professional invoice from, say, 'Acme Office Supplies', and sends the bill to 'Accounts Payable' at some random company. Most small companies – those without full-time accounting staffs – simply pay any bill presented to them. Sally in Accounting always assumes that someone in the company, somewhere, has bought something. The bills are typically for small amounts – $100 here, $250 there. But carried over long enough periods of time, across hundreds of companies, a criminal can make a nice living at it.

But the sham vendor scam I've just uncovered is more ambitious than that. This is an inside job. Someone at Tao is presenting invoices to the Accounting Department, pretending that they are for services rendered to the company. This criminal probably has an outside accomplice, someone who rents a post office box under the name International Tradeshow Services, and who answers the telephone if someone at Tao gets suspicious and decides to call the mysterious company.

Now David Paris is staring at me, waiting for me to say more. When he decides I will say nothing further, he squints quizzically. 'I'm afraid I don't understand you, Jim.'

'International Tradeshow Services,' I say. 'They're a vendor. The marketing department – that's your department, isn't it? – is spending a lot of money on their services. Who are they? What do they do for us?'

David looks puzzled. He glances down at his feet, wrinkles his brow. He has a look of quiet desperation, the look of a man who wants to please, but has no idea how. Finally, he admits softly: 'I'm sorry. I don't know the name.'

'International Tradeshow Services,' I repeat, for the fourth time. 'Marketing has spent three million dollars on them over the past twelve months.'

David's face shows a glimmer of understanding. He realizes now – perhaps for the first time – that he is being accused of corporate larceny.

'No!' he shouts, too loudly. He's standing at the entrance to my office, on the edge of the bullpen, and his voice carries. From my perspective, I can't see many people in the office, but I sense the background noise grow mute. Conversations stop; people listen to the excitement emanating from the boss's room. David must sense the change, too. He takes a step closer and lowers his voice. Softer now, but still insistent: 'Jim, I have never heard of that company.'

I hand him Joan's report. He stares at the first page. He's a marketing executive, and not very au fait with accounting statements. I watch his eyes flutter over the endless rows of numbers, as he tries to figure out exactly what I want him to look at. Finally, he navigates the page. His little elf-like eyebrows shoot upward and disappear under his hairline. 'No,' he mutters, mostly to himself. 'No, no, no.'

He looks up at me. 'Jim,' he says, softly but with great conviction, 'I have no idea what these payments are for. I have never heard of this company before today. International Tradeshow Services.' He repeats the company name slowly, spitting it out, as if it's a filthy word.

'You didn't submit these expense reports?'

'No,' he says. His voice is quiet but firm. 'Absolutely not.'

'You didn't authorize these payments?'

'No, I did not.'

'It's three million dollars,' I say. 'Tao Software paid that company three million dollars. Where did it all go?'

'How should I know?'

'David,' I say, lowering my voice. I adopt the tone of a father gently reprimanding a favourite son. 'I want you to come clean with me. I can help you, but only if you tell me the truth. We can avoid taking this to the authorities. We can settle this quietly. I have no desire to make this into a criminal matter. Let's just work this out, man to man.'

He turns aggrieved. 'Jim, I don't know what you're accusing me of. But I have nothing to do with this. Besides, I couldn't get those expenses approved without sign-off. Ask Joan. There'd be paperwork.'

Of course there would be. Even at a rinky-dink operation like Tao, no one signs a cheque for fifty grand without *someone's* approval.

I dismiss David with a wave of my hand. He leaves my office in a huff, muttering to himself. I dial Joan.

I say, 'Joan, I see a vendor here...'

'International Tradeshow Services?' she asks.

'Who are they?'

'No idea.'

'Did David authorize those payments?'

'There's no paperwork. I already looked. Someone cut those cheques, but it wasn't me.'

'Who wrote the cheques?'

'I don't know.'

'Get me any information you have on the company. Phone number, address, anything—'

'Last page of the packet,' she says. '"Vendor Details". All the way on the bottom...'

I flip to the last page. Again, Joan is one step ahead of me. She has thoughtfully included the mailing address and phone number of International Tradeshow Services. It's a 941 area code, and a Naples, Florida street address that looks suspiciously like a commercial post office box – 'Suite 3524' in a town without any thirty-five-storey buildings.

'Thanks, Joan,' I say. 'Got it.'

I tap down the receiver, hang up on Joan, and dial the number for International Tradeshow Services.

A female voice answers. 'ITS. How may I help you?'

I come up with the most unlikely name I can think of. 'Tanisha Rockefeller Margarita please.'

'I'm sorry, she's not available. Can I take a message?'

This confirms my suspicion. I am speaking not to a real secretary, not to someone who knows the names of her fellow employees, but, rather, to an answering service. I ask: 'Where are you located?'

'Who's calling please?'

I hang up.

I blow out a long breath. I'm astounded. In my days parachuting into troubled companies, I have seen a lot of incompetence, and a lot of petty thievery. But I have never seen anything so brazen. Usually a sham vendor asks for a few thousand dollars here, a few thousand there. The idea is to keep the amounts small enough so that they fly under the radar. But *three million dollars*? What the hell were they thinking? That I wouldn't notice three million missing dollars?

Well, I have a little surprise for the thieves. They probably don't expect the CEO of Tao Software to show up on their doorstep. But this is exactly what I intend to do.

First things first. I need their address – their *real* address, not the postal box that they rent in Naples.

I take the Manila envelope that held Joan's expense report. I stick a piece of unread junk mail inside, just to give it some realistic heft. Then, on the outside of the envelope, in bold pen strokes, I scrawl: 'ITS' and the postal box address Joan provided.

I seal the envelope, dial Amanda at the front desk, and ask her to come right away. When she does, I hand her the envelope. 'Priority Overnight,' I say. 'I want this delivered first thing in the morning.'

Tomorrow morning I'll have my answer.

CHAPTER 10

I arrive home at six thirty that evening. Still early enough, I hope, to surprise Libby, who is accustomed to my returning home quite late during my turnaround assignments – usually at ten or eleven o'clock, long after she eats dinner alone. Tonight, I have a different plan: to enjoy a leisurely evening with my wife – to cook dinner together, watch TV, maybe even make love. The unfolding train wreck that is Tao Software can wait until morning.

But when I pull into my driveway, I'm surprised that Libby's Jeep is missing. Inside the house, there's no sign of her. No note on the kitchen table, nothing stuck to the refrigerator door.

I climb the stairs, calling her name.

The bedroom is empty. The fan above the bed whirls slowly, squeaking. I go to the sliding glass door at the far side of the room, step onto the veranda. Down below I see the backyard and the swimming pool. But no Libby.

The cool, clean swimming pool gives me an idea. Back in the bedroom, I peel off my clothes – funky with sweat – and toss them into a pile on the floor. I find a bathing suit in my bureau and pad downstairs, barefoot, to the pool.

The pool is not large – just twenty feet across and seven feet wide – meant for one person to swim laps. There's a low diving board at the deep end, which holds eleven feet of water. I was a diver in high school, probably good enough to compete in college. But I decided not to.

There comes an age when most men realize it is unseemly to compete publicly at *anything* while wearing a tiny Speedo. It just took me longer than most.

I climb up the five steps of the ladder, patter out to the rough end of the diving board, wrap my toes around the edge, and – without thinking – let myself fall forward. That's the secret to a good dive – pretending that you're dead. 'Fall like a corpse, boys!' Coach Kramp used to yell to us, 'Fall like a corpse!'

So I do.

I slice the water, propel myself forward, and swim the length of the pool without coming up for air. At the far wall, still submerged, I flip and turn.

That's when I see him.

My eyes burn from the chlorine, and bubbles cling to my lashes, forcing me to squint, and I'm moving fast through the water, so my vision is blurred.

But I do see him.

I'm as sure of the dark form, floating in the water before me, as I am of the blue sky up above. The little body is back-lit, just a silhouette, a shadow, wavering at the water's surface, sunlight dappling around it.

There's no doubt who it is, though. That yellow hair, spread in a wide arc around his head, lit from behind like a golden halo in a medieval manuscript illumination. The little arms, stretched along the water surface.

No doubt who it is.

It's Cole. Floating, right in front of me. I plant my feet on the rough cement below, stand up, and yell. I don't shout his name, or any real word at all – my yell is just an inarticulate cry – a phlegmy shout. I cough up water, too, which somehow slid down my throat in my surprise, and for a moment I think I'm going to puke in my new pool.

I catch my breath, rub my eyes, wipe the water out, and look again.

Whatever I *thought* I saw – isn't there. The pool is empty. No floating little boys, of course. No corpses. Nothing but water.

I shake my head.

I consider leaving the pool, but I know that if I do, I'll never swim in it again. It's not exactly pride that I feel, or adult embarrassment about a childish fear. That's not what keeps me here. It's different. It's primitive. I feel like an animal, an animal whose territory has been encroached. I know, without putting the feeling into words, that if I leave here – if I give up this bit of territory to my dark thoughts, they won't stop here. They'll press in, find another room to surprise me in – maybe the living room, or the bedroom. They can have my dreams, if they want. They've already won that bit of real estate. But they can't have my waking hours, too. Those are mine.

So I take a deep breath, and stubbornly continue to swim.

I swim laps, trying to put that vision – and all memories of that night – out of my mind. I concentrate instead on the sheer physicality of swimming. I listen to my own breathing. I feel my own heart. I hear the sound of the water splashing against the sides of the cement. I try to gauge my body's response to exercise. I'm surprised – and a little depressed – that I'm winded by the tenth lap, and I am unable to continue by the fifteenth. I sigh. Years of self-abuse have caught up with me.

I look up, arch my back, and float on the surface of the water. I stare at the cloudless blue sky. I try to clear my mind, to think about nothing. I'm not sure how long I stay in this floating position. The water slaps and gurgles in my ears, so that I don't hear Libby's car pulling into the driveway, just on the other side of the fence.

But she must have arrived, because when I glance down at the house, almost by accident, I see Libby walking briskly inside, past the sliding glass doors, with great purposefulness. She is, I think, carrying something in her hands – what looks like a package the size of a jewellery box, wrapped in plain white butcher paper. Then she disappears out of view.

I stand, feel the grout under my toes, shake the water from my ears. 'Libby?' I call. 'I'm out here.'

Maybe she doesn't hear me, because she's gone for quite some time, perhaps three or four minutes. I'm about to climb from the pool to search for her, when she finally appears at the sliding door. Her hands are now empty. She looks surprised to see me. She slides open the glass, steps onto the patio. 'There you are,' she says.

I try to leave the pool in a brisk, manly fashion. I put both hands on the concrete edge and jump. I swing one of my legs over the side, just barely, and for a moment I'm balanced precariously between success and failure. Luckily my momentum carries me forward, and I pull my other leg onto dry land. I hop to a standing position, hoping she hasn't noticed my decrepitude.

Now, facing my wife, my bathing suit dripping, I realize, too late, that I forgot to bring a towel with me. I am embarrassed by my flabby stomach – that damned Egg McMuffin! – or was it two Egg McMuffins? – I can't quite remember. I don't want to look down at my stomach or call attention to it. Instead I try to keep my gaze steady, at my wife's face. I hear water dripping from my hair onto the stonework below. I say, mostly to keep the attention away from my gut, 'Where were you?'

She shrugs. 'Just shopping.'

'For what?'

'Clothes.'

'The stuff still in the car?' I ask this because when I saw her walk into the house, she wasn't carrying any large bags of merchandise – but rather, just a small package wrapped in white paper.

She smiles, as if my question is queer. 'No, Sherlock. I'm having everything delivered.' She stares at me. 'It's good to see you swimming,' she says.

She sounds sincere. Before I can reply, she goes on, 'I'll start dinner. You must be hungry,' and she retreats into the house.

*

I sit at the table as Libby stands near the stove. She's sautéing a quartered chicken in a frying pan, and the smell of onions and garlic fills the kitchen. I've showered and dressed, in jeans and a soft button-down shirt, and feel more comfortable now that I'm clothed and my wife cannot see my naked body in daylight.

'How was your swim?' she asks.

For just a moment, I consider telling her about the imagined dead boy floating in our pool. It's tempting. I want to be close to my wife. I want to share things with her, even if it's only despair.

But of course I know better. Some things are best left unsaid. Particularly if they concern your dead son. The son you let drown.

'Perfect,' I say.

'I'm so glad,' she says. But she doesn't look up from the chicken. And she doesn't sound glad. She stares into the frying pan.

'It's a nice house,' I say.

'Is it?' She continues staring stubbornly at the chicken, refusing to meet my gaze.

'You don't like it here,' I say. 'Do you?'

Finally, she looks up. 'I like it fine,' she lies.

'It doesn't matter,' I say softly. 'We won't be here very long.'

I mean this as a comfort. But Libby's expression changes. She looks nervous. 'What do you mean by that?'

'I mean... the company's a mess. We only have seven weeks of cash in the bank. That's it.'

'You can ask Tad for more, can't you?'

'Sure, I can *ask*. But he'll say no. In fact, he already did.' I recall that conversation with Tad, yesterday evening. 'When I asked him for money, he said something very odd. He said I should protect him.'

'Protect him from what?'

'I guess from myself, asking for money. I don't know. He said, "Protect me. Protect my investment." And then he refused to invest another dollar.'

87

She says nothing. She thinks, for what seems like a long time. Finally: 'Strange.'

'What is?'

'That he went through all the trouble of hiring you, and bringing you down here, and he doesn't want you to succeed.'

'Of course he wants me to succeed.'

'Putting you in charge of a company with only seven weeks of cash. Refusing to give you more. It sounds like he wants you to fail.'

I am about to protest. To tell her that she's wrong.

But then I don't. Because she's not.

What she says is true. Why *is* Tad installing me in a company that's doomed to fail? Why is he refusing to put money into it, if he really wants it to be turned around?

Perhaps Libby senses that she hasn't sounded sufficiently supportive of her husband. She says quickly, 'Well, he must think you can do it. He must really believe in you.'

The preposterousness of this statement escapes neither of us. No one in the world believes in me. Not Tad. Not Libby. Not even, come to think of it, me. Mercifully, she doesn't snort with laughter and roll her eyes after she says this.

'You know what I found out today?' I say. 'Somebody has been stealing money from the company.'

'Who?'

'I'm not sure yet. But I'll find out tomorrow.' I add: 'Three million dollars, at least.'

'Wow,' she says, to the chicken. She pokes a thigh with a fork, stares at the juice burbling out. 'Three million dollars.'

'That's why I said, don't get too comfortable. I'm not sure I can make this work.'

My wife looks up at me. Her face takes on a new hardness, like chiselled stone. 'Jimmy,' she says. And she stares for a long time, as if sizing me up. 'You *have* to make this work. This is your last chance.'

I think about her words. What *is* she saying, exactly? That this is the last chance I will be given in the technology industry?

Or that this is the last chance *she* is going to give me – that after being dragged across the country three thousand miles, after having her life uprooted with some vague promise of a new start – that she has finally had enough, and that she is done with me?

Either way, does it matter? 'Yes,' I say. 'I understand.'

'You *have* to make this work,' she says again, and then goes on cooking dinner, staring at the chicken, not looking up at me again for some time.

CHAPTER 11

The next morning, I arrive in the office early, so that I can continue investigating the thief in our midst.

By now, the priority overnight package that I sent to 'International Tradeshow Services' – or at least to the commercial mailbox rented by that fictitious entity – has arrived.

I open a web browser and Google the street address that Joan gave me for International Tradeshow Services: 15266 Collier Boulevard, Naples, Florida, 34119. Google returns a half-dozen companies sharing the exact same address. A plumber, a dog-walking service, an architect, a time-management consultant, and two corporations of unspecified trade. All reside at 15266 Collier, in different suite numbers. My suspicions are confirmed: it's a commercial post office box facility – a Mailboxes Etc., or similar chain.

I pick up the phone, dial information, and ask for Mailboxes Etc. at 15266 Collier, in Naples. The operator, a helpful woman no doubt speaking to me from sultry Bangalore, explains that there is no Mailboxes Etc. at that address, but there is a Postal Plus. Would I like that number?

Yes, I certainly would.

The operator reads the phone number and connects the call. The line rings three times. A man eventually answers. 'Postal Plus,' he says, sounding aggrieved.

'Hi,' I say. 'It's me – from International Tradeshow? I'm expecting that important FedEx from Tao Software. Has it arrived?'

'Just put it in your box.'

'Damn it,' I say. 'How many times do I have to go over this with you? I want all FedExes forwarded directly to me. Didn't we talk about this already?'

'No.'

'You have my address on file, don't you?'

'I'm not sure.'

'Let me guess. You probably lost that, too. Why aren't I surprised? Last time you gave my FedEx to the goddamned dog-walkers.' Then, as an afterthought: 'Do you know where to send it or not?'

A brief pause. I picture a man flipping desperately through a little box of handwritten index cards. He says finally: '56 Windmere Avenue, on Sanibel, right?'

'That's right,' I say, and scribble the address on a sheet of paper. 'Send it right away. Thank you.' I hang up.

So: at 56 Windmere Avenue, wherever that is, I'll find the employee who has been stealing from Tao. What will I do when I learn his identity? I'm not sure. At a minimum, I'll try to recover the money. If it means jail time for the perpetrator, so be it.

I stand up, fold the paper with the Windmere address, and slide it into my pants pocket. I am about to leave the office, to continue my investigation, when Dom Vanderbeek appears in my doorway.

'You ready?' he asks.

'For what?'

He smiles. It's the mean smile of a school bully about to hang the weak kid by his underwear in a locker. 'We're on,' Vanderbeek says. 'Twelve o'clock sales meeting at Old Dominion Bank. You still want to come, don't you?' Almost a taunt. Just yesterday I told Vanderbeek to set up a meeting with any retail bank that would be able to sign a cheque for a half-million dollars. And I insisted that I should come along to run the meeting.

'I'll come,' I say.

'Great,' Vanderbeek says. 'I'm looking forward to seeing you in action.'

CHAPTER 12

Desperate times call for desperate measures, do they not?

What else but a desperate measure could you call this: Asking Randy Williams, my moronic Engineering VP, and Darryl Gaspar, his long-haired programmer, to come along on a sales meeting to Old Dominion Bank, in Tampa – the sales meeting upon which the entire fate of Tao Software now rests?

I ask them to bring a demo of P-Scan. This, it turns out, is just Darryl's beat-up laptop computer, and an old digital camera. The set-up performed adequately two days ago, so I'm hoping lightning can strike twice.

We take Vanderbeek's car. It is a stylish BMW 7 Series sedan. Sticker price: $80,000. I can't help noticing these sorts of things, with the mysterious corporate embezzler still in the back of my mind.

Vanderbeek drives the way he talks, smoothly and authoritatively, weaving through highway traffic, ignoring the people around him, pushing them aside and slicing into their lanes. The drive takes just over ninety minutes. I spend much of the time role-playing with Vanderbeek, learning the names of the people who will attend the meeting: Samir Singh, Old Dominion's VP of Consumer Privacy; Stan Pontin, their CTO; maybe even (although this is not confirmed) Sandy Golden, Old Dominion's CEO.

The agenda for the meeting, I explain to my colleagues, is simple. We will tell Old Dominion that P-Scan is almost ready for commercial release. We will say that Tao wants to deploy the software in a handful of retail bank branches, as a pilot project. We will require a $500,000 commitment from Old Dominion, which will be used to fund final development of the software, and pay for setting up the software in the banks. In exchange, Old Dominion will buy a small piece of Tao Software.

Because we will deploy our astounding technology in Old Dominion's branches – and not branches owned by its rivals – Old Dominion will garner all the favourable media attention that is sure to come from the project. Even better, Old Dominion will share in the profits when Tao sells its product to Old Dominion's competitors. (Nothing delights an executive so much as discovering a way to have his competitors pay him money.)

That's the plan, anyway. It is, I must admit, a long shot. But if we can somehow pull it off – if we can somehow convince Samir Singh, Stan Pontin, and Sandy Golden to write a cheque for $500,000, Tao will gain a few additional weeks of life. Even better, with a modest success to our credit, we may then be able to convince Tad Billups and Bedrock Ventures to sink another five or ten million into Tao.

We arrive in Tampa at eleven thirty. We park in the underground garage below Old Dominion's headquarters, a tall round office tower that looks like a mirrored cigarette. We take the elevator to the fifteenth floor.

The elevator empties into an executive suite, which was clearly designed to convey a message to visitors. The message goes something like this: 'If you did not choose retail banking as your profession, you chose incorrectly.'

The reception area has plush carpet, thickly upholstered chairs, and a cherry-wood table polished to high gloss. On the table, industry trade rags have been carefully fanned out: *American Banker*, *CTO Magazine*, *Retail Branch Specialist*. Perhaps not surprisingly, their pages seem virginal, untouched.

A little before twelve, we're led into the conference room. The receptionist is a young blonde girl who surely can't be older than twenty. Nevertheless she's a pro – when she observes our laptop computer and camera, she offers us a few minutes to set up our presentation before she calls in her bosses. She shows us the power outlets hidden beneath the table, points to the video input jack, and presses a button on the wall. A large projector screen descends from the ceiling with a motorized whir. Then she smiles and leaves. I'm pretty sure the Christians saw a similar smile from the centurions as they were led to the Coliseum stage entrance.

Randy and Darryl plug the digital camera into the laptop port. They boot the computer. They're quiet and nervous. Maybe they've never been on a sales call before? Vanderbeek, in contrast, has that delighted, expectant look you see on the face of a fight fan just before a heavyweight bout. He knows he's about to see a knockout – of me, no doubt. He glances at his big Rolex, as thick as a money roll, as if he can't wait for the bout to begin.

After a few minutes, two men enter the room. They have that hurried, distracted air of executives trying to show that they are too busy to stay for long, and so we ought to prepare ourselves for their imminent departure. Both men are far younger than I expected. One, a handsome dark-complexioned Indian man, must be in his early thirties. He introduces himself as Samir Singh. The other – blond, with stylish wire-framed spectacles – introduces himself as the Chief Technology Officer, Stan Pontin. The two of them standing together look like a welcoming committee at a college fraternity. I have a disconcerting realization: it wasn't long ago that I was the youngest man in any business meeting. Now I'm the oldest. Time marches on.

We go through all the mathematical permutations of shaking each other's hands, sit down across the conference table from each other, and slide business cards back and forth. They skim over the table surface like air-hockey pucks. Stan Pontin arranges our cards into a neat row in front of him, makes sure the top edges are perfectly aligned. Staring at the cards, he says that Sandy – he means his boss, the CEO, Sandy Golden – will try to join the meeting, if he can. 'If he can' is sales-meeting code for: If you guys prove to me and Samir that you aren't assholes.

I say that sounds wonderful, and hopefully Sandy can make it.

They nod.

Finally, with introductions out of the way, and the visiting team's expectations suitably lowered, I kick off the meeting by saying, 'So let me tell you why we're here.'

I cut right to the chase. There's no point in labouring it. Either the gamble will work, or it won't. Business isn't like making love to a woman, where your chances improve the slower you go. The pros and cons are right there in front of you. Either the pluses outweigh the minuses, or they don't. An extra hour of bullshit up front won't get you laid.

I start speaking as if I'm at a dinner party, recounting an amusing tale that I am confident will delight everyone. I'm the new CEO at Tao, I say, and I've been hired to 'turbocharge' Tao's performance. I give a sidelong glance at Vanderbeek, to see his reaction to this bit of bravado. But he keeps a pleasant half-smile on his face, and doesn't react.

I continue my pitch. Tao originally designed its technologies for the consumer market, I say, but we're moving aggressively into a new vertical – retail banking. Within a year, Tao's P-Scan technology will be in use at most retail banks across the country. It's a passive identification and security system. It keeps track of anyone who enters a retail branch – from employees to customers. The technology is so important, and improves account-holder security to such a high degree, that soon almost every bank will use it. In fact, there's a good chance the federal government will *require* its use, in all retail branches, for the purposes of AML compliance.

I pause, let this scenario sink in. It's preposterous, really, and I almost feel embarrassed saying it out loud, but what the hell. It's our one shot.

I continue. We're looking for one bank, I say, just one, that wants to share the spotlight with us. The bank that we choose – whichever it turns out to be – will bask in the initial press frenzy that's sure to accompany the introduction of P-Scan. Americans love new technology. And what's more, this bank will be paid royalties by all of its competitors when those other banks are required to use P-Scan. And, oh yes (almost offhandedly) – this bank will invest $500,000 in Tao, up-front, in order to seal this win-win deal, and become our equity partner.

I stop talking, and let the two young men from Old Dominion digest this. There's a long silence. As I sit, I have a vision, that both Samir Singh and Stan Pontin will burst out laughing. They will slap the table with their palms and guffaw at the outlandishness of my proposal: that Old Dominion pay a half-million dollars to some chicken-shit start-up with a meth-addict CEO on loan from the treatment centre.

But nothing of the sort happens. Instead, they nod respectfully at me, as if my proposal is quite reasonable and is exactly what they expected.

Then they turn to each other. Samir speaks, and at first I think he's talking to his colleague, but the words are really meant for me. 'Yeah, that sounds about right,' he says. 'We've been anxious to roll something like this out. We're playing catch-up in the Georgia market, after the SunTrust merger.' He turns to me. 'We'll roll it out there, first. Metro Atlanta.'

'Yeah, it's perfect,' Pontin says. 'Exactly what Sandy wants.' He has the earnest, guileless face of a technologist. It's a face that says: Surely there's an answer, somewhere, if we only put our minds to it! He adds: 'And that five hundred thousand dollars isn't a problem. It's well within our budget. We can get that done ASAP.'

Then that's it. No point in continuing the pitch. When someone agrees with you, and tells you they will give you everything you asked for, and more, you get out – fast – before they can change their minds.

'Excellent,' I say. 'Well, then.' I rise from my seat.

Samir also stands. He looks down at my business card. It was actually Charles Adams's business card, but I've crossed out the old CEO's name, telephone, and email and replaced them with my own. Classless, I guess, but there wasn't enough time to order reprints before the meeting. Samir says: 'Jim, I'll have our corporate counsel get in touch this afternoon. His name is Mark Sally. He'll email you an MOU. We can get this done by the end of the week.'

'That'll be fine,' I say. I refuse to look at Vanderbeek. But in the corner of my eye, I see that he is standing, too. He also is a pro. He understands: take the money and run. Now we simply need to leave the room. Easy enough.

I reach my hand across the table. Unsure of the pecking order, I offer it to the exact geometric midpoint between Samir and Stan. I smile, but I'm careful to make sure it's not too broad. Not a cat-got-the-canary smile. More like a well-that-was-a-worthwhile-meeting smile. Samir is the first to take my hand. He pumps. Then I turn to Stan Pontin, and shake his. Vanderbeek joins the hand-shaking.

I'm about to move away from the table when a voice, on my right, speaks. It's Darryl. He says: 'But what about my demo?'

I continue to stare straight ahead, hoping that my perfectly modulated grin doesn't waver. I'm about to say, 'Don't worry about it, Darryl,' but then Stan Pontin raises his palms and says, 'Oh, my' – as if he has been terribly thoughtless and rude. He says, 'I'm so sorry. You came all the way here to give us a demo of your product, and we're rushing you out the door, without even seeing it.'

I say, 'Well it's nothing, really. Hardly even a full demo. We can save it for next time.'

But now Samir is staring at the camera and the laptop sitting at the end of the conference table with intense curiosity. He says, 'No, no. We'd be remiss. If Sandy asks us about the demo and we didn't see it... '

He shrugs, as if to say: You know what it's like to work for a tough boss.

'Right,' I say. 'OK.'

Everyone sits back down.

I turn to Darryl. He is slumped in his chair, with his legs outstretched, staring at the presentation screen, as if he's impatient for a movie to begin. All he needs to complete the effect is a bucket of popcorn and box of Jujyfruits. I say gently, 'Darryl, why don't you run the demo?'

He looks baffled for a moment, then says, 'Oh,' and scrambles to his feet. He pushes a long strand of greasy hair behind his ear. He says: 'Great!' and smiles. 'Let me show you Tao's P-Scan 2.0 technology!'

But of course you know what happens next, don't you?

Darryl hands the digital camera to Samir, and tells him to take a picture of anyone in the room – 'anyone he wants'. Samir looks at the camera as if he's been handed a newborn baby, and the responsibility that comes with it. 'Doesn't matter who,' Darryl reassures him.

Samir looks around the room with wavering uncertainty. He points the camera first at Randy, then at Vanderbeek. At last, he makes a decision.

He points the camera at me.

I freeze.

In that moment – that instant between Samir aiming the lens at my face, and clicking the digital shutter – my mind whirs through the distressing possibilities. I am not a famous man, exactly – not in the traditional sense of the word – and yet many of my most colourful moments have been memorialized on film.

There was, for instance, the mug shot after my Menlo Park DWI. I was going eighty in a school zone. The only thing that saved me from serious jail time was that schools are not in session at 2.30 a.m. The incident is not something I'm proud of – not something I like to reminisce about – but then again, the cops don't give you a choice about whether you want your mug shot taken. They just simply take it.

Surely that photo, from the Santa Clara County Jail, circa 2003, is available for download, and now resides in Tao Software's photographic database, ready to be identified and displayed on the huge screen in this fifteenth-floor conference room?

As alarming as this possibility seems, surely it would be better than seeing my *other* mug shot – the one from that night in LA, five years ago, when I was arrested after a bar-room brawl. At least, I think it was in a bar room. The *brawl* part I'm pretty sure about. I was so cranked up, that I didn't sleep for forty-eight hours afterward. It's not every day that your picture appears in your hometown newspaper with *two* black eyes. That photo will surely have tongues wagging in the SunTrust executive lunchroom. Now *there's* a CEO we should stake our reputation on, they will say, studying my photograph, noting the blood-encrusted hair and the meth-enhanced eyeballs popping from my skull.

But before Samir can commit to taking my photograph, there's a commotion at the front of the room. Samir lowers the camera. The door opens, and the young blonde receptionist enters, leading the way for an older gentleman, right behind her. 'Here they are, Sandy,' she says. 'See, you're not late, just like I promised.'

'Thank you, Margie,' he says gruffly. The blonde leaves, shutting the door as she goes.

The older man is portly, with the jowls of someone who has been enjoying fine wine and good steaks for as long as he can remember. He introduces himself – needlessly – as Sandy Golden, CEO of Old Dominion. I notice his tie, a beautiful azure silk Hermes, which sparkles electrically in the sunlight that streams through the conference-room windows. He wears an impeccable suit of dark wool. It occurs to me that the only people in Florida who can get away with this kind of outfit are those who are ushered from air-conditioned conference room to air-conditioned limousine to air-conditioned restaurant. Sandy Golden is a man who hasn't perspired in twenty years.

Golden turns to his lieutenants and says: 'What did I miss, guys?'

Samir summarizes the meeting economically. 'Tao has what we've been looking for, Sandy. Passive image scanning. We can pop it in at our branches. Back of the envelope, I'm guessing it'll reduce liability and compliance costs by thirty per cent, minimum. As far as the deal, we can do a small equity tranche, half-million, and they can use Metro Atlanta as the pilot platform.' He indicates the camera in his hands. 'They wanted to give us a quick demo.'

'Ah, good!' Golden says. He has the booming voice of a man who is used to being in charge. 'Just in time for the show.' He looks at Samir. 'Go for it, Sammy.'

His tone is somewhere between good fun and impatience. Samir gets the hint. He lifts the camera, points it at his boss, and snaps a digital photo.

The camera beams the photo into the laptop, which in turn sends it to the screen at the front of the conference table. Sandy Golden's photograph appears larger than life, accentuating his beefy jowls and the flesh that overhangs his collar like a turkey giblet. God, I think to myself, I hope the P-Scan software doesn't highlight *that*.

Even so, I'm relieved at the turn of events. Surely the software will be able to identify Sandy Golden. He is one of the financial industry's most recognizable CEOs, and there are countless newspaper and magazine articles about him, many recent photographs of his hobnobbing with politicians and treasury officials and other industry bigwigs. And the photograph that Samir just snapped is perfect – a close-up, head-on, in sunlight. His face will be impossible to get wrong.

Darryl says, 'OK, Sandy.' I cringe at my programmer's use of the CEO's first name. 'Let me tell you how this works. We're going to digitize your photograph – you're a handsome man, by the way – congratulations – and then convert it into a series of measurements. Basically, we're turning your picture into numbers, and then we're going to use those numbers to search our database. Think of it like a visual search engine.'

Please, I silently pray. *Please stop talking now.*

'It's really a clever algorithm,' Darryl continues. 'I suppose it isn't going to seem like very much to you – I mean, you're kind of famous, actually, so it's no big deal to identify you – right? But still. You need to use your imagination a bit, Sandy. What you're about to see here – you should imagine it taking place in *all* your bank branches, with thousands of your customers experiencing what you're about to experience.'

Lord, save me, I think. And for a moment, I wonder if I've accidentally said this out loud. I glance around the room. No one is staring at me, so I must have spoken silently.

Darryl says: 'OK, so let's see if we can identify the mystery man on the screen.'

He winks at his audience and types a few keystrokes.

The P-Scan algorithm kicks in. On screen, Sandy's photograph is converted into granular grey blocks. The software identifies his most salient visual characteristics; I grimace as I watch Sandy's fleshy neck being highlighted in yellow. But when I look around the room, no one seems to notice.

On-screen, the software begins announcing which databases it is scanning: first, the state-by-state DMV records, the local newspapers, Facebook, YouTube…

The scanning continues.

I think to myself, with growing concern, that surely the program will arrive at the correct identification at any moment. After all, it is analyzing a photograph of Sandy Golden. A *perfect* photograph. Of *the* Sandy Golden. Industry Titan. Famous, and publicity-hungry, CEO.

No answer comes. P-Scan continues scanning. Thinking.

Another list of databases crawls down the screen: *Crain's New York Business… Fortune* magazine… *Bloomberg Businessweek…*

Ah, I think to myself. *Closing in on the answer. Closing in. Here it comes.* We wait one moment longer.

Finally text appears on the screen: 'Identity Confirmed. Probability: 98.3%.'

Below this definitive statement of great certitude is a photograph of the man that P-Scan has conclusively determined is the same man who is seated in the conference room.

It is a driver's licence photograph. In defence of the P-Scan algorithm, I will admit that the man on the screen in front of us shares a similar build and heft to the Old Dominion CEO. The man in the photo too has a fleshy neck that hangs pendulously beneath his chin. There, alas, the similarities end. The man in the photo is black, weighs about three hundred pounds, has two gold front teeth, and sports a gigantic 1970s afro. His name, according to the text beneath the photo, is 'Anthony B. Tybee', and he lives in South Carolina, or at least he did when the photo was taken, two years ago.

We descend from the fifteenth floor to the parking garage in silence. Even Randy Williams, who lacks any business sense, knows enough not to speak, and instead stares down at his shoes, which are, I notice dishearteningly, white Keds. Dom Vanderbeek isn't smiling exactly, but his lips are twisted puckishly, like an altar boy trying not to laugh when the priest lets slip a fart. Darryl looks from face to face, sensing that he is the subject of some as-of-yet undetermined emotion. He's not sure what he has done wrong, but he knows it's *something.*

The floor indicator counts down from 3, 2, L, and then finally P1. The chime sounds, and the door opens. The four of us exit the elevator and step into the dark parking garage. The air is humid. As I turn to look for Vanderbeek's BMW, a figure slips past us and steps into the elevator. Behind us, the elevator doors rattle and start to close.

I didn't get a good look at the man, but caught enough of a glimpse to realize he was familiar. I'm not sure where I've seen him before, but

I know I have. Recently. So I turn, to get a better look.

By now the elevator doors have almost closed, and – here's something odd – the man who entered – whom I'm trying to get a good look at – is standing off to one side of the elevator, as if to stay out of view. The doors clank shut, and I'm left looking at my own misshapen reflection in the polished wood and brass of the doors.

I look at the floor indicator just above my head. It rises past L, without stopping, and keeps ascending. It stops finally on 15 – the floor from which we just came – and pauses there for a while, before it begins its descent back to the lobby.

'Jim?' I hear someone behind me say. I turn, startled. It's Dom Vanderbeek. Now he's grinning broadly. His mirth is unmistakable: Boss loses sale. Boss freaks out in parking garage, stares at elevator. Good story to tell when we return to the office. 'Everything OK?' he asks.

'Fine,' I say. 'Let's go.' I lead them to the car. As I walk, I realize at last whose face I just saw – who it was that ascended to the Old Dominion executive suite. The face was that of my neighbour – the man across the street, the carnivorous velociraptor with the bulbous head and feral eyes.

But that's impossible. I saw the face for only an instant, and my brain – overtired, burdened by our recent humiliation at the sales meeting upstairs – surely must be playing a trick on me. As I climb into the passenger seat of Vanderbeek's car, I try to put the episode out of my mind.

By the time we pull into Tao's parking lot, an hour and a half later, I've succeeded, and I think no more about the man in the elevator, or the failed meeting, or the imminent termination of my short-lived career as a corporate turnaround specialist.

CHAPTER 13

Back in my office, I check my voicemail. There is just a solitary message from Gordon Kramer, 'checking in' and making sure I kept my appointment with Dr Liago yesterday – 'or else'. I call Gordon back right away, and leave him a message that the appointment went fine. The last thing I need is for Gordon to think I went AWOL, and have him show up with a set of handcuffs at the Tao office building.

I glance at my watch. While this morning's failed meeting at Old Dominion means I won't be bringing any new cash in through the front door, at least I can stop it from leaving out the back.

It's time to pay a visit to the corporate embezzler who has been stealing millions of dollars from my company. I finger the piece of paper where I wrote the address of the thief – the real address, where the money actually winds up: 56 Windmere Avenue, Sanibel.

It's time to pay a visit to 56 Windmere Avenue.

My phone rings. It's a soft muted tone. The Caller ID says 'Reception'.

I pick up. 'Yes, Amanda?'

'You have a second, Jim?'

I'm already on my feet, the phone receiver wedged against my shoulder, the paper with the Windmere address clutched in my hand. 'Actually I'm on my way out the door—'

'There's someone who wants to see you.'

'Now?' I have no appointments scheduled. It must be a salesman –

someone selling printer toner or payroll services. 'I don't have time. Just take a card and tell him I'll be in touch.'

'Jim,' Amanda says, and I realize now that her voice sounds urgent. 'His name is Tom Mitchell. He's from the police. He wants to ask you some questions.'

I meet Tom Mitchell in the boardroom. He's a handsome man – broad-shouldered and trim. His hair is the colour of pewter, like old, heavy silverware your grandmother leaves you when she dies. In contrast, his eyebrows are jet black, and they arch theatrically, as if Tom Mitchell hasn't believed a word *anyone* has said since 1992.

He is not, technically, 'from the police', as Amanda claimed, but rather (I learn this from his impressive business card) an agent from the Special Crimes Unit of the Federal Bureau of Investigation, Tampa Field Office.

We sit across from each other at the long black conference table. After he hands me his card, he says, 'Thank you for meeting with me. I know you must be up to your eyeballs in work.' He has a Panhandle accent – *ah-balls* for eyeballs – and his honeyed lilt makes each word sound like a gentle caress.

'Not a problem.'

'So.' He smiles at me. 'You're the new guy in town.'

'I suppose.'

'When did you arrive?'

'Two days ago.'

'And how do you like Florida, Mr Thane?'

'Well, to be honest, it's very hot.'

'Ain't it though.' He places his hands on the surface of the table, drums his fingers, and stares at me for what feels like a long time. Finally, he says: 'You probably know why I'm here.'

'You code in Java, and you're looking for a programming job.'

'Ha,' he says, in a tone that does not sound much like laughter. But then again, it wasn't much of a joke. 'Not exactly. No. You may have heard that I'm looking into the Charles Adams case. Did they tell you about him – about what happened?'

'Just that he disappeared.'

'That sums it up perfectly,' he says, and smiles. He sounds strangely upbeat, considering he's talking about a man's disappearance. Maybe he's happy that he doesn't have to explain any intricacies of the case to me, since there are no intricacies – the case being exactly this: *Man walks out of front door of house. Man vanishes.*

I wait for Tom Mitchell to say more about Charles Adams. But he doesn't. Instead, he looks at me, smiling, as if inviting me to volunteer my own information. I have no idea what he's waiting for. That I'll rise from my chair and shout, 'It was me! I did it'?

But I don't. Instead I look down at his business card. 'Special Crimes Unit,' I say, reading the title under the embossed logo. 'What is that – some kind of super investigative agency?'

'Yes,' Mitchell says. 'A super agency. I work closely with Aquaman and Green Lantern. They're waiting for me in the car.'

Now it's my turn to laugh.

'Seriously,' Mitchell says, 'it's not very glamorous. The way I describe my little group is that we investigate the things that fall between the cracks. Crimes that don't quite belong anywhere else.'

'Oh?' I say, trying to sound interested.

'For example, crimes that cross jurisdictions. Crimes that are politically sensitive. Things that politicians want to seem upset about. Things like gambling, racketeering, child pornography, that sort of thing.'

'And missing CEOs?'

Do I see a flash of anger on his face – for just an instant? As if he's not sure why he's on the Adams case, either? If I did see it, it's gone in a moment, and he's a good soldier again. He shrugs. 'Well, now, not all our cases are high profile. Sometimes we just look into things that don't belong anywhere else. Charles Adams being a good example.'

I lean back in my chair, make a show of glancing at my watch. 'So how can I help you, Agent Mitchell?'

'Well I'm not sure,' he says. He thinks about it, as if he truly is trying to figure out how I might help him. After a moment of this theatrical pondering, he says: 'I guess I'd like to know if you've noticed anything since you've been here.'

'Noticed anything?'

'Anything *unsavoury*?'

I am suddenly conscious of the sheet of paper in my pants pocket, the note with the sharp crease digging into my thigh like a guilty memory. On this paper is scribbled an address: 56 Windmere Avenue, Sanibel. And at this address, I will find the person who has embezzled millions of dollars from Tao Software. Yet despite my awareness of this paper, and despite its digging insistently into my thigh, I hear myself say to Tom Mitchell: 'No. I can't think of anything worth mentioning.'

'The reason I ask,' Mitchell says, and he leans forward, as if confiding a secret, 'is that we suspect Mr Adams was mixed up in some unpleasantness. He knew some very nasty people.'

'Venture capitalists?'

'No,' he says. He doesn't crack a smile. He stares at me. Then, quite suddenly, he asks: 'Have you ever heard of Ghol Gedrosian?'

I shake my head. 'Is that some kind of... some kind of lamb dish?'

'It's a person, Mr Thane. He's a person. A person of interest.'

'Whose interest?'

'That's an expression. It means he's someone we'd like to talk to.'

'What's stopping you?'

'Just the fact that we don't know where he is.'

'You have two missing people, then.'

He spreads his palms in a small gesture, something between an admission of failure and a plea for forgiveness. 'I suppose you're right.'

'I wish I could help you,' I say. 'But I've never heard of him.'

'No,' Mitchell says. 'I wouldn't expect that you had. He's not exactly part of your milieu.' He lingers on the word milieu, insinuating that I'm the kind of man who might just use such a word, maybe over lunch at the country club. I want to tell him that no one at AA uses the word milieu, unless it's a kind of French liqueur I haven't yet discovered.

Mitchell rises from his seat. 'I won't take any more of your time, Mr Thane. I came mostly as a courtesy, to let you know we haven't given up on Charles Adams. We're going to keep looking for him.'

'That's very reassuring, Agent Mitchell. Thank you.'

'Do me a favour, though, will you? If you notice anything – anything at all – I want you to give me a call. My number's on that card.' He leans over, taps his own business card, which is lying on the table in front of me.

I look at the card, dumbfounded. 'Is *that* what these things are for?'

He smiles and wags his finger at me. 'You're a funny man, Mr Thane.'

'That's what they tell me. Would you believe it hasn't helped me in my life at all – not a single bit?'

'I *do* believe it. No one likes funny people. We think you're hiding something.'

'Maybe we're hiding the fact that we're not really funny.'

'See?' he says. 'There you go again.' He points and shakes his head. 'You're like a nightclub act.'

A nightclub with a ten-drink minimum, I want to say.

But I merely rise from my chair and shake his hand.

'I promise to keep you informed, Agent Mitchell,' I say. 'If I notice anything at all.'

Ten minutes later I'm driving West on Route 867, over the Sanibel Causeway, to the island of the same name off the Florida coast. I lied to Agent Mitchell when I told him I hadn't noticed anything 'unsavoury' at Tao. In fact I've noticed three million unsavoury things – those dollars stolen from my company's bank account and delivered to an imaginary firm called ITS.

Of course there's no mystery behind the missing money. The culprit was Charles Adams. I knew it even before Agent Mitchell showed up and told me that the former CEO was mixed up with dangerous people. All the evidence pointed to Charles Adams. No one else at Tao – no one other than the CEO – had the authority to sign cheques for such large amounts. Joan Leggett could find no paperwork supporting the ITS cheques – no invoices, no receipts – because there was no paperwork.

Charles Adams skulked into his office late at night, or early in the morning, entered bills into the corporate accounting system, and printed and signed the cheques himself. The cheques that came out of his laser printer travelled through the US mail, to a Naples post office box, and then into the hands of... *someone*. Who? Charles Adams himself? More likely, one of his mysterious associates – one of those 'dangerous men' that Joan Leggett had seen waiting for him at Tao.

Why didn't I tell Agent Mitchell any of this? Partly it was because of Tad Billups's warning to me, to 'protect' him, and to protect his investment. But there's something else too. I feel a peculiar closeness to Charles Adams – a man I've never met, a man who's likely dead. I've walked in his shoes: owed money to frightening men, felt the walls closing in around me. I understand men like him. Because I am one.

Sanibel Island is – despite the best efforts of its Chamber of Commerce and its Rotary Club to portray it as a young person's paradise – really just a large retirement community floating in the middle of the ocean. It sits there, in the Gulf of Mexico, stocked with old people at varying levels of decrepitude.

As far as retirement cities go, it's an odd one. You notice it as soon as you cross the Causeway. What you notice is: it's not quite rich, and it's not quite poor. Looking at the houses, I can't decide whether the island is an aspiration, or a cautionary tale. Maybe it's a little of both – a place where people travelling in opposite directions meet in the last years of their lives.

It's no Nantucket, no Sea Island. There are no estates, no rolling lawns. It was built too long ago for that, in an age before air conditioning, and so the houses are crowded and small, from a different era – the era before McMansions and three-car garages. It's a snowbird community, filled with people who flee brutal winters or needy grandchildren. It's crowded in December, packed in January. But today, in the middle of July, it's hot – very hot – and most of the houses I pass are deserted and shuttered.

The house where I finally arrive – 56 Windmere – is about what I expected: a run-down ranch-style box, aluminium siding, a screened-in side porch, and brown, overgrown grass that hasn't been mowed in many weeks. How many weeks? I try to estimate. Maybe six – maybe the same period of time that Charles Adams has been missing.

I drive past the house, turn the corner, and park a block away. I'm not sure what I'm going to do at 56 Windmere, or who I'm going to find there, but I don't want anyone to see my car, or find me snooping around.

I leave my car unlocked. I trudge through stultifying heat, listening to cicadas scratching out mating cries in the grass. How the hell do insects have the energy to screw when it's this hot? No wonder there are so many bugs.

I approach the house. There are no cars in the driveway, and the windows are dark. I ring the doorbell.

No answer. I wait, ring it again, knock loudly.

A minute goes by, then two – enough time for even an elderly person to make his way off the crapper and come to the door. But no one does. Either the elderly occupant is physically stuck to the seat, perhaps due to an unfortunate suction accident, or there is no one home.

I try the knob. It's locked. I retreat down the steps and wander through overgrown lawn, around the perimeter of the house, my shoes swishing through dry grass, nettles catching on my chinos. I circle the screened-in porch. If someone approaches me, and asks what I'm doing here, I still have a plausible excuse: Why, I'm just checking to see if my friend is at home, napping on the porch. Of course, if anyone bothered to quiz me about my friend's name, I'd soon be led away in handcuffs. Not for the first time, mind you.

But the porch is dark and empty. My friend is not napping on it. In fact, I doubt my friend, or anyone else, has slept in this house for a long time. It has a forlorn, abandoned look.

I circle to the backyard. Now I've crossed a line. If someone confronts me, I will have no excuse. Even friends don't peek through their friends' rear windows.

Florida doesn't have basements, because you can't dig a cellar in a swamp. So most houses are built on raised concrete platforms. I stand on my tiptoes and peer into a double-hung window.

I see a small, dark bedroom. I know it's a bedroom because there's exactly one item that is bedroom-like within it: a thin scraggly futon on the floor. No sheets, no blankets, no box spring. The carpet is water-stained and threadbare. A cheap desk is pushed up against the far wall.

My investigation would probably end here – really *should* end here – except that I notice that the window's sash lock is unfastened. I'm no expert at home intrusion, but it doesn't take much to see it: the top and bottom windows are misaligned by half an inch, almost as if someone is inviting me in. Anyone standing this close could see the window was unlocked. Anyone would be tempted to enter. Anyone.

So I tug the window upward. I expect an alarm to blare, but it stays quiet. The window rises smoothly in its track, opening wide enough to allow entry even to my portly frame.

I give one more glance behind me, making sure that no nosy neighbour watches, then I hoist myself up. I fall inward, onto the floor, and wheelbarrow with my hands onto the carpet. I pull myself into the house. My feet land with a thump. I'm in.

I've made a lot of stupid choices in my life. Most of them were made under the influence of alcohol, or pills, or crystal meth, or just sheer desperation. But at least my stupid choices have, until this point, been based on some kind of reasoning. It's true that my reasoning may have been degraded and flawed – you can't parse constitutional law when you're jacked up on Wild Turkey and coke – but at least I *had* reasons – misguided ones, drug-induced ones – but they were still reasons.

In contrast, standing in this dark bedroom at 56 Windmere, I can't for the life of me come up with one plausible excuse as to why I'm here. I have just broken into someone's house. How in the world can I justify that? And then the reason comes to me, and it's worse than having no reason at all. I'm doing the thing that I always do: I'm fucking everything up. I'm destroying my own life.

I can imagine the newspaper headlines: 'Software Executive Breaks into House'. I can imagine the conversation with Tad Billups: 'Yes, Tad, I'm aware that you gave me one last chance to get my life together, but you see, I had to find out what was in that old abandoned house.'

But here I am. So I might as well. These words ought to be etched onto my tombstone – probably will be – '*Might as well*' – because they sum up my life perfectly, and surely will explain my death. It's my reason for doing everything I have ever done.

Might as well.

It's the motto of every hooker, of every addict, of every tattooed two-bit thug, of hapless death-row inmates, of crank whores lost on drugs. It's how we got to where we are.

Might as well.

All right, Jimmy. Since you're here, you *might as well* have a peek inside that desk.

Desks make for good peeking. Desks have papers inside them. And papers have names. And a name is what I seek. The name of the person who has been stealing from my company.

I go to the desk, and the floorboard creaks. I stop and listen. Surely it would be obvious by now if someone else were in the house with me – wouldn't it? – but I stand very still nevertheless, counting to twenty.

I listen for footsteps, for snoring, for water running through pipes, for the murmur of soft daytime TV. But I hear nothing.

The desk is a cheap IKEA model, one of those particleboard designs that you assemble yourself just once in your life, maybe when you're twenty, and then – after you finish – vow that from now on, you'll splurge the extra fifty bucks to have someone do it for you. There's a wide drawer along the top, and three narrow ones to the side. I look inside the big drawer. Just dust, a chewed pen, a dead spider. The other drawers are empty, too. Whatever I was hoping to find isn't here.

I go into the hall. The carpet is a burnt orange colour that hasn't been popular since the 1970s. Even in the half-light, it's clearly filthy, with a path trodden deep into the pile. Whoever owns this house doesn't spend much on upkeep.

From the hall, I can survey the lay of the place. Just above me is an attic trap door. There are two bedrooms off the corridor – the one I just explored, and a second, which I peek into now, and which is empty except for a bookcase without any books.

I give the rest of the house a similarly cursory inspection. There's a single small bathroom. It contains: a plastic bathtub, a floral shower curtain, and a toilet – seat up – with a rust ring in the bowl, and dried yellow piss on the rim. Down the hall, near the front door, there's a kitchen with a linoleum floor that curls up at the edges like an old man's toenails.

The kitchen is conclusive proof that no one lives in this house. The little telltale signs that kitchens usually hold – the ones that mark human habitation – are nowhere to be found: no dishes in the sink, no newspapers on the butcher's block table, no half-drunk glasses of orange juice. A quick glance inside the fridge confirms this: the fridge itself is empty, but the light bulb still glows. Someone has paid the electricity bill within the last several months. But no one bothers to keep food here.

Whatever I hoped to find at 56 Windmere – whether an incriminating document, or maybe even Charles Adams's corpse slumped on the kitchen floor, in a pool of brains, with a shotgun in its hands – I do not find. There is no document. There is no dead CEO.

I decide to bring my little breaking and entering adventure to an end. I am about to walk out of the front door, and return to my humdrum existence as a turnaround executive. I'll have other opportunities to ruin my life in the future. It won't happen today, apparently.

But as I approach the entry foyer, something occurs to me. There is one place left to explore, one area in the house that I haven't looked at. And it's bothering me. After all, I've come this far, haven't I? So I might as well.

Might as well.

I return through the hall, to that attic door tucked into the ceiling. There's a short pull chain. I tug, and the door glides open on a hydraulic hinge. A compact stepladder is telescoped against the back of the trap. I extend it down, and it reaches to the ground.

Heavy, humid air pours out of the opening, and it smells like mothballs. Up the ladder I climb, poking my head into a black crawl space. Far away in the darkness, three slits of light glow – a ventilation grille. My hand grazes a light switch. I flip it. A single bulb in an enamel socket illuminates the attic. The room is A-shaped, just tall enough at the apex to allow a man of normal height to walk, stooped over. I pick my way over the unfinished floors, careful not to trip on exposed beams. There are no boxes, no crates, no family heirlooms, no furniture that someone can't bear to throw out. There are no dead CEOs, either. There is only one item in the attic. I see it at the far side: a black, heavy plastic garbage bag – 'hefty' size, they call it – the kind of bag used for the disposal of lawn clippings or construction debris.

I walk to it, bent over, careful to avoid the exposed rusty nails poking out of the roof's two-by-fours. I kneel down next to the bag, spread it open.

114

I've never seen this much cash, in one place, in my entire life. The bag is filled with hundred-dollar bills, stacked and banded into tight bricks. I reach deep into the bag, pick one of these bricks at random, flip through the bills to be sure they are all Ben Franklins. I'm not a counterfeiter, and wouldn't know the difference between a real hundred-dollar bill and a fake, but these look as real as any money I've ever seen.

When you work as a commission-based sales executive, as I once did, you become extraordinarily skilled at a certain type of arithmetic. This is because your entire life is based upon it: how much food you can eat, how big a mortgage you can afford, how much pussy you can get on the side. You begin to solve these types of equations in your head, as proficiently as a NASA scientist.

They go something like this: 'If I have one hundred sales prospects, and I close a sale ten per cent of the time, and each sale is worth one hundred and fifty thousand dollars, and I earn forty per cent commission, well then, I'm going to bring home $600K. You've got to figure taxes, of course, and the tax rate on that kind of income – federal and state – is about forty per cent, which leaves me with $360K.'

Now, a similar set of equations runs through my head, automatically, as I stare at the pile of cash at my feet. A brick of hundred-dollar bills is worth, I guess, twenty grand. Two hundred bricks is worth four million dollars. You've got to figure taxes, of course, and the tax rate on a bunch of cash sitting in a plastic garbage bag is… well, it's zero.

It occurs to me, as I stare at this four million dollars of cash in a garbage bag, that I'm looking at Tao Software's missing venture capital. I don't have evidence for this, of course, but the numbers fit, and this is the address where Tao's cheques were sent. The mechanism by which those legal above-ground dollars were converted into underground cash eludes me, but surely the police and Agent Mitchell will be able to figure it out.

Assuming I live long enough to tell them.

Which – I suddenly discover – is not a sure thing.

From outside the house, I hear sounds in rapid succession: two car doors slamming, heavy footsteps on the front walk, and keys jingling in the entry door. I freeze.

I consider retreating further into the attic, hiding in the dark recess at the far side of the room, hiding until whoever is visiting 56 Windmere finally leaves. That thought lasts exactly two seconds. This attic isn't a hiding place. This attic is a dead end. Maybe literally. Whoever is visiting this house means to come right here, to this attic. There is only one thing in this house worth visiting. It's not the empty IKEA desk, or the bookcase with no books. It's the plastic bag at my feet.

So I turn and I flee. This is a two-step process – turning and fleeing – and I execute the first part with competence, maybe even grace, turning my body with the litheness of a gazelle. Next, I flee. Here is the part where I fail. I lunge towards the attic exit, with all the speed and power I can muster. Unfortunately, I forget about the low ceiling, and the exposed rusty nails. My head slams into a beam, and sharp metal punctures the skin of my forehead. I see a flash of white light, and I hear the ocean. I stand motionless, dazed, my hands gripping my head, trying to remember where I am, and where I'm going.

I regain my bearings. I'm in an attic, and I'm standing next to a garbage bag of cash that I'm not supposed to see, and there are men coming to retrieve it. Presumably these men will be surprised to find me here. Men who come for four million dollars of cash in a garbage bag probably do not like to be surprised.

More carefully now, I try again to flee – slower this time. I flip off the light and scramble down the stepladder.

I jump down into the hall. I need to get the hell out of here, but I can't just turn and run. I must re-fold the stepladder and close the attic. I glance into the hallway. I can't see the front foyer from here, but I hear the door opening. I try to stay calm, keep my motions small. Fumbling makes things take longer. I telescope up the ladder, segment by segment, until it fits neatly behind the attic door. I push the entire apparatus upward, into the ceiling. It's heavier than I expected. The door closes on its hydraulic hinges and clicks shut.

There are voices now, in the foyer, near, indistinct and male, more than one.

I lunge from the hall, into the safety of the nearest door, which turns out to be the bathroom. Bad choice. The one window here is small, and stuck shut with dried paint. I could probably open it, if I banged it loose. But banging is not a good idea. I hear footsteps approach in the hall.

I step into the shower and pull the curtain closed, slowly. I remove my fingers from the plastic liner just as I hear a voice in the bathroom doorway. For an instant I fear I have been discovered, because the voice speaks directly to me. But the language is not English, and the tone, though loud, is not aggressive. It's a man calling out to a friend – a hint of laughter in his voice.

His footsteps trudge into the bathroom, and they stop just inches from the shower curtain. I can hear the man's breathing. He sounds big, like a bear. There's a metallic *clank*. Then I hear a zipper and the splash of urine in the toilet bowl. 'Ahhh,' the man sighs, in that universal language of men who have waited too long for a car ride to end.

The piss continues for some time. Outside the bathroom, the other man's voice calls. Again, not English. It sounds Eastern European, maybe Russian. The man who is urinating says something in response, but keeps on pissing. I don't speak Russian, but I do piss, and so I get the general idea: 'Give me a minute. I'm taking a piss.'

I move my head slightly, one inch to the right, to expand my field of vision. Now I can see the top of the toilet tank, just barely. It isn't much of a view, but it does help explain the metallic *clank* I heard just before the man began to urinate. The man was carrying something in his waistband, something that he removed and lay on the ceramic tank. A gun. A very large, black gun. Which I now stare at, as it lies on the back of the toilet.

I hold my breath. The gambler inside me suddenly doesn't like these odds. Indeed, the gambler inside me doesn't like any of this. It was a fun little escapade, breaking into a house, because it seemed harmless. Oh sure, there was some downside. I might be arrested. My career might be ruined. Libby might be embarrassed.

Now, the downside seems much steeper than I initially calculated. Not only embarrassment. The downside now includes... well, *death*.

Next to me, the man finally stops urinating. There's a zipper sound, and a toilet flush. 'OK,' the man calls, in accented English. His hand reaches into my field of view, grabs the gun from the toilet, and then he, and his gun, are gone.

I stand very still. There's activity outside the bathroom door: the clanking sound of the attic stepladder being unfolded, then muffled footsteps. I wait for what feels like a long time. Then the footsteps, and the voices, return. The ladder clanks again, and the attic door closes with a click.

I wait, motionless, until long after the sounds of the front door closing and tyres receding from the driveway.

I look down at the bathtub where I stand. Drops of blood spatter around my feet like warm rain. It takes a moment to remember that it's mine. I step out of the tub and look at myself in the bathroom mirror. On my forehead is a lump the size of an egg and the colour of rotting meat. A line of blood streaks from the wound and drips down my face, like a very Catholic depiction of a crown of thorns.

I hold a thick wad of toilet paper against my head, to staunch the blood. It keeps coming, but at least the paper stops it from dripping to the floor. With my left hand holding the paper to my head, I use my right hand to wipe down the tub, erasing the evidence that I've been here.

When I finish cleaning the bathroom, I return to the attic. I am not surprised by what I find. Which is nothing. The attic is empty; the four million dollars are gone.

CHAPTER 14

'Jim, what happened to your head?'

This is the question asked by Amanda when I return to the Tao office. Puzzled faces stare at me through the glass of the conference room; people in the bullpen, hearing the commotion, lean back in their chairs to get a better look at the most exciting thing they've seen all day, maybe all month: the boss in the reception area, with a head wound.

'I'm fine,' I say, loudly. 'Just a little accident. Rusty nail in the head. That's all.'

'Do you need stitches?' Amanda asks. She flips the telephone headset from her ear, stands to get a better look at me. 'Come here.' She grabs my hand and guides me around the reception desk. I want to protest, but her grip is strong and she accepts no opposition. She pushes me down into her chair and stands over me.

Before I can stop her, her fingers are dancing along my scalp, moving aside my hair, gently touching my wound. 'Does that hurt?' she asks.

'No. Ouch. Yes.'

'Look at it,' she says, in something like fascination. 'Was it really a rusty nail?'

'Not sure how rusty. It was kind of dark.'

'Where were you?'

'Long story.'

'Now, Jim, this is a very important question, and you must answer me seriously.' She looks at me sternly.

I'm expecting her to ask if I broke into someone's house and hit my head in their attic. But she asks instead: 'When was your last tetanus shot?'

Tetanus shot? I can't recall my last doctor's appointment. When your medicines tend to be delivered in eight-ball format rather than pill jars, things like health care and doctors take a back seat to other priorities, such as: When can I next get high. But I do not want to explain this, nor do I want to spend the afternoon at Tampa General, waiting for a tetanus vaccination. So I lie. 'Yeah, I had one. Right before I came to Florida.'

'You are very lucky, then,' she says. Amanda's voice is soft, very close to me – her mouth just above my ear. I feel her warm breath against my skin. Her fingers are in my hair. It's strangely intimate. Even though we're in the public reception area, and I know people are watching us, her back shields this private moment from everyone's view.

I glance at her shirt. It's a natural movement of my eyes – I merely try to look straight ahead – but straight ahead in this case means that I look down her loose-fitting camisole. I see her breasts. She wears no bra. Her nipples are pink, round, the size of cherry blossoms. And I see something else, too – something jarring and out of place on this girl's skin that is so smooth and pale. A tattoo, on her left breast, just above her nipple.

The tattoo is not a girly, feminine drawing. It's Cyrillic, blue-black ink, block letters.

Иисус умер за мои грехи.

I glance up, at her face, but it's too late. She has caught me. Done the triangulation. She knows. Exactly where I was looking.

But she stays still, with her shirt hanging down. Her fingers remain on my head; and her touch becomes even softer, more gentle. She leans closer.

'You are very lucky,' she says, again, softly, more breath than voice, and I smell her perfume: floral, like honeysuckle. She pauses. 'Very lucky.'

'Am I?' My voice is hoarse. I look down, to avoid her eyes. I'm firing on all cylinders today: breaking into houses, avoiding Russian mobsters, ogling my employee's breasts. Maybe this afternoon I'll use a cap gun to stick up the local Winn-Dixie. Just for the hell of it.

I stand, and we break contact. She backs off, and we switch places behind the desk.

The moment is gone, and she sits down and puts on her headset. Then, as if nothing has happened, she says: 'Your three o'clock is here. He's in the small conference room.'

'My three o'clock?'

'Pete Bland. He's been waiting for you. You're twenty minutes late.'

I inherited Pete Bland, Tao's attorney, from my predecessor, the same way I inherited Charles Adams's title, and his desk chair, and his tattooed receptionist.

Pete Bland is a partner at Perkins Stillwell, Tampa's pre-eminent white-shoe corporate law firm. This is yet another example of a pattern I've noticed everywhere at Tao since my arrival: for a company that hasn't turned a penny of profit, ever, and relies on the largesse of distant investors, thrift is nowhere to be seen. The sweeping art deco reception area, the designer furniture, the Aeron chairs, the class-A office space, and, now, the fancy attorney – all of these add up to one haemorrhagic burn rate.

But that cash haemorrhage is precisely the reason I called this meeting with Pete Bland – I need to staunch that bleeding. And fast. There's only one way to do that.

I take a Manila folder from a locked drawer in my desk and hurry to the small conference room. I'm expecting to find a corpulent middle-aged man, in an expensive suit and gold cufflinks. Instead, I see a skinny thirty-five-year-old kid with Doc Marten shoes and stylishly long sideburns – I think they still call them 'mutton chops', don't they? – and a colourful neon tie that looks as if it needs its own power generator. I guess when you're born with the name 'Pete Bland', there are two ways you can cope: give in, or resist. Tao's corporate attorney chose the second path. With his shoes, and sideburns, and tie, he looks more pimp than lawyer.

'Jim Thane,' he says, 'great to meet you. I'm Pete Bland.' Despite his unusual dress, he has a standard lawyer's handshake: dry, firm, quick. Lawyers are like taxi drivers; they always want you to know that the meter is running. 'I've heard a lot of good things about you.'

Clearly a lie, which I ignore.

'But I have to ask,' he continues, 'what happened to your head?'

I almost forgot. I touch the wound. It's the size of two eggs now. 'I didn't look where I was going.'

'Story of my life,' Pete Bland agrees. 'That's how we wind up with a mortgage and two kids.' He sits down, pops the lid of his attaché. He removes a yellow legal pad and a pen. 'So,' he says, clicking his pen. 'You want to fire a few people.'

I look behind him, make sure the door is firmly closed. 'More than a few, actually.'

Two things happen after you fire a lot of people. First, you spend less money on salary. Second, you get sued. The two things go hand in hand, and one follows the other like caboose after locomotive. That is the reason for my meeting with our company attorney: I want the first, but not the second.

Pete Bland asks: 'You have that list we talked about?'

I open the Manila folder I brought, and hand him a single typewritten page. On it is a double-spaced list of names. No bold typographical heading, by the way, saying: 'To Be Fired Next Wednesday'. That's one of those little CEO tricks you learn after many years of accidentally leaving papers on the photocopier.

'Before we start,' Pete says, 'maybe we should call your HR person in here and have her join us?'

I tap my index finger next to one of the names on the list – Kathleen Rossi, Director of HR.

'Ah,' he says.

I nod grimly.

He looks over the list. 'OK, let's cut to the chase. Forty names. How many of them are black, how many women?'

'Zero black, four women.'

'How many women will be left after you fire everyone on this list?'

'Two,' I answer.

'No good,' he says, quickly. 'Take all four women off the list.'

'You're shitting me.'

'I shit thee not,' Pete says. He doesn't look up. He's busy drawing a line through each of the obviously female names. 'You'll save whatever you think you'll save on salary, but you'll pay it back ten times, first to me, then to the EEOC.' He looks up. 'Now, tell me about the old folks. How many on the list?'

'How do you classify "old folks"?'

'People over forty.'

'Ouch.'

Pete leans back in his chair and studies me through slitted eyes. He has the look of a doctor trying to decide whether a patient is ready for grim news. He tosses his pen onto the table. 'Clark Rogers, he's the partner at Stillwell who handles employment law? – you probably know him?' He doesn't wait for an answer. 'He has a saying. You wanna hear it?'

'No. I don't think so.'

'"*When an employee looks ugly, things get ugly.*" That's his saying.'

'Classy.'

'You said you wanted to hear it.'

'Actually, I didn't.'

123

He shrugs.

'There are six people on that page over forty,' I say. '"Old folks", to use your fancy legal jargon.'

'So let's do the math. Six people means fifteen per cent of all the people being fired,' Pete says. 'How many old folks are employed at Tao currently?'

'Seven.'

'See the problem?' Pete Bland asks. 'They make up eight per cent of the workforce, but fifteen per cent of the lay-offs. Might as well cut a cheque right now. Write it out to "Aggrieved Old Persons Class Action Trust". How much money you got in the bank?'

'Not much.'

'Enough to pay my bill?'

'I wouldn't sit on our invoice, if I were you.'

He looks at me warily, to see if I'm joking. I am not. He slides the list to my side of the table, gingerly, a train robber passing a stick of dynamite. 'Here's what you do. Take three of the old folks off the list.'

'Which three?'

'I don't care. Flip a coin.'

'I'm firing them for a reason. They're terrible.'

'Of course they're terrible,' Pete says. 'They're old. When people get old, they get lazy. That's why we want to fire them. But you can't do it. Not in this country.'

He stares at me, lets his point sink in.

Then he goes on: 'Once you make the changes that I'm recommending – the girls and the old folks – you'll be OK. The WARN Act doesn't apply here. You can just terminate at will. When's the big day?'

'Wednesday, next week.'

He nods glumly. 'I *am* sorry,' he says. 'I know this is the hard part of your job.'

Actually, I want to tell him, the hard part of my job is figuring out who *not* to fire. This company is like a high-tech grease trap – all drippings, no meat. But I put on a dour expression and say, 'Yes, it's going to be very difficult.'

Pete Bland attempts to commiserate with me, for exactly five seconds, by not speaking, and nodding. Then, his mourning complete, he clicks his pen smartly, as if snapping the head off a particularly annoying insect. He rises from his chair, puts his pad back into his attaché. 'You married?'

'Yes.'

'We should go out. Me, you, the wives. There's this little place on the water, only the natives know about it. It's called the Gator Hut. Ever been?'

'No.'

'It's great,' Pete says. 'I'll have my assistant set something up.'

'Sounds like fun,' I say. An image comes to me: of Libby, seated at the table with Pete and his wife. My wife wears a morose expression, and her arms are crossed, and she stares sullenly, refusing to speak or to eat, like a political prisoner on a hunger strike. 'A lot of fun,' I repeat.

'Good,' he says. We shake hands.

I escort him to the door. 'There is one other thing,' I say, as if it's an afterthought. 'Someone at Tao is embezzling money from the company. Would you mind doing a little fact-finding?'

'Fact-finding?' He raises an eyebrow.

'The money is being sent to a house on Sanibel. I want to know who owns the house.'

I hand him a piece of paper with the 56 Windmere address.

'Easy enough,' he says. 'I'll have someone run a search.'

CHAPTER 15

I leave the office at six thirty and arrive home ten minutes later. When I climb from my car, I notice my neighbour across the street – the velociraptor with the overbite and the protruding forehead.

He's pacing on his front porch, speaking into a cellphone, gesturing with his free hand, which holds the stub of a cigar.

He's far enough away that I can't make out his words distinctly, but I hear the murmur of his voice, the rhythm and flow of his words. I am about to turn and walk into my own house. A breeze catches my neighbour's voice, and carries it to me. Something clicks, and now I know why I couldn't understand him. He is speaking Russian.

He turns to look at me, and our eyes lock. I feel guilty, as if I've been caught spying. He says something into his phone – but now the breeze is gone and I can't hear him – and he snaps his cellphone shut, and drops it into his pocket. He throws his cigar to the ground, crushes it with his heel, and walks inside.

I search for Libby in the kitchen first, and then in the bedroom. I do not find her in either place. I wander back outside, into the front yard, to look for her in the vegetable garden. But the garden too is empty. The soil is flat and virginal, without a single footprint.

I go to the side of the house. A chorus of cicadas ululate around me. Twenty yards away, behind the pool, there's a garden shed, on a raised wooden platform. The door of the shed is open. Inside is dark. When I approach, I see my wife, kneeling in the shadows of the shed, her back to me.

'Libby?' I call.

My wife turns to me. 'Jimmy,' she says, sounding startled. She pushes a bag of topsoil quickly onto a metal shelf.

She rises to her feet, slaps her palms. Then, without looking back, she leaves the shed, and closes the door behind her. 'You're home early,' she says. It sounds remarkably like an accusation.

'What are you doing?'

'Just gardening.'

I think about the garden I just passed, its flat soil and lack of footprints.

'What happened to your head?' she asks.

'Accident.'

'What kind of accident?'

Admitting that I broke into someone's house, or that I found four million dollars of cash in a stranger's attic, or that I hid behind a shower curtain from a man with a gun, will probably not build my wife's confidence in my good judgement.

So I say, 'Supply closet at work. Would you believe all I wanted was a lousy pen, and this is what I got?'

She looks dubious. But then she smiles. She takes my hand and guides me into the house.

We order pizza from Domino's. We sit on the little veranda just off the master bedroom, above the pool. There are two chaise longues here, but we share a single one. We sit cross-legged, facing each other, with the grease-soaked pizza box between us.

I tell Libby about my day – most of it, but not everything. I tell her about my meeting with Pete Bland, and his neon tie, and his Doc Martens, and his long sideburns. I recount how Pete described people over forty as 'old folks', about his advice that Tao fire people in a precise mathematical ratio, according to sex and race.

I do not tell Libby about my trip to 56 Windmere, or my discovery in the Sanibel attic.

Things feels right and comfortable between us – maybe for the first time since I arrived. Not great, exactly, but comfortable. How many times have we sat this way, facing each other, with a pizza box between us? How many meals have we shared? Many, surely, and these are the moments that make up a marriage – these small events of no great note. It's *these* moments – not the big dramatic ones – that determine the fate of a relationship. I'm happy finally to have a quiet, boring evening with my wife.Our lives could use a little less drama.

We finish the pizza. I get up from the chaise, stretch my legs, and look through the glass door, back into the bedroom. 'Should we go inside?' I ask.

This was not really meant as a question, of course. It was more a statement. What I really meant was: Time to go inside now, Libby.

But Libby looks into the bedroom in a way that suggests she is actually deciding whether to join me there. Whether to return inside. *Ever*. A strange expression crosses her face – a momentary darkness – like a shadow of cloud racing across a sunlit meadow. 'I wish we didn't have to go back in there,' she mutters.

I look through the glass again, trying to understand what she means. I stare at the bedroom. There is nothing in the bedroom, save for the bed, of course, and a few bureaus, and a ceiling fan. Is it possible that I misunderstood her? I say, 'You don't like the bedroom?'

'I don't like the house,' she replies.

But then, as suddenly as the darkness appeared, it is gone, and she laughs, throwing back her head, showing me the pale white curve of her throat. 'Oh never mind!' she says, and smiles. 'I'm sorry. It's just… I like it out here. I like the fresh air.'

She takes my hand, and starts to lead me to the door. But I pull away from her, and I lay my palm on the door handle, to keep her from opening it.

'Wait,' I say.

Something tells me not to let this moment pass. Maybe this is Libby's way of reaching out to me. Maybe this is her way of letting me know that she is ready to talk about that night. The night that Cole died.

I say, 'Sometimes I see him, Libby.'

She looks at me. Her face is wary. 'You see him?' she repeats.

'Our son,' I say.

'Oh.' She nods. 'Of course.'

'I know you blame me for that night. And you should. Of course you should, but...'

'Please,' she says, and grabs my hand. 'Please, Jimmy. Let's not talk about it.'

'We lost our child, Libby. How long can we not talk about it?'

Libby looks beyond me, into the distance, to someplace very far away. To a different time. To a different place.

She remains silent. Staring. Distant. What is she thinking about?

When she speaks, at last, her voice is just a whisper. 'Something we share,' she says.

'What is?'

'Losing a child.'

'Of course it is,' I say.

But before I can say more, or ask what she means, she steps forward, and kisses my cheek, very softly. Very sadly.

She turns, and goes back into the bedroom, leaving me alone on the veranda, as if it were I who resisted returning to the house in the first place.

Downstairs we watch TV – one of those reality shows where people try to act naturally while performing for cameras that they pretend do not exist. An hour of this is enough to convince us to go back to our own reality show, and so we climb the stairs, back to the bedroom.

We undress for bed. My wife stays on the opposite side of the room, keeps the bed between us, her back turned to me. As she slides on her T-shirt, I catch a glimpse of her naked breast, in profile, and – despite myself – am aroused.

She slides into boxer shorts – men's boxer shorts – there's nothing sexier than a woman in men's boxer shorts, is there? – and she climbs under the covers, and turns off her nightstand light. 'Good night, Jimmy,' she says. 'I'm tired.'

Not tonight then. Another image comes to me, unbidden, of my receptionist's breasts, her small, pink nipples, that weird tattoo.

I turn off my own nightstand light, and we lie together in the dark. I listen to the creaking electric ceiling fan above us.

'There's something I didn't tell you,' I say, into the darkness. 'About how I hurt my head.'

I know immediately that I've made a mistake, that I've chosen a path that will lead to conflict. But there was an instant tonight, out on the veranda, when Libby connected with me – or *nearly* did. It lasted just a moment, but maybe that's what I'm searching for now, again – another moment of intimacy – a connection with this woman who always seems so far away.

'You said it was the supply closet at work,' she says.

'I lied. It was a house, actually. I broke into someone's house.' I have that familiar feeling now: that I'm ruining things – the pleasant evening we just shared, the pizza on the chaise longue, the moment of intimacy on the veranda – all the closeness, all the comfort. I just can't leave things alone. Here comes Jimmy Thane, with a torch, ready to burn it all down. 'I climbed into the attic. I found a bag filled with cash.'

I tell her the story: about 56 Windmere, about the cheques written by someone at Tao and sent to that address, about how I slipped into the house through a back window, and found cash in a garbage bag, and was almost discovered by men speaking Russian, men with guns.

When I finish, she is silent.

Silent for so long, in fact, that I wonder if she fell asleep during my recounting of the tale. But no, I feel her sitting upright beside me in the dark. She is awake. But silent. Completely silent.

I must admit: I was not expecting silence. I was expecting a reaction, *some* kind of reaction, because that's what a wife does when her husband tells a story about breaking into a house and finding four million dollars of cash in a garbage bag – she reacts, somehow. *How* she reacts is beside the point. Maybe she is titillated. 'You broke into a house?' she might say. '*You*? Jimmy Thane?'

Or maybe she is angry. 'What a terrible risk you took!' she might say. 'You could have been hurt! They had guns!'

But silence? I was not expecting silence.

This silence continues for a long time.

Finally, I say, 'Libby?'

She whispers, 'Jimmy.'

I can't read her tone.

'What are you doing, Jimmy?' She sounds sad, disappointed. She mutters, mostly to herself, 'Jimmy, Jimmy, Jimmy.'

'What?'

'Why do you ruin things?'

'I don't ruin things,' I say, even though she's right, even though this is the exact thought I had about myself, just a moment ago. I tried to ruin things this afternoon when I broke into the house; and when that didn't work, I tried ruining things again, just now, lying in bed, when I insisted on telling Libby about the house and the money. I couldn't leave things alone. I couldn't let our nice evening together end... nicely.

'I just wanted to find out who's stealing money from the company. I need to figure out who's responsible. It's my job.'

'Your job?' she repeats. She turns on her nightstand lamp. In the sudden brightness, her skin is pale and lined, her face haggard.

She stares at the teak fan blades, spinning lazily above us, and addresses her next words to the fan, not to me. 'Why do you think you were hired, Jimmy?'

'Because Tad Billups—'

'Tad Billups *what*?' she spits. 'He thinks you're a great CEO? Is that what he thinks, Jimmy? That you're a great turnaround artist? He hired you because you're the best candidate? In all of Silicon Valley, you were the best one he could find? You're his last great hope?'

'No,' I say weakly.

'What did Tad tell you when he hired you? Do you remember what you told me? "Protect me", he said. "Protect me, Jimmy."'

'What does that have to do with anything?' I ask. But even as the words leave my mouth, I know. As usual, I am one step behind her. As usual, she understands things long before I do.

But she continues, relentless, pressing her advantage. She stares at me the way an entomologist stares at a beetle she's about to pin to a specimen board. 'We finally have a chance, Jimmy. After everything you've done to us, we still have a chance. God only knows how.'

'Libby... ' I croak.

'We still have a chance,' she goes on. 'But you want to ruin it. Tell me something. If you keep digging, what do you think you're going to find? Do you honestly think you're some genius detective, uncovering a big secret? There *is* no secret, Jimmy. Why do you think you're here? I tried telling you before, but you didn't listen. Why do you think Tad Billups, your so-called friend, who practically gave you up for dead – why do you think he gave *you* this job in Florida, to save some crappy company that he knows can't be saved? Because of your impressive pedigree?'

I'm shocked into silence. When I look at my wife, I see an anger and intelligence I never recognized before. Where is that soft waitress I flirted with at The Goose, so many years ago? Where's the girl who knew nothing about venture capital when we married, or high technology, or CEOs, or corporate turnarounds? She is gone. She has been replaced, by someone else. Someone new.

Lying in the bed beside me is a clever and hard woman.

I say, 'I just want to know what's going on.'

'You don't know what's going on?' she asks. '*I* know what's going on, and I'm your wife. Should I lay it out for you?'

I stay silent.

'All right,' she says. 'Here's what's going on, Jimmy. You were *not* hired to dig and investigate what's happening at Tao. You were hired to be so goddamned grateful you're there, that you ignore whatever the hell you see. You were hired to shut up and act stupid. That shouldn't be too hard for you, Jimmy, should it?'

'Libby…'

'Four million dollars stolen from your company, Jimmy. Four million dollars in a garbage bag. Who do you think is behind it?'

'Tad?'

She smiles. Not a mean smile. It's much worse than that. A smile of compassion. The smile that smart people make for dumb people, strong people for weak. A patronizing smile. When I see that smile on my wife's face, I think I might cry.

Maybe she realizes she has gone too far. She takes my hand. Her voice is soft and warm. 'Jimmy, listen to me. We're not going to get another chance. This is it.'

'I know that.'

'You were hired *not* to notice missing money. You were hired *not* to investigate. That is why Tad selected you. Because you owe him everything. Do you see now?'

I nod.

'Jimmy.' Her voice is gentle, and I want to roll over and melt into her. How I love this woman. 'Jimmy, you can do this. If you give Tad what he wants, he'll reward you. I know he will. He wants you to keep things quiet. So keep them quiet. No bankruptcy, no lawyers, no accountants poring over the books. You see? When everything blows over, when it's all quiet and no one's looking, he'll shut the company down. And then, he'll owe you. He'll owe you big time. He'll find a way to thank you. Maybe he'll give you a real company to run. Maybe back home. In California. You see?'

I do. What was I thinking, exactly? It seems crazy now. Skulking around in attics, hiding behind shower curtains. My wife is right. Of course she's right. Tad Billups knew I'd discover the missing four million dollars. How could I not? He didn't hire me to *find* it. He hired me to ignore it.

'You know the definition of insanity, Jimmy?' Libby asks.

'No.'

'Doing the same thing, over and over. Doing it again and again, despite all the evidence in the world that it isn't working.'

'What are you saying?'

'Not saying. Asking. *Begging.*' She squeezes my hand. 'I'm begging you, Jimmy. Don't make the same mistake again. This is our chance. This is our way back.'

CHAPTER 16

The next morning, when I arrive in the office, Amanda is manning the reception desk, smiling beatifically, happy with everything in the world.

'Good morning, Jim,' she practically sings. 'Your head looks healthy today.'

'Only on the outside,' I say, as I brush past. I want no further discussion about my head wound. I will put away all memories of yesterday – of dark attics filled with garbage bags of cash, of looking down Amanda's shirt. My bedtime conversation with Libby has inspired me. I will be a good soldier, a good CEO. I will lead Tao quietly and efficiently, to the best of my ability. I will keep the company afloat for as long as I can. I will protect Tad Billups. No more rusty nails in my forehead. No more self-destruction.

'You missed a phone call,' Amanda says. She hands me a pink message slip. 'Just a minute ago. He said it was urgent.'

I glance at the note. 'Sandy Golden,' the paper says, and a phone number. I walk into the bullpen, studying the message. *The* Sandy Golden? From Old Dominion? What on earth could he want?

'Good morning, Jim,' someone says.

David Paris's head pops over a cube wall.

'Morning, David.'

'Jim… ' he starts, and before I can walk away, he leaps from his cube like a thoroughbred from the starting gate. He's off, bounding towards me, waving a white pad of paper, which I notice – even from this distance – is filled with copious notes and sketches, the jottings of a man locked in a mental institution. 'I really want to show you this, if you have some time.'

'Unfortunately I don't have a lot of time, David.' I keep moving towards my office.

'But you don't even know what it is,' he whines. He sounds hurt.

His analysis is true; I don't know what is written in that tiny handwriting on his pad. But there is something I *do* know, which David does not – which is that, next Wednesday afternoon, he will be one of the forty people escorted from the office. So there's no point in building bridges, or reaching out to him, or even feigning interest in his notes.

'Some other time,' I say.

'When, Jim?' He yammers like a relentless little terrier nipping at my ankles. 'When? When exactly?'

'Thursday,' I say. 'Next week, Thursday. Schedule a meeting with me in our online calendar.'

'Very good, Jim,' he says. He grins, a happy elf again.

He retreats quickly, before I can change my mind, backing away towards his desk. I'm only halfway into my own office, one foot still in the bullpen, when I hear an electronic ding from my computer. I look to see a new meeting request on my computer screen: Will I accept a meeting with David Paris, the screen asks, 'to discuss cost-effective marketing initiatives'? Coincidentally, I am about to implement my own cost-effective marketing initiative, which is to axe the entire Marketing Department. But what the hell. I go to my desk, slide the computer mouse, and click that I do indeed accept David's meeting.

'Thank you, Jim,' David shouts across the bullpen, into my office. So much for electronic messaging.

'No problem, David,' I shout back.

I put my briefcase down on the desk, beside the ornately-framed photograph of me and Libby and the red demon lurking behind us. I really do need to get rid of that picture.

I dial the phone number on the message slip. I'm expecting to navigate a series of corporate gatekeepers – first the receptionist at Old Dominion, then Sandy Golden's personal assistant – and then perhaps to wait on hold for Sandy to 'be connected' with me – which is corporate-speak for 'please cool your heels while the other fellow picks his nose, or finishes taking a dump, or whatever else he needs to do to establish his telephone dominance over you'.

But the voice that answers on the first ring is the same gravelly bass I remember from our disastrous meeting in downtown Tampa. 'Sandy, here,' the voice says. He's talking through a cloud of static, which tells me that I've reached Sandy on his private cellphone – no receptionists, no assistants.

'Sandy, it's Jim Thane. I got your message.'

A long pause. I think that Sandy's cellphone has been disconnected. But then his voice returns. 'Jim,' he says finally. 'I'm very happy to tell you that you've got the contract. We've discussed it internally here, and everyone agrees that your company's technology is just what we need. So we're in. In fact, we're so excited, we'd like to up the ante. We want to invest an even one million dollars. Same pre-money valuation as we discussed. That sound all right to you, Jim?'

I try to keep my voice flat, not to sound surprised. 'That sounds all right.'

'We can do it on a handshake. Save the legal. I'll have a deal memo on your desk by the end of the day. Payment wired by Monday.'

'That's great,' I say. 'I'm delighted.' But I try not to sound too delighted. It's a negotiating tactic you learn over time: try not to laugh uproariously at the schmuck who actually accepts your offer.

'So we're square?' Sandy asks. A strange question, asked in a strange tone of voice. For a man who claims to be 'so excited' about this deal, he doesn't sound very enthusiastic. He sounds like a man settling a tab with a bookie.

'Sure,' I say. 'We're square.'

'Good. Goodbye, then.' And with that, he's gone – no telephone niceties, no promise of 'a mutually beneficial partnership', or of 'exciting things to come' – none of the usual corporate crap that everyone blows into each other's assholes at the end of every conversation, in order to keep the wheels of commerce lubricated. I'm left holding a dead phone.

I replace the receiver softly. I'm still standing at my desk – haven't sat down since arriving.

I walk over to Dom Vanderbeek's office. Since the day I came to Tao, when I embarrassed Dom in front of the rest of the employees, he has beat me into the building every morning. His precious BMW 7 Series is always there when I arrive, parked in the space nearest the entry door, a shiny black middle finger pointing in my direction when I enter.

Dom's office is the biggest in the building. It didn't surprise me when he claimed Charles Adams's private office for himself, after I declined it. Not one for egalitarian symbolism, apparently. Now he's sitting in a sleek grey chair, leaning backwards with his feet on his desk, listening to someone on the phone. He notices me in the doorway, waves me in with self-important nonchalance. He rolls his eyes and makes a chattering-mouth gesture with his hand, to indicate that his telephone partner won't stop talking.

'All right, buddy,' Vanderbeek says, finally, into the phone. 'We're on for next Tuesday. I'll see you at Derousher's at noon. I'm buying.' A few more pleasantries, some more silent listening by Vanderbeek, another roll of his eyes. 'All right, then,' Vanderbeek says again. 'All right. Take care. Later.'

Vanderbeek hangs up.

'Guess who that was,' he says to me.

'No idea.'

'Guess.'

'No idea.'

'Hank Staller. Wells Fargo. He's interested.'

I wonder silently if he's interested in buying Tao's P-Scan technology, or if he's interested in poaching Tao's VP of Sales. Either would make me happy. 'Excellent,' I say.

Vanderbeek waits, maybe for more compliments. So I add, 'Really, excellent. I'm impressed.'

Vanderbeek mulls this over, wondering whether I'm being sarcastic. Finally he points to the chair across from his desk, inviting me to sit. He removes his feet from my face, sits up straight. 'So, what's up?' he says. He rubs the area around the black Rolex Submariner on his wrist, to indicate that his watch is so expensive and heavy, it tires his wrist.

'I just got off the phone with Sandy Golden,' I say.

'He took your call?'

'Actually, he called me. They're going to do the deal. Old Dominion will pay us one million dollars, in exchange for rolling out P-Scan in the south-east branches.'

Vanderbeek squints. 'For real?'

I shrug.

'Well,' he says. I see the gears spinning in his head. He's trying to decide how to feel. He's happy, obviously, because Old Dominion was his lead in the first place, and so he'll net a piece of the sale – maybe as much as a quarter-million dollars. On the other hand, the meeting with Sandy Golden was instigated by me, and I ran the show. So some of the credit – not the cash – needs to be directed my way. Which obviously pains him. And then, finally, there's some amount of bewilderment. He was at the same meeting I was: the meeting where our technology didn't work. And that raises the question: What the hell is going on?

'I just thought you'd like to know,' I say.

'Congratulations.'

'To both of us,' I try.

He stares at me.

Still, I play nice. 'It'll give us some runway, Dom,' I say. 'A million dollars means more breathing room, if we can get spending under control. An extra month, maybe, if we can—'

The phone on Vanderbeek's desk rings, cutting me short. He holds up a finger to silence me, and lifts the receiver. 'Vanderbeek here,' he says. He listens for a moment, then says into the phone, 'Hang on a second.' He cups the mouthpiece, looks at me. 'I have to take this, Jim. You mind?'

As I turn to leave he says, 'Jim, do me a favour, will you? Close the door on your way out?' Into the phone: 'Hey, buddy, what's up?'

I shut the door and go.

CHAPTER 17

Given the way Vanderbeek studiously ignored the news of our amazing sales success at Old Dominion, I'm surprised when, late in the afternoon, I hear the sound of champagne bottles popping in the lunchroom.

I've been poring over next Wednesday's upcoming termination list all afternoon, trying to run the numbers and figure out who, given the additional cash from Old Dominion, can be struck from the list (the answer, I realize sadly, is no one; no one at all).

The sound of champagne corks in the lunchroom makes me curious, though, and so I leave my office and slip between the foosball table and the Ms. Pac-Man machine, through a bullpen that is strangely empty. No one is at their desk.

When I get to the lunchroom, the Mystery of the Empty Desks is solved: the room is crowded with Tao employees, virtually all of them, and belatedly I understand what's happening: a celebration. Four magnums of cheap champagne are being passed around the crowd, the necks of the green bottles throttled like chickens, bubbly gurgling into tiny plastic cups and sloshing onto the linoleum floor.

'Here he is,' Vanderbeek calls out loudly, when he sees me in the doorway. 'The man of the hour!'

A smattering of applause.

'What's this—' I start to say, but too late. Vanderbeek barrels on.

'Let's hear it for the man who single-handedly closed the Old

Dominion deal!' He shouts like a carnival barker. 'Let's hear it for the man who gave Tao one million dollars in the bank, and another month of breathing room. Isn't that what you called it, Jim? "A month of breathing room"?' Before I can answer, he shouts: 'Let's hear it for our new CEO, Jim Thane, the man who can close million-dollar deals with his eyes closed, before breakfast.' And to ensure the proper response, Vanderbeek begins to chant, leading the crowd, pumping his fist: 'Jim! Jim! Jim! Jim!'

Maybe there hasn't been much to celebrate lately at Tao, because people take up the chant with surprising alacrity. 'Jim! Jim! Jim!' they cheer.

'Listen,' I say. 'It's not exactly...' My voice trails off. I'm not sure how to extricate myself from this. Next Wednesday, I'm going to fire almost every person in this room. To gush publicly about an extra million dollars in the bank, when that million barely buys us another month of time... to celebrate a great personal triumph, to pop champagne corks and declare victory, when a few days from now these same forty people will be escorted into the front parking lot, carrying boxes filled with their belongings – would be an amazingly heartless and tactless gesture – a tone-deaf move of epic proportion.

Which is certainly why Vanderbeek arranged this.

'Jim! Jim! Jim! Jim!' the crowd chants. Their smiles are good-natured, not cynical. They want to have good news. How strange it is, that – after two centuries of capitalism – with the evidence laid out starkly in front of us like a prosecutor's summation – we Americans still believe in all the corporate bullshit; we still treat our companies like sports teams for which we're important players, cheering our mutual successes, blissfully unaware that all of us – from the highest to the lowest – are just cogs in a vast, industrial, unthinking machine, grinding everything and everyone into a fine powder of unimportance.

'Pass him a drink!' Vanderbeek shouts, over the chant. He's smiling, that wolf's smile, and it occurs to me at this instant that he *knows*

– of course he knows: the community of high-technology people is small, and Vanderbeek has friends in the Valley, people who know all about my colourful past – about my drunken outbursts, my downward spirals, my crash landings in rehab. He has talked to those people, shared stories. He knows all about me – knows that I'm an alcoholic and an addict.

One of Vanderbeek's henchmen – a sales guy whose name I almost but not quite recall as Rick or Dirk or Rich – something masculine and Waspy – grabs the champagne bottle from Rosita and careens across the room towards me. He sticks it in my face, smiling wide. 'Drink up, boss!' he shouts. 'Drink.'

Vanderbeek changes his cheer. 'Drink! Drink! Drink! Drink!'

And the rest of the employees do, too. 'Drink! Drink! Drink!' they shout.

I glance across the room, and my eyes lock with Amanda's. Her expression is more curious than happy – she's studying me the way a scientist might, sincerely interested in my reaction to this latest probe. Almost the same instant that I realize Vanderbeek knows my secret, I sense that Amanda does too, and that my secret is her secret, also. I recall that tattoo, on her left breast, that intricate Cyrillic writing, and I know it tells a long, sad story, one that will not be unfamiliar when I finally hear it.

I take the champagne from Rick or Dirk or Rich, put it to my lips, and drink.

It's not like in the movies, you know, where everything changes the moment you taste alcohol again. It's not *Dr Jekyll and Mr Hyde*. You don't start foaming at the lips, launching into a bender, groping girls' asses right there in the lunchroom, out of control and maniacal.

You just sip. One sip. And that is all.

And then you hand the bottle back to Rick or Dirk or Rich, who is smiling broadly, as if he knows too. Could Vanderbeek have told him?

Across the room, Vanderbeek is nodding at me, with a warm smile, as if I've passed his test, and I haven't let him down.

I look back to where Amanda was standing, but she's gone. I just catch a glimpse of her, through the kitchen doorway, as she sashays back to her reception desk, to man the phones. It's impossible to read her reaction, of course, because her back is towards me, and I can't see her face, and you can't determine someone's emotions from the way they walk – can you?

Yet she seems disappointed in me.

She has the walk of the brokenhearted.

CHAPTER 18

I leave the celebration early, and let Vanderbeek run the show. Once I depart, though, his game is won, and he too soon retreats.

With Vanderbeek gone, the room deflates. Employees scud away like ocean foam, drifting off in little clumps, away from the lunchroom, back to their desks and their make-work, pretending to be busy and productive.

In my own office, my mind wanders, and I find myself looking at that silver-framed photograph, of me, Libby, and the horned satyr. I pick it up and stare. The frame is solid and heavy. I try to recall the night the photograph was taken – the party, the brick-walled loft, my drunken pass at the hostess. I can't remember much about that night. Nothing at all, in fact, except that it *happened*.

'Jim?'

I look up to see Joan Leggett peering into my office. She's wearing some awful pants ensemble, with a big colourful silk bow tie on her blouse. The outfit makes her look like an old vaudeville act, a sad clown about to be sprayed by seltzer.

'What is it, Joan?'

'There's something I need to tell you.'

I gesture to a chair. She closes the door and sits. Her eyes flit to the photograph of me, Libby, and the satyr.

'I know,' I say, pre-emptively, 'like a kidnapping.'

'Actually, I think you look... *nice*.' Maybe she means younger. Or less battle-scarred. It was two rehabs ago, come to think of it. She continues, 'I'm not sure I should even tell you this. Probably it's not important.'

'*What's* not important?'

'Last night, I came into the office. About eleven o'clock. I couldn't sleep, so I thought I'd do the bank recs.'

I can imagine Joan Leggett's life: forty-something, divorced, living alone. With so little else, other than this lousy job at this shitty company, that she rises from her bed near midnight to perform bank reconciliations.

She goes on, 'I thought the office was empty. But when I got to my cube, there was someone in it.'

She waits for me to guess.

'Vanderbeek,' I say, without much surprise.

'He was using my computer. Going through the financials. I'm sure of it. He was very apologetic. He had an excuse – he was just getting ready for a sales meeting, and his computer wasn't working, and so he needed to use mine.' She pauses. 'But I didn't believe him. He had that smile. You know the smile I mean?'

'Like a wolf.'

She nods. 'I didn't want to bother you about it. I mean: there are no real secrets at the company, right? Everyone knows what's going on.'

I keep my voice steady. 'What do you mean, Joan?'

'I mean the money,' she says.

I keep my eyes fixed on her, try not to move. Try not to breathe.

'Well it's not a surprise, Jim,' she goes on.

'It's not?'

'People know cuts are coming. Headcount has to be reduced. How else can we do it? Everyone sees the writing on the wall.'

'I suppose,' I say. I feel myself relax.

But she's waiting for more. I understand finally what she wants. Maybe even the real purpose of this conversation. She wants comfort.

'You're staying, Joan,' I tell her. 'You're not on the list.'

She smiles, realizes it's unseemly, then tries to look dour. It doesn't work, so after a struggle, she just smiles again. 'Thank you, Jim. That means a lot to me.'

'Don't thank me yet.'

She rises. 'Well… I know you have a lot of work to do.' She mutters more thanks and retreats from my office.

The day drags on, and when its end finally comes, it's a relief.

The truth is, I don't have much work to do. That's the dirty secret of being a CEO. Like a British monarch, your role is mostly ceremonial – handshakes and public pronouncements, showing up in the right room at the right time on the right day. You are the face of the company, both to the outside world, and to the inside. Supposedly, you are in charge of 'big' decisions, but you learn pretty quickly that whatever big decisions you make are never implemented anyway. Your pronouncements are like those of the Oracle of Delphi: you declare something, and the people around you fight about what it means, or how to carry it out, and at the end of the process, nothing much happens as a result.

So I sit at my desk, makings lists and outlines, reordering priorities, assigning tasks. After Wednesday's lay-offs, only a handful of people will remain at the company, and so it's probably worth figuring out who they will be, and what they will do.

David Paris, the VP of Marketing, will go, because you can't market a product that doesn't exist.

Darryl, the long-haired programmer, will stay, despite his failure at the Old Dominion meeting. I need at least one programmer to develop our product, and he seems the least incompetent of the lot.

Other than this rearguard action, software development will effectively stop. There won't be any version 3.0 of our P-Scan software. We'll try to milk what we have, whatever it is, and stop pouring cash down the development rat hole.

147

Which means Darryl will effectively replace his boss, Randy Williams, VP of Engineering, who, come Wednesday, will be unceremoniously escorted into the parking lot. Randy will continue doing the job he did at Tao Software, which was nothing at all; but at least he'll get to do it from the comfort of his own home, in slippers and a bath robe, and he won't be burdened by the inconvenience of having to deposit a weekly paycheque.

That means Dmitri Sustev will go, too, because we don't need a Quality Assurance department. I already know the quality of our product; no assurance is required.

Kathleen Rossi, VP of Human Resources, will go, because HR's job is to hire and fire. There's no chance in hell that we'll do any hiring soon, and come next Wednesday, there won't be anyone left to fire.

Joan Leggett, our CFO, will stay, as I promised her, because I need someone to wring a few more weeks out of our dwindling cash.

Dom Vanderbeek will have to go, of course. A highly-paid sales executive is an extravagance. We can implement a channel strategy instead. We can find corporate partners to do our selling on our behalf. This will allow us to cut commission costs, cut T&E, cut overheads, and...

No. I'm lying, of course.

Dom Vanderbeek will be fired because he knows too much.

The conversation with Libby still echoes in my mind: my job is to save the company if I can – but more importantly, to keep things quiet. To make sure there's no trouble for Tad. Not to look too deeply into whatever is going on. Vanderbeek is a loose end, a wildcard. I can't have Vanderbeek hanging around, digging into our general ledger, looking at cash disbursements. And those antics he pulled in the lunchroom this afternoon – the drinking and the cheering – that was the last straw. He knows too much about the money, and he knows too much about me. This afternoon he signed his own death warrant.

And Amanda the receptionist will stay, because—

I think about this one. Why will she stay, exactly? Because we need a receptionist. That's why.

That she happens to be pretty, and sexy in a strange and exotic way, and maybe even a bit wild – what kind of things won't a girl do who inks a tattoo above her nipple? – that has nothing to do with it. We need someone to answer the telephones. That is all.

I pick up my own phone, dial my house. No answer. Where is Libby at seven o'clock on a Thursday night? Maybe it's unfair to expect her to stand by the phone, eagerly awaiting my call.

But still.

I dial again, her cellphone this time. It rings four times, then I hear her voicemail message. I hang up.

It occurs to me now, as I feel the first pang of doubt about my wife's fidelity, that maybe I shouldn't have spent that final week before I came to Florida on Orcas Island, enjoying a solitary vacation, while sending Libby here, to prepare for my arrival, as if I were some kind of colonial potentate.

Every now and then I have moments of clarity like this, and I understand what a terrible person I am – how flawed and selfish. The problem is that these moments of clarity come too late – after I've done the deed, behaved thoughtlessly, pushed away those who love me. I never seem to have this clarity *before* I commit the wrong, when I still have time to avoid the mistake. Maybe that's why I always make the same mistakes, over and over.

I call it a day. I stack my papers neatly – so many to-do lists, schedules, and action plans – pen scribbles decreeing the fate of dozens of human beings. I lock the pages in my desk drawer. I pack my bag and head across the bullpen floor. Only two cubes are still occupied, and I note with some pleasure that one of them is Darryl's. Perhaps I made a good choice to keep him. Come next Thursday, he's going to run the Engineering Department. Actually, come Thursday, he'll *be* the Engineering Department.

I pass the front reception desk and see that Amanda's gone. With some discomfort, I note the strange feeling that passes through me when I see her empty desk. What is it, exactly?

Disappointment.

That's what it is.

In the parking lot, the sky is bruised, with purple clouds swelling on the horizon.

'Hey,' she says. She's sitting in her car, a beat-up cabriolet, which is parked next to mine, and her window is rolled down. The cabriolet's motor is off. I hadn't noticed her. Has she been waiting for me?

'Amanda,' I say, trying to keep the delight out of my voice. 'Why are you sitting in the middle of a hot parking lot?'

'It's cooler today,' she says. But in fact my shirt is already sticking to the small of my back, and the air suffocates me like a wet towel pressed to my face. If it's somehow cooler, as Amanda claims, then it's some tiny gradation that my body can't recognize. Maybe it's like the Inuit and their thousand words for snow – maybe the people of Florida can discern subtle tones of oppressive humidity.

'Well, have a good night,' I say.

'Actually, I was waiting for you.'

My car keys dangle in my hand. I look at her carefully. Am I misinterpreting her?

Every now and then, we middle-aged men have to ask ourselves this question, particularly when we're speaking to an attractive woman, twenty years our junior. It's easy to forget, when you're locked inside your body, how you really look, who you really are.

She leans over, pops the passenger door of her car. 'Get in, Jim. I want to take you somewhere.'

No, I am not misinterpreting her. For the first time, I realize I'm attracted to her. But at the same time, I know with awful clarity that this is a Bad Idea.

'All right,' I say.

Libby's not expecting me back at the house. Hell, she's not even home. And though I try not to think about it, I can't stop myself: Libby *does* seem to disappear an awful lot, and her absences are never satisfactorily explained. For instance. Where is she tonight? Why didn't she answer the house phone? Why didn't she answer her cell? Where is she? With whom?

I look at Amanda. 'Where are we going?' I ask, as I climb into her car. 'You'll see.'

She smiles. Her hair is down. The tight bun that she wore during the day has been unfurled past her shoulders into loose waves of auburn, the colour of new pennies just unwrapped from the bank, the colour of promise and fresh starts.

She cranks her engine, and the cabriolet whines in complaint. She backs up and then out onto Route 30. It's a five-lane road with a shared turn lane as a median. It's painted crazily with thick white arrows, hash marks, lines like angry punctuation. Amanda ignores the lane marks, as if they are mere suggestions. We weave in and out of traffic. A car behind us honks angrily. Amanda does not notice.

We drive for a long time, not speaking. The road grows less busy, the restaurants less expensive, the asphalt less smooth.

She says, 'I think it's funny how you are.'

'How am I?'

'Not you personally. Men, I mean. When we take you out of the office, without your big desk and a fancy chair to protect you, you get nervous, like little boys.'

Again, I notice her accent, just barely there, a thin crystal of frost at the edge of a November window pane – pellucid and angular. Not that I'm any sort of detective. Libby convinced me of that. The real hint was that Cyrillic tattoo just above Amanda's breast. Yes, perhaps I detect a trace of Russian in her voice.

'Where are you from?' I ask.

'Most recently? Tallahassee.'

'How about less recently.'

She glances at me. 'I came here a long time ago. I have my Green Card, if that's what you are asking,' she pauses, then turns the knife, '*boss.*'

'Please don't call me that.'

'OK,' she says, easily.

'I want you to call me... *Mr* Boss.'

She laughs. She has a loud, confident, ringing laugh. 'All right. Mr Boss. I like that.'

I notice her teeth – another clue – uneven, like smooth little pebbles. Americans – even poor ones – get braces when they're young. I say, 'But you didn't tell me where you're from.'

'No, I didn't.'

'A woman with secrets.'

'You have no idea,' she says, and her voice is filled with such sadness, such exhaustion, that I turn again to look at her, to make sure that the woman driving has not aged forty years since the last traffic light.

She must recognize her voice has betrayed her, for instantly she turns far too gay. 'Well, there I go, acting like a drama queen. Of course we all have secrets. You have secrets too, don't you, Jim?'

She says it casually, as if it's just meaningless conversation, but I know her question is sincere and she's seeking an answer. 'I do.'

'And I know what they are.'

We drive silently. This quiet, rather than feeling awkward, is intimate, a sign of comfort between us.

Finally, she says: 'We're almost there, Mr Boss.'

We pull off the main road, onto a two-lane street. Typical Florida zoning policy – or lack of it, more precisely – is evident around us. There is no order, no logic, to the neighbourhood. We pass fast-food restaurants, RV parks, little white houses stacked tightly like gingerbreads.

A half-mile down the road, we pull into a church parking lot. The church is marked by a roadside light-board, the same kind of glowing sign that rises above a Wendy's to advertise 99-cent cheeseburgers. 'Golgotha Church,' it says, 'Evening Service, 7.30 p.m. We all make mistakes. Ask the Lord for forgiveness.'

Amanda pulls into one of the empty spaces. There are a surprisingly large number of cars here for a Thursday evening service.

'Oh, Amanda,' I say, gently. 'This isn't really my thing.'

'Is there someplace you'd rather be?'

'I'm married,' I explain.

'Married?' She laughs. 'We're sitting in a church parking lot! I won't do anything to you... ' With one quick motion, she snaps open her door handle and says, 'yet', so softly that the word is lost in the noise of the door; and the moment I hear it, I'm not even sure she really said it.

She darts from the car, slams the door shut behind her, and circles around to let me out. 'Come on, Mr Boss,' she says, holding the door open for me gallantly. 'You'll like this. I know you will.'

'I don't really want to go in,' I say. I look up at her, refusing to budge. The fun has drained from my voice. I was lured into her cabriolet under false pretences. Now I'm trapped in a church parking lot with a girl who suddenly seems a lot less exciting than she did twenty minutes ago.

'Please,' she says. 'Do it for me.'

Church is not, as I told Amanda, my thing.

My thing usually comes in bottles. I have, on occasion, snorted my thing, or even lit my thing with a match. There was a time, back in California, when I injected my thing, but that got too intense and so I went back to drinking my thing, or sucking on a pipe with my thing inside.

But Amanda is persistent. She guides me from the car, down into the church basement. Thirty people are there, sitting on metal folding chairs in a low-ceilinged room with no windows. The chairs are arranged in an arc, and a pastor sits at the centre. He's young, far too young, with a bowl-shaped haircut shellacked into place with thick and shiny hairspray. His eyes are watery and red, as if he's been crying. Maybe he caught a glimpse of himself in the mirror and saw his haircut.

He smiles at Amanda when she enters, and the other churchgoers do, too. There's an easy familiarity in the room, with people slumped back, collars loosened, legs outstretched. Most of the people seem working class, in retail and fast-food uniforms, one in a white nurse's outfit. But there are men in suits, too, and they look particularly interested to see me when I enter.

'Hello, Amanda,' the pastor says. His accent is Southern, as thick as his hairspray. 'I see you've brought someone. No need for names.'

'Yes,' she says. She looks at me mischievously and says: 'But you can call him Mr Boss.'

'There's only one boss in this world,' the pastor says, stiffly. He senses, a bit late, the chill brought into the room by his humourlessness, and so he adds quickly, 'But, all right, Mr Boss. I'm Brother Sam. Welcome to our little party.'

'Welcome,' someone shouts from the back of the room.

Amanda and I step across the floor, over feet and purses and briefcases, to two empty chairs.

Brother Sam waits for us to settle. 'Let us begin,' he says. 'Let us pray for Jesus to enter our hearts.'

Brother Sam clenches his eyes tightly shut. 'Oh Jesus,' he says, raising his chin to the ceiling, 'we are all of us sinners, all of us seeking your forgiveness and love.'

Everyone in the room closes their eyes. A few people lift their palms, halfheartedly, towards the ceiling.

I leave my eyes open. How else can I watch the show?

'Jesus,' Brother Sam continues, his rheumy eyes squeezed tightly shut, as if afflicted by some terrible allergy. 'Thank you for filling our hearts with your love. Thank you for attending our meeting. Thank you for blessing us.'

Amanda opens her eyes. She sees me staring. She shakes her head as if I am a very naughty child. She put her fingers near her eyes and makes a shutting gesture, in case I don't understand.

I close my eyes.

'Jesus,' continues Brother Sam, 'we are born in sin, and we live in sin, and we wallow in sin like pigs at a trough. Only with your grace and mercy can we be reborn. So many of us look for answers. We look to drinking, and to drugs, and to pornography.' His voice lilts and caresses this last word in that peculiar Southern fashion that sounds like so much intimate familiarity – por-*nah*-graphy – and I picture Brother Sam pulling his own pud in a rectory, a sticky magazine in his lap. I try to dispel this disturbing image.

He continues, 'Jesus, your love is the only way. Your love is the only path. There is no other way to be cleansed of our sinning natures. Amen.'

'Amen,' everyone says, and so do I. I open my eyes.

'Now,' Brother Sam says. 'Who would like to testify?'

The nurse in the white outfit volunteers. She's overweight and unattractive, with little eyes and a tiny chin lost in a mound of fat, but she has that well-scrubbed look of someone trying her best with severely depleted assets. She tells the story of how, this week, John Junior stole from her, *again*, and spent her entire paycheque on booze, but she forgave him, thanks to the grace of Jesus. It's not clear if John Junior is her husband, or her son, or perhaps her father, but the people in the room nod knowingly, as if they've heard this story before, maybe from her, maybe even last week, and there's nothing terribly surprising about any of it.

Brother Sam pretends to listen. Finally, he asks, 'May I cast out Satan from you, my dear?'

'Yes, Brother Sam,' she says, eagerly. 'Yes, please.'

The preacher walks to where she stands and lays his hand on her

155

sweaty face. 'Jesus,' he intones. 'Enter the body of this woman. Bless her.' He shuts his eyes and begins to speak in a gibberish that sounds like a made-up children's language. A pig-Latin, but with a drawl. '*Katanya edanah, katanya edanah,*' he repeats. I realize that he's speaking in tongues. '*Katanya edanah, katanya edanah!*'

He presses the woman's head back, tilting her little chin to the ceiling. Her body stretches backwards, as if she's playing limbo.

'Satan, get out!' Brother Sam screams. 'Get out, Satan. I command you in the name of Jesus. I cast you out!' Two burly men position themselves behind the woman. When they're ready, they exchange a signal with Brother Sam, a little nod, and the preacher pushes the woman's face with great force, so that she is shoved back into the men's waiting arms. 'Satan, be gone!' he yells. The men catch her, and she opens her eyes, and smiles with surprise and delight.

'He's out!' she screams. 'He's out!'

'God bless you,' Brother Sam says.

'Amen!' the other people say.

Amanda calls out, too. 'Amen,' she says.

The men lead the fat woman back to her chair. It squeaks under her bulk when she sits. If Satan was indeed cast out from her, he must not weigh a lot.

The meeting continues like this for some time, with other testimonies – a black man who was tempted to drink but didn't, a muscular tweaker with tats running down his arms, who speaks a million miles a minute and shifts in his seat, but who insists he's been clean since prison. Looking around the room, I sense no one believes him.

I've been to a dozen meetings like this. All twelve-step programmes are the same – a lot of heartfelt stories about unrelenting personal failure. The squinty-eyed-Jesus stuff, and the speaking in tongues, is novel enough, I have to admit, and more entertaining than anything back in California, but it's still really the same old show. I've seen it all before.

Which is why I'm anxious to leave this basement. I'm practically at the edge of my seat, ready to bolt and call a cab – Amanda be damned, sexy tattoo or not – when Brother Sam says, 'Are you ready to be healed, Mr Boss, and to accept Jesus as your personal saviour?'

Everyone looks at me. I'm ready for many things, but not that.

'I'm not sure,' I say. 'That sounds like a pretty big commitment.'

'It *is*, Mr Boss,' he says, approaching me. 'It is a wonderful commitment. It is a commitment from you to Jesus. And from Jesus to you. A *permanent* commitment.'

'Right,' I say. 'Gotcha. It's just that—'

'He loves you,' Brother Sam says, interrupting. 'He forgives you. Whatever you have done, he understands. Have you done bad things, Mr Boss?'

'Oh yes,' I say, quite truthfully. As I speak the words, the images come too – a rush of them, a slipstream of tragedy and failure: Libby's tear-streaked face the night Cole died; his wet blue corpse floating in the water; the black hooker with the blonde wig that I visited that night; the white meth smoke curling in the glass pipe; Gordon Kramer punching me in the face, knocking out my tooth – everything out of order and jumbled, but all of it painful, and all of it my fault.

Brother Sam says, 'There is no sin too large. He ate with whores. He died on the cross beside thieves. He is the god of sinners and broken men. Anyone can be reborn. Anyone.'

'Anyone?' I say, my voice hoarse. More images from that night come back to me. I recall the long walk down the corridor, how I carried Cole's body in my outstretched arms, how I laid him gently down on his bed; how I stood over him for hours, his room lit only by the moon in the window. How long did I stand there, over him? It couldn't have been hours. But everything about that night seems wrong. All sense of time twisted. I had left him alone only for a few minutes. Only a few minutes in the bath. I was coming right back. I just needed a few minutes.

Brother Sam lays his hand upon my shoulder. 'Rise, sir. Accept Jesus as your saviour.'

Everyone is staring now, and I feel extraordinary pressure to conform. One of the things about being an atheist is that you always find yourself in bad company, with cranks and know-it-alls – people who take every opportunity to ruin everyone else's comfort, by telling everyone how stupid they really are. I do not want to be one of these people. After all, if you don't believe – if you *can't* believe – why not just go along for the ride?

Which is what I do. I stand. There are smiles and nods of appreciation. Brother Sam lifts his palm, and puts his sweaty fingertips on my face. 'Close your eyes, Mr Boss,' he says, in a stage whisper. Louder, now: 'Jesus, enter into the body of this man, whatever be his true name. Cast out Satan from him.' He starts speaking in tongues again – '*Katanya edanah katanya edanah*' – repeating the phrase over and over, louder each time.

'Cast out Satan from this man!' Brother Sam shouts. 'Satan, be gone! Satan, be gone! Be gone, Satan! Be gone!'

His voice bounds along, faster, graceful and athletic, like a gazelle leaping through savannah. '*Katanya edanah!*' he shouts. He puts his face close to mine. He yells: 'Be gone, Satan! Get out of this man! I feel you inside. Get out! I can feel you, Satan. Get out, you beast! Leave this man. I command you to leave him!' His spittle dots my cheek. '*Katanya edanah katanya edanah.*' His breath smells like garlic. 'Satan, be gone! Get out! I feel you, Satan! I feel you in this man! I feel you! I feel—'

He stops mid-sentence. He opens his eyes and looks at me.

And what I see in his eyes – there is no other word for it. I see horror. He is staring at me with horror.

His skin is suddenly as pale as moonlight. He glistens with sweat. His eyes are open wide now – not rheumy slits any more – wide, as if he has stumbled accidentally upon an abomination in this very church.

He takes his hand from my cheek, quickly, as if from a hot stove. He backs up a step, off-balance, nearly trips on the leg of a folding chair. A man sitting nearby reaches up to offer support.

Brother Sam bats the man's hand away, not very politely, and backs up another step, away from me farther still.

Then, suddenly, he seems to remember where he is – a church basement – and who I am – a sinner – and what is expected of him. He looks down, embarrassed. 'Forgive me,' he mumbles. 'I must not be feeling well. I think… ' He glances around the room.

'Brother Sam,' a man nearby says, 'are you all right?'

'Yes, of course. But… but… ' He stops, collects himself. 'I'm sorry. I think we should end here for tonight.'

No one in the basement speaks, but I feel the force of silent stares upon me.

Despite his words, Brother Sam remains still. He does not move. He does not step closer to me. He does not look at me. He does not offer me a hand, nor make a gesture of apology. He stays as far away from me as he can, as if he wants to be sure that he remains out of my grasp.

I look over to Amanda. She regards me thoughtfully, her head tilted to the side, as if a new and interesting quality has been revealed in me, one that impresses her very much.

Now we're in her car, heading back to the office, so that I can pick up my own Ford and return home. It's nine o'clock. I can still make it back to Libby at a reasonable hour. Perhaps – if I play it right – I won't even have to explain to my wife where I went, or with whom.

'Well that was interesting,' Amanda says drily.

I stay silent.

'I know you don't believe,' Amanda says, staring straight ahead as she drives. 'But it's real, you know.'

'If you say so,' I say, agreeably.

'He changed my life,' she continues.

'Brother Sam?'

'Jesus.'

'Oh,' I say.

'He can change yours, too,' she goes on. 'What do you think of that?'

What I think is that Amanda is becoming less sexy with each passing second. Another minute, and my bra-less receptionist with the breast tattoo will be singing hymns and trussing a corset. I'd like to be back home in my own bed before then.

'Hey,' I say, as we speed past the Tao Software office building. In the rearview mirror, I see my Ford grow distant and then recede over the horizon. 'I think you passed the office.'

'We're going someplace else.'

'Where?'

'My apartment.'

'Why?'

She looks at me, sidelong.

'What about Jesus?' I ask.

'He'll come too.'

She lives in a complex called Plantation Manor, two miles from the office. Despite its regal name, the place has a decrepit look. It's a three-storey building, timber and cement, with open walkways exposed to the weather, overlooking a parking lot. There's a swimming pool off to the side, fenced in, teeming with debris, and surrounded by rusting sun loungers.

From one of the balconies hangs a vinyl sign that screams, 'No Deposit – No Credit Check – First Month Free!'

Amanda leads me up two flights of stairs. The air is humid, and halfway up the first flight, I'm out of breath. I hear the thrum of cars from the highway, just beyond a concrete noise abatement fence, which doesn't seem to be doing much abating.

At the top of the stairs, she leads me down a long hallway. We stop at the apartment marked '309'. She fiddles with a key in the lock, then shoves the door with her shoulder. I follow her in. We're hit by a blast of wintry air. An air conditioner roars in the window like a jet.

'What do you think?' she asks, standing aside to give me a better view.

'I think electricity must be included in your rent,' I say, shivering.

'I leave it on,' she says. 'Because I like the cold.'

'You moved to the wrong state.'

'Sit down,' she says. 'I will pee.'

She disappears around a corner. I sit on the couch as instructed. I look around. It's a standard sunbelt apartment: white stucco plaster ceiling, a medium-pile beige carpet, a breakfast bar overlooking a tiny galley kitchen, and a sliding glass door with Levolor blinds leading to a patio. No photographs, no books. It's simultaneously clean, and depressing: the apartment of a woman who is one part hard-worker, and one part flight-risk.

I hear the sound of urine tinkling on porcelain. 'So now I will tell you my story,' she calls from the other room, as she pees. I wonder whether she has left the bathroom door open. I peer around the corner, but can't see.

'Maybe you want to finish up first,' I suggest.

She ignores this. 'I was born in Russia. You knew that, didn't you?'

'You have an accent,' I say. 'Just a slight one.'

'When I was twelve, I ran away to Moscow. There was a man. He told me I should model for magazines.'

The toilet flushes. I hear water in the basin, and then the sound of rapid soapy hand-washing. Soon she's back, rejoining me in the living room. 'He called himself an agent,' she continues. 'But he wasn't, not really.' She sits on the couch beside me, on her knees, with her feet behind her. 'I visited him one night, so that he could evaluate me. That's what he called it: "evaluate". He did evaluate me, in a way. There were a lot of men, not just him. I won't tell you everything. But you can imagine.'

'I'm sorry.'

She waves her hand, dismissing sentiment. 'I never saw my family again. They brought me to different houses, and different cities, and soon I didn't know where I was. After a few months, they brought me to this country. I worked for them. Do you know what I mean?'

'I think so.'

'They called me a dancer. But I did more than dance. I did everything. Whatever they told me.'

'Why didn't you… ' I stop before I utter the words. But it's too late. She knows what I'm going to say.

'Escape?' she suggests, and laughs. I nod.

'Let me tell you a story. On the first night, they picked one girl from the group. Just at random. I remember the one they chose. She was standing right next to me. She had blonde hair, and she was very young and very pretty. They unrolled plastic sheets, onto the ground, and they told her to stand on the middle of the sheets, because they didn't want to clean the carpet. No one understood what they meant. They told all the girls to gather around and watch. They took out a gun, and put it into the young girl's mouth, and they shot her. Just like that. And then they said to the rest of us, 'This is what happens. If anyone tries to leave, this is what we do. We'll kill you, and we'll kill your family in Russia, too, because we know where they live. But—' She raises a finger, and pauses. Her face takes on a stony hard look. 'But, if you're good, and you do what we say, you can earn your freedom.'

She slinks closer to me on the couch. Part of me wants to comfort her – to put an arm around her, to hold her – this girl from another land, who was taken from her home. But I know not to. She does not seek my comfort. She does not seek any man's comfort.

'I will tell you a secret,' she says. 'Do you want to hear my secret?'

'All right.'

'It doesn't matter how they threaten, because soon you don't *want* to escape. They give you things, to make you like being there. You *want* to stay. Do you understand?'

'Drugs,' I say. I try to sound clinical, but my voice is thin and excited despite myself, the way you sound when you try to speak casually the name of an old lover.

'Yes.' She comes closer. 'Oh yes,' she purrs. 'How nice it was.' I can feel her warm skin next to mine. 'You know that feeling, don't you, Jim?'

'Yes.'

'You've tried.'

Not a question. 'Yes.'

'From that first day at the company, I knew. We can recognize each other. Can't we, Jim?'

It's true. Being an addict is like being in a club. Once you're in, you're in. It's something straights can't understand. When I walk down the street, I know. Just looking at strangers, I know – I know who is on, and who is off, and who is heading back. There's something in our eyes. We're searching. We never find it, but we're always looking. It's a hollow, haunted, hungry look. Amanda has it, too. Some part of me always knew that.

Amanda continues, 'I did terrible things. I wish I could... ' She shakes her head. 'I wish I could take them out of here.' She points to her skull.

'I know that feeling.'

She leans over. For a moment I think she's going to kiss me. But then she turns away. She says, 'Jesus rescued me.'

I repeat stupidly: 'Jesus... rescued you?'

I sit there, squinting, trying to picture Jesus, with flowing white robes, leading some kind of Delta Force extraction of Amanda from a Russian's compound, abseiling down walls and evading laser-scoped rifles.

'I prayed,' she says, 'and he saved me. He gave me a new life.'

'But... how did you escape?'

She shakes her head and waves her hand, as if that subject is uninteresting – mere logistics. 'It doesn't matter. Once you decide you want to leave, there's always a way. The hard part is deciding. But I did. And then I came to Florida. I moved in with a girl – a college girl. She taught me what to do, and how to act, and how to get a job. I got a GED. I fixed my English. I took a receptionist job. Men like hiring pretty girls for their front desks. Have you noticed that, Jim? That's how I found Tao.'

'Well I'm glad you're here.'

'What a *boss* thing to say,' she scoffs. 'You're "glad I'm here". Why on earth would you be glad I'm here, answering your telephone?'

I search for an answer. After a long moment: 'We *do* get a lot of calls.'

She laughs. 'You see how you hide?'

'Hide?'

'Behind jokes, Jim. You try to distract people. You're very devious.'

'I didn't know I was devious.'

'A devious man. You always avoid the question. Even now, you are avoiding it.'

'What question is that?'

She leans close, lowers her voice. 'You know the question.'

I don't. Not really.

She says: 'Here you are, a married man, on a Thursday night, in your receptionist's apartment. On her couch. And she's very close to you. Very close. She could be naked at any moment.'

'But she's not.'

'But she could be,' she whispers. She leans in, and her lips brush my ear. She whispers, so close and soft, that her words are just warm breath against my skin. 'The question is: What are you going to do?'

'It is a very good question,' I admit. 'Tricky.'

'I've seen your wife's photograph. She is so pretty.' I can smell her perfume. It's the scent of flowers, rich and sweet, like a funeral spray.

Amanda leans forward to kiss me. Her tongue slides across mine. We remain still, mouths pressed together, gently. She breaks off the kiss, and looks at me.

'What's the matter?' she asks.

I lean back, away from her.

'You know what's funny?' I say. 'I was talking to my shrink. I told him that I wanted to become a new man. A better man. I think the *old* Jimmy Thane would have wanted to fuck you.'

'And the *new* Jimmy Thane?'

'The new Jimmy Thane wants to fuck you, too. That's why I'm beginning to suspect my shrink is no good.'

And then, because it's the only decent thing to say: 'I have to leave now, Amanda. I have to go home to my wife.'

She looks me over for a long time. For a moment I think she's going to slap me, or cry, or yell, 'Then get the hell out!' But she does none of those things. She says, brightly, 'You see? I told you he would be here tonight.'

'Who?'

'Jesus. I told you he would be here, in this apartment. Now you see for yourself. He is inside you.'

'Oh,' I say. 'I don't feel Jesus inside me. But then again, I don't feel much of anything inside me. I'm just tired. So tired.

I stand up, head to the door. Amanda follows.

'I need a ride back to the office, Amanda,' I say. 'Would you mind?'

She grabs her car keys from the side table and tosses them to me. 'Take my car. Leave it in the office. I'll get a ride in the morning.'

'Thank you.'

I turn to leave. She grabs my arm. 'Jim,' she says, with a grin. 'Don't you want to ask?'

'Ask what?'

She takes my hand, and guides my fingers to her breast. Her nipple stiffens under my touch. She keeps her palm over mine, preventing me from moving. 'Ask me what it means.' She presses my fingers down, on the place where I saw her tattoo. 'I saw you looking. Can you read Russian?'

'No.'

'Do you want to know what it means?'

'What does it mean?' I ask dutifully.

'"Jesus died for my sins."'

'*That's* what it means? Why do you… ' I pause. 'Why do you have that tattooed on your breast?'

'So that I can *remember* it,' she says, emphatically.

'When I want to remember something, I just use Post-it Notes.'

She laughs. 'You see?' She removes her hand from mine. Reluctantly I lift my fingers from her breast. 'Do you see how you use jokes? To hide from the truth?'

I'm too tired to argue.

In the parking lot, as I walk to her car, I hear the thrum of tyres on the other side of the noise abatement wall. I feel a strange surge of emotion, something I can't identify at first. It's not regret – regret that I didn't make love to her – which is the feeling I was expecting to have by now. This feeling is something different.

Triumph.

Yes, that's what it is. For the first time I can remember, I didn't give in to my urges. My base, evil urges.

Maybe this is the start. Maybe this is the new Jimmy Thane.

As I climb into her car, I smile. The *new* Jimmy Thane. I like the sound of that.

CHAPTER 19

'Tell me what happened,' Dr Liago says.

We're sitting in his study, that odd room built entirely of leather and wood – oak floors, bookshelves filled with calf-skin bindings, window shades with oak slats shut tight – a room that is somewhere between English gentleman's club and New Jersey funeral parlour. Four days have passed since my visit to Amanda's apartment, four days of relative calm – relative, anyway, for Jimmy Thane – four days without a church-basement exorcism, or an abortive sexual escapade, or a public drinking binge in the office lunchroom.

I glance at the clock on Liago's desk, old-fashioned enough to proclaim 'Electric' proudly on its face. It glows orange.

'Nothing happened,' I say. 'I left her apartment and I went home to my wife.'

'And what did your wife say, when you told her where you went?'

'I didn't tell her.'

'Why not?'

'Why not?' I laugh. 'Are you married, Dr Liago?'

A simple question, I think. A question that requires only 'yes' or 'no' for an answer. But Liago strokes his short white beard and mulls over this question as if I have asked him about the mysteries of string theory or quantum physics. He says, finally, 'I wonder why it is that you want to know that.'

'Just making conversation,' I say.

'Is it important to you? To know whether I'm married?'

'Forget it, Doc. Sorry I asked.'

'I'm not,' he says. 'Married.'

'I didn't tell Libby where I went, because nothing happened, and it wasn't worth the trouble.'

'Hmm,' he says, nodding. 'You've had quite a week. You broke into someone's house and found cash in a garbage bag. You suspect that the man who hired you is involved in some sort of criminal enterprise. And you drank again – drank champagne—'

'I didn't exactly drink,' I insist. 'It was a party, and I was forced to do it.'

'You were *forced* to drink,' he says, in that maddening tone used by psychiatrists and parents – the one where they repeat your words exactly, thereby making you sound ridiculous and guilty.

'That's exactly right.'

'And you looked down your secretary's shirt and saw her breasts. And you kissed her.'

'Right,' I say. 'More or less. The kiss wasn't much. It lasted just for a second.'

'Do you want my opinion?'

'No.'

'These do not sound like the actions of a man who wants to live a quiet and normal life. Do you agree?'

'I suppose.'

'On its own, everything you've told me has a perfectly acceptable explanation. You broke into a house because you wanted to find out who was stealing from your company. You sipped alcohol because your Vice President of Marketing was trying to embarrass you.'

'Vice President of Sales.'

He ignores this. 'You went out last night with your receptionist because… ' He stops. 'Why exactly did you go with her?'

He's got me. I entered her car and let her drive me because I wanted

168

to fuck her. Because I couldn't get that image out of my mind, of her breasts, and that Cyrillic tattoo, and because I wanted to see her outstretched on a bed, naked, with her back arched and her ribcage exposed, so that I could read the writing on her body at my leisure, like a novel with a delicious twist to the ending.

Dr Liago is waiting for me to explain why I got into Amanda's car. But the best I can do is offer a guilty smile.

'You see?' Liago says, triumphantly. 'Even the fact that you are investigating this theft from your company – even that, in itself, is self-destructive. Just as Libby told you it was. You turn over rocks, looking for answers, but the answer is staring at you. You were hired *not* to look for answers. Your venture capitalist, the man who hired you—' He glances down at his pad to search for the name. 'Tad Billups. He doesn't want you poking around, answering policemen's questions about Ghol Gedrosian. He told you this. But what do you do? You poke around. The very fact that you do this is a way of destroying yourself – of denying yourself that fresh start that you deserve. Do you see?'

'Yes.'

'In the same way, you attempt to destroy your relationship with your wife. You do this by… well, let's call it *flirting* – with your receptionist.'

'I see where you're going with this.'

'Do you?' He stares at me. Finally he asks: 'Have you talked to Gordon Kramer yet?'

'About what?'

'About what happened. About the kiss. About the drink.'

'No.'

'Why not?'

Because I'm afraid Gordon will show up at my office with the grim face of a hangman, and that he'll punch me in the jaw, and that he'll handcuff me to a sprinkler.

But out loud I say, 'Because I would prefer to talk to *you* about it.'

'Good,' he nods. He seems genuinely pleased, that we've reached a new level of trust.

But something is bothering me. I try to recall what Liago just said, try to replay his words in my mind.

'That name,' I say.

He looks at me warily, and – is it possible? – do I see a flash of fear in his eyes, that he's been caught in some kind of mistake?

'What name?'

'Ghol Gadro... whatever.'

'Ah,' he says. He looks down at his pad again. 'Ghol Gedrosian,' he reads.

'Did I tell you that name? I don't think I did.'

He smiles. 'Of course you did.' He taps the precise spot on his yellow legal pad where he wrote the name.'

But his scribbling is quite small, and Liago's chair is several feet from mine, and he doesn't offer me the pad to see for myself.

'How else would I know it?' he asks.

'I suppose you're right.'

'From the sound of it, Mr Thane, you've had a very exhausting week.' A polite way of saying: You sound paranoid.

'I *am* pretty tired,' I admit. 'And things will only get worse. Tomorrow I'm going to fire a lot of people. More than half of the people that work at my company.'

'How does that make you feel?'

'Feel? I don't feel anything. It's my job. I have a list in a desk drawer. I fire whoever's on the list.'

'You enjoy that.'

I'm appalled. 'Enjoy it?'

'Having power. A power that you can't exercise over your own life. You – a man who can't refuse a drink at a party, who can't keep his eyes from wandering down an employee's shirt, who can't stop lying to his wife about where he goes at night – you suddenly have a chance to determine other people's fates. Isn't that so?'

170

I squint. 'That's not very charitable, Doc.'

'Perhaps. But is it true?'

Before I can answer, Dr Liago's face widens in surprise. For an instant, I think he is incontinent, because suddenly he has an embarrassed look, and he reaches a hand down to his pants. Then he fishes in his pocket, and finds a cellphone. It vibrates.

'Forgive me,' he says, looking at the screen of the phone. 'This is very… ' His voice trails off. 'I'm afraid it's an emergency. Can you wait here?'

'No problem, Doc.'

He stands, lays the yellow legal pad face-down on his chair, and walks halfway to the door. Then he stops, and – thinking better of it – returns to his chair, and retrieves the pad. Without apology or acknowledgement, he removes the pad from his chair, and carries it with him out of the room. He shuts the door behind him.

I sit very still, trying to listen through the thick wood of the door.

I hear Liago's voice, rising with emotion, but his words are muffled, and I can make out only the most general impression that he's arguing with someone on his cellphone.

Maybe he knows I'm listening, because he says two quick words, and then there's silence, and then I hear his footsteps on the uncarpeted floor in the entry, growing distant. The exterior door of the house opens and shuts. I rise from my chair, go to the slatted window, and peek through.

Liago is walking away from his own house, down the long gravel driveway. He stops next to his Crown Victoria. His back is towards me; I can't see his face. He presses the phone to his ear, gesturing as he speaks.

This continues for a minute – Liago pantomiming, gesturing intently, arguing. When he turns around, though, and I see his expression, I realize something quite different: he's not arguing. He's begging. His face is ashen. His hands shake.

I dart to the side of the window, out of his view, but it doesn't matter; Liago has forgotten about me. He does not even look in my direction. His attention is rapt, held by that phone call.

Which is most welcome, because it gives me the chance I've longed for – which is to snoop through Liago's private belongings.

I have a rule: if you don't want me to see your things, for God's sake, don't leave me alone with them. Especially if you're my psychiatrist. After all, who doesn't want to know the secrets hidden by his own shrink?

Alas, Liago's office doesn't hold much promise for a man like me, being devoid of intimate personal effects. The top of his desk is bare – no pictures, no mementos – and the room is decorated with that sparse movie-set quality that I noticed the first time I was here. It's an office that conveys the *notion* of being a 'psychiatrist's office' without really seeming like a place where an actual human being works or lives. I've met men like Liago before – men who are more interested in portraying themselves to the public, rather than actually living their lives. You see this a lot in the venture capital business, where the walls of private offices are adorned with lucite IPO plaques, listing lead underwriters and the number of millions raised, but contain no pictures of little Johnny playing Pee Wee Football, or the venture capitalist's wife wearing a wedding dress.

I walk to Liago's desk. There are two drawers on the side, and a narrow one on top. I try a side drawer first. It is empty. The second drawer is empty, too.

I despair of finding anything interesting about this drab little man to whom I pay $125 per hour, and to whom I spill my own secrets. But then I pull open that final drawer – the thin long one at the top of the desk.

And I'm glad that I do.

Because there's a big black gun, which slides across the interior of the drawer when I open it, the way a chewed-up Bic pen might slide if you open a drawer too quickly.

Now *that* is interesting. A big black gun. How many shrinks keep big black guns in their desks?

I look at it, warily, from a distance. I wonder what kind of patients Dr Liago sees. They must be very dangerous men.

I close the drawer – much more slowly and gently than I opened it, to be honest – and begin to explore the other side of the room.

What attracts my interest now is the metal filing cabinet, the one with the oversized and intricate lock. This must be where Liago keeps his patient records. This is where, for example, he must keep all those pages from his yellow legal pads – like the pad that he just removed from the office – the pad with all the notes from our conversations.

I am not expecting this cabinet to reveal much – not with that big lock securing the drawer – but I tug anyway. And wouldn't you know it – the drawer glides open easily.

The good news about Dr Liago, I now see, is that he keeps copious and detailed notes about all of his patients.

The bad news about Dr Liago is that he has only one patient. And that is me.

At least, this is the only way I can explain what I see in the filing cabinet. Inside the drawer is a single hanging folder, stuffed thick with yellow sheets of paper. The folder is labelled in a neat hand. 'Thane, Jim', it says.

And that is all.

There is not one other folder. Not one other patient.

Just one: 'Thane, Jim'.

I open the bottom drawer of the filing cabinet, to be certain. That drawer is empty.

Just one folder. Just one patient. 'Thane, Jim'.

I feel a sickness inside me, a dark fear rising from the pit of my stomach, threatening to engulf me. There is something... *wrong* here. Something dangerous. A doctor with a gun. A doctor with only one patient.

My fingers flit through the pages in the hanging folder. The sheets are thick with scribbles, tiny and intricate handwriting, the ravings of a lunatic. There is an impossible amount of writing – too much information to be gleaned from the one session that I spent with Dr Liago.

I read the pages, flipping through them quickly, at random. '*Gordon Kramer*', a paragraph begins, in that tiny crazed writing, and Gordon's name is underlined. The notes continue: 'St. Regis. Garage. Handcuffs. Parking Area 4C. Sobers him up.'

Another paragraph starts: '*Hector Gonzales*. Bookie. What happened to Jim's finger? Libby drives him to hospital. Bloody dish towel around hand. Jack in the Box for hamburger.'

These are incidents from my own life. I remember them clearly. They are seared into my mind. But what I don't remember is telling Dr Liago about them. About any of them.

'Lantek, Ethernet networking – VP of Sales – made drunken pass at *Bob Parker*'s wife while high. San Francisco loft.'

I want to read more about this incident – and all the others recounted in the doctor's notes – but behind me, the door creaks, and I turn to see it opening. I know that I can't make it back to my chair in time. Instead, I return the folder, softly close the filing cabinet, and take just one step away, into the corner of the room, where I pretend to be studying the diploma on the wall. 'Dr George Liago, Doctor of Medicine, Cornell Medical School, 1972', it proclaims.

'Forgive me,' Liago says, entering the room, breathless. 'That was rude of me. I'm sorry, but I had to take that call. An emergency, you know.'

He sees me standing near his desk, which is clearly not where he expected to find me – and his eyes dart around the office, suspiciously, before they return to me.

'No problem,' I say. 'Just admiring your diploma. I always wondered how they make the script so fancy. It must take them an awful long time to write each one by hand. How many people were in your class?'

174

'I think it's a mechanical reproduction, Mr Thane,' he says.

'Is that right?'

'Ah,' he says, trying to smile. 'You're joking.'

'Not much of a joke.'

'No,' he agrees. 'Should we continue?'

I return to my seat.

He sits down in the chair across from me. I try to keep my face blank, try not to telegraph my distress.

For a moment, I think about confronting him – standing up, stomping to the file drawer, wrenching it open, and shouting, 'Where are your other patients? What kind of doctor *are* you?'

But something tells me not to. Just to play dumb. Which isn't terribly hard for a man like me.

'I think I'll just turn this off for now,' Liago says, fiddling with his cellphone. He presses the power button emphatically, to demonstrate how sincerely he hopes we will not be disturbed again.

'Where were we?' he says, looking down at his notes. 'Oh yes,' he says. 'You're going to fire people. Lots of people. Tomorrow. Tell me how that makes you feel.'

CHAPTER 20

Somehow I make it through the session. Liago must sense something is wrong, though, because after a few abortive attempts at conversation, he finally suggests we wrap up early, since my mind 'seems to be elsewhere'.

If my mind is anywhere, it's in that filing cabinet, which holds just a single folder. Or it's in his desk drawer, which contains a gun.

But I don't say either of these things. I just nod mute agreement, and let him lead me from the office. In the foyer, he puts his hand on my arm, and he says he'll see me next week. Almost a question. I mumble agreement. He watches me warily from the front door as I back my Ford out of the driveway. I do it slowly – no flooring the accelerator, no gravel shooting from beneath spinning tyres. I just back up, as if there is nothing wrong in the world, nothing odd in what I just discovered, nothing at all unusual about a doctor who lives alone in a house, and is a specialist. A Jimmy Thane specialist.

I drive, keep my gaze straight ahead. When I get to the highway, I drive for another mile, and then I pull over into the brown grass on the shoulder of the road. Cars whizz by. The Ford hasn't even stopped rolling by the time I finish dialling Gordon Kramer's number on my cell.

'Hello, Jimmy,' he rasps. 'What the hell's the matter now?'

'Oh nothing, Gordon,' I say, with false lightness in my voice. 'Other than the fact that the doctor you recommended to me is a maniac.'

'Maniac doctor, huh?' he says. He doesn't sound too concerned. 'Why is he a maniac doctor, Jimmy?'

'Let's see, where to start? Well, there's a gun in his desk drawer.'

'I have a gun in my desk drawer, Jimmy.'

'You're an ex-cop, Gordon.'

'That's right. My job has me deal with a lot of cranked-up meth-heads. Guess what kind of patients Dr Liago sees.'

'Funny you should mention that. That was my next point. Dr Liago apparently deals with only *one* patient.'

'That's right,' Gordon says. 'You.'

He says this as if it were an obvious fact, one that we've discussed before, and one that should come as no surprise to either of us.

'You know that already?'

'Of course I know that, you moron. I hired him.'

'But—'

'I got him out of mothballs just for you. He was retired. I had to call in a favour. He didn't want to do it, but – well, you know how persuasive I can be.'

'Oh,' I say, suddenly deflated. 'So you knew all about it.'

'All about what?' he says. He sounds truly mystified by this entire conversation. Then, his breath catches, and he has a realization. 'Oh, shit,' he says. 'Oh, shit, Jimmy. Are you tweaking? Are you getting paranoid again?'

'I'm not paranoid. I'm not tweaking.'

'Jimmy...'

'Gordon, he knows things about me. He has hundreds of pages of notes – things that I did not tell him.'

A long silence. When Gordon's voice returns to the line, he sounds disappointed. 'Aw, shit, Jimmy,' he says, again. 'You're using.'

'I am not using.'

'Then why are you being paranoid?'

'I'm not paranoid. I'm just asking how he knows things that—'

'Jimmy, I had him call Doc Curtis, before you saw him. She sent over your entire file. Of course he knows things about you. How else could he possibly treat you?'

'Oh,' I say again. An eighteen-wheeler barrels past the Ford, sucking the window out from the frame as it speeds by. I suddenly feel silly. Here I am, sitting in a car, on the side of a highway. I have just fled from the office of my shrink – literally *fled* – convinced that he was a gun-toting maniac. I am telling this to my sponsor, one continent and three time zones away, and asking him to explain the rather obvious fact that doctors share notes when they treat each other's patients.

'Oh,' I say one more time. Then: 'Gordon, I am deeply embarrassed.'

'"Deeply embarrassed"?' Gordon repeats. 'I don't think I've ever heard you use that one before, Jimmy. '"Shit-faced drunk" – yes. "Cranked Out of My Mind" – yes. But never "Deeply Embarrassed". That's a new one. I like it.' He pauses. 'Go back to work, Jimmy. Stop freaking out, and go back to work. Don't make me get on a plane and come find you. You would not want that. I promise you. You would not want that.'

CHAPTER 21

The next day, the lay-offs come.

In my career as a restart executive, I have fired four hundred and ninety-six people. Mass lay-offs are the first and most important step in any corporate turnaround.

People who don't understand business have the wrong idea about capitalism. They think capitalism is heartless and cruel – that it puts profits above people, that it makes managers do inhumane things – and that this inhumanity is the reason we have corporate lay-offs.

In fact, the opposite is true. Lay-offs are the result of people behaving with too much compassion. Too many managers run their business like a family, and they treat their employees with the same misplaced kindness that we show our sons or daughters. Your twenty-two-year-old son is a fuck-up who lives at home and wants to be a musician? Why not let him stay for a while, rent free, while he finds himself?

The same thing happens in business. Look at Cheryl in Accounting. Oh sure, she's lazy, and her numbers are always wrong, but she's our Cheryl, and she buys us doughnuts on Doughnut Wednesday, so why not let it ride? So much easier than firing her. After all, she might cry.

And so, over the lifetime of a company, hundreds of these small, seemingly inconsequential decisions build, like plaque in corporate veins, hardly noticeable at first, until finally you step back and realize that the system is filled with these deposits – people who don't do their jobs well, or who don't care, or who are lazy – and soon the business seizes up like an arrested heart, and needs to be shocked back to health.

That's my job – to shock a company back to health. To do the painful thing, the necessary thing. If the original executives had possessed the courage to do what I must do, back when it mattered, the company would not be in the situation in which it finds itself. There would be no need for mass lay-offs. Hell, there would be enough profit to allow us to hand out raises instead of pink slips.

But of course no one sees it this way. People who make tough decision are vilified; cowards are praised. This is the nature of the world: we wish things were one way, regret they are another, and blame the difference on someone other than ourselves.

The protocol that I follow when I fire people is the same no matter where I go. First, I wait until Wednesdays. Wednesdays are best, both for the people being fired (so they don't have to stew over the weekend) and for the lucky people who remain (so they can start fresh on the following Monday, the trauma long past).

Typically I do the deed in the afternoon – just after lunch – after nerves have been sated by a big meal – but not too late, because I don't want everyone leaving early for the day, missing the bad news, and then wandering in the next morning, puzzled that their desk has been emptied without explanation.

At some companies, I hire a security guard, to protect both myself and the other remaining employees. I do not bother to do this today, because Tao is a computer software company, and the worst that happens at a software company is the occasional barrage of curse words and maybe a paperweight being thrown into a computer screen.

The one thing that *is* critical at a software company, is that you prevent theft of intellectual property. The only real asset a technology company has is the computer code residing on its hard disks and tape backup systems. You do not want this software to be copied onto a CD-ROM and physically carried out of the building, nor do you want it emailed off the corporate network. In either case there's a good chance the code will wind up in a competitor's hands.

This is why, ten minutes before I'm about to begin the mass firing, I bring Darryl into my office, shut the door, and tell him that lay-offs are imminent, and that I'm going to need his help.

'Wow,' he says. 'When?'

'Ten minutes,' I say.

'Ten minutes?' He does a cartoon double-take. 'Holy shit!'

That's another rule. Never tell people in advance. No one can keep a secret about anything. No one.

I tell Darryl that he will remain at Tao, and that he'll take over Randy's job as VP of Engineering.

'No shit?' he says.

'When you leave this room, you will walk directly into the server room. Do not pass go. Shut down the network so that no emails or files can be transmitted from the LAN. Can you do that?'

'Hell yes.'

'I want RDP shut down, SSH, and telnet. Do you understand?'

'Yes.'

'When you've done that,' I continue, 'I want you to change the password of every user account. No one should have access to his account any more. Do not tell anyone what you're doing. Just do it. Choose a different random password for every account. Write each one on an index card. Do not make a copy of these passwords. Bring them directly to me.'

'OK.'

'Do you have any questions?'

'I need the root password.'

'Who has the root password?' But I don't wait for an answer. 'Randy.'

He nods.

'Bring him in. He can be first.'

*

A minute later, Darryl returns with Randy Williams, VP of Engineering. That is his title, for thirty seconds longer, anyway.

Randy's round Midwestern face still has that big blank expression, a calf on the way to the slaughterhouse, but I see a glimmer of understanding forming behind his eyes.

'Have a seat,' I tell Randy, and I gesture to the chair across from mine.

Darryl is about to leave the room. I say, 'Stay, Darryl. Shut the door.'

Darryl obeys.

To Randy, I say in a firm voice meant to telegraph that I will accept no opposition, 'Randy, I want you to tell me the root password for our network. Write it down here.'

I slide my pad across the table to him.

This is the moment he realizes what is happening. He looks down at the pad, then at me, and then at Darryl.

'What's going on?' he asks, even though he knows. His voice falters. He tries his gap-toothed smile on me. Receiving no response, he lets it droop, then vanish. He shrugs, takes his pen from his shirt, and writes down a string of characters and symbols on my pad.

I tear the page from the pad, hand it to Darryl. 'Make sure it works. If there's no problem, just do what I told you.'

Darryl nods. Randy looks at him pleadingly. '*Et tu*, Darryl?' Randy says.

Darryl opens his mouth, about to answer, then thinks better of it. He looks down at the ground, turns the doorknob, and leaves.

'Randy,' I begin, 'I'm afraid that I have some bad news.'

Once you start, you have to hurry, because the general population soon learns what's going on. The goal of a mass firing is to get it over with, to get people out of the door, quickly, before they can cause mischief – erase hard drives, filch files, destroy property – before they can do anything they'll later regret.

When people leave the death chamber – in this case, my broom-closet office – onlookers, curious about their colleagues' shell-shocked expressions, or their red and puffy eyes, or their tear-streaked cheeks, typically ask what's going on. 'I got canned,' the passive ones say. Or, the angry ones say, 'Cocksucker Jim fired me.' Or something in between.

I go through my list efficiently. Each session takes only a few minutes. By the end, when people enter the room, they know exactly what's coming, and some even do my job for me. 'I'm being fired,' they immediately start. The helpful ones try to assuage any guilt I might have. 'I understand; it's not your fault, Jim,' they say.

In all cases, when I describe the reasons for the person's firing, I stick to the abstract and impersonal: bad decisions were made by previous management, venture capital firms have less cash to fund development, economic times have changed, the identity-management market has become more competitive. I use the passive voice – mistakes were made – and am vague about whom to blame. The time for hard truths and plain speaking has long passed.

Last on my list of forty people is Dom Vanderbeek. He knows what's coming as soon as he walks in. He doesn't even bother shutting the door or sitting down.

Before I can say a word, he leans over my desk, gets in my face and says, 'Fuck you, Jim.'

'I'm sorry, Dom. It just didn't work out.'

'What about our agreement?'

To my credit, I don't laugh in his face and say, 'What agreement?' He's talking about that bargain we struck when I first came to Tao: Vanderbeek would work hard to sell our lousy software if I agreed to recommend him for the CEO position after I left.

But whatever agreement we made – and it wasn't a formal contract, not even a handshake, come to think of it – we made it before I understood my job at Tao. Now that I know my role – to keep things quiet, to keep the police at bay, to overlook the money being shovelled out of the back door – now that I understand these things, keeping Vanderbeek around is both unnecessary and impossible.

'I agreed to try my best,' I say. 'But you didn't deliver on your end of the bargain. I don't see any sales happening because of you. Do you, Dom?'

'You know the product stinks.'

'I'm sorry,' I say again.

He turns, heads to the door, then stops at the threshold. With one arm on the doorframe, he pivots and looks at me. 'I know a lot about you, Jim. A *lot*. And guess what? I know a lot about Tao. About where our money goes, for instance. I wonder if other people would be interested in finding out what I know.'

'I have no idea what you're talking about, Dom.'

'Then you won't care if I make some phone calls.'

'Dom!' I say. But I'm speaking too loudly. The door of my office is open. People are listening. How much of the argument have they heard, out there in the bullpen? I lower my voice. 'Dom,' I say, again, more quietly, 'if I were you, I'd be very careful.'

Immediately I regret this.

A look of pleasure washes over Vanderbeek – this is exactly what he wanted. 'Jim, are you threatening me? Are you fucking threatening me?' He shakes his head, but he's smiling merrily, because I've taken his bait.

'Dom, I'm not threatening you. Be quiet and close the door—'

He raises his voice. 'Are you threatening me, Jim?' He leans out through the door, and yells into the bullpen, 'Hey everyone, Jim just threatened me.' Turning back to me: 'What do you mean, "If I were you, I'd be very careful"? What are you going to do? Beat me up? *Kill* me?'

From my vantage behind the desk, I can only see a sliver of the bullpen – just one of the engineers packing a box of his belongings. There can't be many people left in the office at this point, with the firings almost done – yet I hear murmurs of interest nonetheless. People are listening.

'It's time for you to leave now,' I say. I keep my voice quiet.

Dom nods. 'OK, buddy. OK. But you haven't heard the last of me.'

This would normally be the moment when I would respond with a witty comeback, but my wit – whatever is left of it – is cut short by a female voice shouting from the bullpen: 'No! Don't!'

I jump up from my desk, race past Vanderbeek, into the bullpen, to see what is happening.

David Paris, ex-VP of Marketing, who took the news of his termination with such stoic good grace only twenty minutes ago, is standing on top of his desk, with his naked ass cheeks exposed. His pants are bunched at his ankles, and people are shouting, 'David, no!' And: 'Oh gross!'

As I circle him, I see a stream of urine flowing in a graceful arc from David's impressively large cock to the floor of the bullpen. 'Here you go!' he shouts. 'Here you go! Take it! Take it all!'

He turns, directing his spray this way and that, like a fireman dispatching the last stubborn embers of a blaze. Someone shouts, 'David, what are you doing?'

'Something to remember me by,' he explains.

'Look at it!' Rosita calls gaily, and it's unclear if she's talking about the piss or the huge penis.

David turns to me. 'Here you go, Jim,' he says. He aims his piss at me, but I'm hopelessly far away, and he is nearly drained anyway, just a trickle now.

'All right, David,' I say, trying to sound authoritative, 'that's enough. Put your... thing... away.'

Out of ammunition, David shrugs, pulls up his pants, zips. He leaves his belt unclasped.

I help him down from the desk. He is strangely passive, acting as if nothing unusual has happened. 'Thank you, Jim,' he says, accepting my hand as he jumps off the desk. 'I just had to do that. I don't know why.'

I tell him it's OK, people do strange things at times like these. But he smells like piss, and I see drops of the stuff beading on his left sock, like morning dew, and I want him out of the building before he can cause more trouble.

'You're a good man, Jim,' he says to me, as I escort him to the front door. I accept his thanks, but I'm hardly paying attention. Instead, I'm looking behind him, to the parking lot, where I watch Vanderbeek slide into his BMW, slam the door, and peel onto Route 30, tyres screeching.

CHAPTER 22

I return home at four thirty in the afternoon, which is the earliest I've left the office since starting my job at Tao.

I expect to discover Libby missing, maybe off somewhere having an affair, or doing something to punish me for being a lousy husband, or for sending her to Florida while I vacationed on Orcas Island, or for letting our son drown.

But here she is, in the kitchen, putting away groceries – and the very domesticity of this makes me feel ashamed about my doubting her.

Two shopping bags of food sit on the kitchen table, waiting to be unpacked. One overflows with fresh corn, husks trailing brown silk over the edge of the bag. The other has a folded newspaper, *The News-Press*, peeking over the rim.

I slap my car keys on the table and put down my briefcase. Libby glances up briefly, then goes back to arranging the contents of the kitchen cupboard. 'How did it go?' she asks the cupboard.

'Uneventful.'

She doesn't come over to kiss me, I notice, or to say hello. But at least she's talking.

I sit down behind the shopping bags. 'There was an incident,' I say. That's her cue to ask something like, 'Oh yeah? What kind of incident?' – but she doesn't. I wait. Finally I say: 'Yeah, so one guy pissed on the floor.'

She looks up. 'That's a new one.'

'Stood on top of his desk, and pulled out his dick, and started urinating in my direction.'

'My God. What did you do?'

'I backed up.'

She laughs. I don't tell her about Vanderbeek's threats, or about how he claimed to know that money was being stolen from the company. That would just reopen old wounds – make her worry that I wasn't sticking to the programme. The Protect-Tad-At-All-Costs Programme.

'Who was it?' she asks

'David Paris.'

'Which one is he?'

'Marketing.'

'Oh, Marketing,' she says, knowingly. She takes the newspaper from the grocery bag and throws it on the table in front of me. She begins unloading the bag, lifting cans and Tetra Paks. Two cans of Del Monte peas. One box of Swanson low-fat vegetable broth. One pack of Nature's Goodness aged tofu. I wonder absently if she has invited the Dalai Lama for dinner.

'Don't you have some sort of theory about Marketing VPs?' she says, as she tucks the tofu into the fridge. 'That they're the most unstable people in the company?'

'That was my old theory. I have a *new* theory about Marketing VPs. That they have the biggest cocks in the company.'

'You're disgusting.'

'*I* didn't piss on the carpet, baby.'

My gaze falls on the newspaper in front of me. It's numbingly local: an article about the Lee County school-board election, a full-colour furniture ad offering a no-cash-down living-room set, and a handful of wire stories. But a headline just above the fold catches my eye. 'Bank Executive, 36, Injured in Crash, Dies.'

I pick up the paper.

Stanley Pontin, Chief Technology Officer for Old Dominion Bank, headquartered in Tampa, died of injuries sustained in a car crash that occurred last Thursday morning. Pontin's 2008 Ford Mustang ran off the road on July 23 at approximately 2 a.m. Pontin was found in his car, in a ravine eight miles from his home. The accident left him paralysed and brain dead, his wife, Nadia Pontin, reported.

Police are investigating whether drugs or alcohol played a part in the crash. Pontin called 911 from his car shortly before the accident, and reported that his automobile brakes were not functioning, and requested police assistance. Toxicology reports are due to be released on Friday morning.

'That's disturbing,' I say.

I remember that strange phone call with Sandy Golden – how he agreed to do business with us, even though Tao's software failed during our demonstration; and the way he asked that odd question after agreeing to the deal: 'So we're square?'

From the dates in the newspaper article, he called me a few hours after Stan Pontin's accident.

'What does it say?' Libby asks. She is standing behind me, looking over my shoulder to see which article has caught my attention.

I tap the paper. 'He was a guy I met recently. He died.'

'That's terrible.'

'Young kid. I was just sitting across the table from him, just last week.'

Her eyes scan the article. 'Drunk driving,' she says. Which means: It's his fault. 'A shame.'

'Yeah.' But I don't know a lot of drunk drivers who make the effort to dial the police on their cellphone, or to report malfunctioning brakes.

My cellphone rings. I take it out of my pocket and glance at the Caller ID. PERK STILL ATTNY. Pete Bland's law firm.

I answer and Pete says, 'So, how did the lay-offs go?'

'Fine. No problems.'

'We're still on for tonight? Six o'clock?'

Damn. I forgot about this. Earlier in the week, I received a phone call from Pete Bland's secretary, scheduling tonight's dinner. I suppose the idea was that Pete would cheer me up after a dreadful day firing half the company. A nice gesture, but the truth is that I don't feel particularly dreadful. Firing people comes with my job. You develop a thick skin. And also, I recognize in Pete's invitation a cynical motive too: his desire to bond with a client, to make sure Perkins is retained as law firm, even during a period of cost-cutting.

But still. I wouldn't mind getting out of the house.

Pete says: 'I got us reservations at the Gator Hut. We're bringing our wives, right?'

'I don't know,' I say. 'I better check with Libby.'

I look up at my wife. I make a point not to cover the phone, so that anything she says can be heard by Pete. 'Want to go out to dinner with my lawyer, Pete Bland, and his wife?' I say very loudly.

Her sour face tells me that there is nothing in the world she would like less to do. But she has always been a good corporate wife, always willing to take one for the team. She fills her voice with cheer and says airily, 'That sounds wonderful!' The effect is slightly diminished however when she pantomimes putting a finger down her throat and gagging.

Into the phone, I say: 'Libby says it sounds wonderful. We're on.'

The Gator Hut is a South-west Florida Tradition.

I know this – not because I was born in South-west Florida, nor even because I have spent two weeks here. I know this because the sign above the restaurant proclaims it: 'The Gator Hut – A South-west Florida Tradition'. Ours is the only country in the world where you can invent your own history, by painting it on a billboard.

The Gator Hut is on the other side of the river – the redneck side – in North Fort Myers, about as far east as you can go before you start being glad you're not black. You take I-75 to Bayshore, then follow the signs to a gravel road, and then follow more signs, the gravel beneath your tyres growing progressively finer, until at last it ends up as dirt. Then you park next to the river, at the end of a long driveway. That's where you find the Gator Hut. The restaurant is a squat wooden box, cantilevered over the water, nestled under a canopy of live oaks draped with Spanish moss.

Libby and I park the Jeep. The parking lot is fifty yards from the restaurant. We walk past a small pond surrounded by chain link. A few onlookers stare through the fence.

I follow their gaze. The pond is shallow and muddy. In the centre is a cement island, twelve foot square, atop which sit five alligators, warming their bellies on concrete. The gators stare lazily at me and Libby. A sign on the fence says, 'Feed the Gators – Meat Provided – $5'.

Nearby, a teenage girl in a 'Gator Hut' T-shirt sits on an ice chest, watching us as listlessly as the gators.

'Want to feed the gators?' I ask Libby.

'No.'

'Meat provided,' I try, enticingly.

'Whose meat?' she asks.

'I'm not sure.' I turn to the teenage girl. 'Whose meat?'

'Cow,' she says, chewing her gum morosely.

I hand her five bucks. She reaches into the cooler and gives me a package wrapped in newspaper. 'Y'all watch your fingers, now.'

We stand at the perimeter of the fence, next to a family of four – a mother, father, two kids – each one plumper than the next, like little redneck Matryoshka dolls. The kids are poking their fingers through the fence, dropping balls of raw hamburger onto the ground. But the alligators remain perfectly still, resting on their cement island a dozen yards away, staring at the meat with cold reptilian disinterest. Either they have already been sated by dozens of pounds of hamburger, or they are more intrigued by the two porcine children just beyond their reach, and are biding their time.

'Not very active, are they?' I say, to the father.

'Not yet, but when gators move, they move *fast*. Most vicious animals on earth.'

'Is that right?' I turn to Libby. 'Here you go, baby.' I open the newspaper and hand her a ball of raw meat.

She looks disgusted. 'You'll get salmonella from that.'

'I'm not *eating* it. It's for the gators.'

'I hope you're going to wash your hands,' she says.

'If I don't do it after defecating,' I explain, 'I certainly won't do it after feeding alligators.'

I note to myself that Libby isn't much fun these days – and hasn't been in a few years, come to think of it. So I give up on her and decide to feed the animals myself. I push a large chunk of raw hamburger through the chain-link fence, watching it extrude like Play-Doh.

The meat hits the ground. The suddenness of the gators' movement startles me. Four dive off their concrete island, disappear into the water, and then reappear, just feet from me, on the other side of the fence. They fight for the hamburger, whipping their tails, snapping their jaws. I hear the clack of gator enamel when they bite. When I look at the spot where the meat landed, it is gone.

'You see that, Dad?' the little fat boy shouts, excitedly.

'Yup,' the father says, not sounding impressed.

I hand my remaining stash of hamburger to the little boy. 'Here you go,' I say. With great solemnity I add, 'Now, I want you to share this raw meat with your sister.'

'Thanks, mister,' the boy says.

Libby and I leave them, and go into the Gator Hut to find Pete Bland and his wife. Inside, I do as Libby demands, and wash my hands at the bathroom sink. When I return to the lobby, I see Pete Bland standing near the door, with his arm around the waist of a stunning blonde.

My eyes meet Pete's. He waves. I take Libby's hand and guide her to my lawyer and the blonde.

Pete is wearing jeans and a polo shirt. He looks even younger than I remember, now that he's not wearing a suit. His wife seems younger still – maybe not quite thirty.

'Perfect timing,' Pete says. 'Jim, this is my wife, Karen.'

'Nice to meet you,' I say, making a point to keep my eyes on her face. Not easy, given the body it's attached to.

'And you. I've heard a lot about you,' Karen says, offering her hand. She has a Southern accent – genteel, charming – which I place somewhere between Savannah and Charleston.

'Yes,' I say, 'I'm the sucker who took the job at Tao.'

She laughs. 'That is *exactly* what Pete told me about you!'

I introduce Libby, who responds with a grim smile and tepid handshakes, as if we're meeting in a funeral director's office. We go out to the veranda, where we find a table overlooking the river. There is a gaping round hole cut into the centre of the table, under which sits a garbage can.

'That's for the claws,' Pete explains, as we take our seats. 'Just pump and dump.'

'Funny,' I say. 'That was my nickname in high school.'

When the waitress comes, Pete, Libby, and Karen order a round of beers. I ask for an iced tea. Pete glances at me. 'Trying to cut back,' I explain.

'I hear you,' Pete says. But now he knows. I know that he knows.

Everyone orders the all-you-can-eat crab legs, and soon they arrive, steaming hot, overflowing their wooden serving bowls, like giant alien insect legs.

I am surprised by my own hunger. I crack the claws apart, ravenously, dig inside the shells with a flimsy plastic fork. Working on my second claw, my fork snaps in half. No matter – I keep at it with the remaining half-fork, wielding the broken tool like a shattered prison shiv. I splash meat into melted butter, swallow it whole. Ten thousand years of human civilization slough away, as I find myself sucking arthropod joints and muttering to myself, 'Damn good, damn good,' over and over.

I crack a claw, sending salt water across the table into Karen's eye.

'Ouch,' she says, winking.

'I think your wife is winking at me,' I say to Pete.

'You wouldn't be the first man,' he says calmly, sucking his claw. He takes a swig of beer.

"What do you think?' Pete asks.

'Excellent,' I say. 'They're excellent.'

'Yeah, me and Karen come here a lot with Kyle and Ashley. Any excuse we can get.'

'Kyle and Ashley?' I ask.

'Our children,' Karen says. She beams. She has the face of an angel, and it glows at the mention of her kids. 'They're four and six.'

'Thank god for babysitters,' Pete mutters.

'They don't really eat crabs,' Karen goes on. 'But they love feeding the gators out front.'

'Impressive creatures,' I say. 'The gators, I mean.'

'What about you two?' Karen asks. 'Do you have children?'

It's a question that inevitably comes, and I suppose I should be ready for it, but nevertheless it always feels like a roundhouse punch.

'No,' I say, trying to keep my countenance as placid as a mountain lake. No sadness. No pain. 'We don't have any children.'

I glance at Libby. She is staring at the table – seething, maybe – hating me, certainly – for what I did. For letting Cole drown. For getting high and leaving him in a bathtub.

Pete senses something wrong – God bless him – and he tries to rescue me. 'So anyway,' he says, wiping butter from his lips with a crumpled napkin. 'Tell me. How did you and Libby meet?'

'Oh, it's a very romantic story,' I say, relieved to change the topic, even to one that involves my wife. I turn to her. 'Why don't you tell them, baby?'

She looks at me, warily. 'Why don't *you*?'

'You first,' I say.

'*You* first,' she replies.

'All right,' I say. This is not the first time that Libby has been sullen and uncommunicative in public. But it is strange that she is refusing – utterly refusing – to tell the story about how we met. As if she wants to erase me from her memory. Or maybe already has. 'Libby was my waitress,' I say.

Karen laughs and claps her greasy hands together. 'That's wonderful! What did she serve you, Jim?'

'Scotch,' I say, too happily. Even the name of the drink does something to me. 'Actually, I can't remember. I think it was scotch.'

'If you can't remember,' Pete muses, 'then it probably was.'

'I asked her out four times,' I say.

'Four times!' Karen says. 'You were persistent!'

'Yes I was. If nothing else, I am persistent. Try and try again.' I turn to Libby. 'Remember what you told me the first time I asked you out?'

'No.'

'"Go to hell",' I say. 'That's what she told me, I mean.'

Karen laughs politely. 'If every woman answered as honestly as your wife, I do believe the human race would have died out, long ago.'

'Amen to that,' Pete says. He's still busy with his claws, though, sucking on them with great intensity, and I'm pretty sure he isn't paying much attention to anything anyone is saying.

'And the second time I asked Libby out,' I continue, 'she just laughed at me. "Very funny, Jimmy!" That's what she said. "Very funny!" Like I was joking.'

'But you weren't joking,' Karen says.

'No I wasn't. But I had to convince her, apparently. Now, let me see. Attempt number three... ' I look to the sky, theatrically, pretending to recall that incident long ago. 'Attempt number three – she was at the bar, serving me a drink, and I whispered into her ear.'

'And?' Karen asks. 'What did she say?'

'Nothing. She pretended not to hear me.' I think about it. 'Or maybe she really didn't. The bar *was* very loud.'

'That's three,' Karen says. 'You said there were four tries. How did you finally succeed?'

'The last one – well, that was magic.' I turn again to Libby. 'You want to tell them what happened? Where we finally met?'

My wife looks at me with a curious expression. Not anger, exactly. Not even annoyance. Something like – could it be *fear*?

She rises from her seat, too quickly, knocking over her bowl of butter, which spreads in a slow puddle across the table towards Karen and Pete.

'Oh my,' Karen says, backing away with good grace. To Libby: 'Let me help you.' She drops a stack of napkins on the spilled butter, then hands a clean one to Libby.

'No,' Libby says, too loudly. 'I'm fine.' She turns and leaves the table.

The three of us watch her stalk away, in a half-run, across the patio, into the interior of the restaurant.

Pete says, 'She all right?' He's still got a claw in his mouth, and doesn't look very concerned.

'Maybe it's just a lady's emergency,' Karen offers.

'Oh,' Pete says. 'OK.'

'I should go and find her,' I say tepidly. Half wishing they would tell me not to.

Just then another round of crab legs arrives.

'Sit,' Pete says. 'Have a crab. Libby's fine.'

I love Pete Bland, I decide; and I will retain him as our company's lawyer for as long as I can.

The three of us continue eating, and Karen talks about how she met Pete – 'at a corporate event' – whatever that means – and how it was love at first sight.

'Then she got to know me,' Pete says. 'And it was all downhill from there.' Pete and Karen both burst into laughter at the same instant. Even their laughs sound weirdly alike – little rhythmic snorts through buttery noses. Karen playfully pushes her shoulder into Pete's side.

It's at this moment that I feel the pang – something like sadness – that my marriage is so different from theirs, my wife so different from Karen. Libby is hiding in the bathroom, sulking about some perceived slight that I must have perpetrated, but which I do not yet understand and probably never will.

As if on cue, Libby returns to the table. She wears the expression of a boxer, steeling herself to go one more brutal round.

'You all right?' I say.

'Fine,' she says. 'Just needed a minute.'

We all eat quietly, and let the moment pass.

Pete finishes his second plate of crabs, dumps the shells into the centre garbage hole.

'Hey that works pretty good,' I say. 'We should cut one of these holes into our kitchen table, Libby.'

My wife smiles wanly.

'Who needs a hole?' Pete says. 'At home, me and Karen just toss them on the floor.'

Soon the conversation breaks into two, the men talking business – about the lay-offs, the prospects for turning the company around – not good, I admit to Pete; and the women talking between themselves. I half listen to them, chatting beside us, murmuring about Florida, and the heat, and the best beaches, and the shells on Sanibel, and shopping in Naples.

The third serving of crab legs soon arrives. As I eat, I watch Libby methodically dispatch her crabs. Is there anything sexier than watching your wife suck meat out of a claw? Things seem normal again, and I almost forgive Libby for the way she acted tonight – almost love her more for it. My fragile, volatile, intelligent wife. It's just Libby being... *Libby*, after all.

197

In the end, we finish three portions each; and when our waitress asks if we're ready for our fourth plate, we all raise our hands in surrender. 'No mas,' I say.

We sponge off with postage-stamp sized towelettes, scented like lemon, and courteously provided 'for free' (as the waitress explains graciously when she hands them to us). We decline her offer of pecan pie for dessert, and Pete and I settle the bill. The entire feast costs less than the price of four fish tacos in San Francisco. At least there are some perks when you relocate to the middle of nowhere.

We waddle from the restaurant, sated, and buttery too; and I watch Libby from behind as she and Karen walk in front of me and Pete, past the alligator pond. I compare the two wives' asses. I must admit, Libby looks damned good, even in a T-shirt and jeans. Karen may be ten years her junior, but my wife is holding up. I wonder if Karen will look this good, when she reaches Libby's age. I find this observation – sexist and detestable as it is – weirdly heartening. Maybe things aren't so bad after all.

'DeeDee?' calls a woman's voice from behind us.

Karen turns, and so does Pete, but Libby ignores the voice, and keeps walking. The woman calls again, louder, more insistent. 'DeeDee? Is that you?'

Footsteps approach from behind, and now there's no ignoring her. A woman, about my wife's age – late thirties – but worn, terribly worn, with circles under her eyes, blonde hair turning grey – jogs towards us. Libby keeps walking, leaving me, and Karen, and Pete to face the woman alone.

'I'm sorry,' the woman says. She's peering past me, at my wife, who barrels on, ignoring her. 'DeeDee? Is that you?' she calls.

Libby has no choice. She turns to the woman. Libby stands a dozen feet away, shoulders squared and ready for confrontation.

'It *is* you,' the woman says. 'I knew it. I told my husband, "That's DeeDee." What in the world are you doing in Florida?'

Uncomfortable silence. Libby regards the woman coldly. I've been on the receiving end of that look before: it's the look you get when you say something stupid to a very smart wife. Like, for example, when you explain that you broke into someone's house and found cash in the attic. *That* look.

The stranger must be a masochist, because she doesn't catch on to what I know is merely Libby's warning glance. 'It's *me*,' the woman insists, 'Kimmy.'

'I'm sorry... *Kimmy*,' Libby says, spitting the name. 'I don't know who the hell you are.'

Something clicks, and the woman blushes. 'Oh, I'm sorry,' she says, quickly. 'I'm so sorry.' She looks to me and Pete, and then to Karen. She backs away. Muttering embarrassed apologies, her face crimson, the woman named Kimmy disappears back into the Gator Hut.

'That was weird,' I say.

Pete turns to Libby. 'You know her, Libby?'

'No,' Libby says, and turns a venomous gaze to Pete.

Karen says soothingly, 'Nowadays you can't be too friendly to strangers. You just don't know what they're up to.'

A valiant attempt to make my wife's behaviour palatable. But an unsuccessful one, we all know.

In the parking lot, we say goodbyes, and we promise to do this again, since it was, Karen insists, 'so much fun.'

'Take care,' Pete says to me. He shakes my hand and looks me in the eye meaningfully, man to man, as if to say, 'I don't envy your job... *or* your home life.' I turn to Libby, but she's already gone, twenty yards away, climbing into our car, rushing to escape.

CHAPTER 23

During the ride home, we don't talk about what happened in the restaurant. Libby sits in the passenger seat, staring straight ahead, with that expression that I've become so familiar with over the last decade. It means: I may be sitting just inches away from you, but do not dare to speak to me.

So I stay silent as I drive, flipping through the radio channels, trying to find a station at once innocuous and soothing. I settle finally on Christian contemporary music – which fills practically every channel on the dial – and we listen to a song about Jesus and his love for all men. The ride passes quickly enough.

Back in the house, Libby wanders around downstairs, performing her night-time rituals, straightening pillows on the couch, wiping down counters, starting the dishwasher, checking that the sliding doors to the patio are securely locked. She is delaying what inevitably must come next – being alone with me, with nothing left to distract us.

I follow her from room to room, cautiously trailing behind, not wandering too close, waiting for the right moment to speak.

At last, when she is finished straightening and fiddling, and there is no task left undone, I say, quietly: 'Do you want to talk about it?'

She looks up at me, as if surprised that I'm in the room with her.

'Talk about what?'

'About what happened tonight.'

'No.'

'Because you were behaving kind of... ' I stop. I am about to say, 'strange', but decide at the last instant the word will provoke her. I say instead, '... like you were sad.'

She looks at me. Her eyes are weary, heavy-lidded. Her face is more than sad. It's despondent.

I say, 'You were thinking about... *him*.' I can't use Cole's name in her presence. This was never formally discussed, never explicitly agreed; but one day I noticed I hadn't spoken it in a very long time, and neither had she; and then every day that passed, it became harder to say it.

'Yes,' she says. 'When they started talking about their children, I... ' She shakes her head. 'Well, it doesn't matter.'

I walk to her, and hug her, wrapping my arms around her protectively. I love this woman, and all her faults, and all her meanness and unkindness to me. She has stayed true to me, despite everything – everything that I have done, everything I have destroyed, everything I have taken from her.

She stands motionless, wooden and stiff in my arms.

'I love you,' I say. 'I'm sorry I dragged you to that dinner. You didn't really want to go.'

Silence.

'And I'm sorry I dragged you here. To Florida.'

Still no answer.

'Come upstairs,' I say, raising her chin gently, so that she must look at me. 'Let's make love.'

She stares at me. Her expression is not one of love; I am certain of that. It is not even particularly matrimonial. It is an expression familiar to me, though; I have seen it before. I saw it on the faces of men that night I spent in jail. It's the dull and glassy stare of a prisoner – a look of powerlessness – an expression that says: Do with me as you will.

'I'm so tired, Jimmy,' she says, quietly, without much hope.

'Come,' I say again – still gently, but with more firmness in my voice. 'Come upstairs with me.' I tug her hand.

She lets me lead her up the stairs, to the dark bedroom. I don't bother shutting the bedroom door, or closing the blinds. Outside the window, past the branches of the oak tree, I see our neighbour's house across the street. The velociraptor's attic light is on. What is he doing, on a Wednesday night, in his attic?

'Come here,' I say, and gather Libby close. I pull her T-shirt over her head, drop it to the floor. I unfasten her bra, put my hands on her breasts. I kiss her neck, taste her salt, smell her sweat.

She stands there, stiffly, like a patient under a fluorescent light, in a doctor's examination room.

'What's the matter?' I ask.

'Nothing,' she says sullenly.

I unbutton the top of her jeans, work my half-stub of a pinky into the elastic band of her underpants.

'No,' she whispers. 'Please, Jimmy.'

I ignore her. I unzip her jeans, pull them over the hump of her hips, down to her thighs. Her underwear catches and goes with them. Now she's standing, bound around the thighs by her pants, her pubic hair exposed.

'Please,' she says, louder now. She pushes me away.

'What now?' I ask, finally losing patience. 'What now?'

She's looking past me, to the teak ceiling fan, spinning lazily in the middle of the room.

'I'm just tired, Jimmy,' she says, softly. 'Is that OK? To be tired?'

'You know, Libby,' I say, petulantly, 'it would be nice if, every now and then, you acted like my wife.'

With that, I stomp off to the bathroom, letting the door slam just a bit too loudly. It's my turn to have some drama.

I let the cold water run into the sink, splash my face. I look at myself in the mirror.

I try to do the impossible – evaluate my own appearance with complete honesty: my hair, coarse and greying at the temple; my nose, not overly large, but nevertheless awry, from some long-forgotten drunken stumble or fistfight.

I am not an ugly man. But neither am I handsome. I possess one of those faces that, when woman try to be charitable say, *shows character.* But the character it shows depends entirely on the story that goes with it. Long ago – when I first met Libby, when I was a young executive, on my way up, when Libby and I walked into restaurants together, when we came home after a long day and tugged on each other's pants – this face would have told a story of a businessman, a star on the rise, a young man with talent, and ambition, and the world spread below him, available for his taking.

Now the cragged lines on my face, the disjointed nose, even the missing pinky, tell a different story – a story of wear and waste and attrition. And failure.

The water gurgles into the sink. Outside the bathroom door, I hear sounds. I shut off the sink, and just barely detect the last echo of a telephone ringing in the bedroom. Libby is speaking to someone. I try to listen, to discern the sound of lovers' whispers, of a secret affair, of a hurried, 'I have to go'. But I hear only one or two syllable answers, 'Yes', or 'I know', or 'Please don't', or 'OK'.

I open the bathroom door, just as Libby is replacing the phone in its cradle on the bureau. This is not the act of a guilty woman. She is not trying to hide the telephone from me, nor the fact that she was speaking into it.

'Who was that?' I ask.

She looks at me for a long time before she answers. Finally she says, 'Our neighbour.'

'What neighbour?' I ask, even though I know.

She gestures with her chin, out of the bedroom window, past the gnarled live oak, to the house across the street. When I turn to look,

I'm expecting to see the velociraptor in the attic window, with a pair of binoculars, waving to me. But now the attic light is off, and the house is dark.

'What did he want?'

'Nothing. He noticed our back gate was open. He closed it for us, when we were at dinner.'

'That was nice of him,' I say. 'Have you spoken to him before?'

'Not really,' she says.

'Not really?' I repeat. A strange answer to a simple question. 'What's his name?'

'I don't know,' she says. And then, suddenly: 'Come here.'

'Why?'

'Come here.'

'Libby,' I start, wanting to ask more questions about the neighbour, about what he said on the telephone, about how often he and Libby have spoken... and about *why* they had spoken.

'Shhh,' she says. She walks to where I stand, near the bathroom door. 'I want to suck your cock.'

She kisses me on the lips, hard, with a desperate craziness, and I feel her fingers expertly unfasten my belt, unzip my fly, pull down my pants.

She kneels on the floor in front of me.

'Forget it, Libby,' I say. 'It's not necessary.'

'It *is* necessary,' she corrects me. 'It is *very* necessary.'

She begins to suck me. Libby gives me blow jobs sometimes, but it is not her favourite activity – something akin to rearranging the cans in the pantry – something she does periodically to keep the house running smoothly, but not something she enjoys.

Tonight is different. I have never seen her like this. She has turned ravenous, cannot get enough of me. She forces me into her mouth, pulls me towards her from behind, deeper. She moans something, but her words are lost.

204

'Libby,' I say, 'forget it. It's OK.' A part of me wants to spurn her, to walk away so that she can't make everything OK, not so fast, not like this, but then the reptilian part of me, the animal, doesn't pull away. Not at all.

She lets me slide from her mouth. 'Is that better?' she asks. 'Is that better?' And then she starts again, more violently. Things are getting a bit weird now. She's moving her head back and forth, spastically, violently – and her motion is more epileptic than sensual.

I grip the door frame to steady myself. 'Libby,' I say. 'It's OK. Stop.'

But it feels good. And I don't want her to stop. Not really.

She releases me from her mouth again. 'Is this better?' she says, practically shouting. 'Is this better?' And I see that she's crying – are those tears of sadness? – and she's looking up – not at me, but at the ceiling fan, which is spinning lazily like a giant lascivious winking eye. 'Is this better?' she shouts at the fan.

She sticks me back into her mouth, and pumps her head back and forth, like an automaton. There is nothing loving or kind in what she does to me. There is nothing warm. It's barely human, barely biological – she is a machine, with gears and pinions and wheels.

But that doesn't stop me. I grab her head from behind, gently at first, then with something approaching violence, and I finish in her mouth, pumping, and then I hold her head in place, and I see that she's looking up with vacant eyes, her gaze fixed on the ceiling fan. After a moment, I release her. She stays on her knees, and wipes the tears from her eyes. Then she crawls onto the bed and lies down. 'Is that what you want?' she asks.

'Yes,' I say, in a hoarse whisper.

'Then you have what you want.' She pulls the pillow over her face.

I look across the street, at our neighbour's house, and the lights are off, and I see no one in the window.

CHAPTER 24

That night, I see Cole again, but this time, my dream is different.

I am in a house. I walk up a flight of stairs. Moonlight casts the way, spilling through banister slats at my feet. At the top landing, there's a hallway. I hear the sound of a boy, laughing, splashing water. I follow the sound. My feet are silent in the carpeted hall. Why am I sneaking? Darkness, all around. At the end of the hall, I come to a closed door. I can see a thin line of yellow light beneath it. Behind it, the sound of a little boy's laughter.

I open the door. Cole is in the bathtub. He's alive – sitting and smiling and playing with a red plastic boat. I must surprise him. He looks up at me, stops playing.

His face changes to confusion. Then fear. He doesn't recognize me. Who is this man standing in the door?

He opens his mouth. He screams.

I wake, my own scream strangled in my throat.

Libby is sleeping beside me, breathing slowly, a dark shadow barely moving on the bed. The branches of the live oak tap the window pane.

'Libby,' I whisper.

No answer.

'Libby?' Her breathing stutters, then starts again. She hasn't moved, but I know she's awake now. Listening.

'I'm sorry, Libby,' I say. 'I'm sorry for everything I've done. Everything that I've lost for us.'

She is silent. Though her body is turned from me, I somehow can picture her. I somehow know exactly how she appears. She's awake. Her eyes are open. She is staring into the dark.

I want to say more. I want to tell her about the dream – how my own son did not recognize me. And how, sometimes – like tonight – I don't recognize myself. How I can't stop being a monster.

But these words don't come. I think them. I hear them in my mind. I desire to speak them aloud. But nothing comes. After a few minutes of sitting upright, in dumbstruck silence, I lay my head down beside my wife. I listen to her breathe.

And soon I sleep.

CHAPTER 25

It's Thursday morning, the day after the lay-offs.

When I arrive at Tao, the parking lot is deserted – just a few cars, no sign of human activity. The only thing the scene lacks is a dusty wind and a tumbleweed rolling past my feet.

In the reception area, Amanda greets me with sleepy eyes. 'Good morning, Jim,' she says. Since last week, neither of us has acknowledged our church-basement date, our kiss, or my brush with Jesus in her apartment.

'Morning, Amanda,' I say, trying to sound chipper and boss-like. 'How are things?'

'Lonely,' she sighs.

The complaint of a spurned lover? The gripe of an employee? When you're in charge of a company and you can't tell the difference, that's probably a warning sign.

'Things will get better,' I say, vaguely – an answer that works in either case.

'Sure, Jim,' she says.

'You know what they say,' I begin, 'it's always darkest before...' but Amanda holds up her index finger – the workplace gesture that translates roughly to: 'Shut up, you boring load' – and she presses a key on her telephone console, and says into the headset, 'Tao Software. How may I help you?' And then: 'Let me see if he's available.'

She looks to me. 'Tad Billups.'

'In my office,' I say, and I race to meet the call as she transfers it to my desk.

I shut the office door.

'Hi, Tad,' I say, easing into my chair. 'What's up?'

'You tell me, champ,' Tad says. 'How did it go?'

He means the lay-offs, and did anyone get killed.

'Fine,' I say. 'Fine. I did what was required.'

'I knew your would, champ,' he says. 'That's why I hired you. Now I'm going to give you some good news. Do you want good news?'

'Sure I do.'

'Are you near a computer?'

'Yes.'

'Look in your bank account. Your personal bank account. Not the Tao Software bank account. We already know the balance there, right?' He laughs. 'Zero!'

'Tad,' I begin, 'I'm glad you brought that up. I know you said there would be no further investment by your firm, but I think you should reconsider. We just need a little bit more runway, Tad. That's all we need, just some runway. I thought maybe if you could talk to your partners and—'

'Did you look yet?'

'Look at what?'

'Your bank account.'

'No.'

'Do it. Right now. While I'm on the phone.'

I sigh. On my desktop computer, I launch a web browser, log in to the Wells Fargo account belonging to me and Libby.

'There,' Tad says. 'See it yet?'

At first I think I have made a mistake, that I have somehow accessed the wrong bank account – someone *else's* bank account. When I understand this is impossible, I have a second thought: that the bank has made a monumental error, and that I must hang up with Tad and report this *immediately*. Isn't it true that not reporting a bank error is the equivalent to stealing – that you can be thrown in jail for it? That's all I need to put the finishing touch on my résumé – seven to twelve years in a federal penitentiary.

'Hello, hotshot, are you there?' Tad's voice calls me back. 'You see your account?'

I *do* see my account. The screen says that my cash balance, which – just Monday morning, when I last paid my bills, was $22,100.12 – is now, at 9.36 on Thursday morning, $2,022,100.12. Between Monday and today, I have made two million dollars.

'Tad,' I say. I try to keep my voice calm. I sense that something in my life is changing, and not for the better. Before this moment, I had fears and doubts and suspicions. I *suspected* that Tad Billups was involved in… what was the word I used, when I voiced my doubts to Libby? – *shenanigans*. But shenanigans are the acts of drunk fraternity brothers – short-sheeting the pledges, dabbing warm water on their wrists while they sleep. Two million dollars in a bank account is not a shenanigan. It is something different. Very different. It is something related to cash in garbage bags, to missing CEOs, to Russian gangsters.

'What is this, Tad?'

'What does it look like, hotshot? It's money. M – O – N – E… money.'

'You forgot the Y.'

'There is no *why* in money, Jimmy. Get my point?'

'No.'

'Well, here's how I'll put it. This is my way of thanking you. Of saying, you're doing a good job. Keep it up.'

'But I'm not doing a good job. I can't save this company, Tad. It can't be saved.'

'I think you must know,' he says, and pauses, 'that's not what I mean. That's not what I care about.'

'What *do* you care about?'

'Come on, Jimmy,' he says, and for the first time I hear a human being at the other end of the phone. It's the voice of an old friend, a man who began as my peer, long ago, but whose career has since surpassed mine. It's the voice of compassion, and charity, and patience – the voice of a man who has slowed down for me, just for a moment, and who has reached out his hand, one last time, to help. He continues, 'You're a lot of things, Jimmy. You're a drunk, and you're a cheat, and you don't pass up blow if it's free at a party. But you're not stupid. Are you?'

'No.'

'Are you?' he asks again.

'No.'

'Well then.' A long silence. He's calling me from his cellphone – the connection has that radio-from-the-moon quality, but the line is quiet; he's not calling from a moving car, or from a busy sidewalk. He's sitting in a room somewhere, a quiet room, with the door locked behind him. He's alone.

'Here's what I want you to do,' he says softly. 'That lovely wife of yours. She is a lovely girl, and I must tell you that if you don't want her, I'll take her for myself. I want you to hang up the phone with me, and get into your car, and drive down to the nearest Bloomingdales. They do have Bloomingdales out there, don't they, Jimmy?'

'I'm not sure.'

'They have *something*. Whatever they have, go there. And buy that wife of yours something wonderful. What would she like?'

'A new husband.'

'Nu-uh,' he says, clucking his tongue. 'No can do. She's stuck with you. And you're stuck with her. So do the right thing, for once. Buy her something expensive. Ah, to hell with Bloomingdales. Go to the Mercedes dealer, and buy her one of those convertibles. She like Mercedes?'

'I guess.'

'Of course she does! All women like Mercedes. They like driving around with the top down in the sunshine, while their husband is at work. Reminds them why they put up with the fat pig in the dark.'

'I can't keep it, Tad.'

'Keep what?'

'The money.'

Another long silence. 'Why not?'

Why not, indeed? I'm not sure what to answer. Before this morning, when I had a mere suspicion of illegal activity at Tao, I was just a bystander – maybe a bystander who was encouraged to look the other way – but still a bystander. By accepting this money, I become something else. An accomplice. Two million dollars in my bank account. Exactly half of the amount missing from the company's coffers.

'Listen, partner,' Tad says. His choice of word chills me. *Partner*. 'Here's what you have to understand. You're a businessman. I'm a businessman. It's all business. In business, there's give and there's take. I'm going to give to you, and you're going to take.'

'Tad—'

'Listen,' he snaps. 'I'm not finished.' More gently: 'Now, after this gig is over, there'll be other companies. Bigger companies. That's what's great about your line of work, Jimmy – the supply of human weakness is unlimited. There's always more garbage for you to clean up! And, after Tao, you'll have a track record. You'll get bigger jobs. More important jobs. I'll help you get them. For now, just keep quiet and make everyone happy.'

'Who is everyone?' I ask, suddenly emboldened. 'Who? You and who else?'

'My partners,' Tad says.

'Who are your partners?'

'You know,' Tad says quietly, with a chill in his voice.

I have met the three other partners at Tad's venture-capital firm, Bedrock Ventures. I have pitched all three of them my cockamamie business ideas, have sat in board meetings with them, and have – when things were going badly – requested desperate lunch appointments. There's Steve Burnham, a software entrepreneur and MIT grad, who made two hundred million dollars selling a piece-of-shit start-up to Yahoo, exactly one year before Yahoo shut down the unit and wrote it off as worthless. There's Biram Sanjay, the ex-BCG consultant, whose area of specialization, as far as I can tell, based on my interaction with him, is to show up at board meetings, draw four squares on a whiteboard, and tell CEOs that they ought to 'move to the upper right quadrant'. There's Tench Worthington, nicknamed (behind his back, of course) Tench Worth-a-Ton – Harvard undergrad and MBA, lineage back to the *Mayflower*, nose like a Roman statue – whose function at Bedrock Ventures is that of a skeleton key: he opens a lot of doors – at endowments, state pensions, family offices – and convinces important people to sign cheques.

Each of Tad's partners is insufferable in a different way – and none is a person I want to spend an hour with. But not one is a criminal. Not a single one would sign up for this plan: to drain cash from Bedrock's investments, and have it flow into the pockets of Tad and myself. After all, the cash is *their* cash. The money I now possess came from them.

'Tad,' I ask again, 'who do you work for?'

'Too many questions, hotshot.' A pause. 'Dangerous questions. *N'est-ce pas?*'

'Tad—'

'Listen, my friend. Men like you, how many chances do you think you're going to get? Two? Three? Five? What number are you on, anyway?'

'Maybe ten.'

'"Maybe ten,"' he mimics me, using a pansy voice. 'Try maybe twelve or thirteen. And this is it, Jimmy. Last stop on the Loser Express. Guess what, buddy? You don't have the luxury of picking your gigs. Take what you get. And that means taking the people who come with it. Me, my partners, the whole ball of wax. We're a package.'

'I'm just asking who they are.'

'And I'm just telling you to stop asking. Now, listen, I have to go.

213

I have an appointment. A manicure, if you can believe that. Does that make me gay? I hope, sincerely hope, you stop being so curious. This isn't a game, Jimmy. The people we're talking about – they aren't Silicon Valley people. They haven't drunk the Kool-Aid. They don't buy into the "Let's ask lots of questions and see if we can do better by questioning all our assumptions" bullshit. These people do not like questions. So don't ask them.'

'Is that what happened to Charles Adams?'

'Goddamn it, Jimmy!' he yells. 'I tell you to stop asking questions, and what do you do? You ask another question. Now, remember what I told you.'

'Not to ask questions.'

'No, you misogynistic pig. To buy your wife a Mercedes. If you're in doubt about the colour, try black. It'll go great with Libby's hair.'

'All right, Tad.'

'*Ciao*, hotshot.'

Before I can say *ciao*, the line is dead, and he's gone.

CHAPTER 26

Have you ever done this?

Have you ever pulled into the driveway of your house, in a brand new Mercedes SL550 Roadster, with the top down, after spending exactly thirty-two minutes at a dealership negotiating the car's purchase – that negotiation consisting exactly of this: asking the sticker price of the car, nodding dumb agreement, and writing a personal cheque for the entire six-figure amount?

If you have never done this, you should try it sometime. It is nice to see how the other part of humanity lives. By 'the other part of humanity', I mean the insanely rich, or the seriously criminal, or those who reside in the intersection between the two – the place where I now curiously find myself.

I park this new Mercedes in the driveway, cut the motor, and use my cell to call Libby. 'I have a surprise for you,' I tell her. 'Come outside.'

Soon the door opens, and Libby walks onto the porch. When she sees the car, she staggers back, maybe in surprise. Or maybe it's just the heat – it's only three p.m., and the sun is high and incandescent.

'What in the world?' she says, although of course she knows exactly what in the world.

She trundles down the stairs. I climb out of the car, leaving the door open. 'For you.'

'Me?'

'My way of saying thank you... for putting up with me. All my trouble. All my shit.'

'Oh, Jimmy,' she says, 'you don't have to thank me.' I notice she doesn't disagree about the trouble and shit part – just the thanks.

One week has passed since that night in the restaurant, and since Tad's phone call. Things have been quiet since then – quiet at work, and even quieter at home: no anger, no conflict – just a numbness, as if the house where Libby and I live is bathed in a mist of anaesthesia.

Libby touches my arm and slides into the car, and the leather seat crinkles under her cotton sundress, and she wraps her slender fingers around the hand-stitched steering wheel. 'It's beautiful,' she murmurs. She pushes back into the seat, looks at herself in the mirror. Casually, an afterthought: 'How did you pay for it?'

'A bonus from Tad.'

She glances at me, sidelong. 'What kind of bonus?'

A Jimmy-should-keep-his-mouth-shut bonus, I think silently. But out loud I say, 'Retention.'

'Does that mean he's happy?'

'Yes, I think so.'

'Good.' She gets out of the car and closes the door. It makes a solid hundred-grand *thunk*. 'Keep them happy, Jimmy. It's so important to keep them happy.'

She gives a quick, almost imperceptible glance across the street, to our neighbour's house. Just for an instant. Or maybe I'm imagining it, because now she's looking at me again, squinting into the sun and staring into my face. She squeezes my hand – a gesture of charity, not gratitude – and rises to her toes, and gives me a chaste peck on the cheek. 'It was nice of you,' she says, 'to buy this for me.'

'I love you.'

She says nothing.

I go on, 'I just want everything to be normal again. That's all I want for you and me, Libby. A normal life.'

'A normal life?' she repeats dully. Her lips twist into one of her mean little smiles, which usually indicates a waspish comment about to come. Maybe something like: If you wanted a normal life, you shouldn't have left your son alone to drown while you got high.

But whatever she is thinking, she does not say. She just walks silently to the house.

I stay behind. Something bothers me. When she's on the porch, I call to her, 'Libby?'

She turns.

I say: 'You said "*them*".'

Her face is blank.

'You said keep *them* happy. Who did you mean by "them"?'

A queer look – both puzzled and annoyed. 'Tad,' she says. 'Tad and… Bedrock Ventures.'

No, I think. *That is not what you meant.*

'Come inside, Jimmy,' she says. 'Let me cook you dinner. A normal dinner. So that we can be normal together. That's what we want, isn't it?'

And then she's gone.

I'm not sure how long I stand there, in the driveway, in the sun, thinking about my wife, and her moods, and her mysteries.

When I told Lance, the salesman at the Mercedes showroom, that the new car would be a gift for my wife – meant as a surprise – he laughed and winked and said, 'You're going to be a lucky man tonight!' I just shook my head and told him, 'You don't know Libby.'

No one knows Libby, including me. Maybe not even Libby herself. She's a Chinese puzzle box, intricate and beautiful, full of secrets. She never reacts the way I expect. When I let our son drown, she claims to forgive me. When I try to love her, she pushes me away. I understand her no better today than I did eleven years ago, the night we first met.

I stand in the driveway, pondering this. I'm in no hurry to go inside, to return to her. Out here, it might be a hundred degrees, something close to hell, but at least I don't have to bear that look from my wife. I hear footsteps behind me.

I turn to see Special Agent Tom Mitchell walking up the drive, looking preposterously crisp and cool in a linen shirt and a knitted cotton tie, despite the heat. His sleeves are rolled; his white suit jacket is slung casually over his shoulder. The only thing he needs to complete the look of a Southern dandy is a straw hat and a mint julep.

'Whoooeee,' he says, half whistling, as he circles the Mercedes, staring lustfully. 'Now *that* is one fine automobile.' With this last word, his transformation into plantation owner is complete: auto-*MO*-beel. 'That a new car, Mr Thane?'

'Brand new,' I say.

'Cost a pretty penny, I bet.' He's still circling the car, shark-like, examining it from every angle.

'It's a gift for my wife.'

'That right?' he says. He purses his lips. 'She must be a special lady.'

He stands on his toes and peers into the car, as if that special lady might be right there, chopped up into pieces on the floor.

'Yes,' I say.

'I thought I'd stop by,' he says, looking at me, smiling. 'I wanted to see how things are going. From the looks of it, not bad.'

He glances at my house, and the wraparound porch, and the fence hiding what must be a swimming pool. I see the gears turning: he's trying to figure out how much all this is worth, and how I afford it.

'Can't complain,' I say. 'What can I do for you, Agent Mitchell?'

'Do you remember that name I mentioned to you, last time we spoke?'

'What name is that?'

'Ghol Gedrosian.'

I do remember, of course. The name sounded strange and foreign, back when I first heard it, weeks ago, in the boardroom at Tao. Today

218

it seems less strange, less foreign. Indeed, I wouldn't be surprised if this was the name of one of Tad Billups's partners. One of his silent partners. And so, I suppose, one of my partners.

'No,' I lie. 'I don't remember that name.'

'You sure now?' He stares at me. '*Ghol Gedrosian.*' He says it again, quite slowly – enunciating each syllable – studying my reaction as he repeats it. 'Remember?'

'Maybe,' I say, uncertainly. 'Maybe.'

'You *do* remember.' His voice is gentle, but there's a hint of accusation.

'Maybe,' I repeat. 'What about him?'

'Well, now. I need to find him. I was hoping you could help.'

As ridiculous as this sounds to me – Jimmy Thane helping an FBI agent to find someone he's never met – I don't laugh. Not out loud. One of the things you learn in business – something they don't teach you when you study for your MBA, but which you figure out pretty fast in the real world – is to be polite and agreeable to any government official who harasses you. No matter how lowly, no matter how uneducated, no matter how unimportant they may seem, always remember that they have the power to destroy you. To ruin you utterly and completely. So be humble. And give them whatever they ask for.

'Help you find him?' I repeat, as if he's talking about a misplaced set of car keys. 'Sure. I'd like to help you any way I can. Maybe first, you can tell me who he is.'

'Who he is?' Mitchell smiles. But it's a strange smile – a smile completely without pleasure – the kind of smile you make when you talk admiringly about the perfection of nature's predators, or when you describe a senseless tragedy at an elementary school, or when you express grim hopelessness about the permanence of evil in the world. That kind of smile. 'Maybe I should tell you a little story,' Agent Mitchell says.

I try to keep a delighted expression planted on my face, as if nothing could please me more. A story! While standing here in my driveway! Under the beating sun! While it's a hundred degrees! 'Yes, please.'

'There was a DA out in California – out in San Joaquin, your neck of the woods, I believe. His name was Bob Callahan. You recall the name?'

'No.'

'One day, Mr Callahan wondered why so much methamphetamine was flooding into his county. It was destroying the town where he lived, Mr Thane. The town where he brought up his children, where he went to church. They're rural out there, and mostly poor. Every other man was selling it or using it or making it. And no one was willing to put a stop to it. It was as if everyone in charge agreed to look the other way. Everyone except for Mr Callahan. So he started asking questions. He found out that all the meth in the valley was being supplied by just one man – a Russian – some two-bit asshole. But no one could even tell Callahan the guy's name. He had different names depending on who you asked. Carl Gadossan. Ghulla Gadrosan. No one could say for sure. Some people said he was Russian. Others said Chechen. Others Armenian. No one knew what he looked like, or where he lived, or who he was. He was… ' He stops. Thinks about it. 'Well, he was a ghost,' he says. 'Even the people that worked for him didn't know shit about him. They took their orders from other people, who took their orders from someone else. He was a clever man, this little chicken-shit meth dealer. Hiding in shadows. Not quite real.'

'What happened?'

'Callahan asked questions. That's all he did, Mr Thane, just ask questions. But that was a mistake.'

'Why's that?'

'They took his daughter first. She was only nine years old, by the way. They walked right into her school, pretending to be police officers, if you can imagine that. Signed her out at the principal's office, drove away with her. A few days later, they sent Callahan a videotape of what they did.'

220

'My God.'

'Callahan knew that he had crossed the wrong man. Maybe this meth dealer wasn't so chicken-shit. So, first thing he did, after he put his daughter into the ground, was to announce his retirement. You see, he still had a son to protect. He wasn't interested in being a hero. He told everyone he was finished. Didn't care about drugs, or gangs, or Russians. And that was that. He thought Ghol Gedrosian would leave him alone.'

'But he didn't?'

'No, sir. The son was twelve years old. They took him next. They sent another video a few days later. I happened to watch it, Mr Thane. I must tell you, I have a fairly strong stomach, but... ' He shakes his head.

'Why?' I ask, a sense of outrage growing within me. 'Why would someone do that? What purpose did it serve?'

'Purpose?' He squints. 'I don't think it served any purpose. None at all.'

He waits for this to sink in. Then he says: 'That was the end of Bob Callahan, of course. He was a broken man. Went into hiding. Just like a criminal. Just like the men he used to pursue. But they found him. Took them only three weeks. This Ghol Gedrosian – that's the name we've settled on – he owns quite a few police out in California. Knew exactly where to find Mr Callahan.'

'He owns the police?'

'Owns them. Yes, sir. Bought them all. And some of the DAs. And quite a few judges.'

'How do you "buy" the police?'

'Why do you ask? Are you in the market?'

'Just curious,' I say, 'on an intellectual level.'

'On an intellectual level?' he repeats, making me feel as if I'm wearing a pince-nez and velvet smoking jacket. 'It's not very hard. You pay someone money that they're not supposed to have. Or you give them something that's illegal. A gift, say. And when they accept it, then you own them.' He stares at me. 'Does any of that seem familiar to you, Mr Thane?'

221

The black Mercedes – which I bought not two hours ago, with money that surely I am not supposed to have – money that was a gift – winks at me in the sun. It seems big and black and obvious. I have an intense desire to distract Agent Mitchell and make him look over his shoulder, so that I can lean into the car, pop it into neutral, and let it roll quietly away, down the driveway, and out of sight.

Mitchell goes on: 'I ask if it's familiar because I think that's exactly what happened to your predecessor at Tao Software.'

'My predecessor?' I say, unable to keep the relief from my voice. 'You mean Charles Adams?'

'Yes. Charles Adams apparently knew Ghol Gedrosian. Knew him quite well.'

Now I recall the stories that Joan Leggett told me, when I first arrived at Tao – how Charles Adams took strange meetings with frightening men. How he returned to Tao Software hurt and scared, and how he locked himself into his office, and hid, and refused to come out for hours. Those stories seemed familiar to me, even when I first heard them. They were stories that could have come from my own past. From my own bad old days.

Agent Mitchell continues, 'I suppose you could say that Charles Adams and Ghol Gedrosian were business associates, in a way.'

A pause. And now, at last, the real reason he's here. Finally. 'Have you personally ever met Ghol Gedrosian, Mr Thane?'

'Me?' I say, quite surprised by his question. 'Met him? No, of course not.'

'Have you ever been contacted by him?'

'No.'

'Have you ever been contacted by any of his associates?'

A note of uncertainty creeps into my voice now, despite my efforts. 'No.'

'Have you had any indication that Ghol Gedrosian is involved in your company in any way, sir? Have you seen any signs?'

'Signs?' I repeat.

Now that he mentions it, I have seen signs. Four million signs, to be exact. Dollar signs. All of them missing from Tao Software's bank account. And two million signs deposited into my own. I think about the cash in the attic in Sanibel, about the Russian pissing into that rust-ringed toilet bowl, and about Tad Billups's mysterious partners.

'No,' I say. 'I haven't seen any signs.'

'You sure now?'

Beads of sweat prickle my forehead. 'Quite sure.'

'Mr Thane, I need you to listen to what I'm about to say to you.'

For an instant, I fear he is about to Miranda me. As in: 'Mr Thane, I need you to listen to what I'm about to say to you. You have the right to remain silent. Anything you say or do can and will be held against you in a court of law.'

But he doesn't say that. He says something worse.

'He's here,' he says.

'Who?'

'Ghol Gedrosian. He's here.'

'Where?'

'*Here*. We've intercepted communications. There's something happening in his organization. Some kind of restructuring, I think you corporate types might call it. Pieces being moved around. Other pieces being made... redundant.'

'Redundant?'

'He's killing people, Mr Thane. People who work for him. He's shutting down his entire operation in California. He's moving it to Florida.'

I look past Mitchell, to the house across the street. The house of the velociraptor. Dark and empty. 'Why would he come here?' I ask.

'That's what I intend to ask him. As soon as I can find out where the hell he is.'

CHAPTER 27

The next day, I spend the morning in the office, trying not to think about the conversation with Agent Mitchell.

I try not to think about the story he told me, about the District Attorney and his children. I try not to think about the Russian mobster, Ghol Gedrosian, or about my predecessor, Charles Adams; or about the fact that the two men apparently knew each other.

This exercise in *not* thinking of course ends in failure. At last, defeated, I pick up the telephone and dial Amanda at the reception desk.

'Yes, Boss?' she says.

'I need you.'

She arrives a moment later, in my doorway, smiling coquettishly. 'You need me?'

'Come in,' I say. 'Close the door behind you.'

This request for privacy must confirm her secret hopes. She shuts the door with a smile. She sashays closer.

'Tell me about Charles Adams,' I say.

Her face drops. She looks uncomfortable. 'What do you mean? What do you want to know?'

'What was he like?'

'Like?'

'What kind of man was he? Was he nice? Was he smart?'

'Very smart,' she says, nodding.

'Did he use?'

'Use?' The word catches her by surprise. But of course she knows what I mean. 'Why are you asking me this, Jim?'

'I heard rumours. I want to know the truth.'

Her lips become a thin pale line. She says nothing.

I sigh. 'All right, Amanda. I see where this is getting me. Absolutely nowhere. Let me just have his file.'

'His file?'

'From Kathleen's office.'

Kathleen Rossi was our VP of Human Resources. Last week, when our company decided to use fewer resources, Kathleen became renewable. She was one of the forty people that I fired.

Now her office sits dark and empty, except for two filing cabinets filled with HR records. They are the kind of documents that businesses like to keep locked away – lists of salaries, stock-option grants, compensation packages, employee reviews – the kind of papers that start revolutions, and lead to CEOs' heads on spikes outside their office doors, when such papers fall into the wrong hands. Which is why, when I fired Kathleen, I asked Amanda to be in charge of that room, and to hold the key, and to make sure no one snooped.

Now, Amanda stands in front of my desk, considering very carefully my request to open Kathleen's office to me. She seems to weigh the pros and cons of this course of action.

At last, she says, 'Fine,' in a way that suggests it is not. 'Follow me, Jim.'

She leads me first to her reception desk. I watch her open the top drawer and rifle through the contents, taking out personal effects, one at a time, slapping each down on the counter. She removes: a make-up compact, a tube of lipstick, a tiny tampon – so small that surely it must use nanotechnology – and her own gold-foil embossed Bible. At the bottom of the drawer, she finds what she's looking for – a fat key ring. She lifts it, triumphantly.

'You keep it *here*?' I say, surprised at this somewhat dubious level of security. 'In your desk?'

'Where should I keep it, Jim?' she asks, deadpan. 'In the Tao Software underground vault?'

Touché.

'Come,' she says, dangling the keys from her fingers. 'I will now let you in.' She says this in a tone of generous benevolence.

I follow her across the bullpen to the shadowy side of the office building. This is the area where, previously, the Marketing Department worked. Now that there is no more Marketing Department, the fluorescent lights on this side are kept dim, and they flicker and hum. This dubious effort at electricity conservation is perhaps more successful at creating an atmosphere of creepy solitude. It feels very private here.

We stop at the door marked, 'Kathleen Rossi, VP Human Resources.'

Amanda tries the knob. Locked. She tries a few keys on the key ring, until she hits the right one. The door opens.

The lights in the room are off, but sun slants through the blinds. I shut the door. The office is small – just enough room for a desk and a visitor's chair. Two large filing cabinets stand against the far wall.

'You want Charles's folder?' she says.

'Please.'

She circles behind the desk to the filing cabinets. She opens the left cabinet, without hesitating. I notice, too, that she knows exactly which drawer to open, and exactly where in the drawer to look – at the very rear. She pulls out a file and holds it out for my inspection. The tab says, 'ADAMS, CHARLES'.

Should I be surprised that Amanda is so familiar with our company's personnel files? But no. It's the same at every company. The receptionist knows everything. About everyone.

I flip the pages of the folder. Amanda waits beside me. There's not enough space for two adults to stand comfortably. Amanda is very close to me, and I smell her perfume, that floral scent I remember from her apartment.

In the folder I find Charles Adams's W-4, which contains the information I'm looking for – his home address. 172 Loria Street, Bonita Springs.

'Was he married?' I ask, still looking down at the papers.

When she doesn't answer, I look up. A strange expression crosses her face. Briefly. But I see it.

Now I understand. 'Amanda,' I say, gently. 'Did you and he ever... ' My voice trails off.

'Did we ever... *what*?'

'Did you ever... '

Defiance flashes in her eyes. 'Fuck?' she says.

So much for my delicate workplace sensitivity. 'Yes,' I say. 'Did you ever fuck your boss?'

'Which one?' she asks.

'What is it with you? Do you come with the job? Are you one of the perks? Like the corporate jet?'

She slaps me. Hard. My cheek stings.

We stand there, facing each other, neither of us moving, neither speaking. I hear her breathing. It sounds loud and ragged and excited.

Finally, she says, 'Are you going to fire me?'

'For what?'

'It was just a few times.' Her voice is quiet again. 'It was a long time ago. Back when I first came here.'

'I just want to talk to his wife,' I say. 'That's all.'

'Are you going to tell her about me?'

'Of course not.'

'Then why do you need to talk to her? What's the point?'

'The point?' I repeat. I look at her. She is always so curious. Always asking me where I'm going, and why. 'It's really none of your business.'

She shrugs. Her expression seems to suggest it's none of mine either. But she says: 'I'm sorry I hit you, Jim.'

'I suppose I deserved it.'

'Yes,' she says. 'You did.' She rises on her toes and kisses me softly on the lips. Before I can decide whether to push her away, or pull her in, she steps back. She leaves the room, without saying another word.

CHAPTER 28

My GPS takes me south to Bonita Springs, an old 1980s subdivision that saw its best days two boom-and-bust cycles ago.

As someone who saw my own best days two boom-and-bust cycles ago, I have an instant liking for the place.

Maybe *liking* is too strong a word – for how can someone truly *like* forlorn streets, or yards bristling with hopeless FOR SALE BY OWNER signs, or withered brown lawns, or scraggly palms that cast no shade? *Comfortable* is more the word. I feel comfortable here. This is the neighbourhood where I ought to be living – maybe the neighbourhood where I will wind up living, after all – after Libby leaves me, or after I lose my job. The houses are small and tightly-packed. The driveways have pickup trucks, wide American cars, fibreglass boats on cinderblocks, trailers with empty hitches.

Charles Adams's house is the least impressive house on an unimpressive block. The lawn is a week overgrown. The stuccoed walls are sun-faded and water-stained. The roof tiles smile like cracked and missing teeth. It is the house of a man who ran out of money, quite suddenly and quite completely.

I park in his driveway – maybe in the same spot that Charles Adams parked his own car, on that day he vanished months ago. As I open my door, and step onto the baking asphalt, I think about the story that Tad Billups told me: one Wednesday morning, Charles Adams backed out of his garage, stopped his car, with the motor still running, and was never seen again.

I walk up a short concrete path to the front door, where I ring the bell. The door opens instantly, just a crack – so quickly that I'm certain I've been watched – that someone has been staring at me from the moment I turned into the driveway.

'Yes?' A woman peers at me through the slit of door, behind a brass chain, still fastened. I see white skin, a pale blue eye, and a wisp of brunette hair.

'Mrs Adams?'

'Yes?' says the pale blue eye.

'My name is Jim Thane. I'm the new CEO of Tao Software.'

'I know who you are.'

The door slams, so near my face that I feel the whiff of air, and I flinch. I stand there, unsure whether to stay or go. But then the chain rattles, and the door opens wide.

The woman in front of me is tall, forty years old. She was beautiful once – with dark hair, blue eyes, a complexion like snow. But now her beauty is gone. Her arms are scarecrow thin, her cheekbones protrude like tent poles. Her paleness has turned morbid and cadaverous. Her hair is streaked with grey. She looks as though someone sneaked into her house, late one night, while she was asleep, and loosened a tiny valve on her body, so that all the colour and energy and life drained from her.

'Come in,' she says.

I follow her inside. Before she shuts the door, she sticks her head out and looks around furtively, like a nervous animal. Whatever it is that she's searching for, she does not find. She closes the door and slides the chain. She locks the deadbolt. Then the second deadbolt.

She leads me into a sunken den. The decor is Miami, 1985, entirely monochromatic. Everything is white – the walls, the ceilings, the pile carpet, the sleek modern coffee table, even the vase that rests upon that table, holding a single white orchid, probably fake.

My eyes adjust, as they might adjust to twilight, and now I can make out a different colour on the far wall – an abstract painting – a tiny splash of beige. In the whiteness of the room, this single small dab is loud, even shocking.

The woman gestures to a modern, angular couch. 'Sit,' she commands.

I do. My thighs land with a thud on what turns out to be plastic – one of those couches that feels like a subway bench.

'Would you like a drink?' she asks.

'No, thank you.'

She walks across the room. Her steps are silent, and mincing, and she seems to float above the carpet. She stops at a bar, a little cubby decorated with white tesserae, which – until she brings it to my attention – was invisible in the room's gloaming. There's a crystal decanter on it. She fills a glass. 'It's five o'clock somewhere,' she mutters, mostly to herself. She lifts the glass, and turns her back, and empties it down her gullet. She fills and repeats. Suitably fortified, she returns to me, with yet another full glass, and sits down in the white chair nearby.

She's very close to me, and I can smell the drink. Sherry. It may be five o'clock somewhere, but here in Florida it's not quite eleven in the morning. She is, I decide, a woman quite after my own heart.

She fixes me with her pale eyes, and says, in a not particularly friendly tone, 'Why are you here, Mr Thane?'

On the table near us I see a photograph of a little girl, with her hair in pigtails. She wears a paper party hat and is blowing out three candles on a birthday cake. I say: 'Your daughter? She's very pretty.'

She looks down at the photo, surprised, as if she forgot it was there. She doesn't reply. Obscurely, I feel that I've said something wrong, but am not sure why.

I say: 'Would you mind if we talked about your husband?'

'My husband?' She straightens in her chair, backing away, as if she wasn't expecting this subject – not at all – and indeed hasn't thought about the man in quite some time. 'My husband is... missing.'

'Yes, I know. And I'm very sorry for that.' Which comes out sounding too much like a condolence, and so I add quickly: 'But I'm sure he'll turn up.'

No. That's much worse. I might as well have said: 'I'm sure he'll turn up *floating in a river*. Or *dug up by a coyote*.'

Mrs Adams doesn't seem to notice the faux pas. She fixes me with pale blue eyes, and says, 'Yes, perhaps you're right.'

Now that she's staring at me, I feel something odd about her gaze. She reminds me of someone. Who, exactly? I study her, trying to discern the similarity. And then, suddenly, it comes to me. Libby. She reminds me of Libby. Indeed, put brown hair on her instead of grey, and restore the curves and flesh that she surely lost when her husband disappeared, and the two women would be very alike. The same pale blue eyes. The same fine bone structure. The same elegant bearing, the same height. It's uncanny.

Mrs Adams breaks my reverie. 'What is it exactly that you want to know?'

What I exactly want to know is her husband's relationship with a man named Ghol Gedrosian. According to the FBI, Charles Adams and Ghol Gedrosian were 'business associates'. It was a business association that apparently ended rather badly, when Mrs. Adams's husband disappeared from the face of the planet.

It's not just morbid curiosity that led me to his widow's house. There's more than a little self-preservation, too. It has occurred to me this past week – and it occurs to me even more now, as I sit and stare at his wife, who looks so much like my own – that I have followed very close in my predecessor's footsteps. Uncomfortably close.

Today, I am doing exactly what Charles Adams did in the weeks before he vanished: running a company on behalf of a Russian mobster. Ignoring cash disbursements and receipts. Trying to keep things quiet on my employer's behalf.

'Did you and your husband ever talk about his work?' I ask.

'We were married, Mr Thane,' she says. 'Husbands and wives share everything together.'

'Of course they do,' I agree. I think about Libby, and her secrets, and her mysteries.

'But yes,' she says, her voice softening. 'We did talk about his work, quite a bit.'

'Did he ever mention anything… *unusual* happening at Tao?'

'"Unusual"?'

Illegal, I want to say. But don't. Instead I ask: 'Did he talk to you about problems he was having?'

'Problems? Oh, my husband had problems. But not the kind you're thinking of.'

'What kind of problems did he have?'

'He was an addict, Mr Thane. Did you know that? Methamphetamine.'

I did not know that. I suspected it, maybe, based on what Joan Leggett told me, when I asked her about Charles Adams. But receiving confirmation from his wife, and now learning his drug of choice – the same as mine – I have a strange feeling. I feel as if I've been transported into Charles Adams's body. No, that's not quite right. I feel like I *am* Charles Adams, seated in my own house, staring at my own wife. So much of our lives in common. Our love of drugs. The similar women that we married. Our employment, or our partnership – or whatever it is – with a man named Ghol Gedrosian.

'He cheated quite a bit, too,' she adds.

And that, as well.

'I think with that receptionist at work,' she says. 'What's her name, again?'

She looks at me, as if I should know that name very well indeed. I say nothing.

'But, you know,' she goes on, with sudden and surprising warmth in her voice, 'when you love someone, you forgive so much.'

'Yes, you do,' I say. And I think of Libby, forgiving me for Cole. And for so much else that I've done. 'Yes, you do.'

'But to answer your question,' she says. She takes a slug of sherry, wipes her lips with the back of her hand. 'He *did* talk about work. He was very depressed about it. Not enough sales. Expenses too high. That sort of thing.'

'It's a hard business,' I say. 'I'm learning that first-hand.'

'I'm sure that you are.' She looks at me significantly. What does she mean by that? She says, 'It was a constant source of stress for Charles. Maybe that's why he did the drugs. To escape.'

'Maybe,' I say. 'Did he ever mention any names to you?'

'Names?' She looks puzzled.

'Unusual names?'

'Unusual?' She stares at me, stupidly. Too stupidly. And it is at this precise moment that I know she's lying. She knows about the Russian. The man with the most unusual name of all. She knows about him. And she's not telling me.

'For example, did he mention the names of any of his investors?'

'Let me think.' Her eyes dart around the room. What is she looking for? When her gaze returns to me, she says, 'No, he never did.'

I wait a decent interval for her to add more, but she doesn't.

I stand from the couch. 'Well, I appreciate your time, Mrs Adams. I should really be going.'

'Yes,' she says, agreeing with this notion entirely. 'Yes, I suppose so.' She offers me her hand. 'Good luck to you, Mr Thane.'

She turns, and starts from the room. But I stay behind, with the distracted air of someone who has just suddenly remembered something. I snap my fingers and say, 'Oh, there is one other thing.'

She's poised at the edge of the room, on the step leading from the sunken den back to the foyer. She turns to me.

'There is one name in particular that I'm interested in,' I say. 'I wonder if you heard it. It's a Russian name. Did your husband ever mention the name… '

But even before I finish, something happens to her. She changes. Her body stiffens. Her face, which was pale before, now completely drains of blood. Her skin turns the grey mottled colour of old melted snow. By the time I finish the question, my words are superfluous, my question already answered. 'Did your husband ever mention the name Ghol Gedrosian?' is what I say.

She tries to recover. She keeps her body motionless. She looks me in the eye and says, 'No. I've never heard that name. Never.'

She turns and walks to the front door. I follow. She unlatches the chain, and then the two deadbolts – *slip clack clack* – and pulls open the door. 'Goodbye, Mr Thane.'

'Goodbye, Mrs Adams. Thank you again.'

But just as I am about to walk from the house, she grabs my arm. I look up, surprised. Her index finger is pressed hard to her lips. She has a crazy, bug-eyed look. She reaches into her pocket, takes out a slip of paper, and hands it to me.

I unfold it. A woman's handwriting says:

Do not speak. Pretend that you have left the house.

She slams the door, and fastens the chain and the bolts, locking me inside with her. She taps a finger to her lips again, and beckons me to follow.

I do. We walk up the stairs, to a second-floor landing. We go down a short hall, passing a little girl's room, all pink and gingham. The bed is neatly made, with dolls arranged on pillows. Toys are piled in the corner – a stuffed dog, and cat, a unicorn. On the bureau is another picture of the same girl that I saw in the photograph downstairs.

Mrs Adams turns, makes sure that I'm directly behind, and touches a finger to her lips again.

We pass another empty bedroom. And a third. The tour has taken us past every room in the small house, and now it's clear that there is no one else here with us – not another soul – no one but me and Mrs

235

Adams. So why her insistence that I remain quiet?

She walks through the last door in the hall. It's a bathroom. I remain at the threshold, wondering whether I should follow.

I have followed a lot of strange women into a lot of strange bathrooms, which is what you tend to do when you need to get high. But something about this day, and this bathroom, and this woman, seems different. Peculiar. Dangerous.

I peer in. Mrs Adams is leaning over the tub. She looks over her shoulder at me, waves for me to join her.

I do. She unscrews both faucets of the tub, as far as they turn. Water gushes.

She edges past me, back to the sink, and opens the faucet, full flow. She closes the bathroom door and locks it.

The sound of rushing water fills the tiny room, loud as a jet. Steam billows up from the bath. When she whispers to me, finally, her voice is so quiet that I can barely hear her words.

'He has ears,' she whispers.

'Who does?'

'*Shh.*'

I say again, more softly, 'Who does?'

'You know who.'

I study her. Is she drunk? She did finish two glasses of sherry. On the other hand, she seems steady on her feet, and, more to the point, seems to be a professional – not an amateur – drinker, someone who could have kept up with me, back in my bad old days.

She asks, 'Has he given you gifts?'

'Who?'

'Stop. You know who I'm talking about. Has he given you gifts?'

I think about it. Two million dollars? A job? Are these gifts?

'There's a price,' she whispers. 'That's what I want to tell you. That's what you can't see yet. Not at first. But he demands his price. I promise you that.'

Before I can say anything, she touches my arm. 'Stay here,' she says. She

236

opens the door and leaves the bathroom. The cool air rushes in, swirling the steam. It condenses on my skin and turns clammy. She returns a half-minute later, holding a shoebox. The bottom has rainbow stripes. The top is purple, with a Stride Rite logo in big childish letters. This box is achingly familiar; my son's closets were filled with shoeboxes like this.

'This is what he gave to Charles.'

'Shoes?'

She holds it out. 'Open it.'

I take the box. I peek under the lid, cautiously. I see only darkness.

'Open it,' she says again.

I remove the lid. Inside are photographs, five by eights. I take out a stack of them. They are colour photos of young boys, nine or ten years old, pre-pubescent, lying naked on a bed. As I flip through the pile, the pictures become worse, more explicit – boys engaged in sexual acts with older men. Horrible acts. Some boys are crying, with tear-streaked faces. Others look confused and lost, with dead eyes. The men – the ones whose faces are visible – have strangely blank expressions. What is it that I see in them? Lust? Fear? It's hard to know.

'No,' I say, and push the pictures back at her.

'Shh!' she hisses. She refuses the photos. 'Look at them,' she whispers. 'These are what he gave to my husband. These were his gifts.'

'Gifts?'

'Even before we married, I knew. In my heart, I suspected. The way Charles looked at boys. Some of the things he said. But he never acted on those urges. Never, Mr Thane. You have to believe me. He was a kind man, a good man. He was weak; I admit it. He had urges. But he never acted on them. Never. Please believe me. Please.'

She looks at me with wide eyes, begging for some kind of forgiveness, some kind of mercy that I cannot give.

'Do you think it makes someone evil,' she asks, 'if he has urges that are locked away, deep inside? If he never acts on them?'

'I don't know,' I say.

'That was Charles. There was someone else inside him. But he kept it locked away. And then one day that man came into our life. And he destroyed my husband.'

'Who did?'

'You know who I'm talking about. Why do you pretend that you don't? The man who knew what was in Charles's heart. He knew his secret. Who gave Charles what he wanted. That's what he does. He gives people what they want.'

'Take these,' I say, handing her the pictures.

'Look at the next one.'

'I don't want to.'

'Please,' she insists.

I look at the next photo. Through the steam, I see a middle-aged man, balding, kissing a young boy's naked chest.

'That's Charles,' she says. I don't have much doubt about which one. The one who's not ten years old. 'That was at the end. Once they had photographs, they owned him. Charles had to do what he was told.'

'Which was what? What was he told to do?'

'To get things ready.'

'Ready?'

'For *you*, Mr Thane. He was told to get things ready for you.'

It occurs to me now, for the first time, standing in this steam-filled bathroom, that the woman beside me is bat-shit crazy. Which explains a lot. The frightened glances. The deadbolts on her doors. The note she slipped into my hand.

Now I know. Now there can be no doubt. She is crazy.

'I need to leave you now, Mrs Adams,' I say gently, and hand her back the photographs. This time she accepts them.

'He was going to turn himself in,' she says. 'We talked about it one night in the bedroom. We thought we were alone. That no one could hear us. We decided. Charles was going to talk to the police. He was going to tell them everything. The photos. The money he was given. He was going to tell them about... ' She stops. 'About that man. He was going to tell them everything he knew about that man.'

'Did he?'

'No. The man found out. He punished us.'

'Punished you?'

'He hears everything. He knows your thoughts. He knows your secrets. He is Satan.'

'He killed your husband?' I say.

'No,' she says. 'He didn't kill Charles. Not right away. That's not what he does. First he makes you suffer.' She looks into my eyes. She seems very sad, very old. 'You saw the picture downstairs,' she says. 'The one of my daughter?'

'Your daughter... ' I stop.

Now I remember what Joan Leggett told me, on that first day that I arrived at Tao, when I asked about Charles Adams. *There was a personal tragedy in his family,* she said. I didn't ask what she meant, but now, something clicks, and it fits: the quiet house. The dark hall. The empty bedroom, preserved like a mausoleum. No child's footsteps. No child's laughter.

She says: 'I left my baby with Charles. My little girl. It was at night. Just for an hour. When I came home, I found Charles on the couch. Passed out.'

'What happened to her?' I say. I feel the dread rise within me.

'Maybe he was drunk, or maybe he was high. Or maybe they *made* him sleep. He can do that, you know. And I found my baby here.'

'Where?'

'*Here*,' she says. She turns to the bathtub, near overflowing. 'They came into the house, and they took my baby. And they brought her here. They held her under the water until she drowned. She was so blue when I found her. That's the one thing I will never forget. How blue she was. And how her eyes were open. As if she was looking for me. And she couldn't find me. She was so blue. So blue.'

239

CHAPTER 29

Later, I don't remember running from her house.

But I must have fled. Whether I said goodbye, or just unlocked the door and ran, I do not know.

It's not until I'm in my car, driving, with my foot hard on the gas, that I notice where I am, or how fast I'm going. Too fast – the speedometer bumping fifty, in a thirty-five zone – and so I brake, and stay in the flow of traffic, whizzing past McDonald's and Walgreens and Macaroni Grill.

She was crazy, of course; I see that now. Her husband was a paedophile, and he was being blackmailed by a Russian mobster.

His wife knew about me. She knew about Jim Thane. That much is clear. She obsessed about me. She read about me somewhere, researched me, uncovered my secret. She knew about Cole, about what happened that night, in the bath. Maybe she read about me in the papers, that flurry of stories that appeared when the DA dropped the charges against me. Or maybe she heard it through the grapevine. The tech community is small, and people talk, and I know that they still whisper, about what happened that night. *His son drowned*, they murmur, when I walk into a room, and they think that I can't hear. *He was high, and his son drowned.*

This can be the only explanation: she blames me for what happened to her husband. She wants to hurt me. For I am the man who replaced her husband.

A part of me understands. She may have been married to a sick man, but she loved him. And he was being tortured in front of her eyes –

blackmailed by someone remote and unassailable. She was unable to strike at the real perpetrator, the man who destroyed her husband – Ghol Gedrosian – and so instead she lashed out at the one man she could find. She saved her hatred for that man, for me, Jimmy Thane.

CHAPTER 30

That night, Libby and I watch television in the living room, stretched on the couch. I soon lose interest in her reality shows, and when I mutter that I wish we could change the channel, she ignores me. I get up from the couch, and stretch, and wander to the sliding glass door leading to the patio.

'Where are you going?' she asks, noticing me at last.

'Just getting some air.'

I walk outside before she can argue. I slide the door shut.

The swimming pool is lit from below, and in the dark night, it casts dancing yellow light on the palm fronds that shield us from our neighbour's gaze.

The pool looks inviting, but I'm too lazy to go back upstairs for swim trunks. So I peel off my sweaty clothes right there, leaving them in a crumpled pile on the patio, and I dive, naked, into the water. I swim five laps.

When I finish, I'm out of breath, but invigorated, and I pull myself from the pool and carry my clothes back into the house.

'You're dripping,' Libby says, not even looking at me.

'Am I?'

'And you're naked.'

I look down. 'Hadn't noticed.' The carpet at my feet is turning dark with puddled water. 'You're acting very strange today, Jimmy.'

'Am I?' Maybe my meeting with Mrs Adams disturbed me more

than I realized. 'I'll get dressed.'

I'm about to leave her, and head upstairs, when my cellphone rings. The trill is sharp and startling. I see the phone glowing on the desk nearby, next to my laptop computer.

I walk to the desk, still dripping. I open the phone, keep it an inch from my ear.

'Hey, hotshot,' says the voice, when I answer.

'Tad?'

'What are you doing right now?'

'Just walking around naked.'

'Good, good,' he says, ignoring me. 'I just got off the phone with someone interesting. Guess who.'

Ghol Gedrosian, I want to say. But instead I say merely: 'Who?'

'Guess.'

'Really, Tad, I can't guess.'

'Dan Yokelson.' He says the name proudly, as if I ought to know who it is, and ought to be deeply impressed. The name *is* familiar, but I can't quite place it.

'Come on, Jimmy,' he says, when I'm silent for too long. 'You know who that is, right?'

'No.'

'White Rock.'

'White Rock?' I say. And then I remember. White Rock is one of the largest hedge funds on the West Coast. A firm that happens to be run by a friend of Tad's. An old Harvard MBA buddy, or so Tad has told me a dozen times. A billionaire. One of the Forbes Top 50 richest men in the world.

'What'd you guys talk about?' I ask.

'You, partner.'

'Me?'

'Well, not you personally,' he admits. 'But Tao. He wants to do a deal.'

'A deal?'

'He'll license your technology. What are you calling it nowadays? P-Scan?'

I'm puzzled by what Tad is telling me, because hedge funds have no conceivable use for Tao's technology. Hedge funds deal with wealthy customers. They handle big money from big institutions. They have meetings over lunch at the Four Seasons. They don't operate retail branches, where strangers walk in from the street, requiring facial identification. There's no conceivable way that Tao's technology could be of any use to a firm like White Rock.

'But they're a hedge fund,' I say.

'They are,' Tad admits, reluctantly. 'They are. But he wants to do it. And I have his personal guarantee. It's a done deal, Jimmy. He'll license it for five million. How does that sound to you?'

'How does that sound to me? It sounds... *crazy*.'

I glance at the couch, catch Libby looking at me. She looks away quickly.

I say to Tad, 'What are they going to do with the technology?'

'How the fuck should I know? Who do I look like, Carnac the Magnificent? He wants to pay you five million dollars. Take his money.'

I think about it. Something doesn't feel right. But then again, nothing about my job at Tao feels right any more.

I give up my effort of keeping the phone dry, and I shove it between my ear and my shoulder. I lean across the desk, dripping onto the surface, and wake my laptop computer with a flick of a finger. I type a name into Google: 'DAN YOKELSON'.

The search returns an avalanche of results for Dan Yokelson.

At the top, I see a section that says: 'Recent news for Dan Yokelson' and a collection of headlines.

Now I understand why the name is so familiar: Dan Yokelson *has* been in the news a lot lately, and not just in the financial press.

The bottom headlines give the backstory: 'White Rock Executive Served With Wells Notice for Fraud' and then 'Possible Jail Time for Yokelson in Insider Trading Probe'.

Those stories are dated four months ago.

I see more recent stories at the top of the page, dated a mere '23 hours ago': 'Key Government Witness in White Rock Case Disappears' and 'SEC Likely to Drop Yokelson Prosecution'.

Tad's voice on the telephone brings me back. 'Jimmy? Are you there?'

'I'm here.'

'You don't sound very grateful. You know what I had to do to convince him?'

'No,' I say. 'What did you have to do?'

'A case of Latour. A *case*, Jimmy. Do you know how much that stuff costs?'

'No.'

'Me neither,' he says, and laughs. 'I probably should have asked before I told them to charge it on my card. But the point is: that's what a Board of Directors does. We get you the deal. No matter what it takes. Remember that.'

'I will, Tad. I'll remember.'

CHAPTER 31

August passes.

Agent Mitchell doesn't call again, and I almost forget about the FBI man, and his search for the Russian meth dealer. I almost forget about Charles Adams, too, and his lunatic wife.

I have pushed these things from my mind. Now they are just tiny dark smudges on the distant horizon – still there, but barely perceptible.

It has been surprisingly easy to forget them, too. Surprisingly easy to focus on my own success.

Success.

What a strange feeling, to be successful. I've spent so many years failing, so many years stumbling from one disaster to the next, that I almost forgot what it's like.

To be a success.

When I arrived at Tao, things seemed hopeless, the company's problems insurmountable. Now, despite the odds, I've turned the company around. I was ruthless, it's true – reducing headcount, cutting costs, changing direction. But my actions, while they hurt some people, saved the company for everyone else.

And, while it's not a sure thing, yet – not by a long shot – I can feel triumph within my grasp.

The trade magazine *Banking Times* runs a small news item about Tao's beta-test with Old Dominion, and the nearly simultaneous deal with White Rock. This one-two punch is the validation we've been waiting for. The floodgates open. Now, every day, I receive new phone calls – from Wells Fargo, Chase, HSBC; it seems that everyone wants to work with Tao, wants to start their own pilot programme, using Tao's amazing P-Scan technology in their own retail banking branches. No one wants to be the last financial institution without state-of-the-art biometrics.

My answer to each request from breathless executives is the same. I explain how difficult it will be to arrange another deal, since Old Dominion bought exclusivity in the south-eastern United States. Oh, what's that? Can we structure a deal that excludes the south-east? Well, I never thought of that. I suppose we can.

The only thing keeping me from laughing aloud, joyously, into the telephone, during each of these calls, is the flickering memory of Stan Pontin, the can-do technologist at Old Dominion, whose untimely death preceded the signing of that very first deal.

But that disturbing thought never lasts long – not when everything else is going so right.

With the money coming into Tao's bank account, no one really cares about the money going out. Joan Leggett stops asking about the cash that vanished under Charles Adams's watch – which is a comfort to me, since it is surely the same cash sitting in my own personal bank account, the same cash that I'm living off, the same cash that I use to pay for our house rental, or the restaurant meals with Libby, or the increasingly preposterous gifts that I buy her: the Mercedes, the diamond earrings, the gold necklace, the Cartier watch, the David Yurman rings.

Tad Billups's weekly telephone calls are always the same – pep talks, really: Keep up the good work, Jimmy; Keep things calm, Jimmy; My partners are watching you, Jimmy, and boy are they impressed. I never ask *which* partners – the Silicon Valley VCs, or the Eastern European meth dealers with the foreign-sounding names. I don't want to know.

Even life around the house has improved. Libby's sulking and night-time crying jags have petered out. Libby's not Miss Sunshine – never has been – but at least nowadays she doesn't seem to hate me – doesn't stare at me as if I'm some stranger who woke up one day, uninvited, in her bed. Or, if I *am* a stranger, at least now I am one she has grown accustomed to.

I see Dr Liago once each week, religiously keeping my appointment with him, not because I like him – or even think him competent – but rather because I want to avoid the wrath of Gordon Kramer. The little whispering doctor performs his mumbo-jumbo hypnotherapy – *Relax and breathe, Mr Thane; Do not take drugs, Mr Thane; Lock the memories of your son away, somewhere safe, Mr Thane* – and even though his sessions are both ridiculous and tedious, they are better than the alternative: a surprise visit from Gordon, and finding myself handcuffed to a parking-garage sprinkler while he screams and punches me and tells me what a good-for-nothing shit I am.

I like this new feeling. I like being happy. I like being successful. It's so new, and so good, and so right, that I ignore the voice, that soft and almost imperceptible voice, that nags on occasion. It comes at night, usually, in the dark, as I fall asleep beside Libby, with the teak-blade fan squeaking overhead. It's a tiny voice. *You're Jimmy Thane*, it says. *You are Shiva, the destroyer. You are the wrecker. You are death. You can't change who you are. You can't start again.*

But that voice is very quiet. And I can ignore it, usually. And I can go to sleep.

PART TWO

PART TWO

CHAPTER 32

The trouble starts on a Tuesday afternoon in September.

I'm seated at my desk, and the phone rings. When I answer, Amanda is on the line. 'Oh, Jim, you're still here,' she says, sounding surprised to hear my voice. 'I wasn't sure that you would be.'

That's a little jab at the new Jimmy Thane office hours. I *have* been taking it easy these past weeks, coming in late in the morning, leaving early in the afternoon – and when I do bother to show up, I tell Amanda airily to 'Hold all calls'. I admit it's hypocritical, coming from the CEO who tore his employees a new asshole that first morning he arrived, when they showed up twenty minutes past nine. But that was before I understood my real job. My real job is simple, and doesn't require effort. It doesn't even – for that matter – require showing up. My job is this: Shut up, take the money, and don't ask questions.

'You have a visitor,' Amanda says. 'Should I send him in?'

Before I can ask who it is, I hear her tell the visitor, 'Go ahead in. He says he wants to see you.'

A moment later there's a knock on my door, and a voice calls, 'Special delivery!'

Pete Bland fills the doorframe, toting a plastic shopping bag. He holds it up. 'Present for you, Jimmy,' he says cheerily. He walks in, without waiting for an invitation. He plops the bag on my desk. It crunches with the sound of ice. 'A dozen stone crabs from the Gator Hut,' he says. 'Now we're Even Steven.'

'Last person who gave me crabs was a hooker named Angel. I still haven't gotten even.'

'Mind if I sit?' he asks, sitting.

'Yes,' I say. 'Actually, I was on my way out.'

He looks at his watch. His eyebrows arch. 'At three o'clock?'

I lift the bag of crabs from my desk, lay it gingerly by my feet. A whiff of its contents wafts to my nostrils. Wharf at low tide. 'You know how it is,' I say. 'Trying not to burn out. Reasonable hours. Work–life balance. All that crap.'

'Oh, OK,' he says, in a voice that indicates that he is trying hard not to pass any judgement. 'OK. Then I'll make it fast. I came here for two reasons.' He holds up two fingers. 'One, to say thank you for all your billable hours. Tao Software is now officially my most important client. All those signed contracts... Good Lord, how are you guys doing it, anyway? Making an offer they can't refuse?' He laughs.

'Something like that.'

'That White Rock contract alone is putting Ashley through college. She wants to start calling you Uncle Jimmy, by the way. You don't mind, do you?' Before I can answer he goes on: 'Don't have a heart attack when you see our August invoice. It's big, Jimmy. Really big. You guys will pay, right?'

'I always pay my debts,' I say. Which is not exactly true. Involuntarily I touch the nub of my missing pinky finger, where Hector the Bookie once educated me about the importance of timely repayment.

'Number two,' he says. 'And this is the real reason for my visit. I mean, besides my desire to give you crabs.' He pauses. 'I found something you might be interested in.'

'Oh?'

He turns in his seat, to look behind him. He reaches for my office door – my room is so small, that he has no problem doing so – and he pushes it closed. He returns his gaze to me and says: 'Remember when you asked me to investigate that house?'

252

'What house?' I'm about to say – but then I do remember. Before the intrusion of Ghol Gedrosian into my life, before that two-million-dollar gift from Tad Billups, before the mass lay-offs at Tao – before all that, I actually cared who was embezzling money from my firm. That was back when I thought my job was to turn the place around. Now I know better: my real job is to keep things quiet, and to keep cashing cheques.

Whoever was stealing from Tao used a house on Sanibel as his base of operations – that house with the low-beamed attic and the preponderance of Russian speakers. I asked Pete Bland to do some digging, and to find out who owns it.

'Well,' Pete continues. 'We ran a search, like you asked. And we found out who owns the house on 56 Windmere. I guess the file got misplaced, with all the excitement over the lay-offs. So I never showed you. Actually I didn't see it myself until this morning.'

'OK. Who owns it?'

Pete looks uncomfortable. 'I want to be honest with you, Jimmy. I feel like we're friends. Are we friends?'

'Sure, Pete, we're friends. Friends that happen to bill each other. But friends.'

'That's why I was disappointed. I felt like maybe we weren't. Like you were testing me.'

'Testing?'

'Or maybe this is what passes for Silicon Valley humour. You know, making the country lawyer do a little jig, while you guys laugh about it in the boardroom?'

'I don't understand. Who owns the house, Pete?'

'Come on, Jimmy.'

'Really,' I say. 'Who owns it?'

'You want some timpani before I make the announcement? A drum roll?'

'Pete—'

'Fine. Hang on to your hat, Jimmy.' He opens his briefcase, takes out a Manila folder, and tosses it onto my desk. 'The house at 56 Windmere is owned by – get this, Jimmy – a Mr James Thane, from Palo Alto, California. That's right. Pick yourself off the floor, Jimmy. *You* own the house. *You've* owned it for three years, free and clear. Paid cash for it back in 2007. As if you didn't know.'

I stumble from my office. I hear Pete behind me, calling, 'Are you OK, Jimmy? Jimmy, what's wrong? Jimmy, you forgot your crabs! You gotta put them in the fridge!'

I ignore him. I need to get out of here. I need to go home. I need to find Libby. I need to tell her.

Before this moment, I could make excuses, could tell myself stories – increasingly elaborate stories, I admit – about what I was doing at Tao. I wasn't proud of my role, but I accepted it: to be window dressing for other people's criminal activity. When I went to sleep at night, I could convince myself that, despite what was going on around me, I was doing my best to run a legitimate company. I was doing my best to save Tao.

But now I know the truth. I'm not here to turn this company around. I'm not here to act as window dressing.

I'm here to take the fall. I'm the mark. I'm going down.

I jog through the bullpen towards the reception area. Ahead, I see Amanda through the door. She is talking to someone. She looks anxious.

But this barely registers. I'm moving fast, and I'm desperate to leave this place and go home to my wife. Three steps into the reception room, I hear the man's voice – familiar, dripping with Southern honey – an accent so thick you could spread it on cornbread with a fork.

'Mr Thane!' Agent Tom Mitchell calls. Then I see him, standing in the corner, practically hiding from me. 'There you are, Mr Thane! I'm so glad I caught you.' An emphasis on the word *caught*. Or maybe I'm imagining it. 'I have a few things I need to discuss with you. How about me and you have a private chat?'

He lassoes me into the boardroom, where he takes a seat at the end of the conference table. I remain standing, as if to show him that I'm not fully committed to being here, not at all, and that I might just choose to flee.

Agent Mitchell slumps back into his chair. He stretches his legs, and clasps his fingers behind his head, revealing dark ovals of perspiration under his arms.

'How've you been, Mr Thane?' he asks, peering down his nose at me.

'Not bad,' I say.

'You look... ' He pauses, staring. He considers. He says, finally, 'Piqued.'

'Yes,' I say. 'It's been pretty stressful around here.'

'I was surprised that I didn't hear from you. Not since we last spoke.'

'I've been busy.'

'Have you?' He smiles. 'It's just that I thought you might call. On the chance that you remembered something. You know, about our friend.'

'Our friend?'

'Our Russian friend. The man I'm looking for. You remember his name, I'm sure. Have you heard from him?'

'No.'

'You would have called me if you had,' he says. 'Right?'

'Of course.'

'I knew I could count on you, Mr Thane. You're a true gentleman.' His face changes – becomes clouded. 'Actually,' he says, 'I'm here for another reason. I'm looking for one of your employees. A Mr Dom Vanderbeek.'

It takes me a moment to process this. I was expecting – even dreading – a question about the house on Sanibel. Or about the money in my bank account. Or about some combination of those two things. Such as: 'Did you take cash from an attic on Sanibel and deposit it into your bank account?'

But that's not what Agent Mitchell asked. He asked about Dom Vanderbeek. He continues, helpfully, as if my silence were caused by forgetfulness: 'Mr Vanderbeek is your VP of Sales, I believe, Mr Thane.'

'Yes,' I say. 'He *was*. But I terminated him.'

'Terminated?' He raises an eyebrow. He leans forward in his chair. 'Now, just checking, Mr Thane. When you say you "terminated" him, that means you *fired* him. Am I right?'

'Of course.'

'Because Mr Vanderbeek is missing.'

'Missing?'

'Disappeared,' he says. He snaps his fingers. 'Just like that. Ten days ago. Wife found his car in the driveway, engine running. But no Dom Vanderbeek inside.' As if he can hear my thoughts, he adds, 'Yes, it's quite a coincidence. So many people leaving their cars running. As if we don't have a terrible oil shortage in this country already.'

'I haven't seen him,' I say.

'Not since you terminated him?'

'Fired him.'

'Fired him,' he agrees, pleasantly enough. 'I was just speaking to that gal in your office – the Spanish one? Big fat girl?'

'Rosita.'

'That's the one. She told me that when you fired Vanderbeek, you two had words together. You threatened him.'

Thanks, Rosita.

'That's not true,' I say, keeping my voice even. 'Dom was very upset when I fired him. But I didn't threaten him.'

'Why did you fire him, Mr Thane?'

Because he was too curious about my company's cash flow, I think.

'Because I didn't like him,' I say, looking Mitchell directly in the eye.

256

He smiles. 'I respect your honesty,' he says. 'I suppose it's none of my business who you fire or why. Chances are, Mr Vanderbeek is just taking a long vacation, and he neglected to tell his wife. Happens more often than you think. Usually the husband turns up in the Keys, with a young lady, and they're drinking margaritas and singing Jimmy Buffett.'

'I hope you're right.'

'I'm sure I am. In fact, if I was a betting man, I'd put money on it. I wonder, Mr Thane… are you a betting man?'

His smile, which was friendly just a moment ago, has curdled. Now it's lupine and sly.

'No,' I say.

From his shirt pocket, he removes a spiral-bound notepad and taps it on his hand. It's already opened to a page of interest. 'See, now, that's an answer I didn't expect. Do you remember, Mr Thane, the last time we met, I asked you about Ghol Gedrosian?'

'Yes.'

'You told me that you didn't know him.'

'I don't know him.'

'That's not what I hear.' He leans closer. 'We made an arrest on Thursday. Out in California. A nasty little Armenian fella. I won't even *try* to do justice to his name. I would just embarrass myself. This man was in charge of Ghol Gedrosian's loan sharking and gambling. A money man. Sort of like your CFO.'

I picture mousy Joan Leggett in a fedora, holding a Tommy gun, wearing a Donna Karan outfit. No, probably not much like my CFO.

'We found documents,' Mitchell says. 'Computer files. There were a lot of names in those files. Who owed money. Who paid money. Generally speaking, when you deal with a man like Ghol Gedrosian, if you're on the first list, you better *hope* you're on the second. You catch my meaning?'

'Yes.'

He's staring at me with an open, friendly expression, as if inviting me to confess something. The boardroom – which is usually air conditioned to meat-locker chill, suddenly feels quite hot, and for the first time, I think I might actually pass out, standing right here, with my head going *thump* against the polished conference table.

'Do you know where I'm going with this yet, Mr Thane?'

'No.'

'Your name was on that list. You owed money to Ghol Gedrosian. You paid him money. Not pocket change, either. Hundreds of thousands of dollars. Amounts that would stick in a man's memory. You are a good customer of his. Gambling, call girls, and – as far as I can make out – I don't really read Russian too well, so I could be wrong about this – a hell of a lot of drugs. Is any of this starting to sound familiar, Mr Thane? Or should I say' – he looks down at his pad – '"J.R. Thane of 22 Waverly Drive" – that was your address back in California – 22 Waverly Drive – wasn't it?'

'Yes,' I say. I reach for the edge of the table, and I'm grateful when it's actually there.

'Anything you want to tell me? Now might be a good time. A really good time.'

'No.'

'Are you an addict, Mr Thane?'

As soon as he asks the question, all the old feelings come back. I don't answer him, not with words, but my body betrays me, and I feel it deflate in front of his eyes. So many months of trying to appear strong, of trying to impress people – all the people in my life – Tad, Libby, Gordon Kramer, Doc Curtis, Dr Liago, even myself; it has been an endless struggle, really it has, every hour of each day – pretending to be someone I am not – and, finally, at this moment, in this hot room, with a hayseed cop glaring at me and accusing me of *something*, although I'm not sure exactly what, it all catches up with me, and I just want to retreat into my dark bedroom, and have a drink, and maybe smoke a pipe, and curl into a ball, and call it a day.

'Gambling?' he asks, gently.

'Sure, gambling,' I agree. My voice is hoarse. 'And drinking. And drugs. And whores, too, if you got any. You offering?' I glance at the door, make sure that it's closed, that no one outside can hear. 'I've been clean for over two years.'

'Good for you,' he says, but he doesn't sound very congratulatory. 'Tell me where can I find Ghol Gedrosian, please, Mr Thane.'

'I can't tell you that.'

'Can't? Or won't?'

'I don't know the man. I've never met him. And I certainly don't know where to find him. That's the God's-honest truth.'

He stares. Maybe he does believe me, after all, because he shrugs, and closes his pad, and drops it into his pocket. He stands.

When he speaks, his voice has become gentle again. 'My daddy was in AA. So I know a little bit about what you've gone through.'

Unless his daddy ever woke up in the Mission District, with an empty wallet and a crack pipe in his hands, he probably doesn't know what I've gone through. But it was humane of him to try.

He leans across the table and gives me his business card. 'You ought to keep this, Mr Thane,' he says. 'Keep it handy. I think you'll be wanting to call me soon. You'll be needing my help. Probably sooner than you like.'

CHAPTER 33

But Agent Mitchell is wrong. There is only one person in the world whose help I need. There is only one person in the world to whom I want to talk.

We've had our problems, Libby and I; that is true. We've suffered. I have betrayed her. I have wrecked her life. I have destroyed what she loved. Yet, after all that, she is still my wife, and we are still partners. We are partners, no matter what comes.

When I arrive at home, though, my partner is gone. Her Mercedes is missing from the driveway. I walk into the house and call her name. 'Libby?' My voice echoes in the empty hall.

It's just past four o'clock. She wasn't expecting me home this early, and I doubt she left a note. But I look for one anyway – on the kitchen table, the refrigerator door, anywhere she might have left a clue.

There is no note. There is no clue.

I try to recall my recent conversations with Libby. Did she mention to me that she had plans this afternoon?

Now, standing in the middle of the kitchen, something occurs to me. It occurs to me that, in fact, I have no idea how Libby spends *any* of her afternoons. She lives alone in a house, in a strange town, in a strange state. She has no job, no friends, no family.

She lives in a house. That is the only thing I know about her, and how she spends her time.

It is as if Libby is a prop on a Broadway stage. When the audience arrives and the spotlight goes on – that is, when I return home from work – the curtain goes up, and her life begins. But when the audience files out at the end of the show – when I leave the house in the morning – things go dark, and her story pauses.

I step outside, onto the porch. Across the street, my neighbour with the bulging forehead and overcrowded teeth waits on his own porch. He stares at me.

I wave to him.

A pause. An uncertain look. He waves back, tentatively.

For a moment, I consider heading across the road, with an outstretched hand, and introducing myself, maybe even asking if he's seen my wife. We've lived across the street for months, in the only two houses on a deserted cul-de-sac, and yet we have never exchanged a single greeting.

Before I can act, though, he takes a cellphone from his pocket, presses a button, and raises it to his ear. He says something I can't hear. He turns his back to me, and disappears into his house, shutting the door.

Back in my own living room, I sit on the couch. Waiting.

I listen to the tick of the grandfather clock. I think about the conversation with Agent Mitchell – about how my name was found in Ghol Gedrosian's list of customers.

Before I took the job at Tao, I never heard the name Ghol Gedrosian. Of this, I am certain. Yet according to Tom Mitchell, I have been a customer of his, a customer of long standing and great value.

How can that be?

Being an addict doesn't mean living in a haze, unaware of your actions, oblivious to people around you. Even today, I have vivid recollections of those mean bad years, those years when I was using – searing and bright memories – as if captured by an old magnesium flash from a 1940s movie: of snorting lines of coke off two hookers' flat young abdomens; of standing outside a Wells Fargo at ten a.m., with trembling hands, waiting for the bank to open, so that I could withdraw the ten Gs that I owed to scary bookies by noon; of touring a backyard in Woodside, under a camo tarp, where a tin Gulfstream hid the portable meth lab from which I was buying in bulk – a drug addict's peculiar approximation of home economy.

These are all very real recollections – indelible and intense. With these memories come specific names: Hector the Bookie; Johnnie Deadpan, who boasted that he played with Dylan at the Newport Folk Festival, and who, forty years later, sold me crank from his trailer; Angel, the hooker who would do anything, and I mean anything, to share my stash of meth. Many memories, and many names, from that long and not-so-glorious catalogue.

But from this list one name is conspicuously missing.

His name is so peculiar – with its odd jumble of consonants and vowels – its sound so foreign and frightening, like a curse in an ancient tongue – that surely I would recall it, had I heard it even once in those years.

Before coming to Florida, I never heard the name Ghol Gedrosian. So how can I be his customer? How can the name Jimmy Thane appear in his files?

And another thing.

Do mobsters keep computer spreadsheets? Is it common for them – after a hard day breaking legs and selling girls into slavery – to fire up Microsoft Excel, and draw little pie charts with coloured slices for each line of business – red for meth, say, blue for hookers, and green for loan-sharking – like earnest McKinsey consultants slouched at the back of the airport Admirals Club sipping Chivas on the rocks? How many criminals keep computerized lists of their customers, anyway? How many of these lists are ever found by police?

None, of course.

Unless the lists are meant to be found. Unless they're planted, designed to incriminate.

I hear the tinkling of keys in the front door, and then Libby stands in the doorway, clutching a single grocery bag. She peers into the room.

'What are you doing home?' she asks, sounding not exactly pleased to see me.

'Where were you?'

'Groceries.' She lifts the bag in her arms, as if to corroborate this story.

Something about the way she does this makes me feel an intense curiosity to examine the contents of that bag. I get up from the couch and approach. Before I can reach her, though, she walks away, into the kitchen, taking the bag with her.

I follow.

'We needed milk,' she explains. She lifts a gallon jug from the bag, to demonstrate, and carries it to the refrigerator.

She puts the milk inside. My eyes flit past, to the top shelf, where I see a gallon already sits, nearly full.

'Libby,' I say, 'we need to talk.'

She turns.

I say, 'I'm being set up.'

She stares at me with a blank, uncomprehending expression.

I continue: 'This job. This city. This house—' I lift my hands to encompass it all. 'It's not real.'

'It's not... *real*?'

'It's a con, Libby. I'm the patsy.'

She looks dumbfounded.

I realize that our marriage has reached a dubious new low. For the first time in ten years – ten years of mistakes, and heartaches, and betrayal – for the first time, I have done something completely new. I have *befuddled* her.

'You're a... *patsy*?' she repeats, not quite sneering at the word, but coming close.

'They arrested a man. A dealer out in California. Guess whose name they found in his papers. Guess whose name was in his list of customers.'

'Yours,' she says, right away, not sounding surprised.

'How did you know?'

'You're an addict, Jimmy. You buy drugs.'

'Used to.'

She shrugs. 'Used to.'

'The man they arrested, I never bought from him. And his boss – this guy named Ghol Gedrosian.' I spit the name. 'I never bought from him, either. I'm sure of that.'

'How do you remember *who* you bought from back then? You can't seem to remember who you fucked.'

'I do remember,' I say, and add, 'who I bought from. Every single person.' Which is true. When you're an addict, one of the things you never forget is your dealer. You might forget to pay your bills, or to call your family, or even to come home at night – but that Rolodex of phone numbers and secret knocks and names you need to mention – those are never forgotten. Never.

'They planted my name, Libby. How else can I be a customer of someone I've never met?'

'I love wearing Gucci. But I never met Tom Ford.'

'Be serious.'

'Fine.' She makes a dour face. 'I'll be serious.'

'There's something else. Something I haven't told you.'

I take her hand, and guide her to the living room. We sit down on the couch, in front of the grandfather clock. It ticks metronomically.

'They gave me money,' I say.

She looks puzzled. 'Who gave you money?'

'Tad. Tad and his partners. They gave me money. A lot of money. I took it. I didn't ask any questions. I just took it.'

'How much money?'

'Does it matter?'

'I think it does.'

'Two million dollars.'

'They gave you two million dollars?' She can't keep the surprise from her voice. 'What for?'

'You tell me.'

'Two million dollars,' she says again, mostly to herself, considering. She looks at me. Her eyes narrow, and I see something new in them – something I haven't seen recently in my wife. Something I haven't seen for years. What is it exactly? *Respect.* Yes, that's what it is.

'Two million dollars,' she repeats.

'Don't you see? That money is in our bank account. Anyone who looks will find it. Tad set me up. He played me. He left clues, to make me look guilty. He put money in my account, to make it look like I'm stealing from Tao. He planted my name in a meth-dealer's house, so it'll look like I'm an addict.'

'You *are* an addict.'

'I am being set up.'

'You sound paranoid, Jimmy.'

'Libby,' I say, trying to keep my voice very calm. It's hard not to sound paranoid after someone tells you that you are. 'Libby. Listen to me.' I speak slowly. 'We need to think about this very carefully. We need to go to the police. We need to give back the money. We need to tell them everything we know. We need to explain what Tad is up to. How he's stealing from the company. Who he's working for. We need to tell them about Ghol Gedrosian.'

'The police?' Libby repeats. She is apparently still stuck on the very first part of my plan.

I take her hand. It is strangely cold. 'Listen. Here's what I think we should do,' I say. 'I think we should go home. I mean, our real home. I think we should go back to California.'

I hardly thought about this idea before I started to speak it, but now, even before the words are out, I am excited by it. More details come to me. I blurt them out, almost breathless. 'Let's leave *tonight*. Let's get on a plane and get the hell out of here. Fuck this job. Fuck this house. Let's just leave. We won't even pack. Let's just drive to the airport – right now – and take the first flight. When we get home, we'll find a lawyer. We'll go to the police. We'll deal with whatever comes. We'll deal with it together. Whatever comes.'

Libby considers.

'What do you think, Libby?' I say. I'm relieved. Relieved that I've told her. Relieved that I've unburdened myself of the secret that I've been keeping. Relieved – most of all – at the idea of escape – at the thought of walking out this front door, locking it behind us, and never seeing this house again. Never stepping foot in Florida again. Going home. 'What do you think, Libby? Let's get on a plane. Let's just leave. Right now. Let's go.'

Libby stares at me. For a moment, I think that I've made quite an impression on her, that she's considering this new plan, maybe even signing up for it: walking out the front door, getting on a plane, going home, telling the police everything. Starting our lives again.

'Think how nice it would be,' I say. 'To go home. Doesn't that sound good to you, Libby? To start again?'

She prises her fingers out of my hand. She stands up and walks to the clock. She stares into its blank glass face, standing with her back to me. I can't see her expression.

'Libby?' I say, quietly. 'What are you thinking?'

'Jimmy,' she whispers, shaking her head.

She seems to consider her next words for a long time. Finally, when she turns to me, she says, 'I never want to threaten you. I never want to be *that* kind of wife.'

'What kind of wife?' I ask, even though I know, because she *is* that kind of wife.

'I've waited so long. You're not an easy man to love. You know that, don't you?'

266

'Yes,' I whisper.

'How many times do I have to forgive you? Your incompetence? Your stupidity? How many times do I have to say, "It's OK, Jimmy. It's OK that you've destroyed everything we've been given"?'

'I'm not destroying anything.'

'You're not? Two million dollars in the bank. A good job. You want to throw it all away.'

'No.' I shake my head. 'No. I'm working for gangsters.'

'And you're so pure?'

'I don't kill people.'

'Really?' Her eyes flash hatred. I see her thoughts. She is remembering that night. The night she came home to find me standing in Cole's bedroom. To find me yelling incoherently, crying, standing over our dead son.

Then, as quickly as it comes, her hatred is gone. She speaks quietly.

'Look at yourself,' she says, staring at me with a pitiless expression. 'You're forty-seven years old. If you walk away from this – assuming they *let* you walk away – what do you think is going to happen next? Tell me what you think is going to happen.'

As soon as she says it, I know *exactly* what will happen. We'll slump back to California, and I'll be unemployed again. Probably unemployable. Without the two million dollars, I'll run out of money, and I'll start using; and Libby will leave me – most certainly she will leave me – that's what she's saying, isn't it? – and I'll wake up in a motel, one more time, with the sun pounding my eyeballs, and I'll wonder where it all went wrong. And I'll know: right here, in this room, right now, talking to Libby, with the grandfather clock ticking off the seconds relentlessly – this is when it happened. This is when it went wrong. Right now. This moment.

As if she knows what I'm thinking, she says, 'You see? You can't throw this away. Not this time. Not again. Not our last chance.'

'But it's wrong,' I say. 'It's all wrong.'

'Of course it's wrong,' she says. Libby's face is drawn and bloodless. I notice – maybe for the first time – that she has narrow ruthless eyes. Which is really something you ought to notice about your wife, before you've been married for ten years. 'Of course it's wrong, Jimmy. But that's not something people like us can worry about. People who aren't addicts – they can worry about right and wrong. People who can find another job – they can worry about right and wrong. People without dead children – they can worry about right and wrong. People like us… ' She shakes her head. She lets the thought hang, unfinished.

I'm dumbfounded. Literally, struck dumb. Unable to speak. The air has left my lungs. My body is frozen. Immobile.

Her voice softens. 'Jimmy,' she says gently, 'you're a good man.'

'Am I?' I whisper.

'Good enough,' she says, not unkindly. 'You deserve better. You finally have your shot. God only knows how you got it, but you finally have it. Accept it. For once, accept what you've been given.'

'But it's a set-up, Libby. I am being set up.'

She sits down beside me. She takes my hand. Her skin is cold and reptilian. 'Of course you're being set up,' she says. 'Of course you are. And when the day comes, you're going to take the fall. You will. But that day might be a long time coming. Or maybe it will never come. And until it does… ' She stops.

'Until it does… *what*?'

'Until it does, we can be together. We can try to be happy. I can try to be your wife. You're being given a gift. Do you see that?'

'A gift?'

'A second chance. How many people get that, after they ruin things the first time around? This is *your* restart. Your second chance. A new life. A new house. Money. A wife who loves you.'

'Do you?'

She looks at me for a long time, as if trying to decide. When she speaks, at last, she answers a different question. 'Here's what I want,' she says. 'I want you to promise me something.'

'What?'

'Promise me you won't ruin this, too. Promise me you won't go to the police.'

'But Libby...'

'Promise me,' she says.

'Libby...'

She screams: 'Promise me!' – so loud and so sudden that her shout echoes on the walls, and the ceiling, and the glass clock – startling me.

Softer now, much softer, but still insistent, she says, 'Promise me. Promise me.'

'Libby...'

'Promise me,' she whispers. 'Promise me.'

She touches my face. Kisses my lips. 'Libby...' I say.

'Promise me. Promise me.'

'I promise,' I say at last. I have no choice. After all that I've done to her, all these years, how can I say anything else? How could anyone?

CHAPTER 34

I wait only fourteen hours to betray her, which is a new land speed record, even for me, even for Jimmy Thane.

Usually it takes weeks or days from the time I make a promise to my wife until the time I break it. Usually, the breaking of that promise involves waking up in a strange bed, in a strange woman's arms; or finding myself at a 'friend's' house at three in the morning – that friend copiously supplied with sandwich baggies bulging yellow crystals.

This morning's betrayal is different.

This morning, when I wake from my dream – the usual dream – the bath, and boy's body, the moonlight – Libby is already downstairs, frying eggs; and there's a fresh pot of coffee dripping into the glass carafe. It's as if she's showing me what life might be like, if I play along: domestic bliss – eggs and coffee every morning, banal conversation in the breakfast nook, each of us reading our favourite section of *The New York Times*.

We don't speak about yesterday, nor about my plan to go to the police. We don't mention the idea of giving back the money, or of turning in Tad Billups, or leading Agent Mitchell to Ghol Gedrosian. Apparently, my promise not to do any of these things is enough for her, and we never need to speak of these matters again. Yesterday is just one more incident that we can lock away and forget, like the night Cole died, or the day she found a hooker in our bed, or the day she left me, or the day she came back.

I eat the fried eggs that she offers, and drink the coffee, gratefully, and when I'm ready to go to the office, I kiss her on the cheek.

'Have a good day,' she says. 'I'll be here when you get back.' A promise, maybe. Or a threat. Or maybe she's just trying the idea on for size – seeing how it fits – that she'll be here when I get back.

I leave the house. I step onto the porch, into the heat. It's eighty degrees before nine o'clock – an impossible temperature – and indeed the weather seems precarious – ready to break. The air feels heavy. Clouds darken the horizon.

I climb into my Ford.

I drive west on the causeway, into the greying sky, out to the island of Sanibel, to the house that I own.

No skulking this time. No sneaking through backyards, no squeezing through open windows. I park in front and walk straight up the path. I expect the door to be locked – maybe even hope that it will be – but it gives easily, and swings open, inviting me in.

I shut the door behind me. The air inside is warm and stale. The lights are off. Sun pushes through brittle yellow window shades, revealing the empty living room to the side, and the shadowy kitchen straight ahead.

Right away, I smell it.

It starts as an undertone. It's cloying and sweet and foul. It's the smell of corruption, of old things under floorboards, of dark shapes at the bottom of sewers on hot summer days.

I walk down the hall, peering into rooms, expecting to see the body sprawled on the carpet. But there is no body. There is just a smell. The rooms are as empty as I remember from my first visit: threadbare futon in the bedroom, rickety desk, bookcase devoid of books.

No body. I pass the bathroom. The smell is stronger here. No mistaking it now, no denying what it is. I retch. I stop moving, as if holding perfectly still might make things better. I take little shallow

271

breaths, only through my mouth, try not to think about the smell.

The hallway ends at a metal door, probably the garage. There are no windows, and the light is diffuse. I look up. In the shadows of the ceiling is the attic trap door. I reach up to the dangling metal ring, and I pull.

Everything happens at once. A rush of warm air on my face. A man jumping from the attic and punching my jaw. My stumbling back and yelling in surprise, arms windmilling.

The man crashes to the ground at my feet, his face turned away from me. But I would know that gelled Caesar haircut anywhere, and that fat Rolex strapped to his wrist, and those Ferragamo pants, crisply pressed as though pulled off the dry-cleaner's rack this very morning.

I circle the body and see the face. It stares at me with vacant eyes. The smile is a blend of mean-spiritedness and rigor mortis – teeth bared, lips snarled. In death, Dom Vanderbeek doesn't look much different from Dom Vanderbeek in life. Maybe a bit angrier. But just as aggrieved, as if he can't believe the unfairness of it all, that I am alive, while he is dead, and yet he clearly is the better man of the two.

I run.

The door slams behind me, and I race out of the house, my shoes scuffing concrete. I fumble with keys and climb into the Ford. I crank the engine and reach for the gear shift, relieved – relieved to be gone from there, relieved to escape the odour, the dead body, the dark house.

That's when I feel the cold metal pressed against the base of my skull. 'Do not move, Mr Thane,' a man says, in a Russian accent. 'You should not have come. You shouldn't have seen that. Now what am I going to do with you?'

CHAPTER 35

When I look in the rearview mirror, I see a man seated behind me, holding a gun to my head. He is young, maybe thirty, with blond hair cut military short. An angry purple scar runs from the bottom of his left cheek to his ear. It's raised, grossly stitched in an XX pattern, like a cheap baseball mitt.

He says, 'Leave the engine running. Get out of the car.'

When I don't move fast enough, he cocks the hammer and shoves the gun hard into my skull. '*Now.*'

I do as he says, opening the door and climbing from the car, leaving the engine idling.

He gets out behind me, keeps his gun pressed into my spine. 'Leave your door open,' he says. 'Come into the house with me.'

I know that if I do as he commands – if I leave the car running, the door open, and go into the house – I will die. Just as Charles Adams did. Just as Dom Vanderbeek did.

'I don't want to shoot you,' he says. The conclusion of this thought is unspoken, but perfectly clear: *But I will.* His gun prods like a bony finger, pushing me forwards, towards the front of the house. At the door he says: 'Open it.'

I glance over my shoulder at the street behind us. No one is on the sidewalk. No one drives past. There is no one to call for help. He says, 'There is no help for you, Mr Thane. Go inside.'

In the house, it smells worse than before. Maybe the Russian wasn't expecting it. He shuts the door and says, '*Ecch.*'

If the smell hinders him, though, it does so only momentarily, because immediately he jabs his gun into my back, and urges me forward, in the direction of the corpse. At the end of the hall we see Vanderbeek crumpled on the carpet. The Russian leans over his body and studies it with something like scientific interest. He taps his toe into Vanderbeek's ribcage – once, then twice. When the corpse doesn't move, he seems satisfied.

He looks up at the attic trap door, still ajar. He says, 'You should not have opened that door. It was closed for a reason.'

'I'm sorry.'

He takes out his cellphone, dials, and holds it to his ear with a huge hand. He says something in Russian and snaps the phone shut.

He turns to me. 'We will need to dispose of the body. You may never come here again. Do you understand?'

These words do not sound like words that a murderer speaks to a man he is about to kill. 'Yes,' I say.

'Mr Vanderbeek was too curious. You see what happens to curious people? People who ask too many questions?'

I nod.

Before he can take this line of reasoning further, he is interrupted by the sound of a car engine outside the house. In a moment, the front door opens, and loud Russian voices are in the foyer, laughing and joking. Two men appear at the end of the hall – big men, stupid-looking men – carrying a roll of carpet between them. When they see me and the blond man, they stop their banter mid-sentence. They nod respectfully at the man with the gun. The blond man waves the barrel at them, beckoning them to approach.

The men lay down the carpet beside Vanderbeek, unfurl it. They each take one end of my Sales VP's corpse, lift him onto the rug, and roll him up. The blond man says something in Russian, and the two bruisers nod, and bend, and lift the load between them. They leave the

274

house without another word.

When they are gone, the blond man turns to me. He sticks his gun back into his belt, and opens his hands wide, a gesture I take to be one of peace and forgiveness.

'My employer has sent me to deliver a message to you,' he says.

'Who is your employer?'

'You know who I work for.'

'Yes,' I say. 'You work for Ghol Gedro—'

He punches me in the stomach. I fall, clutching my guts and saying something like, '*Oof*,' which sounds ridiculous, even to me, even as I fall to the ground. My knees slam onto the floor. There's no padding below the rug – just concrete – and a bolt of pain shoots up my legs. I keel over, and cough – one fist on the ground, trying to catch my breath. The blond slides a knife from a scabbard on his belt – where the hell did *that* come from? – a big sawtoothed blade – and he reaches down and grabs my hair, very hard, and pulls my head upwards and back, exposing my throat. He presses the blade under my chin. 'Never say his name,' he whispers. 'Never.'

'I'm sorry.'

He lets me go, and I crumple. He stands. For a moment, I am relieved. Alas, the relief does not last very long, because he kicks me in the ribs. 'Ungrateful,' he says, and kicks again. 'Ungrateful!' Another kick. I curl into a foetal position, put my hands over my head, wait for the next kick.

When it doesn't come, I peer through a crack in my fingers. He's kneeling beside me, looking concerned, as if he happened to wander by and find me here. 'Are you hurt?' he asks gently. 'Can you sit up?'

I do. My ribs ache. The blond man sticks his face just inches from mine, so close that I am able to study the scar on his cheek. 'Do you know that he has given you a gift, Mr Thane?'

'The money?'

'More than the money. Your house, your job, your wife. Everything a man could want.'

'Libby?' I say, surprised.

'He has given her to you. Have you enjoyed her?'

'Actually… ' I start. But then I think better of it.

'Everything you have, was once his. Everything you have, he can take away. Even your life. Do you understand?'

I nod.

'Say it. Say you understand.'

'I understand.'

'You must accept his gifts,' he says, 'and be grateful for them.'

'Yes.'

'Say it.'

'I accept his gifts. I am grateful for them.'

'His power is vast. More vast than you can imagine.'

'Yes,' I say.

'Say it.'

'His power is vast. More vast than I can imagine.'

'That's right.' He nods. He stands. He stares at me. 'Look at you. Pathetic. Fat. Disgusting. Weak. Yet he wants to protect you.'

'Protect me?'

He slides his knife back into its sheath. 'Vanderbeek will not bother you again,' he says. 'Obviously.'

'Obviously.'

'And as for you,' he says. 'There must be no more investigating. No more questions. No more thinking. Do you understand these words? No more thinking, Mr Thane.' He taps my forehead with his huge thumb, to demonstrate where my thinking must not take place. 'Thinking is for dead men.'

'I'm not a big fan of thinking,' I admit.

'No more going to widow's houses. No more asking your little secretary for secret files. Do you understand what I tell you?'

To help me understand what he tells me, he gives me one last kick in the ribs, a hard one, and I hear a crack as his toe connects with bone, and I fall backwards, and I yell, 'Oh shit! Fuck! Please stop.'

'Did that hurt?' he asks.

'Yes.'

'Good. This makes me happy. Go back to work. If you see me ever again, it means I've come to kill you.'

CHAPTER 36

I go back to work.

It hurts when I breathe, but at least there's no blood, and Amanda barely looks at me as I limp into the reception area, and head back to my office.

I'm vaguely aware that this is how Charles Adams behaved during his final days on the planet – taking meetings with scary men, slinking back to his office, shutting his door and hiding within.

I shut my door. I collapse into my chair.

'*He wants to protect you,*' the blond man said. I touch my ribs. They do not feel protected, not at this moment, and I pull my shirt from my pants, and stare at the purplish black bruises that have appeared on my chest. I press one. It hurts. No, I do not feel protected.

But he did not kill me. Maybe that is Ghol Gedrosian's idea of protection. Not killing you.

I open my desk drawer, remove the business card belonging to Agent Tom Mitchell. I study it carefully, as if the telephone numbers and street address are ancient runes that require deciphering – answers to long asked, never answered, questions. I stare at the telephone on my desk. For exactly three seconds, I consider lifting the receiver, and calling Agent Mitchell. I would tell him about Dom Vanderbeek, and the corpse in the house, and how I work for a Russian mobster, and how I've been paid millions of dollars to look the other way while Ghol Gedrosian steals money from the company that I supposedly run.

But of course I don't. I don't tell him these things. I don't pick up the phone.

I slide Agent Mitchell's card into my wallet. Again I think back to the story he told me, of the DA in California, and what happened to him, and his children. I know that if I pick up the phone, the same will happen to me. That's what the blond man meant: *If you see me ever again, it means I've come to kill you.*

If I pick up the phone, I *will* see the blond man again. Maybe tonight, in my house, leaning over my bed, when I open my eyes for the last time. Or maybe at Tao, this afternoon, in reception, seated on a chair like a photocopier salesman, waiting for me to leave the office. Or maybe in my car, as I pull out of my driveway tomorrow morning.

Somehow, Ghol Gedrosian will know if I lift this phone to speak to the FBI. Just as he knows everything that I've done since I've come to Florida.

How *did* the blond man know that I drove to Sanibel? I told no one that I was going to the house on 56 Windmere. It was a spur-of-the-moment decision… one that I made when Pete Bland walked into my office, and shut the door, and told me that I owned that house.

The blond man's words come back to me: *No more going to widow's houses. No more asking your little secretary for secret files.*

He knew about that too. About my visit to Charles Adams's widow. About my conversation with Amanda – the conversation that took place right here, in this office, with the door shut, the two of us alone…

And Dom Vanderbeek, too. It was here that he threatened me – standing *right here* – in the doorway to my office.

I feel a chill. I'm being watched. I keep my body very still. My eyes glide around the room. Searching.

Searching.

He hears everything, Mrs Adams told me. *He has ears.*

The ravings of a mad woman.

Or was it something else?

I rise from my chair, slowly, trying to make the gesture seem natural, as if I'm just stretching my legs. I glance casually at the ceiling, the smoke detector, the coat hook behind the door, the power outlets in the wall. A hundred places to hide a listening device. A thousand spots to bury a microphone.

But it's not buried, is it? It's not hidden. It's right here. Right in front of me.

From my desk, I lift the photograph with the ornate silver frame. The photograph of me and Libby and Satan. The frame that's so heavy and peculiar and large.

I stare at it – one final time – that curious photo, which has always seemed so wrong to me – doctored, perhaps – or staged. I lay it on the floor, and I lift my shoe, and I slam down my heel. The glass shatters.

I kneel beside it. The metal frame has cracked, not being solid metal at all. Poking from the hidden compartment are black wires, which are attached to something that looks very much like a microphone, and a camera, and a thin metal antenna.

Now I recall that morning long ago, when I first arrived at Tao, how Libby insisted that I bring this photograph – this particular one – to the office. 'Because it has us together,' she explained, and I believed her. As I have believed Libby for so many years.

Now everything makes sense: her meanness, her sulking. Her standing beside me, despite the fact that she so certainly hates me.

She works for Tad Billups. She has always worked for Tad.

Maybe she is sleeping with him, too. That would explain a great deal. My wife, and my best friend, fucking, and plotting against me.

And then, a thought comes. It arrives uninvited, and it surprises me with its clarity and its pureness.

It is: *You deserve it, Jimmy.*

Everything you've got, you had coming. Everything you have, you deserve.

CHAPTER 37

Each time I have spoken to Tad Billups on the telephone since I arrived in Florida, I have been on the receiving end of his call to me.

Now it's my turn to play offence, my turn to surprise him. I'm not even sure what I'm going to say to him – 'How do you like fucking my wife?' perhaps – or maybe nothing of the kind. I'm not worried. I'll know what to say to my old friend as soon as I hear his voice.

I peck around my computer for his office telephone number and I dial. The receptionist who answers has that smoky, heard-it-all-before voice that venture capital firms love to use as gatekeepers: sexy, yes; friendly, a bit – but not *too* friendly; always a hint of wariness – thanks for your call, but who the hell *are* you exactly?

'Hello, thank you for calling Bedrock Ventures. This is Alicia speaking. How may I direct your call?'

'Tad Billups, please.'

A long silence. Finally: 'Who's calling?'

'Jimmy Thane.'

Another silence. Which leads me to think I need to add more detail. Like who I am. 'Alicia, I'm Jim Thane from Tao Software. I'm sure you know that I am the CEO at one of your portfolio companies.' My voice is meant to convey certainty, and seriousness, and more than a hint of impatience. 'Let me talk to Tad please.'

Another pause, as if I've just announced that I am calling from Planet Mars, on behalf of General Mixilplc, to discuss recalibrating the cosmic ray gun.

Finally, after what seems like for ever, the smoky voice responds, 'Please hold.'

She is replaced by music – the Beatles' 'Penny Lane', reimagined as muzak on a pan flute. After a minute, the music stops abruptly, and a male voice comes on the line.

'This is Tench. Who am I speaking to?'

Tench Worth-a-Ton – Tad's partner. Every venture capital firm has a Tench, a man who can speak the language of the wealthy nincompoops whose money they need to finagle. You can't send a dark-skinned Indian or a mysterious Chinaman into a family office in the deep woods of Akron – even if it is these exotic specimens who will actually manage the money on behalf of the fourth-generation steel barons of Ohio.

You need a Tench. Every firm does. Dumb as a wall, but with blood that goes back to the Mayflower, and a Yale degree, and a Harvard MBA. And a mean forehand in squash.

'Tench?' I say, trying to lather up some enthusiasm for the bastard. 'It's me, Jimmy.'

'Jimmy?' As if he has no idea who I am.

'Jimmy Thane. Tad there?'

'Tad?'

Jesus, I think to myself, I'm trying to reach the man who's cuckolding me, and Tench wants to play Twenty Questions.

'Yeah, *Tad*. Tad Billups. I asked your receptionist to connect me. I'm not sure why she put me through to you. How ya' doing, Tench?'

'*Who* is this?'

'Jimmy Thane.'

At the other end of the phone, there's a noise, a sudden explosion of breath. It sounds suspiciously like a laugh. A laugh of disbelief.

I continue nevertheless. 'That's right. CEO of Tao Software. It's part of your portfolio, Tench. I'm sure you're aware of that.'

This last statement is meant as a joke – or at least is as much sarcasm as I can muster, given the circumstances – because even the laziest VC knows every company in his portfolio, knows it intimately, just as he knows every single entrepreneur working at these portfolio companies – working for *him*, effectively. These entrepreneurs, after all, are entrusted with a large portion of the VC's net worth, and are trying to make that VC rich.

But Tench Worthington does not treat my statement as a joke. In fact, he is silent for a long time. I'm about to ask him if he's still on the line, when he finally says, 'Jimmy Thane, the *drunk*?'

If I weren't sitting down, securely in my chair, I'd reel backwards across the room. Instead, I feel merely light-headed, as if something in the world has changed, something fundamental, like the direction the earth rotates around the sun, or whether it does so at all. But I say, agreeably, 'Drunk, sure. And don't forget about the womanizing and the coke, Tench. So will you get Tad on the phone for me?'

'Jimmy, what are you saying? Where are you?'

'Jesus Christ, you piece of shit,' I say, finally losing all patience. 'I'm in fucking East Buttfuck, Florida, you asshole. I'm sweating my ass off for your cheating double-crossing partner, and it's one hundred fucking degrees. Are you telling me he hasn't even bothered to let you know that I'm working for you?'

'Jimmy Thane,' he says, in quiet wonder, half to himself. 'I never thought I'd hear from you. Not after what happened.' He clears his throat. 'Jimmy, we wrote off Tao Software last year. Dead loss. Goose eggs. We decided to shut the company down. Is this some kind of – I don't know – some kind of joke?'

'Fuck you, Tench,' I say, and only after I say it do I realize I'm not joking. Not a bit. 'Put your cocksucker partner on the phone. Put Tad on.'

'Tad,' he says, as if the name is interesting, worth repeating. 'Tad, Tad, Tad. Well, here's the thing, Jimmy.'

'What's the thing, Tench?'

'The thing is, Tad took a voluntary leave of absence. It was a long time ago. Early last year. He hasn't been with Bedrock since 09. You know, after the incident, everyone thought it might be best.'

'What incident?'

'I'm sure you heard. About the babysitter? The girl that got strangled with her own underwear?'

'No.'

'Well, until a court decides, we won't know for sure. But we all mutually agreed that, until a jury makes a determination about guilt or innocence…'

'What jury? What the fuck are you talking about? Where is Tad? He fucking *hired* me.'

'I don't know, Jimmy. I haven't spoken to Tad in over a year. He doesn't work here. He hasn't worked here for a long time. And he never will. And I can assure you, no one at my firm would ever hire you. Not to run anything. Not to run around the block.' He pauses, then adds: 'No offence.'

'None taken, asshole.'

'But if I see him,' Tench says, 'which I doubt I will, since I don't plan on visiting prison, should I tell him you called?'

CHAPTER 38

It's raining when I arrive home.

It started softly – just a few drops on the windshield as I pulled out of the office parking lot – but by the time I step from my car, in the driveway, it's steady and threatening more. I look up. Just past noon, but the sky is black. Water spatters the gravel at my feet, kicking up the smell of hot summer dust. In the distance, a grumble of thunder.

Libby's Mercedes is gone. But I didn't expect her to be home. How can you stay in a house, waiting for your husband, when you're leading a secret life, working for someone else, fucking someone else?

Inside, I walk up the stairs, to our bedroom. I start in her underwear drawer – because that's where women keep their secrets. I run my hands through her clothes. I'm not sure what I'm looking for: the sharp foil edge of a condom, or the soft bulk of a secret diary, or the crinkling paper of a letter from a lover. Maybe a letter written by Tad. Or maybe a letter penned in Cyrillic.

I find none of these things. Just underwear, and not even much of that.

I move to the closet. I start at the top shelves, feeling between sweaters. Then I kneel, and peer into her shoe-boxes and purses. I find nothing: no notes, no letters, no secrets.

I pad down the stairs into the kitchen, where I open the drawers in quick sequence, flipping through the crap that kitchens accumulate: corkscrews, can openers, dull knives, spatulas, a ball of twine. I look inside the cabinets next, into the nooks behind the dishes and glassware. I dump into the sink the contents of a ceramic canister filled with flour. A Tupperware of sugar.

Outside, the rain starts to pour. It drums against the roof. Lightning flashes and, seconds later, thunder booms over the house, rattling the windows in their sashes.

There's another flash, just as I'm looking through the pane of glass, and it illuminates the vegetable plot, and, behind it, the garden shed.

The garden shed. Of course.

I walk out of the front door of the house, leaving it open, and trudge into the rain. It's coming down hard, pelting my scalp, painfully, soaking my shirt, washing the sweat from my face, pooling in my shoes.

My feet sink into mud. Rivulets of water race past.

I go to the side of the house. The garden shed is unlocked. I pull the handle. The corrugated tin door screeches in the rusted track.

I find it where I knew it would be, right on the bottom shelf, where I once observed Libby kneeling: a small package, wrapped in white butcher paper.

My hand shakes as I lift it from the shelf. I know I've found the answer, even though I don't yet know the question. I pick at the butcher paper. My fingers are wet, and the paper is soggy, and it rips under my thumbnail. Inside is a set of three computer DVDs, branded with the Hewlett-Packard logo and the company's slogan: 'Invent'.

Each DVD has a handwritten date scrawled in indelible marker: 'June 2' and 'July 12' and 'July 19'.

Back in the living room, I slide the first disc into the DVD player – the disc marked 'June 2'.

It plays immediately. Even without a title, I recognize the genre right away. The clues are obvious: high-contrast video, hot orange skin tone, rough rasping breath on microphones. I've seen it a hundred times, as every American man has.

But something about this pornography – for it *is* pornography, surely – is wrong. Something about it is different.

It's too real.

The video is of a young girl, maybe fifteen. Her face is familiar. I've seen her before, but can't recall where. Her hair is plastered against her head. She lies on a plastic sheet, drenched in sweat. She is naked, spreadeagled, probably bound to bedposts that are off-camera. A gag – it looks like a nylon neck tie – is stuffed into her mouth. A brutal strap of black electrical tape is wrapped across her forehead, keeping her skull stationary. Her eyes are filled with tears.

A male voice, off-camera, speaks. 'Do you know what is going to happen to you?' He speaks softly and very slowly. He has a Russian accent. 'We are going to cut you. We are going to hurt you. Is that what you want?'

The girl tries to shake her head, frantically, but the electrical tape stops her. Her movements are just small violent twitches.

'You are so quiet, Lisa. Say something for the camera.'

Her eyes glide sideways and look at me. I've never seen a stare like that. I hope never to see it again.

The Russian voice says, languidly, 'More soon, dear.' The screen goes black.

I stare at the dark television for a long time. Part of me doesn't want to put the next DVD into the player, because I already know what I'm going to see, and I have no interest in seeing it. I want to wrap the DVDs in the butcher paper, and return them to the shed, and never look at them, or think about them, again.

But I can't. Because I have to know Libby's secret.

The next DVD is worse. The same girl, the same room – even the same camera angle, but time has passed. Enough time for horrible things to have happened. The girl is no longer scared. There is little life left in her at all. She is catatonic. She's still strapped and taped to the bed. Though she is alive, and her eyes are open, and she breathes steadily, she does not move. Snot and blood and God knows what else are caked on her face. Her cheeks are bruised, her small breasts red

287

and swollen. The fair white skin I saw in the last video is pocked with black circles oozing puss. Cigarette burns, I somehow know.

The Russian speaks. 'Such a poor girl,' he says. He makes a *tsk-tsk* sound. 'Poor, poor, girl. If you had listened to us, she would be safe. She'd be in school, enjoying homework and dating, like we promised. But you do a bad job. We gave you instructions, and you failed. You are a stupid girl. He does not believe you. He does not trust you. You must do better. Next time, you will not like what you see.'

The Russian's prediction is terrifyingly accurate. The third and last video is the most disturbing thing I have ever seen. The girl is still alive – they've apparently made a point to keep her that way – something that couldn't have been easy. There's not much left of her, mentally or physically. She doesn't look like the pretty young girl of the first video. She looks hardly human at all. Within what was once her face, her eyes are white and bright and open, but they no longer seem to see.

The Russian, off-camera, says, 'Do you see what you've done? Do you know why we've hurt her? Because of you. All because of you. He still does not believe you. This is your last warning. Our next movie will have a new star. The star will be you.'

From behind me comes Libby's voice, startling me. 'What are you doing, Jimmy?' she asks.

I turn. She stands in the doorway of the foyer, clutching the wall for support. She is soaked with rain, her hair clumped in wet strings. She doesn't sound angry. Just exhausted. Maybe even relieved, that I've finally found it. 'You shouldn't have done this,' she says. 'You shouldn't have looked.'

'Who is that girl?' I say, pointing at the TV, as if there might be doubt about which girl I refer to; but the video has ended, and the screen is black.

'You don't understand,' she says. 'You don't understand what you've done.'

'Who is it?'

'Please, stop.'

'Who is it?'

'Jimmy—'

I yell: 'Who the fuck is it?'

She opens her mouth to answer, then stops. She looks at me, considering, and then turns and walks away.

I find her upstairs, in the bedroom. She is staring out of the window. 'I found the picture frame,' I tell her. 'I know that you work for Tad.'

She remains still, with her back to me, not turning, not speaking.

'Who was that girl?' I ask.

When she doesn't answer, I say gently – more gently than she deserves, 'Libby, please. Tell me. Who was she?'

She turns. Her skin is pale, thin like paper, and I see blue veins beneath her eyes. Her lips are pressed together. She looks cold. She answers, just a whisper, 'My daughter.'

'Your... *daughter*?' I shake my head. 'You don't have a daughter. You never had a—' I stop. 'You had a child before me.'

She says nothing.

'Why were they doing that to her?' I ask.

'It's a long story, Jimmy. And I don't think we have the time any more.'

'I have plenty of time.'

'No,' she says. 'No you don't.'

'Everything was a lie,' I say, as understanding dawns at last. 'Your past... everything you told me... it was all a lie. Am I right, Libby?' When I say her name, I think about that night in the restaurant, and the woman who insisted my wife was called something else. 'My God. Is that even your name? Libby?'

Her eyes move slowly across the room, as if inviting me to follow, and they stop at the ceiling fan. It spins lazily above us, churning the stagnant air.

'Tell me,' I say. 'Tell me what's going on. Maybe I can help you.'

'Help me?' She laughs. 'No, Jimmy, I'm quite sure you can't help me.'

'Who made those videos? They're blackmailing you. Why? What do they want?'

She stays silent, but it doesn't matter. I understand now. 'You don't work for Tad,' I say. 'You work for Ghol Gedrosian. You've always worked for him. Where is he? He's here, isn't he?'

She puts a finger to her lips. 'Shhh.' She whispers, so softly that I can barely hear the sound through the pelting rain on the roof. 'Don't say his name.'

'Where is he?' I ask, raising my voice. 'Where is Ghol Gedrosian?'

Silence.

'I trusted you. How long have you worked for him? How many years?'

She stares at me with a strange, inscrutable expression. What is it, exactly? Anger? Hatred? Fear?

No, I realize, with a creeping unease. No.

It's pity. She pities me.

'You still have no idea what they've done to you,' she says. 'Do you?'

'Why is he blackmailing you? What does he want?'

She walks to me and takes my hand. She leans very close. I feel her breath in my ear. It's our last moment of intimacy, I know, our last moment as husband and wife. She whispers, 'We have to leave here. If you want to live, we have to leave this house. Right now. You have to trust me.'

I shove her in the chest. She stumbles back. 'Trust you?' I shout. 'Get away from me!'

She looks disappointed in me and, for the first time... afraid. Her eyes flit to the ceiling fan.

There is something about that fan – something evil. It is like an eye – a lazy, leering, winking eye – taking in this sordid spectacle, this final conflict between man and wife, surely their last.

290

'What are you looking at?' I ask. 'Why do you keep looking—'
I stop.

I go to the nightstand, grab the first thing I see with any heft – a brass bookend, cast in the shape of an elephant head, the size of a brick – a knick-knack that was in the house when we arrived. I climb onto the bed, stand at the edge of the mattress, lean out to the fan.

'What are you doing?' she asks.

I swing the bookend with all my might against the centre of the fan. The plastic eye cracks open. The entire apparatus – teak blades, centre eye, metal mounts – is knocked from the braces in the ceiling. It drops three inches, snags on electrical wires, then hangs limp. White plaster dust rains down. I peer into the fan's centre. There is no mistaking what I see. In the middle, behind what used to be smoked plastic, a camera lens stares back at me, unblinking.

'What the fuck is going on?' I yell. I swing the bookend again. Wires snap. The fan crashes to the floor, leaving a fine cloud of white dust hanging in the air.

'It's him, isn't it?' I point accusingly out of the bedroom window, through the rain, at the dark house across the street. 'He's the one.'

'Jimmy, listen. Let me explain what's going on.'

'He's Ghol Gedrosian,' I say, finally understanding.

'No, Jimmy – You're wrong. Listen... We have to leave this house! They're coming. They hear you.'

I ignore her. I jump from the bed, push her roughly out of my way, and run from the room, gripping the heavy metal elephant in my hand.

She calls after me, 'Jimmy, don't do it! They'll kill you.'

I bound down the stairs, into the living room. Now, everywhere I look, I see hidden cameras. The grandfather clock in the corner of the room. How many times have Libby and I lain on that couch, directly in front of it?

I peer into the clock. The glass reflects my own face: dark circles under my eyes, wet hair, the bump of my broken nose. I see no camera, but instead see an insane man filled with rage. I lift the metal bookend and swing it at the clock face.

Glass shatters. A shard flies, missing my eye by an inch, nicks my cheek. Like a Saturday-morning cartoon, springs literally fly out of the clock. Then I see it: behind the clock hands, behind the warped metal facing, is the dark staring eye of a camera lens.

'Jimmy, listen to me.' Libby has appeared at the bottom of the stairs. She glances at the bookend in my hand. 'They're going to kill me, now. You've just signed my death warrant.'

'Who is going to kill you?'

'You know who.'

'Say his name.'

She shakes her head.

I march past her, into the foyer, and out of the front door. She yells behind me, 'Jimmy, no!'

I stomp onto the porch, and down into the rain.

I pass Libby's Mercedes, which she parked behind my Ford. It's askew, uneven in the driveway, parked in a hurry. She left the convertible soft-top open. Rain pours in. I keep walking. The water pelts my scalp and face and eyelids so hard that I can barely open them enough to see. I march in a straight line, through thunder and sheets of rain, and I cross the street. In the distance, a set of headlights cuts through the rain. I ignore them. I clomp across my neighbour's yard, my feet sinking ankle-deep into mud.

I climb his stairs, onto his porch. On the patio, at last I'm shielded from the storm. I pound the door with the metal bookend. The sound is loud and violent, a Gestapo knock at midnight. The metal leaves deep gouges in the wood.

'Let me in!' I shout. 'Let me in!'

The door opens. My velociraptor neighbour stands there, blocking the doorframe, looking at me curiously. He wears a wife-beater undershirt. Up close, he seems lean and toned, much more muscular than I remember, with the tapered torso of a professional athlete.

'Yes?' he says. 'May I help you?' His accent is Russian.

'I'm your neighbour, Jim Thane,' I say, not sounding particularly neighbourly. 'Let me the fuck in.' I shove him in the chest with my fist, which surprises him as much as me, and he stumbles back and away from the door, giving me entrance.

His house is a mirror image of mine – with his living room to the left of the foyer instead of to the right; and beyond it, a staircase spiralling up to the bedrooms.

I glance past the velociraptor. He seems tentative, maybe even afraid. I stare into his living room. I can't believe what I see.

In my version of the house – the one across the street, where I live – the living room is cluttered with: a couch, an entertainment centre, a TV, a grandfather clock in the corner, and a coffee table where I sometimes rest my can of Sprite and a crossword puzzle.

In this mirror-image house, the one owned by my neighbour who looks feral and carnivorous, the living room is filled with: audio visual equipment.

Just audio visual equipment.

Rows of it – electronics and machines – enough to fill a small recording studio. Because that is exactly what I am looking at. A recording studio. Consoles run along the edge of the room. Twelve large television monitors line the walls, all high-definition screens displaying different images.

'What the fuck—' I start, but don't get very far, because I stop speaking the instant I see the images on the screens.

They are images of me. And of Libby. And of our house.

Frozen on one monitor, paused perhaps so that it can be enjoyed, is the picture of Libby on her knees, giving me a blow job. I recall the night that happened – it was weeks ago – the strangeness of those events, the way the sex turned violent and mechanical, not at all erotic. On other monitors I see more recent images: a close-up of me – which I recognize as taken from the point of view of the grandfather clock, just minutes ago, right before I smashed it. On another screen, a running video, with a time-stamp ticking off seconds in the lower-right corner: infrared video of me searching our bedroom, from an hour before. On-screen, my ghostly green blur rummages through Libby's underwear drawer, then walks to the closet to continue the search.

I turn to the velociraptor, who is looking at me now with a strange expression, one of amused anticipation, as if he sincerely is interested in what my reaction to all this will be.

'Who are you?' I say. 'Are you Ghol Gedrosian?'

He laughs. 'Mr Thane, please. You have it all wrong. I can explain everything.'

'OK,' I say. 'Explain everything. Start by explaining this.' I wave my hand to indicate the screens. I grip the heavy brass bookend in my palm and step towards him. He doesn't flinch. He stares at me, very still, watchful but unafraid.

I hear something outside, through the open door. A bang, then a woman's scream. It's Libby. 'Jimmy, help!' she yells.

I run back into the foyer and out through the front door.

Behind me, the Russian is following, calmly saying, 'Mr Thane, please listen. This is all a very funny misunderstanding. I want to explain it to you before you get the wrong idea.'

I run from his porch, into the rain. Across the street, in my driveway, a set of high-beams cuts through the gloom. I see two dark figures pushing someone into a car. A muffled scream tells me it's Libby. I run across my neighbour's yard, towards my own house. At the edge of the yard, my shoe slips in the mud, and I slam down on my ass. Pain wracks my ribs. I sink deep into the wet dirt, and lie there, catching my breath. A rivulet of water sluices past, washing over my hands and legs. I scramble to my feet just as the tyres in my driveway spin, kicking out gravel, and then the car pulls away. I run towards it – an anonymous black sedan – but it speeds off, past me, just an arm's length away – and down the street.

'Stop!' I yell after the car. But it disappears into the rain.

'Mr Thane, please, come back inside,' the voice behind me calls. I turn to see the velociraptor. He's standing on his porch. I notice he's dressed now in a waterproof navy windbreaker. His right hand rests in the jacket pocket. 'There's been a terrible misunderstanding,' he calls, over the rain. 'And I would like to take the opportunity to explain exactly what is happening.'

He edges towards me as he speaks. He does so slowly, almost imperceptibly.

I look to my own house. The door is open, and the light from the foyer – yellow and welcoming – spills onto the porch. The velociraptor is coming closer, walking slowly down his stairs, into his yard. 'This is all very interesting, you see,' he says, 'I would like to explain it to you over a hot cup of coffee, yes? As neighbours, yes? Would you join me for some coffee, please?' His hand is in his windbreaker, but now he's close enough for me to see that there is too much bulk in that pocket to be explained by a hand alone.

I turn and run, across the street, my feet splashing ankle-high water, which is overflowing from storm sewers; then I run up the incline of my own yard. I glance over my shoulder, and I see the Russian break into a run after me. So much for conversation over coffee. I slip on the wet grass, hydroplaning, losing my footing. I am about to flip onto my ass for the second time. But at the last moment, I regain my balance, and keep stumbling forward. I run up the wooden steps of the porch, and into the house. I slam the door behind me, just as the Russian, racing after, reaches for it.

I bolt the lock. I lean my back against the door, catch my breath, then remember the bulky thing in the man's pocket. I edge away from the centre of the door.

But the knock, when it comes, is gentle – almost neighbourly. The man shouts through the wood, 'Mr Thane, I'm not going to hurt you. I just want to talk to you, OK? You have my word as a gentleman.'

I look around the foyer. Libby's wet car keys lie on the side table. I pick them up and slide them into my pocket.

'Mr Thane,' comes the voice through the door. 'Let's sit down and have a drink together, yes?'

'Go away,' I shout through the door. 'I don't want a drink. Just leave me alone.'

I know that I am safe as long as the Russian is on the other side of this thick door, and as long as I can hear his voice, and as long as I know exactly where he is.

'Just go away!' I shout again.

No answer this time.

I step to the door and look through the peephole. The porch is empty. The Russian is gone.

I take a quick inventory of the downstairs. In the kitchen, I see windows, securely closed and locked. But in the living room, the patio door is slightly ajar. I make a dash for it, across the foyer, into the living room, and past the couch. I grab the door handle and shove it closed. The tiny lock clicks. Outside, a flash of lightning illuminates the sky, and lights up the Russian, standing just inches from me, on the other side of the glass. His fingers are on the door handle. He tugs at it. 'Please, Mr Thane,' he says, his voice muffled by the glass, 'let me in.'

I see another shadowy figure moving around in the vegetable garden. And there's a third man, on the other side of the house, marching past the kitchen window. At least three of them – maybe more – only moments away from swarming into the lower floor of the house.

I run back to the foyer. As I pass the front door, I see the knob jiggling. I race up the stairs and into the bedroom and slam the door. My fingers flit across the knob, searching for the lock. But there is no lock.

Voices in the foyer below. 'He's upstairs,' someone says. 'In the bedroom.'

How the hell did they know that so fast, I wonder. I look around the room. The ceiling fan has been smashed and probably no longer works, but I see at least two other suspicious objects. The clock radio on Libby's nightstand – weirdly bulky, with a Chinese-sounding brand name I am unfamiliar with. A bookshelf, filled with books – any of which could house a camera, or a microphone. I grab the telephone from the cradle on the bureau. My fingers, wet with rain, jam the keypad. I bang out 9-1-1.

On the line, there's a ring, a click, and a voice. Male. With a Russian accent. 'Mr Thane, please listen to us. We're coming into the room now. We don't want you to get hurt—'

I slam the phone and back away, as if the Russians might reach through the receiver to grab me. But it turns out that there is no need for this bit of magic, because they can do it the old-fashioned way. Like this: the doorknob is turning, and the bedroom door is opening.

I run to the veranda door and tug the sliding glass. The door is heavy, and sticks in the track, and I open it just enough to squeeze through. On the patio, in the rain, I pull the door closed. I peer through the rain-slicked glass into the bedroom. Two men trudge past the bed, looking around.

The veranda on which I stand is tiny – just space enough for two sun loungers and a small glass table. Twenty feet below are flagstones and the pool. No escape.

'Over here,' one of the Russians says, and I see him on the other side of the glass, pointing calmly at me, as if he's talking to a colleague about a Manila folder he misplaced on his desk.

The Russians start towards me. They're both large, muscular, bursting out of wet jeans and T-shirts. The bigger one slides the patio door open three inches, puts his fingers through the opening, and wraps them around the edge of the door.

'Mr Thane—' he starts.

With all my strength, I grab the door and wrench it shut. The heavy frame slams on his fingers, and I hear a sickening wet crunch, and he screams.

297

I scramble up onto the balustrade, my shoes scuffing wet cement – slippery from rain – and I stand straight, precariously balancing on the edge, twenty inches above the patio behind me, and twenty feet above the flagstones in front. Rain falls from the sky, and the water blurs my vision, and I can barely see what I am about to do. Which is probably for the best.

I dive.

A long, graceful dive, arms extended, feet rising above my head – beautiful, probably.

A splash, and chlorine floods my nose, burning; and my fingers scrape concrete, and I jam my knuckles into the pool floor so hard that maybe I've broken my hand, but then I come up for air, and stand up straight, quite alive and not crippled.

I bound along the pool floor, my clothes weighing me down like armour, and I vault over the edge of the pool and onto the patio.

'He's down there,' a voice above me shouts. I look up to see a Russian leaning over the balustrade, daintily. He's muscular, and wily, and physically fit – a natural predator. But he's not suicidal. He merely bends over the railing, looking down. 'Alexi!' he calls out – probably to the velociraptor, still somewhere on the ground floor nearby – 'He's in the back, near the pool!'

I scamper through the gate, to the side of the house, and towards Libby's Mercedes, its convertible roof open, welcoming the rain.

'I see him!' a voice shouts behind me. I hear footsteps clomping on wet gravel, and heavy breathing, and grunts.

I run. My wet clothes and saturated shoes slow me down, and my ribs hurt, and it feels as if I'm running through molasses. It's like something from a nightmare – running as hard as I can, but slowly nevertheless – and behind me, I hear ragged breathing and heavy footsteps, getting closer. Closer.

I expect to feel a hand on my shoulder, someone grabbing my wet shirt, whipping me down to the ground. I wrench the Mercedes door open, heave my body into the seat, shove the key into the ignition, and turn it.

I have never loved Germans so much as I do at this moment. All that unpleasantness between 1914 and 1945? – I am willing to overlook that now. No nation is perfect, and, damn, can they build a car. It starts with a purr, despite the fact that the seats, and dashboard, and carpets are soaked, and despite the fact that the floor sits beneath an inch of water, like some exotic aquarium in the lobby of a Las Vegas hotel.

The engine roars to life, and I press the gas, and the tyres spin, and the car shoots back down the driveway just as the Russian reaches for my car door. I look down to see the velociraptor's big hand resting on the door frame, mere inches from my shoulder. It's a moment of strange frozen intimacy – that instant before he lifts his hand and I speed away. But during this moment, I look down at his fingers, and see something odd – that he is missing the last joint of his pinky. It's a red stub, just like mine.

The Russian lifts his palm, and he raises his hand and shouts after me, 'Wait, wait, Mr Thane! Please come here!' – ludicrously, as if I might stop the car, and turn around, and say, 'Oh, did you want to talk to me about something?'

A second Russian runs towards the first, and stops short beside him. There the two of them stand, next to each other, staring after me. My car bangs down into the street, metal scraping asphalt. I wrench the wheel, put it into drive, and floor it. The tyres spin, and I ease off, and then the rubber catches, and the car speeds down the road.

Even though no one follows, I keep going, merging from one rain-slicked suburban road to another, and then onto the highway. I refuse to slow down. I refuse to stop. I just keep going, convinced that motion, any motion, is safer than standing still.

CHAPTER 39

Something is wrong.

It takes ten minutes for the adrenaline buzz to fade. Then another five to understand what bothers me.

No one is following. No one even tried.

They just watched me career out of the driveway, and I saw them in the rearview mirror, two big Russians standing in the rain, very still, next to each other, staring after my tail lights – like a married couple watching their youngest son drive off to college for the first time.

Now, with time and distance between us, I understand why that image of two Russians standing motionless and merely watching me go feels so wrong.

These are men who bugged my house, who inserted listening devices into my office, who spied on my phone calls, who put cameras in my bedroom. Would they allow me to drive away without bothering to pursue?

No. They do not follow me because they do not need to. They have no fear of losing track of me. They know exactly where I am. Even now, they watch me. Perhaps I am a green dot flashing on a computer map, or a phosphorescent arrow blinking on a GPS.

They'll watch me go, and when I stop moving, they'll come and retrieve me.

I dig my cellphone out of my pants pocket. Steering with my left hand, I press the power with my right. The phone stays dark; it died when I jumped in the pool. But that doesn't mean the thing they put inside is dead too.

I toss the phone over my shoulder, and watch in the rearview mirror as it skitters across pavement, cartwheeling and breaking into pieces.

Now, for the car itself.

I can't just park it. They'll see little blinking Jimmy Thane has stopped moving. They'll come and get me then.

What I have to do: I have to ditch the car, but somehow make sure that it keeps moving. Visions come to me now – preposterous visions, born of a million implausible movies: a brick carefully placed on the accelerator, me jumping from the moving car, the Mercedes continuing its driverless progress, through the streets of downtown Fort Myers.

But no. Of course not.

I'm on Cleveland Avenue now, heading north. I see a sign for the Greyhound terminus. Which gives me a better idea.

The rain is tapering now, changing from apocalyptic to drizzle. I head downtown, following the signs to the Greyhound. Some of the hardier drunks have ventured back to the street. Two watch me drive by from below the awning of a liquor store. Only weeks ago, I would have looked at them, standing there in the rain, with pity. Now they stare at me, curious, the roof of my convertible open in a rainstorm, my hair dripping. Who's pitying whom?

The Greyhound terminus is like every other bus station I've ever seen. It's in the wrong part of town: the part that no one wants to come to, the part that no one can afford to leave. The building is large, probably empty, with an angular cantilevered roof protruding over a warehouse-like interior. Three Hispanic men sit out front, crowding under the overhang to keep dry. I stop the Mercedes in front of them, in the passenger drop-off circle.

'Hey, *chico*,' I shout.

The three of them look up at me. The one who's probably their leader – head shaved like Mr Clean, tats running down his arms like inky cobwebs, a mesh shirt revealing muscled guns – tilts his head and cracks his neck. He pauses, insect-like, as he evaluates whether I'm predator or prey. I feel sympathy for him, because surely it can't be easy to know: a white guy, out of shape, in an Oxford button-down shirt and chinos, driving a car worth more than all the crack he's ever smoked; but then again, my convertible top is down during a thunderstorm, and my clothes are soaked, and here I am in the middle of downtown, probably at the tail end of a binge that didn't start very well, and likely won't end any better.

'Yeah, you,' I call. 'Come here.'

Maybe he's not used to being spoken to in this way. He exchanges a can-you-believe-this-guy look with his two buddies, then slowly gets up from the ground. He sidles over to my car, his body turned in profile, maybe to present a smaller target, should I whip out a gun and prove to be as insane as I look.

'Yeah?' he says, suspiciously. He keeps a three-foot distance.

'When's the next bus out of here?'

'What do I look like, asshole, a fucking schedule? How the fuck should I know?'

'I need to get to a very important meeting,' I say. I stick the car into park. 'I'll be gone for a few hours. Do me a favour. Park my car, and keep an eye on it for me. I'll give you a hundred bucks for your time.'

I pop my door and get out. I toss him the keys. He catches them with a surprised swipe. He looks down at his hand, can't believe what he's holding.

'I can trust you,' I say, 'right?'

In my wallet, I find five twenties, water-logged, but serviceable, and hold them out, across the car.

He takes them. He glances back at his friends, who smile at him and nod. He says to me, 'Yeah, sure, homey. You can trust me.'

'You have an honest face,' I explain. 'Just find a safe spot to park it. I hear this isn't the best neighbourhood.'

'No, man, it's OK,' he says, suddenly sounding like a real-estate agent. 'It has good and bad, like every place else.'

'Right on, *hermano*,' I say. 'I'll be a few hours. You'll be here when I get back, right?'

'Sure,' he says. 'Sure I will.'

Sitting by the entrance, his friends laugh.

'*Hasta la vista*,' I say.

For the first time since I arrived in this godforsaken state, luck is with me, because a taxi pulls up in the drop-off circle, just yards away. I hold open the door of the cab for a young European-looking man, too pale to be native, clutching a metal-framed backpack, and a *Lonely Planet: Florida* guidebook in his hand. 'When is train next to Fort Lauderdale?' he asks me in an almost impenetrable accent.

'You're in luck,' I say. 'Right now. But you better hurry.'

He hands the driver crumpled cash and scurries off without bothering with change.

I slide into the taxi he just vacated and pull the door shut.

The Haitian driver, glistening with sweat and wafting Technicolor BO, turns to me. 'Where to, mister?'

I realize I have no idea where to. My house is bugged. My wife has been kidnapped. Russian gangsters chase me.

Probably I should go to the police. But not yet. Not until I figure out what's going on, and what to do next.

'Where to, mister?' the Haitian asks again, with growing impatience.

'You know Fort Myers Beach?' I ask.

When he snarls yes, of course he does, but do I have money for the trip, I show him a wad of wet twenties and direct him to Amanda's apartment.

CHAPTER 40

When I arrive, Amanda is not home.

In the covered walkway of her apartment building, I lie down on her doorstep, exhausted and cold. I fall asleep. I wake to the sound of footsteps scuffing up the stairs, and then tinkling keys, and Amanda is standing over me, looking not particularly surprised to see me – as if it's perfectly reasonable to arrive home to find your boss curled in a foetal position at your door.

'Jim,' she says, 'why are you lying on the ground?'

'No couch.'

She kneels down and takes my hand. Her voice is gentle. 'Come inside.' She helps me to my feet. She unlocks the door and shoves it with her shoulder. Inside, the room is freezing, the way she likes it, the air conditioner churning in the window.

She deposits me onto the couch, where I collapse into the cushions. 'Jesus, it's cold,' I mutter.

'I'll turn it off.'

She goes to the air conditioner and turns it off. The room is suddenly quiet and still.

'Lock the door,' I say.

'Yes, all right,' she says, in that agreeable tone one reserves for the agitated or the mentally ill. She goes to the door, secures the lock, and returns to me on the couch. She touches my shoulder. 'Why are you so wet, Jim?'

'I need a place to stay, Amanda.'

'Yes, of course.'

'Something happened to Libby.'

'Libby?' Then she remembers. 'Ah, your wife. What happened?'

'She was kidnapped.'

'Kidnapped?' I see the first glimmer of doubt in her eyes. 'Jim, I don't understand. Who... *kidnapped* your wife?' She stumbles over the word *kidnapped*, as if she can't bring herself to say it.

I take her hand. 'Listen. There's something I need to tell you.'

She lets me hold her fingers, but they stay limp. Uncommitted.

'Tao Software is a front,' I say. 'It's being used by a mobster. He's laundering drug money. He's taking cash from one place, and then he's...'

Here I stop. Now that I try to explain it, I realize I have no idea what I'm talking about. What exactly *are* the Russians trying to do? I can't construct any conceivable narrative – financial, legal, logistical – which makes any sense, which explains what the Russians are doing at Tao. Laundering money? Selling drugs? Neither is true, so far as I can see. So then what are they doing? Why is the Russian named Ghol Gedrosian involved in my company? What does he want?

After a long silence, I conclude lamely, 'Well, the point is, Libby is working for them. She's working for gangsters.'

'I see,' Amanda says. But she doesn't see. She sounds nervous. Her eyes dart to the door, measuring the distance to escape. I realize, too late, that she wonders if I harmed Libby. She wonders if I killed her.

'Amanda,' I say, letting go of her hand. 'I didn't hurt my wife, if that's what you're thinking. There's a man. A criminal. He's a Russian. He killed Charles Adams, and he killed Dom Vanderbeek. He's framing me. He's making it look like I've done these things. I'm not sure why. His name is Ghol Gedrosian. I don't know why he's —'

But I stop. Amanda has become very white.

'You know that name,' I say.

'Yes,' she whispers.

'How?'

'He was the one.'

'The one?' But even as I say it, I know. He was the man who took Amanda when she was a child. The man who imprisoned her, who brought her to this country. The man who did unspeakable things to her.

'He was the one,' she says again.

She looks at my hand. She takes it in hers, and stares. 'Look.'

She places her hand on top of mine.

She has only nine fingers. Her pinky is missing. What remains is a grotesque red stub, scarred and mutilated, just like my own.

CHAPTER 41

She has made hot tea for me, and I cup the ceramic mug in my palms, and I notice that my hands still shake.

She sits beside me on the couch. She has changed clothes. Gone is her daytime attire, replaced with a soft linen shirt and pair of worn jeans. The barrette that kept her hair in a severe bun has disappeared, and her long copper tresses sit loose on her shoulders. Her make-up is gone, too, and her face is scrubbed. She looks older now. But somehow prettier.

'I will tell you what I know,' she says. 'Some people say he is ex-KGB. Others say that he was a colonel in the army – the unit that interrogated prisoners in Chechnya. I've heard other stories too, very strange stories.'

'Like what?'

'That he's religious. That he thinks he's god. Or maybe he's insane.'

'What does he look like?'

'I never saw him. No one does. The men who took me – they never saw him. They worked for someone else, who worked for someone else, who worked for someone else still.'

She holds up the stub of her pinky. 'This is how he marks property. Anyone who works for him, or who owes him money, or who receives a favour – he takes their finger. He keeps it somewhere. It's like marking cattle.'

She touches my mutilated finger. I pull it away. 'No,' I say. 'This is not the same. Mine was done by a bookie. I owed money to a guy. His name was Hector. It happened years ago.'

I stare at my missing finger. Now that I think about it, I'm not so sure. I don't actually remember *what* happened that night. Libby told me a story about coming home with a bloody dish towel wrapped around my hand, and insisting that she drive me to Jack in the Box for a hamburger. But I don't remember it. Did it really happen like that?

'You don't remember,' Amanda says.

'No.'

She nudges closer to me. 'You're shivering, Jim. Come here.' She leads me from the couch, into the bathroom. The sink and counter are filled with feminine bottles – shampoos and rinses and facial scrubs. 'I will tell you what to do. You need a hot shower,' she says. 'You smell very bad. You'll feel better.' She leans into the shower, turns the knobs, adjusts the temperature, still holding my hand lightly, so that I can't escape. 'There,' she says, satisfied with the temperature. She slides the sanded glass door. 'Go in. I'll find some dry clothes for you.'

She disappears from the bathroom, closing the door softly behind her.

I undress and step into the shower. I let the warm water pelt my back, my neck, my bruised ribs, my scalp. I close my eyes. I think about what to do next. I'll call the police. I'll talk to Agent Mitchell. I'll find Libby. I'll accept the consequences, whatever they are, and fight whatever crime they accuse me of. I'm innocent, of everything, except stupidity.

The shower door slides open, and Amanda steps inside, naked. She presses up behind me, and her arms reach around my chest. She pulls me tightly. It hurts. I feel her breasts on my back, her rough pubic hair, her toes pressing against the edge of my feet.

'What are you doing?' I say.

She doesn't answer. Instead, she guides my shoulders, and turns me to face her. She pulls my head down, kisses me. I taste her, and the warm water, and her perfume, washing from her skin. 'You see?' she says, when she breaks off the kiss. 'We are meant to be together. This is what he intended.'

'*Who* intended? Jesus?'

'No, silly,' she whispers. She takes the stub of my half-pinky, presses it against her own, closes her hand around both, and squeezes. 'You see? We're his. He owns us both.'

'What are you talking about?'

'*He* wanted this. That's why he led us here, together. That's why he let me go. It's no accident. This is what he wanted.'

I want to tell her that she's crazy, but then she presses up against me, and slides me inside her, and so I shut up for about five minutes, which is all the time I need.

CHAPTER 42

The drugs come next.

I suppose I should be surprised, that a girl who found Jesus in a church basement, who tattooed Cyrillic on her breast that He died for her sins, who protested too much that her life had changed after she found Him – I suppose I should be surprised when she brings out a glass pipe and a butane lighter from the shelf in her closet, and when she leads me to her bedroom, and when she starts the music playing on her computer, and says, 'Can we do it, just once?'

There is no *just once* for people like me and Amanda. There is never a last time that you use. There are only pauses, and lulls, and intermissions. That is why restarting is always easy: because using is as much a part of life as quitting. To the addict, these are not opposite poles of existence – quitting versus using, good versus bad – but rather different outward expressions of the same single inner truth. Using, quitting. High, straight. It's all the same – just an open field upon which we dance and play.

Amanda lights a row of honeycomb beeswax candles on the bureau near her bed, and turns off the overhead lamp. The room is dark except for the soft golden circles of candlelight.

For the first time, I realize that she's beautiful, and that I love her. Her age has always been a mystery to me, since the first day I saw her. It depended on the lighting, her clothing, her make-up, the angle at which she was viewed. Sometimes she looked weary, her eyes ancient;

and other times she was sexy, and knowing, and cunning – a worn girl who'd seen it all, who couldn't be surprised, and who would try anything once.

Tonight, in the candlelight, flushed from sex just finished, anticipating a rush about to begin, she is timeless, glowing, her face alive with anticipation, her body taut, thrumming like a bowstring.

She unwraps a tiny wad of toilet paper, revealing flakes of yellow crystal that look like salt, and she taps them into the pipe. She holds the pipe gingerly, expertly, along its fluted glass neck. She flicks the butane lighter and holds the flame underneath for almost a minute. Inside the glass bulb, a crackling sound, and white smoke swirls. She hands the pipe to me. When I take it, the glass burns my fingertips, but I don't flinch. I put the mouthpiece to my lips, and breathe.

I cough, a chemical cough, and mutter: 'Oh fuck yes, fuck yes, fuck yes.'

There are no words for this. It's bliss. It's what you feel when you're a child, in your mother's arms, and I think it's probably what you feel the moment you die, when you decide it's OK to rest at last. It's peace, the feeling that it's all right, that the world can go on just fine without you.

How long has it been since I've felt this way? Years?

The weight lifts. The concerns about career and marriage, about Libby's safety, even about the Russian mob and Ghol Gedrosian – they flit away like glassy-winged insects into moonlight, barely visible for a moment, twinkling reflections, and then gone.

The pleasure surges, liquid, through me. It's an orgasm that never stops.

Amanda takes the pipe from my hands and brings it to her own mouth. I watch her eyes, the way her pupils grow into black buttons, like a doll's, and she slumps over sideways, still holding the hot glass in her fingers, not noticing the pain.

'Oh Jesus,' she says, and I'm not sure if she's moaning or invoking.

She leans over and kisses me. Her tongue and mouth taste chemical and hot, day-old menthol.

The one thing about crystal meth – the most important thing – is that you want to fuck. It's the only thing you can do well while on the drug, and the only thing you desire.

I remember the first time I tried meth. I was alone in a hotel, on a business trip away from Libby. I lit up, and breathed in, and then I couldn't stop having orgasms. It was like a switch had been tripped, and stuck in the on position. I opened my notebook computer, and I pulled up a pornography site, and I played a movie, and I jerked off in about a minute. Then I hit the refresh button on my computer, and watched the same movie again, and came again; and then I did it a third time, and a fourth.

That's meth. That's what it does. It's one giant orgasm crashing over you, again and again, and you can't stop coming. You want to know why people do crank, even though it destroys them? Next time you come, imagine making it feel ten times as good. Now, imagine making it last for three hours. Now you know.

Lying with Amanda in her apartment, on her bed, the idea of time, of relentless forward motion, disappears. It is replaced by ebbs and flows of pleasure. When I become aware again, maybe minutes later, maybe hours, Amanda is sitting beside me on the mattress. She is naked, and her hair is wet from sweat. She is using the long metal clasp of her barrette to scrape the inside of her pipe, to brush the residue baked onto the glass into a tiny pile of powder. She lights the pipe again. This time, all courtesy is gone, and she puts the pipe to her own mouth first, and inhales greedily. I see her orgasm. Her body shudders, again and again, without end, and she says, 'Oh Jesus Jesus Jesus.'

When it subsides, I take the pipe from her, and I suck. And then I'm gone, too, and I don't know what happens next, until I wake up hours later, naked, in her bed, in her arms.

CHAPTER 43

In the morning, when the sunlight wakes me, she is gone from the bed, and I find her in the tiny galley kitchen, frying bacon in a pan.

'I called work,' she says cheerily, 'and told them I'd be in late. Do you think my boss will mind?'

'Not if you share your bacon with him.'

I walk to her. I'm naked. She's wearing a white T-shirt and boxer shorts. She looks tired, with dark circles under her eyes. I probably don't look much better. My mouth tastes like garbage; my head burns like a roadside flare.

'What will you do?' she asks. When she sees my blank expression, she says, 'About your wife.'

It comes back to me: the rainstorm, the listening devices and cameras in my office and house, the Russians across the street, Libby's scream, the black sedan racing away, with Libby inside.

'I need to go to the police.'

'Yes,' she says, stiffly.

'You don't agree?'

She shrugs. 'Maybe you should,' she says, in a way that suggests that maybe I shouldn't.

I squeeze into the galley kitchen beside her. I'm not sure about our level of intimacy. Last night we fucked ten times and did crystal meth, but this morning I don't know if I'm allowed to touch her shoulder.

'What's wrong?' I ask, brushing the back of her neck with my fingers. I am relieved that she doesn't flinch. She presses close to me and pushes her breasts against my chest.

'I just want you to be careful. You don't know him the way I do.'

'I thought you said that no one knows him.'

'Of course, you're right. But still. I've heard stories. Terrible stories.' She turns away.

I think about pressing the point, asking what she does know about him, but isn't telling me. But I don't. I ask, 'Can I use your phone?'

She goes to the living room and finds her purse. She takes her cellphone and brings it to me.

From my wallet I retrieve Agent Mitchell's business card, still damp and waterlogged, but legible. I dial, and I am surprised that he answers directly.

'It's Jim Thane,' I say.

'Mr Thane,' he says, sounding relieved. 'Where the hell are you?'

'I'm staying at a friend's house,' I say. And then: 'I need your help, Agent Mitchell. Something happened.'

'What's wrong?'

'It's my wife. Gedrosian took her.'

'Gedrosian?' He sounds incredulous. 'He… *took* her?'

'His men. Not him… ' I say, as if this makes my words sound less improbable. 'They live in the house across the street. He's been spying on me – watching me – ever since I came to Florida.'

There's a noise on the other end of the line – a sudden breath. Is he laughing?

'Mr Thane, let me get this straight. Ghol Gedrosian lives across the street from you. All this time that I've been searching for him, trudging across thirteen states, and forty-six counties, with a task force of a dozen men – all this time, you boys have been next-door neighbours, borrowing sugar from each other.'

'No,' I say.

'And he came over and – what was it? – kidnapped your wife?'

'No,' I say, again. 'No. That's not what I'm saying. He wasn't the one that kidnapped my wife. Not personally. His men did it.'

'I see. He asked his men to kidnap your wife,' he says.

'Yes. And I can show you.'

'Can you?' he says. 'All right, then.'

'Meet me at my house.'

'I'll be there in an hour.'

I wolf down three slices of bacon. Amanda gives me a granola oatmeal bar, which I shove into my mouth, hoping it will tamp down the pounding in my head. It doesn't. It's like the bad old days, all over again. Now I remember: that feeling you have, after you use, how you start thinking about crank every second – how you need it, just to make yourself feel normal. It's not like heroin, or Percocet, where you have a leisurely week or two to decide whether you're fully committed to the addict lifestyle, where you can quit after a few benders, achy but still sober.

No, meth is different. It's in your face, demanding. It's like a jealous girlfriend, a crazed lover. It requires your full, undivided attention. It wants commitment. *Now.*

'Jim,' Amanda says. She had disappeared from the kitchen, and now has returned, cradling something in her hands, gently, like a fragile baby bird. 'Take this.'

I look down. It's a pistol. It's black and angular, with the profile of a wasp.

'What is it?' I ask.

'It's a gun, stupid. You use it to shoot people.'

'I don't use guns to shoot people.'

'You don't know who you're dealing with. Look.'

She holds it out in front of us, muzzle pointing away. 'This is the safety,' she explains, touching a black lever on the side of the grip. 'Push it down with your thumb before you shoot.'

'I won't be doing any shooting.'

'There's a round in the chamber,' she says, ignoring me. 'All you need to do is flip the safety and pull the trigger. You understand?'

'Amanda—'

'Safety off, then shoot,' she says.

'Amanda—'

'Take it.' She pushes it into my hands. I take it. I'm surprised by how heavy it is.

'Where did you get a gun?'

'From a friend,' she says. 'For protection.'

'In case he comes for you.'

'Not "in case". *When*.'

I put the gun into my pocket. It fits snugly, and feels heavy on my thigh. 'I won't be long,' I say. 'Just stay here. Wait for me.'

I kiss her primly on the cheek, the way you kiss an aunt. When I pull away, she reaches out, puts her hand behind my head, and reels me back in. She kisses me, open-mouthed, holding me tight and hard. It's a desperate, crazed kiss – the kiss of a woman who'll never see you again. Not exactly reassuring.

'You're freaking me out a little,' I admit, when I extract myself from her.

'Take this too,' she says, and hands me her cell. 'If there's any trouble, call me.'

'I'm just going to talk to the police, Amanda. The *police*. They're the good guys.'

'Yes,' she says. 'I know.'

CHAPTER 44

I take Amanda's cabriolet and drive it to my house. I park at the foot of my driveway.

The last time I was here, torrential rain poured from the dark sky, my wife was shoved into a car, and I barely escaped from Russian thugs by diving head-first from a first-floor window. This morning, the yard is bright and sunny, the house immaculate. It looks like any other happy suburban house – ready for children and lawn croquet and freshly-baked cookies on the kitchen windowsill.

Agent Mitchell hasn't arrived. Which means there's still time to make the phone call I have delayed making for as long as I possibly could.

I dial the number from memory. When Gordon Kramer answers, I say, 'Gordon, it's Jimmy.'

'What's wrong?' he snarls, by way of greeting. 'A phone call from Jimmy Thane at eight in the morning. That means you need to make bail. How much?'

'No bail,' I say.

'Are you drunk?'

'No.'

'High?'

'No, Gordon.' Which is technically true. *Technically*. As in: not high at this particular moment.

'Do I need to buy a plane ticket and come get you?'

'No,' I say. 'No. It's not that. It's something else.'

'I'm listening.'

'It's... police stuff.'

'Police stuff?' he repeats. He doesn't like the sound of that. It's as if I said, *ballerina stuff.* 'What does that mean, "police stuff"?'

'Gordon, I'm about to tell you something. I just need you to listen. Promise to hear me out. Promise you'll let me explain everything.'

'All right.'

'You promise that you'll listen? You'll let me finish?'

'I promise.'

'All right.' I take a deep breath. 'The company that hired me... it's really a front for a Russian mobster. It's run by a meth dealer—'

'Goddamn it, Jimmy!' Gordon yells. 'You son of a bitch! You're using!'

'You promised you'd let me finish.'

'I lied, motherfucker. Just like you lied when you told me you'd stay clean.'

'I *am* clean,' I say. 'Will you just listen? Please, Gordon. Let me finish.'

'Finish.'

'The Russian is named Ghol Gedrosian. Have you heard of him?'

'What's his name?'

'Ghol Gedrosian,' I repeat.

'No. Never.'

'He's stealing cash from the company. He's paying me to look the other way. He's blackmailing Libby. He's making her keep tabs on me. He put bugs in our house.'

'He put what?'

'Bugs, Gordon. Listening devices. Cameras. They've been watching me. They're spying. They're—'

'Jimmy,' he says, cutting me off. 'Jimmy, I have to be honest with you. This conversation – it's not exactly reassuring. This is not what I call a reassuring conversation.'

'He took Libby, Gordon.'

'Took Libby?'

'Kidnapped.'

'Aw, fuck you, Jimmy,' he says, but very quietly. He sounds sad. Disappointed. 'You're high.'

'No,' I say. 'What I'm telling you is real. I'm about to meet with the FBI. There's an agent here, who's looking for Gedrosian. He's in the Special Crimes Unit, out of Tampa. You can look him up. He knows all about Ghol Gedrosian. He'll vouch for me. His name is Tom Mitchell.'

I look across the street. 'Here he is now,' I say. In fact, I would have lied to Gordon, and merely pretended that Tom Mitchell had arrived, so that I could end this conversation; but Agent Mitchell's Chevy Impala really does pull up on the other side of the road. He is alone in the car. When he sees me, he waves through his window. 'I have to go, Gordon. Just do me a favour.'

'What, Jimmy?'

'Find out everything you can about this Ghol Gedrosian. I need to know who I'm up against.'

'Jimmy...'

'Please, Gordon. Just this once... trust me.'

There's a knock on my car window. Agent Mitchell stands outside my door.

'Yeah, all right,' Gordon says, and sighs. He doesn't sound very trusting. 'Jimmy, why do I have a feeling this isn't going to end well for you?'

'Because it never does, Gordon.'

'No,' he agrees. 'It never does.'

'Call me at this number,' I say. 'My other cellphone was... Well, I had to get rid of it.'

He laughs. He thinks that my other cellphone was sold. Or exchanged. For yellow crystals in a plastic baggie.

'Yeah, all right, Jimmy,' he says. 'Whatever.' He hangs up.

'Jesus, Mr Thane,' the FBI man says, when I step out of the car. 'You look like shit.'

'Do I?' I touch my face. 'I guess what they say is true. Bingeing on crystal meth isn't good for your complexion.'

'I'm glad you still have that sense of humour,' he says. 'I thought you might have lost it.'

He offers his hand, and we shake. He continues, 'Now then, tell me about your wife.'

'They took her.'

'Who did?'

I point to the house across the street, where the Russians set up their All-Jimmy-Thane-Twenty-Four-Hour-A-Day TV channel. The driveway is empty, the curtains drawn. There is no light in the windows. 'They've been spying on me. They put cameras in my house. They've been watching me and Libby ever since we moved to Florida.'

Mitchell tilts his head and stares at me. He looks wary. Is this a joke designed to make him look foolish? 'Watching you?' he repeats.

'I'll show you.'

I lead him to the front of my house. The door is unlocked. I push it open and we enter. The foyer is cool and dark.

'Look,' I say, directing him into the living room. 'The grandfather clock, it's really—'

But in the living room, the grandfather clock, which I last saw shattered and broken, is gone. There are no springs or shards of glass or warped metal on the floor. There's just a small indentation in the carpet, barely visible, the shape of the clock's base.

'It was right here,' I say.

'What was, Mr Thane?'

I do not answer. I run up the stairs into the bedroom. The ceiling fan is gone, too: no longer on the floor, where I left it. The plaster above the bed has been repaired – touched up, painted, perfectly dry.

'Mr Thane?' Mitchell asks, from behind me. I turn to see him in the doorway, holding out a piece of paper. 'Is this what you're looking for?'

He hands it to me. It's a single sheet, from the magnetic pad that Libby stuck on the refrigerator. It's a picture of a cartoon bear, jumping into the air, trying to grab a beehive dripping with honey, but not quite reaching it. Below the picture is printed: 'If at first you don't succeed, bear with it and try again.'

Below this inspirational message is a woman's handwriting.

Jimmy –
I've had enough. I can't live with your violence any more. First Cole.
Now this. You scare the hell out of me. I need some time alone.
Don't come after me. I'll find you when I'm ready

Mitchell explains, 'It was on the kitchen counter. That her handwriting?'

'Yes,' I say. 'But she didn't write it. They took her. I saw them.'

'Who took her?'

'The Russians.'

'Who's Cole, Mr Thane?'

'My son.'

'You have a son?'

'No,' I say. Then: 'You don't believe me.'

No answer.

I say, 'I'll show you their house. Come with me. You'll see for yourself.' Even as I say it, though, I'm losing confidence. I know exactly what we will find in the Russians' house.

But I lead him downstairs, and through the foyer, and back into the blast-furnace heat. I walk through the front yard, and across the street, to the velociraptor's house.

'Where are we going, Mr Thane?' Mitchell calls out behind me.

'Trust me,' I say, trying to sound confident.

I wait for the agent to join me on the Russians' porch. He walks slowly, looking uncomfortable and wary.

I knock at the Russians' door. There is no answer.

'Let's go inside,' I say.

'Now, listen, Mr Thane, I can't just walk into someone's house—'

I turn the doorknob. The door opens easily, gliding on its well-oiled hinges, revealing a dark empty foyer. There is no furniture in the room.

Mitchell peers through the open door. 'Looks empty.'

I go inside. The room is warm. No air conditioning. Mitchell remains at the threshold, considering. Then he shrugs and follows. The foyer, and every room visible from it, is empty. No furniture. No sign of habitation at all. No Russians. No Libby.

'They lived here,' I insist.

'Who did, Mr Thane?'

'Ghol Gedrosian's men.'

He arches his eyebrows dramatically. 'Ghol Gedrosian's men? They all lived together? In this house? Sort of like a college fraternity?' His voice is full of mirth. 'Why on earth would they do that?'

'To watch me.'

'To watch you?'

I walk to the living room, where just yesterday I saw banks of recording equipment and rows of flat-screen televisions on the wall. 'See?' I say. I point to the wall, triumphantly, where there are still unmistakable signs of screw holes in the plaster, at the exact level where the televisions were mounted.

'See *what*?'

'The holes. That's where they put the TV monitors.'

'Mr Thane, I think we ought to leave here. First of all, I don't have a warrant, and second of all... ' He shrugs. 'Well, second of all, it's goddamned empty.'

He takes my shoulder and urges me from the house, shutting the door behind us. We're back in the heat again. 'Now, Mr Thane,' he says. 'I'm going to be honest with you. Because I like you. I actually do. Which surprises the hell out of me. I'm not sure what's going on, and

I'm not sure why you called me here. But I will tell you something. You do seem a bit... *peculiar* today.'

'I'm telling the truth. Ghol Gedrosian's men kidnapped my wife.'

'I know,' he says. 'That's what you're telling me. But this note seems to imply something else.' He holds up the note from Libby.

'You think I'm lying?'

'I don't know what to think. I think you smell pretty bad, and your eyes look red as the devil's. What would *you* think, given your history, if you were me?'

Before I can reply, the phone in Mitchell's shirt pocket rings. He takes it out, glances at the incoming number, holds up a finger to me. 'I have to take this,' he says, and answers the phone. 'Yeah.' A pause. 'Yeah, he's right here. Black Mercedes?' Another pause as he listens to the other end of the conversation. 'Yeah, all right. What's her name?' He listens in silence, nodding. 'All right. I think that's a good idea. We'll be right over.'

He hangs up. He looks at me thoughtfully.

'Where's your wife's car, Mr Thane? That beautiful new Mercedes you bought for her?'

I'm about to answer, 'I left it in the Fort Myers Greyhound terminus,' but something about his face, and the tone of his voice, tells me not to.

'I'm not sure,' I say. 'It wasn't in the driveway when I got here.'

'Well, they found it,' he says. 'It was over on Pine Island.' He looks intently at me. 'The problem is there were three people in it. Two dead Mexicans in the back seat, and a hooker with her throat cut, in the trunk.'

CHAPTER 45

'The Mexicans are *Zetas*,' Mitchell explains, driving his Chevy Impala onto the Crosstown Expressway and merging recklessly into traffic. 'Now, the Zetas started in California, but they're everywhere today, Mr Thane, including Miami and Tampa. Even here in Fort Myers, it turns out.'

I'm in the passenger seat. Mitchell steers casually, just his right fist against the wheel, and he's craning to look at me every few seconds, gauging my reaction to his gangland sociology lecture. I nod politely, but between last night's meth, my recent discovery of cameras in my house, and their subsequent disappearance, I'm ready to hurl my granola bar into his lap.

I fasten my seat belt.

Mitchell continues, 'These boys we found, they were just thugs, three weeks out of Raiford. No great loss to the State of Florida, if I may be so blunt.'

'What happened to them?'

'What happened?' He gives me a sidelong glance. 'I won't lie to you, Mr Thane. You're probably going to want to get your upholstery replaced. Whoever did it had a field day with those hombres. I'm guessing they needed some information. Poor assholes didn't stand a chance.' He shakes his head. 'Now, the girl – she's more interesting. Especially considering what you've been telling me. You want her life story, or just the highlights?'

'Highlights.'

'According to my colleague – that was my partner on the phone; he's part of the Gedrosian Task Force I told you about – the girl is a hooker from Vegas. Well, not really a hooker. I guess you'd say she was in the hospitality industry. Worked for Gedrosian, servicing high rollers. Ten or fifteen Gs for one night. Good Lord, Mr Thane, what the hell does a woman do that's worth fifteen thousand dollars a night? Don't answer that.' He holds up his palm. 'Anyway, she goes by the name – well, *went* by the name… Danielle Diamond. Ever hear of her?'

'Why would I know a Las Vegas hooker?'

He gives me a mischievous look, as if to ask, Why *wouldn't* you know a Las Vegas hooker? Out loud he merely suggests, 'I thought, since you were a customer of Mr Gedrosian's, maybe you two had met.'

I don't take the bait, and remain silent.

'Anyway,' he goes on, 'I thought we would swing by, take a looksee. That way you can tell me if you recognize the girl. They didn't torture her, if that's a concern. Afterwards, you and I can head over to my office and file a report.'

'Report?'

'Missing Persons, Mr Thane. For your wife. If you still want to go through with it, that is.' His meaning is clear. *If you still want to insist you didn't threaten her and make her run away from you.*

Twenty minutes later, we arrive at a pink limestone building, square and institutional, with a sign that says: 'County Medical Examiner'. The building is set far back from the road, behind a tall chain-link fence and a wide grass border, as if the place were designed to withstand an onslaught of people clamouring to visit the morgue. Or an onslaught of bodies clamouring to get out.

We park in the gated lot, and I follow Mitchell into the building. I notice that, as we enter, he stops chattering, and he drops the aw-shucks good-ol'-boy banter. Maybe he feels the same queasiness about morgues and dead people as I do.

At the front desk he flashes his ID to the rent-a-cop, and signs in. We're waved through a buzzing electric door. On the other side, we nearly run headlong into a big bearded man, who comes racing towards us from around a corner. Everything about the man is huge: his head, his ham hands, his barrel stomach that pops over his belt, his oversized white lab coat.

The big man stops suddenly, just inches from Agent Mitchell's nose.

'Whoa there, Ryan,' Mitchell says calmly, holding very still and making a point not to flinch.

'Damnit, Tom,' Grizzly Adams in a Lab Coat says. 'You have the worst timing. You caught me on my way to the candy machine. Walk with me, will you?'

From his heft, it appears that we had a good chance of catching him on his way to the candy machine, no matter what time we showed up. He leads us down the corridor. The air is chilled. The walls are painted cinderblock. Mitchell says, 'I suppose I should introduce you two. Ryan Pearce, this is Jim Thane.'

Ryan Pearce nods, not bothering to slow down. 'Nice to meet you.' He's clearly got candy on the brain.

Mitchell adds, 'It was Mr Thane's Mercedes.'

Pearce stops. He turns to me with a look of deep concern. 'Aw, shit,' he says. 'I'm truly sorry about that.'

'Mr Thane hasn't seen his car yet,' Mitchell explains. 'It was brand new, though. A gift for his wife.'

'You're shitting me,' Pearce says. He makes a *tsk-tsk* sound, and begins walking again. 'Ain't that the damndest thing? Maybe you can return it. There's some kind of lemon law, isn't there? Less than thirty days and you get your money back? Just claim you didn't notice the bloodstains when you drove it off the lot.'

At the end of the hall he stops at the candy machine. 'Three Musketeers?' Pearce says, looking at me first, then Mitchell. 'My treat.'

In fact, a candy bar sounds good right now. I crave sugar. You always do, after a night on crank. But I shake my head.

Pearce shrugs. He sticks a dollar into the machine, presses the button, and a 3 Musketeers plops into the dispenser below.

He peels it open and pops it into his mouth. Two bites and it's gone. 'Damn, I love nougat,' he says, through a mouth full of the stuff. 'No idea what the hell it is, but it's so goddamned good.'

'Hate to cut into your lunch, Ryan,' Mitchell says, 'but we're a bit pressed for time. We gotta file a missing persons after this. You mind showing us the girl?'

'Oh, sure,' Pearce says, agreeable now that he has had his chocolate. 'You bet. Come with me.'

The big man leads us back down the hallway, the way we came, and we turn left at the main entrance, following a sign that says, 'Cooler 1'. We pass two sets of automatic hydraulic doors that glide open as we approach.

At the end of the long hall, Pearce pushes a heavy metal door; and we find ourselves in a walk-in cooler. The air is cold and burns the inside of my nose. In front of us are six rows of small doors in the wall, twenty across. These hold bodies.

'I'm hoping Mr Thane might recognize her,' Mitchell says.

Pearce licks his chocolatey fingers, wipes them on his white smock. 'All right, let me show you. Autopsy's not 'til tomorrow. But I think the cause of death will be pretty obvious. They were very thorough.'

He walks to the coolers. There's a tag on one of them, scribbled in a messy hand, 'Danielle Diamond'.

Pearce wraps his beefy fingers on the door handle, twists, and pulls out a platform that slides towards him on metal rollers. A body lies beneath a white sheet.

Pearce says: 'We're positive on the ID. Matched her prints. She has quite a record. Twelve arrests for prostitution in the past five years. Vegas is cracking down. Trying to be more family friendly. More Disney, less blow jobs.'

'Now that's a slogan I can get behind,' Mitchell says. 'More Disney, less blow jobs. Wonder what that sounds like in Latin.'

'*Magis Disney, minus BJs,*' Pearce suggests. He looks down at the corpse. He gestures to Mitchell, a polite 'after you' twirl of the fingers.

Mitchell grabs the sheet, near the dead woman's shoulder. He turns to me. 'Now I hope you can help us out here, Mr Thane. Maybe you can recognize this girl from your... well, your various travels. Maybe in California, maybe in Florida. Who knows – maybe you two met in Las Vegas. On some sort of business trip, away from the wife.' He clears his throat. 'Mr Thane, may I introduce you to Danielle Diamond, aka Sandra Love, aka Dierdra Starr, aka DeeDee Starr.' He pulls the sheet.

My wife, Libby Thane, lies lifeless on the gurney. Her eyes are closed. A long black slit, the colour of road tar, stretches across her neck, a wound so deep that a tap on her head would sever it from the body and send it rolling to the ground. Her skin is pale and bloodless, as white as the sheet that hid her.

'Mr Thane,' Agent Mitchell says, 'do you know this woman?'

I use every bit of self control I can muster to stay perfectly still, to keep my feet planted firmly beneath my shoulders. I feel the earth shifting, and for a moment I think I will faint and hit the cement with my chin. But I take a breath, and I stay upright, and I turn to Agent Mitchell, who is staring at me. I return his stare.

'No,' I say. 'I have no idea who this woman is.'

CHAPTER 46

I rush out of the morgue. I slam the door of the cooler room, race down the hall. Agent Mitchell runs after me, trying to keep up. 'Mr Thane,' he calls. 'Mr Thane, wait!'

I don't slow. I don't stop. I just run, past the security door, into the tiny lobby, and into the heat.

Five steps across the parking lot and I hear Mitchell calling for me. 'Mr Thane, please!'

I let him catch up. He's sweating and out of breath. 'Mr Thane, wait. Are you all right?'

'I'm sorry,' I say. 'I'm not used to seeing things like that.'

'No, sir. No one is.' He regards me thoughtfully. 'I guess you don't recognize her, then.'

'No.'

He looks at me cautiously, as if he doesn't quite believe me. But then again, who can blame him? They just found two dead Mexicans and a murdered whore in my car. I'm not exactly in the running for Citizen of the Year.

'Come on then, Mr Thane. Let's head over to my office, and we'll start the paperwork.'

'Paperwork?'

'Missing Persons. Isn't that what you wanted? To find your wife, Libby?'

The answer to his question is that I have already found my wife Libby. She is lying on a gurney, with her throat open. Except maybe

329

her name isn't Libby. And maybe there never was a Libby. And maybe the woman I married ten years ago, the woman who was a waitress at The Goose, back at Stanford – maybe she never really was a waitress – but instead was a hooker named, variously, Danielle Diamond, or DeeDee Star.

'Of course I want to find her,' I say.

Mitchell puts his hand on my shoulder. We walk together to his car. I'm about to let him guide me into the passenger seat when a loud musical trill startles me. It's Amanda's cellphone, in my pocket; its ring is unfamiliar. I look down at the incoming number. Gordon Kramer.

I step away from the car, and away from Mitchell, and gesture for the FBI agent to wait. 'Hello, Gordon,' I say.

Gordon's voice does not sound the way I expect. What I expect is the typical Gordon Kramer: gruff, take-no-bullshit, Roman Centurion, drop-and-give-me-twenty. What I hear is high and strained – quavering with some emotion that I can't quite identify. 'Jimmy,' he says, 'are you with him? Is the FBI agent with you right now?'

I look at Agent Mitchell. He's standing a few yards away, on the other side of the car, staring into the sky.

'Yes,' I say. 'We're about to drive over to his office.'

'Listen, Jimmy,' Gordon says, and now finally I recognize the emotion in his voice. It is something I have never heard before in Gordon Kramer.

It is fear.

'I asked around,' Gordon says. 'That name you told me. The Russian. You should have told me before. Damn it, Jimmy, you should have told me right away! You should have told me everything. I could have helped you. I could have prevented all this—'

He stops. I can picture him at the other end of the line, pacing, rubbing his huge hand over close-cropped grey hair, the way you rub down a deerhound after a good hard hunt.

He says: 'Jimmy, listen to me. Just answer yes or no. Don't say anything else. Just yes or no. The man you're with right now – you said his name is Tom Mitchell. Is that right?'

'Yes.'

Agent Tom Mitchell is smiling politely at me, waiting for me to finish my call. He takes out a pad and a ballpoint pen from his pocket. He clicks the top of his pen. *Click.*

'You said he was from the FBI. Are you sure you got that right? He's on the Special Crimes Unit? At the Tampa Field Office? You sure about that?'

'Yes.'

Agent Mitchell pushes his pen again. *Click.*

'Listen carefully. I called my friend at the FBI. There is no Special Crimes Unit, Jimmy. There is no agent named Tom Mitchell. Not any more. Agent Tom Mitchell was killed five years ago, in Long Beach, doing undercover work. Do you understand what I'm saying?'

I manage to squeeze a sound from my throat, just a whisper. 'Yes.'

'You need to get away from him. Do not get in his car. Do not be alone with him. Can you get away?'

I look around. We're standing in the middle of a parking lot. It is surrounded by chain-link fence. A red Honda pulls into the lot. Two middle-aged black women are in the car.

'I think I can make it,' I say, nonchalantly, as if I'm agreeing to meet him for drinks after work.

'I'm coming in on the red-eye,' Gordon says. 'I'll be there first thing in the morning. I'll call you when I land. We can deal with this together, Jimmy. I'll get you out of this mess, I promise.'

'Thank you, Gordon.'

'I've worked too hard on you. You're the fucking salvage operation of the century. I'll be damned if I'm going to find you cut up into little pieces in a plastic bag. Now get the hell away from that asshole.'

'Right,' I say. 'I will. Talk later.'

I hang up, put the phone in my pocket. 'Sorry about that,' I say to the man who calls himself Tom Mitchell.

He shrugs. His voice is polite, melodious – a true Southern gentleman's. 'No problem, Mr Thane. You ready to go, now? I'll take you over to my office. If you'd be so kind as to seat yourself in my automobile.'

He clicks the top of his pen once more. *Click.*

That's when I see his hand. How did I not notice it before? His right hand – the one gripping the pen – consists of four fully-formed fingers, and one mutilated remnant – a pinky that is just a red raw stump.

I step away.

'What's the matter, Mr Thane?' he says, smiling. 'You look a bit feverish. Why don't you have a seat in my car. I don't want you to faint from this heat.'

He circles around the car, towards me.

'Get away,' I say.

'Mr Thane? What's wrong?'

'I have to go.'

'Go?' He holds up his hands, to encompass the parking lot and the empty streets beyond. '*Go where?*'

I run.

'Mr Thane, you don't have a car!' he calls after me, sounding more amused than menacing.

I sprint past rows of cars, towards the parking lot exit. Just past the fence, a black Lincoln Town Car pulls up, and waits at the front gate, blocking my path. Through tinted glass, I barely make out the driver. It's Ryan Pearce, the medical examiner.

I turn to the other direction. Agent Mitchell is coming my way, approaching slowly and deliberately, with his hand in his jacket pocket. 'Mr Thane,' he calls out calmly. 'You know who I'm looking for, don't you? I simply need your help to find him.'

Nearby, the red Honda pulls into a parking spot and cuts its motor.

The two black women – both large, in colourful blouses – hoist themselves from the car. Each holds a big Starbucks cup.

'Ladies!' I call out to them, as I sprint in their direction. 'Ladies, a moment of your time!'

They look up. Like all women, they're prepared to be polite to any man who calls them 'ladies', with a gentle voice. Indeed their faces have expectant, almost radiant expressions.

Then they see me. I imagine how I must look to them: sweat-drenched, red-eyed, crazed – probably high – and racing towards them. Their faces abruptly change.

The woman nearest the driver-side door is overweight and she wears big owl-eyed sunglasses, giving her a surprised and wide-eyed look. I stick Amanda's gun to her head. 'I need your car keys.'

She glances across the parking lot at Agent Mitchell. He's running towards us, arms pumping.

'Now!' I yell. I slap the Starbucks cup from her hand, as if that's the one thing preventing a brisk response. Warm caramel macchiato splashes my pants, and I look down to see a dollop of whipped cream on my shoe.

But the slap seems to do the trick. 'All right,' she says, handing me her car keys.

Agent Mitchell yells, 'Stop that man! Stop him!'

The owl-eyed woman looks to him, her expression managing to convey the impracticality of his request. I squeeze past her, into the Honda. The seat is too close and I bang my knees on the steering wheel. I twist the ignition, put the car into reverse, and peel out.

Smashing into the car behind me.

There's a crash, and crunching metal. My head smacks the head-rest. I pull the gear back down into drive, and the car surges forwards. I cut the wheel, turn, and floor it.

The Honda races through the parking lot, its little engine whining. Up ahead, the wooden gate arm is down, and beyond it, the black

Lincoln waits, parked perpendicularly across the exit. As I accelerate, I see Pearce's fat face behind the tinted window, as it changes from merely self-satisfied, to alarmed, to – at the very last second – quite terrified and rigid, as he grips the steering wheel and braces for impact.

The Honda crashes into the gate arm, sending wood splintering, and then into the hood of the Lincoln.

I hit the Town Car sidelong at the wheel well – and the bigger car spins ninety degrees, like a compass needle on a magnet. I scrape past, metal rubbing metal, chrome peeling and curling from the Lincoln's right side.

In the rearview, I see Agent Mitchell running towards the Town Car. He pulls open the passenger door and leans inside. That's the last I see of him, or Ryan Pearce, because I turn left, and speed down the empty street; and when I next look behind me, they're gone.

CHAPTER 47

When I return to Amanda's apartment, I know immediately that something's wrong. I knock on her door, but there's no answer. I try the knob, and it opens.

The apartment is empty. There's no sign of a struggle, but, even so, things don't look right. The air conditioner is off. The lights are on. The pillows are askew on the couch. Her purse lies in the middle of the floor, as if dropped precipitously.

Amanda is gone.

I go to the window and peer through the Levolor blinds. Are they waiting for me outside? There are two dozen cars in a parking lot, an asphalt basketball court, two black men shooting hoops. No Russians that I can see.

The cellphone in my pocket rings. The Caller ID says: 'Anonymous'.

I answer. 'Hello?'

'Mr Thane?' The voice on the line is male, quiet, precise – not someone I recognize.

'Who is this?'

'You know who I work for.'

'Yes. You work for—'

'Please, Mr Thane. Don't say his name.' A pause. 'I'm watching you right now.'

I step away from the window, push my back against the wall.

'Not through the window, Mr Thane.'

I look around Amanda's apartment. There are a dozen places to conceal a camera: the framed watercolour that hangs over the couch, the thermostat on the wall, the metal clock on the coffee table, the smoke detector on the ceiling.

'Yes,' the voice says, 'a lot of possibilities.'

'What do you want?'

'I'm very sorry about your wife. I'm sorry you had to see that.'

'Why did you do that?'

'Things have gotten a little… ' He pauses, searches for the right words. 'Out of hand,' he says. 'I'm sorry for that. But we can fix them. We can make everything right again Mr Thane.'

'How can you do that?'

'Come, and I will explain. We're all waiting for you. Amanda, too.'

'Where?'

'Look down at the table.'

I glance at the coffee table next to me.

'Not that table,' he says. 'To your left.'

I turn in the other direction, to the end table near the couch. On it lies a single piece of paper. It's the same stationery that Agent Mitchell found in my house – the cuddly bear jumping for honey. If at first you don't succeed, bear with it and try again.

On the paper, written in cursive woman's handwriting, is an address: 17258 Pine Ridge Road. It's not Libby's handwriting.

'That's where you'll find her,' the voice says.

'Did you hurt her?'

'Not yet,' he says.

CHAPTER 48

Of course it's a trap. Why else would they call, and tell me where to find her, if not to lure me to a place I should not go?

But I don't care. I feel a desperate craziness – the same craziness I feel when I'm high: I'm ready to tangle with anyone, to try anything – wild sex, sloppy bar-room fights, more drugs – it doesn't matter – bring it on.

I'd like to take Amanda's gun from my pocket, feel its heft, be comforted by it. I have never fired a gun in my life, yet it somehow feels familiar hidden there. I go to Amanda's computer, and use Google Maps to find the address where I've been told to go. I study the route intently. Then I'm off, back downstairs, and into the Honda.

I drive for fifteen minutes, following the directions I have memorized. The route takes me through dense residential streets, into commercial neighbourhoods, and then into sparse areas barely inhabited at all – dark brown fields, empty office parks, industrial buildings with few cars and no people.

The place I've been told to go is a desolate building in a wide expanse of brown grass. It is some kind of warehouse – a box of corrugated steel, hangar-sized, with four tractor-trailer-height loading bays in front. No windows. No signs. The lot is surrounded by fence, which is topped by razor wire. There are two gates – front and back – but both are open. I drive into the front, and park beside three other cars in the lot.

I get out of the Honda. I take the gun from my pocket, and I approach the building.

Three of the bay loading doors are shut tight against the heat; but the fourth door is half-open, rolled three feet off the ground, invitingly. I bend under the door.

Inside, the building is almost dark. I am assaulted by the smell of cat piss. The only light comes from the door I just entered; sunlight spills onto concrete in a perfect rectangle at my feet. Beyond that rectangle, I can just see a wall of black PVC strips, hanging in a curtain from the ceiling – a baffle to keep cold air inside during loading and unloading. I push aside the strips, and walk through.

It's darker here, and my eyes still haven't adjusted from the brilliance of the sun. I squint. Through the gloom I can make out what look like long rows of tables and benches, industrial equipment stacked on top, piles of garbage on the floor. The smell of ammonia is overpowering. It's not cat piss, I know. I've visited too many secret apartments, too many houses that smelled like urine, too many kitchens where glass beakers and Bunsen burners sit on countertops beside loaves of Wonderbread and Milano cookies. The smell of ammonia means one thing. A meth lab. The smell of *this* much ammonia means something else. A meth lab of industrial proportions.

They know I'm here, of course. So there's no point in sneaking around. I shout into the darkness, 'Hello? Who's here?'

My voice echoes. The room sounds hard – metal and glass and concrete.

'Amanda?'

I walk further into the building, my left hand outstretched into the dark, my right hand holding Amanda's gun. Twenty yards in, the blackness is total. My foot steps onto something glass; it pops and shatters. Pieces of glass tinkle on the ground, and my shoes crunch as I walk.

'Amanda?'

338

I advance into the darkness. I trip on something. It's metal, and I kick it as I regain my balance. It skitters across the concrete. 'Who's here?' A noise ahead – human. Breathing maybe, or crying.

'Amanda? Is that you?'

I follow the sound, deeper into the warehouse. My foot kicks something soft. I stop and kneel. In the darkness, I can barely make out a human form. I reach out to it. It feels wet. There's something sticky on my fingers. The thing is breathing under my touch, laboured, and I hear wet bubbles in its lungs. 'Amanda?' I whisper.

But it's not Amanda; I know that. It's too big, and it wears some kind of man's jacket. I stand. At the far side of the room, I see a crack of light – a doorway.

I go to the light. I feel with my fingertips along the wall. The wall is steel, warm from the sun outside. My hand brushes a light switch. It flips with an industrial *click*, and then, above me, sodium lamps buzz, and the room is awash in cold white light.

There are long metal tables that run in parallel along the room. The tops are cluttered with beakers, tall metal stands that trail rubber tubes down to the ground, brown glass bottles that look like huge mason jars. Canisters of paint thinner are stacked beneath the tables, hundreds of them, and dozens of propane tanks the size of small dirigibles. There's garbage everywhere: discarded bottles, empty tins, rubber tubes and stoppers on the floor.

In the centre of the long aisle lies the man that I kicked. He is crumpled on the floor, between two of the metal tables. His face is turned away from me.

On the far side of the room, near the PVC curtain where I first entered, three men sit in a row, slumped against the wall. I walked past them in the dark, unaware of their presence.

They have black bullet holes in their foreheads. There are circular powder burns around each wound, like little puckered lips in their skin.

They were shot execution style, while standing. I know this because on the wall behind each man is a circle of blood and brains, head height, and then a vertical line of blood made when each man slid to the ground. It looks like graffiti, like three upside down exclamation marks – marks of surprise – maybe the surprise the men felt when the bullets came.

Next to the dead men, Amanda sits. Her eyes are open. She is breathing. She stares straight ahead. She doesn't seem to notice me.

'Amanda?' I run to her.

She looks up. There's a glimmer of recognition. 'Jim… ' she says, very softly. Then she buries her face in her hands, and starts to cry. It's a silent cry – her body shudders and she rubs her eyes – but no sound escapes. I notice her hands are coated with dried blood.

I kneel down beside her. 'Are you hurt?'

She hugs me. 'No.' She buries her face into my shoulder. 'Oh God… Oh God… '

'What happened?'

'It was terrible… ' Her body shakes, wracked by sobbing. 'It was horrible… What they did… '

'Who did?'

'They came to my apartment,' she whispers. 'They had guns. They took me. They told me they were going to kill you.'

'*Who* did?'

'They did,' she says. She points at the three men beside her.

'*They* did?' I look at the men. They don't seem very dangerous. Because they're dead. 'If they brought you here, then who killed *them*?'

She shakes her head. 'I don't know. It was… ' She stops. 'It was a man. He was tall. He had long dark hair. He was dressed in black. He told me to shut my eyes. He spoke in Russian. I thought he was going to kill me. But he just… '

'He just what?'

'Disappeared.'

'Disappeared?' I say. I am uncertain. What does she mean? That the man hid in the shadows? That he *vanished*?

Across the warehouse, someone moans. It's the man that I kicked in the dark. He's still lying on the ground, struggling to pull himself along the floor.

I leave Amanda and go to him. I keep my gun pointed at his head. His face is turned away from me. His body rests at the end of a long trail of blood. He has crawled a dozen yards, swabbing the floor with the wound in his chest. A puddle of blood grows around where he lies.

I tap him with my foot.

'You,' I say. 'Look at me.'

He turns. It's the velociraptor – my neighbour from across the street.

His eyes are missing. They are just purple oozing slits – swollen and empty. Jelly and blood are smeared across his cheeks.

'Who is that?' he asks. He grabs my pants leg.

I step away from his grasp. 'Jim Thane,' I say.

'Jim Thane,' he repeats, and smiles, as if my name is funny. 'Jim Thane,' he says again. He reaches out, but his fingers can't find me.

'Who did this to you?'

'Who do *you* think did this to me, Jim Thane?'

I feel someone behind me. I turn to see Amanda. She has wiped the tears from her eyes, but the blood from her fingers has left faint pink lines, barely visible on her white skin.

I turn back to the velociraptor: 'Why were you spying on me?'

'I was told to keep an eye on you,' he says. 'A funny expression. To keep an eye. Don't you think? Given the circumstances?'

'Where is he? Where do I find him?'

'You don't want to find him. Trust me. No one wants to find him. He will find you, when it's time. I know he will.'

'What does he look like?'

'I have never seen him.'

'How can you work for someone you don't see?'

341

'Ah,' he says, with something like delight. 'Would you like to hear how I met him?'

'Yes.'

He smiles. 'Come closer.'

'Jim, be careful,' Amanda says.

I step into the puddle of blood spreading across the cement. I keep the gun pointed at the man's head. 'Tell me.'

'There was a man once,' he says. 'His name was Kopec. He was the one who hired me. Me and my friend – the one over there, with the bullet in his head – do you see him?'

I could ask, 'Which one?' – but I don't. 'Yes,' I say.

'We were in Modesto, doing our thing. Buying a little, selling a little. We came to his attention. Maybe we sold a little too much. Yes? You understand?'

'Yes.'

'One day, Kopec found us. He came to us and he said, "This territory is owned by my employer, whose name I cannot say. So now you have a choice. You can work for him. Or I can kill you." Of course we chose to work for him. You see?'

'Yes.'

'Kopec gave us jobs. Maybe they were tests. To see what we could do. A delivery. A pickup. An execution. Yes? Each week Kopec came, and each week he handed me an envelope. Inside the envelope was money, and a description of the job we needed to do. Kopec never knew what was in the envelope. He just handed it to me. He was the messenger. That was all.'

He coughs. Blood bubbles from his lips.

'One day,' he says, 'Kopec came. The envelope was heavy. He told me to open it. Inside was a cellphone, and a gun, and a piece of paper. On the paper was my assignment. Just two words. Do you know what it said?'

'No.'

'It said: "Shoot Kopec". So I did. Right in the head. You see? And then the cellphone rang, and I answered, and a voice said: "Congratulations. From now on, your name is Kopec." *That* is how he works. He controls everyone. He knows everything. He listens. He watches. But he stays hidden. No one knows anything about him. No one knows where he lives. Or what he looks like. Or how old he is. Or even if he's Russian, or Armenian, or Chechen. And if you talk to him, or if you know someone who talks to him, then he will kill you. If you even say his name out loud, he will kill you. Everyone knows these rules.'

'What does he want from me? Tell me what you know.'

'What I know?' he says. 'I know nothing. My job was to watch you. To make sure your wife pleased you. To make sure that you succeeded in your business. My job was to protect Jim Thane.'

'Protect me?' I think about Stan Pontin, and the car accident, and Sandy Golden's sudden and inexplicable decision to invest in Tao Software. And about Dom Vanderbeek, in the attic, and his necklace of purple thumbprints. 'Why did you kill my wife?'

'No,' he says. 'That was not me. Maybe it was someone else. We are not the only team. There's always another team. That's how he controls you. One team watching another. Watching another. Until you don't know for sure who is who.'

'Is Tom Mitchell on your team?'

'Tom Mitchell?' he says. 'Ah, the FBI agent. No. I don't think he works for my employer. I think he wants to *find* my employer. So many people do. He has made so many enemies.'

'Why are you telling me all this?'

He smiles. His empty eye sockets squint merrily. Red tears ooze from the corners. 'Come closer and I will show you.'

'Don't, Jim,' Amanda warns.

I remain still.

The man says: 'I'm missing my eyes, Jim Thane. I can't hurt you. Come closer. I will show you something. Something you will remember for the rest of your life.'

I inch closer to him. I touch his shoulder. 'What is it?' I say, softly, into his ear.

I hear his breath, laboured and ragged, and I feel the life draining from him, gathering in a pool at my feet.

'My jacket,' he whispers. His voice is very soft. Almost inaudible. 'Reach inside.'

I hand my gun to Amanda. She points it at his head. I reach into the man's pocket. It feels wet.

'Do you feel it?'

There is something there – a sharp edge of paper against my finger. I remove an envelope. The corner is stained with blood. On the envelope is written: 'To Kopec.'

'I was given that,' he says, 'by the one who put out my eyes. First I had to read it. It was the last thing I saw. Look at it.'

I open the envelope. Inside is a single sheet of paper, folded into thirds. A paperclip attaches a school photograph of a young girl, perhaps seven years old. She wears a blue velvet dress. Her hands are clasped in her lap. She smiles at the camera.

'My daughter,' he explains.

I open the page attached to the photo. It is typewritten. The machine that typed it was an old manual typewriter, maybe antique. Ink is gummed between the crossbars; the letters run unevenly across the page.

It says:


```
Your last assignment. Tell Jim Thane how you
were hired. Tell him about Kopec. Tell Jim Thane
everything he asks. Answer all his questions. Show
him this page.
Then kill yourself. I am watching you.
(Remember that I watch your daughter.)
```

'You see now?' the velociraptor whispers. 'He knows everything. He controls everything. I think truly he is... God.'

Before I understand what I have read, or what is happening, he brings out the gun he has been hiding. He sticks it in his mouth. He bites down, and I hear the clack of enamel on metal. The back of his head explodes into red mist.

'No!' I yell, too late, and my words are swallowed by the echo of the gunshot.

I step back.

'Oh Jesus,' Amanda says.

In the distance I hear the sound of police sirens.

'We have to leave,' I say, backing away. I take Amanda's hand, and I pull her towards the exit. But she stands there, resisting, unwilling to move, staring fixedly at the corpse.

'Amanda,' I say.

'Wait.' She takes her hand from mine and kneels down next to the dead man.

'What are you doing?'

She leans over, pressing her body to his, her face nearly touching his shattered skull. She feels around inside his bloody jacket.

'Amanda...'

The sirens grow louder. They come towards us.

Amanda is fishing, groping in pockets, searching for something.

'Found it!' she says excitedly. She holds up what she was looking for: a plastic sandwich bag, pinched closed with a rubber band. It contains yellow crystals and a glass pipe.

'Come on,' I say.

I pull her from the corpse, and this time she lets me, and she stands, and she sticks the bag into the front of her jeans.

We run across the warehouse and push through the PVC curtain. We hop off the loading dock, and into the bright sun. The sirens are louder. I climb into the Honda, and Amanda runs to the passenger side.

We drive out through the rear exit, onto the street. Two police cars are pulling into the front gate as we leave, sirens blaring, red and blue lights flashing. For a moment, I expect screeching tyres, and wild U-turns, and hot pursuit, but when I look in the rearview mirror, I see the cruisers pulling to a gentle stop in front of the loading docks.

They ignore the Honda with the blood-spattered man and woman – or maybe they never saw it – and we speed west, cresting over a hill and out of sight.

CHAPTER 49

We check in at the Best Western on Daniels Parkway, which is the first hotel we find near the airport. We take a room on the third floor, overlooking the parking lot. As soon as we shut the door and double-lock it, I head for the bed, and I'm asleep in ten minutes.

When I wake, the room is dark, and it's night outside. I hear Amanda beside me, snoring. The digital clock on the nightstand says two a.m.

Something is bothering me. It has been bothering me, I realize, since I walked into that meth lab and found the dead men shot execution-style, and a man with no eyes.

'Amanda?'

She stirs.

'Are you awake?'

'Mmm,' she says.

'Why didn't he kill you?'

'Who?'

'At the warehouse. The man you told me about. The man with long hair. Dressed in black. He killed everyone else. But not you.'

'I don't know,' she says, in the darkness. A long silence. I feel her shift in the bed. She says finally: 'You don't trust me.'

'I trust you.'

But he didn't kill you. He killed everyone else, and not you.

'Promise?' Amanda asks.

And the blood on your fingers. And the Russian man who was missing his eyes.

But I say, 'I promise.' Because what's a promise between two addicts?

She seals this promise by climbing on top of me. She kisses me hard, slides her tongue into my mouth. She unbuckles my pants, pulls them down over my hips. She mounts me, and I'm surprised by this – surprised that she's ready for me, and surprised that I can respond – that we are going to fuck just hours after everything that has happened, hours after seeing my dead wife Libby, who was not really named Libby, and after seeing a man with no eyes sucking on a gun.

The sex is fast and hard: no romance today – just desperation. The moment I come, I'm disgusted by it all: by my own body – by the blood on my hands and my face; by Amanda, who – before she mounted me – pressed herself on top of a dead man who was missing his brains, in order to find his stash.

We shower together, washing off blood and semen, which disappear down the drain like a bad dream in morning light.

Back in the room, she kneels naked on the floor beside her jeans, which are still wet with blood, and she retrieves the plastic bag she stole from the dead man. She joins me on the bed with the stash. She drops a pinch of yellow crystal into the base of the glass pipe, and she holds a lighter underneath. The crystals vanish into white smoke. She twirls the bowl, continuing to heat it, swirling the smoke. She inhales. She smiles at me, holds out the pipe and lighter.

I know I shouldn't, not with everything that has just happened. But I tell myself that I will stop soon. Just not yet. Just not today.

I flick the lighter, heat the black cinders stuck to the glass. I inhale. It tastes like burnt smoke, like cold winter, and then I feel the surge of pleasure, the relaxation and calm and happiness.

A few minutes later, we're having sex again, and this time I don't feel disgusted. We do it for hours, thinking about nothing except fucking, until we're interrupted by the sound of a cellphone ringing.

It takes me a moment to find the phone – it was in my pants – and then to remember where I am, and then to collect myself enough to finally answer. 'Hello?' I say, trying to sound normal, which is getting increasingly difficult, day by day, hour by hour.

'I'm here, Jimmy,' a voice says. And then I remember: I'm running from an Eastern gangster, and from someone who claims to be from the FBI; and my wife is dead – my wife who wasn't really named Libby.

The voice at the other end of the phone is anchored in reality, and it tugs me back – I was floating away – and it belongs to Gordon Kramer, the only person left in the world that I trust. That he is also the man to whom I have made a solemn promise never to use again, is an irony that even I recognize – even in this addled state – even as I stare at the glass pipe on the floor nearby.

'Gordon?'

'You all right, Jimmy? Did I wake you?'

'No.'

Behind me, Amanda touches my shoulder. I turn to her, covering the mouthpiece of the phone, and whisper, 'A friend.'

'I'm at the airport,' Gordon says. 'Come and get me. We'll rent a car, and we'll get the hell out of here.'

'He killed Libby, Gordon.'

'Who did?'

'Ghol Gedrosian. He killed Libby.'

Silence. Then, he says softly: 'Fuck, Jimmy. I don't know what to say. I'm sorry.'

'She was working for him this whole time. Her name wasn't Libby. She was… someone else.'

A long silence as he considers. This is normally the moment when Gordon should growl into the phone: 'Are you fucking using again, Jimmy? Because you sound crazy!' – but this time, oddly, he says nothing. I hear his breathing. Finally he speaks, and his voice is more gentle than I can remember it ever being. 'Just come to the airport,' he says softly. He gives me the flight number. 'Meet me at baggage. We'll figure this out together.'

'I'm near,' I say. 'I'll be just a few minutes.'

'I'll be waiting.'

When I hang up, Amanda asks, 'Where are we going?'

'*We?*' I say. 'We are not going anywhere.' This comes out sounding mean and suspicious – which I didn't intend – and so I add, 'I'm going alone. It'll be safer. I'll bring him back here.'

'Who?'

'His name is Gordon. He's my friend. We can trust him.' I look around the room. 'Do me a favour, though. Make the bed. And hide the crank. He's my sponsor.'

CHAPTER 50

I roll the cuffs of my pants, to hide the blood. I move quickly through the hotel lobby, so that no one can get a good look at me. But it's early morning, and the lobby is empty, except for the night clerk, who doesn't seem to notice anything unusual about a man with bloodshot eyes and pants stained dark. He has seen worse, apparently.

I grab a stale croissant on my way out, part of the courtesy continental breakfast that my fifty-nine bucks bought. My jaws work on it mechanically.

The complimentary airport shuttle waits outside, beneath an awning. When I board, the driver looks up from his newspaper, vaguely annoyed.

We wait together in the van. It is hot. I am the only passenger. Apparently the driver has been instructed not to make the trip to the airport until more than one rider boards. He studies his newspaper with grim concentration, reviewing the world news carefully, as if preparing for an appearance on the Sunday-morning talk shows.

Five minutes pass, then ten, and when I finally suggest we ought to be going, he mutters something under his breath and pulls the door closed. The van rumbles onto Daniels Parkway.

It's two miles to the Southwest Florida International Airport, and it takes only a few minutes to get there. It's a grandly named place for so small an airport. I hop off the van, and ten steps later I'm already in the Departures Area. A quick trip down an escalator brings me to Baggage Claim.

There are only four carousels. Gordon Kramer stands at the last one, on the far side of the room. He's forty yards away, talking to someone on his cellphone – he hasn't noticed me yet. I feel relief the moment I see his etched-stone face and his brutally-short military haircut. There is something real and solid and familiar about him. He's not a friend, exactly – I did use that term with Amanda, but it wasn't true. A friend is someone you don't care about disappointing. I do care when I let Gordon down.

Which is why I so often find myself caring about him – because my life is an endless stream of failure, a Nile River of Fiasco, ebbing and flowing with annual monotony. Yet Gordon Kramer wades fearlessly in to save me, knee-deep, year after year.

Imagine having a father that you love, and then imagine that your father knows your abject self, the basest truth about who you are, and what you do, and how you think; and then you'll understand why I love Gordon Kramer. Because even though he knows my shameful secrets, I have not yet managed to drive him away. Not yet.

'Gordon!' I call.

He turns. His eyes twinkle. But he doesn't smile. He never smiles. He says something into his cellphone, presses a button, and puts it away. He walks to me.

'Jimmy,' he says, his voice gruff but warm. Just hearing that voice, in person, beside me, tells me that I am safe. Gordon is strong and smart and tough. He is a San Jose cop and an ex-marine. He has killed men with his bare hands, has battled alcohol, has faced down demons of his own. Every battle he accepts, he wins. Ghol Gedrosian is no match for Gordon Kramer. Of that, I am certain.

'You're alive,' he says, in typical Gordon style, sounding not very pleased.

I put an arm around his back. We hug.

'You have a bag?' I ask.

'Just this,' he says. He picks up an old aluminium-sided Samsonite, with machine-tooled ridges that look as if they were carved by a lathe – more toolbox than overnight bag.

'When did you land?' I ask.

'Oh, right before I called you,' he says. But he seems distracted. His eyes are scanning the room behind me, ever vigilant for threat. We start walking towards the sign that says 'Ground Transportation'.

'Do you have a car?' he asks.

'No.'

'Good. I have a limo out front. It's already arranged. It'll take us to Miami. I know a cop there. A good guy. Ex-marine. He's clean, Jimmy. We can trust him. He knows all about this Gedrosian character. He can help.'

'That's great, Gordon,' I say. I am relieved – glad to share my burden at last, glad to let someone else handle things from now on. Gordon has already begun to solve problems. 'Before we go, I just need to pick up my friend. She's at the hotel where I stayed last night.'

'Sure, Jimmy,' he says agreeably.

Gordon's last words strike me as peculiarly accommodating – very un-Gordon-like, in fact – that he doesn't ask me who the friend is, or why we have to pick *her* up. He must be exhausted from the red-eye. He's losing his edge: not questioning me about who I'm associating with, or what I'm doing in a hotel room, or why my eyes are bloodshot, and why my pants cuffs are rolled so high, and so clearly stained ochre.

We pass a baggage carousel – the only one in the terminal with its belt spinning – and the sign above it indicates that the bags just arrived from Dallas.

'You fly through Dallas?' I ask Gordon, mostly to fill the silence as we walk, but also because it occurs to me that Gordon's carousel was not spinning, and that there was no 'Arriving From' sign above the carousel where I found him.

'Straight from SFO,' he says. 'Eight hours. What a goddamned trip.' Out of the corner of my eye I see him look at me quickly, as if he just said something wrong, and wants to detect if my expression changed. But I keep my eyes fixed straight ahead, my face addled and stupid-looking – not a hard thing for me to pull off, given all the practice.

We step out of the terminal, into the sunlight. The air feels hotter now than I remember it being when I entered the terminal, just minutes ago. As if on cue, a black limousine pulls up alongside us. The driver, wearing a dark suit and chauffeur's cap, gets out of the car and quickly circles towards me and Gordon.

'Hello,' Gordon says to the driver.

The driver doesn't speak. He just nods and opens the back door for us. I notice he doesn't offer to take Gordon's metal suitcase, either. That's what limousine drivers do, usually – isn't it? – they offer to take your case? Not this one, though.

'Why don't you just get in, Jimmy,' Gordon says, with a surprising amount of warmth in his voice, as if he is suggesting that I slip into a nice cuddly sweater. He points to the open limousine door. The driver smiles at me and nods. He too would like me just to get in, apparently.

I notice something odd about this man – this driver who holds open the door. He is muscular. Practically bursting out of that polyester suit jacket, in fact. But he's trim, and well-conditioned. No fat, just muscle. Not what you'd expect from a man who sits on his ass all day.

'Hey, Gordon,' I say, and I turn with a friendly smile to my mentor. 'Shake my hand.'

I hold out my hand, inviting him to shake. Gordon's right palm is gripped tightly around his machine-tooled suitcase. So tightly, in fact, that I can't see his fingers. Or count how many he has.

Gordon looks at me for a long moment, perfectly still and expressionless. Then he seems to make a decision. He breaks out into a broad toothy grin.

I've known Gordon Kramer for nearly eight years. This is the first time in my memory that he has ever smiled at me.

He puts down his metal suitcase slowly. He unfurls his hand. He reaches out to mine.

That he is missing his pinky finger does not surprise me. Maybe I knew it, minutes ago, when he didn't remark on the smell of my clothes as we hugged. The Gordon Kramer I know – the *real* Gordon Kramer – the cop who would move mountains to keep me from danger, typically self-inflicted – would have asked me what the fuck I had been smoking, and with whom, and why my eyes were red, and why my breath smelled like crank.

This Gordon Kramer merely grins. His mouth moves, and he says words that I can't understand, and it takes a moment to realize he has spoken these words in Russian. I am about to curse at him, but then there's something wet on my face, a handkerchief pressed violently against my nose and mouth by the driver, who is now standing behind me; and the smell cuts like turpentine, chemical and metallic, and then I'm being shoved into the limousine, and my forehead slams against the top of the door frame, and then everything goes black.

CHAPTER 51

The dream starts like this.

I am in a dark house. The house is familiar, but it is not mine. I walk up a spiral staircase.

Even though the house is not mine, and it is dark, I am not afraid. It feels right to be here, in this house – this dark house, climbing this long staircase.

I stop at the landing at the top of the stairs. Far off, at the end of a hall, I see a door.

I walk to the door. The floorboards creak beneath my feet. I turn the knob, and enter.

I am in a child's room. A boy's room: blue wallpaper, a Superman action figure on the bureau, a plastic Tupperware container filled with Matchbox cars.

The boy is asleep on his bed. He is breathing. He is alive. He is lit by moonlight. He wears blue flannel pyjamas with grey feet. He has blond hair, too long for a boy; and when I lift him from the bed, and carry him, still sleeping in my arms, his head lolls, and his hair hangs down.

He doesn't wake. He breathes softly. I carry him through the dark hall, to another door. A line of yellow light glows beneath it. Through the door, I hear a sound. A rumble, like machinery, or distant thunder.

My hands are full of little boy, and so I push the door with the bottom of my shoe. It opens easily.

Now I know the sound that I heard. Running water. It gushes from a faucet and pours into an overflowing bathtub. It sluices over the side of the tub, and onto the white floor tiles, where it gathers an inch deep.

There is a man leaning over the tub. He wears dark clothes. His hair is long and black, straight and past his shoulders. Stringy hair, dirty hair, like a man who has been dead for a very long time.

He speaks to me without turning. 'You've brought your boy,' he says. Then after he speaks, I wonder if he said the words aloud, or if I am just listening to his thoughts.

I step into the bathroom, and my shoes splash in the water. I carry the boy to the stranger. His back is to me.

'His name is Cole,' I tell the man dressed in black. 'He's my son. My only son.'

'Put him in the water,' the stranger says. I crane my neck to try to see the stranger's face. But it remains hidden. I see only long dark dead hair.

'I don't understand,' I tell the stranger.

But he doesn't answer. I feel myself moving, carrying the boy to the bath, despite my wish to remain still. I bend over the kneeling stranger, and I lay Cole gently in the water. He floats, still asleep, on the surface.

'Leave us now,' the stranger says.

I step aside.

The stranger reaches down to the boy. I stare at the stranger's hand as it pokes from his black sleeve. It is bone. No skin on it.

He lays his bone hand on Cole's chest, and shoves down on the boy with surprising violence.

The little boy is pushed to the bottom of the tub. His eyes open, and he tries to scream, but the sound is inaudible, just a bubble that floats from his mouth and breaks on the surface. He sucks water. His eyes open wide. He screams silently, shaking his head back and forth. His tiny fingers scratch at the stranger's bone hand. The boy breathes water into his lungs.

The stranger holds down the boy. The man is strong and relentless. The struggle is brief: the boy kicks and flails his arms, but he's pinned to the bottom by the bone hand. I watch the boy's face as the life leaves him. He stares at me as he dies, his eyes still open wide. When the boy's fingers stop twitching, the stranger lifts his bone hand. The corpse floats to the surface.

'You can have him now,' the stranger says, still not turning to me. 'He is your son.'

'Be gentle,' a man's voice says softly in my ear.

When I open my eyes, I'm not in a bathroom, and it's not the black-haired stranger that speaks. There's no water at my feet, no bathtub, no little boy.

I'm sitting in a chair. The room is very cold, and I'm shivering, and everything around me is blurry and out of focus. I try to rub the grit from my eyes, but my arm is stopped by a restraint. I can't move. I'm bound to the chair.

My eyes focus. The room is wood panelled, with heavy wooden shutters in the windows, blocking the sunlight. There's a big desk, a filing cabinet in the corner, a diploma on the wall. I know the place: Dr Liago's office.

'Is he awake?' another voice says – a woman's.

I turn to the woman. I recognize her. She has short grey hair, cropped close in a middle-aged matronly dyke style. Her colourless grey eyes stare at me without expression. How can this be? It's Doc Curtis, my shrink from back in California. She stands beside Dr Liago, the little man with the white beard. What are they doing together? Why is she in Florida?

'I came to see you,' she answers, and I realize that I spoke the question out loud. 'I came to help you. You need help. Things have gotten out of control.'

'What's happening?' I ask. I remember now: the airport, Gordon

Kramer, his missing finger, the limo driver, the chloroformed handkerchief…

'You need our help, Jimmy,' comes that gruff, familiar voice. I try to turn to it. But my chest is bound to the back of the chair. I hear footsteps on the wooden floor, and then Gordon walks into view.

'What are you doing?' I ask.

'Jimmy, you fucked up,' Gordon says.

'Is it Jimmy then?' Doc Curtis asks. 'Still Jimmy Thane?'

'That's what it says,' Liago explains. He holds a sheaf of typewritten pages in his hands, and he's scanning the pages quickly, flipping through them, searching for something. '"Jimmy Thane", it says.'

'But we tried that,' Doc Curtis begins. 'And look at what—'

'Just do what it says,' Gordon interrupts. 'Don't ask questions. Do exactly what it says. Jimmy Thane.'

Doc Curtis pushes her lips together. She wants to argue, but she knows better.

Dr Liago walks to his desk. On the surface is the metal Samsonite that Gordon Kramer brought to the airport. The doctor clicks the latches on the suitcase and opens it. He takes out a roll of black fabric. He pushes the suitcase aside, and unfurls the fabric on the desk, revealing a set of syringes strapped by elastic. He removes a glass vial from one of its pockets, and chooses a syringe. He tears open the sterile wrapping, removes the plastic cap, and fills the syringe with liquid from the vial. When the syringe is full, he holds it to the light, and taps.

'What are you doing?' I say, with growing alarm. 'Gordon, what is he doing?'

'Jimmy, you know you fucked up, don't you? We're just trying to help. You want to stay alive, don't you?'

'What are you going to do to me?'

'You should have listened,' Gordon says. 'You had everything, Jimmy. He gave you everything. A job, a wife, money. What the fuck were you *thinking*, you stupid asshole?'

'I'm sorry,' I say. I'm not quite sure what I'm sorry about, but it's clear that I've done something awful. 'Just let me go. Let me go back home. I won't fuck up again, Gordon. I promise.'

'Too late now,' Gordon says. 'You've gone off the rails, my friend. Off the fucking rails. Just like the real Jimmy Thane would have done. Out of control. Completely unreliable.' He turns to Liago. 'You did too good a job, Doc. Just like the real Jimmy Thane.'

'Thank you,' the doctor says weakly, but he sounds more frightened than pleased.

Gordon Kramer has done wicked things to me in the past. He has punched me in the face when I lied to him; he has stuck my head in a toilet bowl when he caught me doing heroin; he has chained me to a fire sprinkler in an underground parking garage; he has locked me in a forty-five-day rehab programme in San Bruno against my will, threatening me with jail if I refused to be committed; and he has poured $10,000-worth of my hard-earned wealth down the kitchen sink in the form of cocaine, after he searched my house and found it in the cupboard, behind the Honey Nut Cheerios.

But what is happening now is an entirely new level of sponsor intervention. With Gordon's blessing, Dr Liago is walking to me with a syringe held in front of him, the needle glistening.

Liago says: 'This won't hurt, Mr...' He stops. After some hesitation he says, 'Mr Thane.' He taps the syringe. 'Not if you remain very still.'

I look down. Both my arms are strapped to the chair with black electrical tape, but they are wrist-down, veins hidden.

Liago says, 'Help me loosen this. Keep him still.'

I try to wrench my arms free. I shake violently and yell, 'Let me go!' I strain against the tape.

Liago stands in front of me, watching me flail. He looks at Gordon.

Gordon issues a loud rasping command. His words make no sense, until I realize they're in Russian. Someone behind me answers in the same language, and the limousine driver appears just behind my shoulder. He no longer wears the ridiculous chauffeur's cap – that should have been my first clue, when I saw him, that silly hat, which no real driver still wears, not for the last fifteen years – and he walks around my chair, takes out a pocket knife, and slices through the electrical tape binding my right arm.

My arm flies free –just for an instant. The limo driver grabs it with two huge hands. He wrenches my wrist violently down, twisting it and exposing the white skin of my forearm. He presses my arm down, holding it rock-steady against the wooden chair.

'If you move, it will take longer, and it will hurt,' Dr Liago says.

Gordon Kramer rasps, 'We'll chloroform you again, if you keep this up, Jimmy.'

My head throbs from the first ether handkerchief. I don't want any more. I stop struggling.

'Are you going to kill me?' I ask.

'God, no, Jimmy,' Gordon says, with a smile. 'We're just going to make everything better.'

Liago says, 'Make a fist please.'

I do. 'Why are you doing this to me?' I ask.

'To make you happy,' Liago says. 'That's what he wants. To make you happy.'

'Who wants?'

He doesn't answer. He taps the vein near the bend of my arm. I look away, and I feel a prick, and then liquid spurts into my vein. My arm feels heavy. The heaviness creeps upwards, into my shoulder, and into my head. 'There,' Liago says, sounding immensely satisfied. 'There, there. You'll be very relaxed in a minute, Mr Thane. Then we can begin our therapy.'

Indeed, I am relaxed. And before I can answer him, my eyes flutter shut.

I hear my own heartbeat, and my own breathing.

I am dreaming now. It's a violent dream. In the dream, I hear crashing glass, and the screams of Doc Curtis and the limousine driver, and then Gordon's voice speaking rapid guttural Russian, and then a pounding noise. The noise pounds again, beside my ear. Pots banging, or firecrackers, or a mallet striking an anvil. *Bang bang bang*. Right next to me.

Some part of my mind – that little glimmering portion that hasn't shut down – deduces that these pounding noises are not mallets or anvils. They are gunshots. They are very close to me.

Bang, says a gun. Disturbing my sleep.

Bang.

There's screaming now, and then another *bang*, and then the screaming stops, and finally I can rest.

How long do I sleep? I do not know, but when I wake, I'm seated in the same chair, soaked with sweat, despite the humming air conditioner that blows freezing air on the back of my neck. I feel nauseous. My shirt sticks to my skin. I try to move, but I'm bound in place. I look down at my right arm. It's the only part of my body that is not taped down. There's a little bruise on the vein near my elbow.

'Well, look at this,' says a familiar voice. 'Like Lazarus rising from the dead.'

I follow that familiar voice, and focus on the blurry figure seated in the overstuffed leather chair – the same chair where I spent so many hours, talking to Dr Liago. It's Agent Tom Mitchell. He looks cool and casual, his shirtsleeves rolled up, his feet stretched out before him, crossed at the ankle. 'How do you feel right now, Mr Thane?'

I feel like there's a power drill behind my skull, and someone is using it to try desperately to drill his way out. 'I don't feel too good,' I say. My voice is hoarse, my mouth cotton.

I look around the room. Gordon Kramer is lying, face down, in a pool of blood that has spread from his skull. The pool is not growing; he's been dead for a while.

So too has Doc Curtis, who is missing half her face, which I believe was blown off by a heavy-gauge shot delivered from close range. Dr Liago is in the corner, slumped against the wall, in his own bloody puddle. I can't see the limousine driver, but I'd lay odds that his driving days are over.

'You don't look too good either,' Mitchell says, still using that ridiculous Southern accent – *ee-thah* – even though I am perfectly aware that *his* Georgia isn't the place that grows peaches and debutantes.

Someone is pacing behind me. I try to turn, but I'm strapped to the chair, and I can't rotate my body. As if to be polite, Ryan Pearce, the big Grizzly Adams from the morgue, steps into view and waves at me. 'Hello,' he says, cheerfully.

'What's going on?' I ask Agent Mitchell.

'I was about to ask you the same question,' Mitchell says. 'Why are all these people tying you to a chair and injecting you with magic potions?'

'I don't know,' I say. Which is the truth.

'But you do know why I'm here, don't you, Mr Thane? Or whatever your name really is. You know who I'm looking for, don't you?'

'Yes.'

'Where can I find that person?'

'I don't know.'

He shakes his head. 'Now, see, I have a hard time believing that. I've been tracking Ghol Gedrosian for many years. Too long, if truth be told. I'm getting very close to him. I know him now. He's like a friend to me. I've read his emails, I've seen his private papers, I've listened to his cellphones. And you know what I think? You want to know what all the evidence tells me?'

'What's that?'

'He's here.'

'Yes, I know. You told me. He's in Florida.'

'No, Mr Thane,' he says, 'you don't understand. Ghol Gedrosian is here. Ghol Gedrosian works at Tao Software.'

'At Tao?' I try to make sense of his words. I shake my head. The anaesthesia, or the drug, or whatever it was that they gave me, is obscuring my thoughts – making me slow and stupid. 'At Tao?' I say again.

From the corner of the room, just behind me, comes a groan. Mitchell looks towards the noise. Gordon Kramer's limousine driver crawls into view. He's down on the floor, pulling himself with one arm, unable to lift his face from the wood. His cheek stretches along the hardwood as he pulls himself, making his face look like a mollusc on the side of an aquarium. He moans, 'Help me, please.'

Mitchell takes a gun from his pocket – a huge gun with a giant phallic barrel – and points it at the man. He pulls the trigger. The driver's head explodes in a cloud of grey mist.

Mitchell turns back to me as if he has just brushed a piece of lint from his shirt. 'Now, Mr Thane, I have to warn you, because I do like you. You're a very funny man, and I appreciate your waggish sense of humour, truly I do. But if you don't tell me everything you know about Ghol Gedrosian, and where I can find him, I will have to carry out some rather unpleasant interrogation techniques. Believe you me, neither of us wants that to happen.'

'Why do you need to find him?'

'That's my concern,' he snaps. But then he considers. His voice softens. 'Do you think, Mr Thane, that Satan walks among us, pretending to be a man?'

'I think,' I say, 'that I don't give a shit. I have my own crap to deal with.'

He considers my answer. He purses his lips, thinks about it. Finally he smiles. 'Maybe you're right. Ghol Gedrosian is a man, then. Just an evil man. A man who has done horrible things. A man who has hurt my friends. A man who has killed men and women that I love. His acts cry out for vengeance. I am vengeance. He thinks he can hide behind other people. He's wrong, Mr Thane. He's at the end of the road now.

There's no one left to hide behind. That's why he left California. That's why he came to Florida. He's running from *me*. He's scared. Because I have found him.'

'Yeah? If you've found him, why are you sitting here pointing a gun at me and asking me where he is?'

'Well,' he says, and smiles, as if I just caught him in a fib. 'I should say I *almost* found him. *Almost.*' His smile disappears. He raises his gun to my face. 'Where is Ghol Gedrosian, Mr Thane?'

'I don't have a clue.'

'Let me ask it a different way. Where is your girlfriend? What's the name she's using nowadays?'

'Who?'

'Your so-called secretary.'

'My assistant,' I say, automatically, as though it matters. 'Amanda.'

'Amanda. Where is Amanda?'

So he didn't find her. That's good, at least. Amanda is safe.

'Mr Thane, this is your final chance. Where can I find Ghol Gedrosian? Where can I find Amanda?'

My mind tries to process his questions. They seem disjointed – they make no sense when put together, side by side. Where is Ghol Gedrosian? Where is Amanda? Two plus two is five.

'Cut off his hand,' Mitchell says. The command is so sudden, that I'm not sure who he's talking to, or what he means, until I turn and see Ryan Pearce holding up a junior hacksaw, forged steel, a thin wire blade glinting like a wicked surgical instrument. He steps towards me, smiling.

'Now wait a second,' I say, but it's too late. Pearce is a huge man – hugely strong – and he holds down my right hand – my free hand – against the chair, so painfully tight, that I think he might actually be crushing the bones within it. He lays the saw blade against my wrist. He looks to Agent Mitchell, who is sitting, leaning comfortably back in the leather seat, with his legs out, ankles crossed.

'Mr Thane?' Mitchell says. 'Last chance. Where is Amanda? Where is Ghol Gedrosian?'

Before I can answer, there's a tap on the glass of the window. Mitchell rises from his chair. He looks to Pearce. Pearce releases my hand. He puts down the hacksaw on the desk, and moves with surprising grace to the window. He stands to the side. The wooden shutter is closed, with thin lines of sunlight pushing through.

Another tap on the glass outside.

Mitchell nods to Pearce.

Pearce reaches out, pulls on the vertical lever in the middle of the shutter, opening the slats and letting sunlight flood the room. The sun forms bright yellow rectangles on the dark wooden floor. One of the rectangles highlights Doc Curtis's skull, a chunk missing from the side.

Everyone stares at the window. I am bound to the chair, seated too low to see anything outside the house, other than bright Florida sky; but Pearce turns to Mitchell and says, 'There's no one there. It's completely emp—'

The sound of cracking glass. Pearce alone stands bravely in the middle of the window, without reacting to the sound of the breaking glass, while Mitchell and I both flinch. Pearce stands motionless for a long time. He turns to Tom Mitchell, and opens his mouth, as if to speak. Then we see the black bullet hole, like a tiny cigarette burn, in the middle of his forehead. He collapses to the ground.

Mitchell scrambles from the centre of the room, towards the wall, out of view of the shooter outside. His gun is out, moving quickly back and forth, searching for a target. He swings it to me. I think he's going to shoot, but he says very calmly, 'I think we have company out there, Mr Thane.'

He sidles along the wall, to the second window. He pops his head up, looks out quickly, then ducks back down.

I remember the pistol in Dr Liago's drawer. My eyes flit to the desk. What's the probability that it's still there? That it's actually loaded? That the safety is off? Can I reach for the drawer, pull it open, grab the gun, and turn it upon Mitchell, with one free hand, before he can react? It seems unlikely. But it may be my only chance.

'Mr Thane,' Mitchell says politely, still crouching low beneath the window. 'I'd like you to do me a personal kindness. I'm going to fire this gun, just once, thereby making a loud gunshot noise. After I do that, I'd like you to shout out that you're fine, and that you've killed me. I'll hide right over there, in that corner.' He points to the side of the room. From that vantage, he'll be able to line up a perfect shot at whoever enters Liago's study through the only door. 'When your friend comes running to help, I'll solve our problem, and then we can continue our conversation. Does that sound like a plan, partner?'

'Why would I help you?'

'Remember how I said that I'm going to fire this gun, just once, to make a loud gunshot noise?'

'Yes.'

'The "just once" part is negotiable.'

He points his gun at my leg, which is strapped to the chair. He pulls the trigger. Everything happens out of sequence. There's a kick at my leg, as if someone has swung a mallet at my shin, cracking bone; and then there's an orange flame of gas shooting out of the gun muzzle, and then there's the report of a gunshot, loud in my ears. The pain comes later, a tremendous white hot burst of it, starting at my ankle and exploding up into my thigh.

I scream and wrench against the restraints of the chair.

Mitchell crawls along the floor, past me, ignoring my yells, and he hides in the corner of the room, down low, where no one can see him through the windows. From this new position he'll be able to shoot at whoever comes to my rescue.

'Ready, Mr Thane?' he says. 'I need you to shout out that you've killed me, and that you can't move, and that you need help, right away. Put a little melodrama into it, if you don't mind.'

'No,' I grunt.

'Mr Thane, I have more bullets than you have legs. I assure you, I do. And then let's not forget about that hacksaw sitting right over there.' He gestures with his chin to the desk. 'It takes a very special man to last more than a minute, when there's bladework involved. Remember, you're just a software man.' He emphasizes *soft*. 'You understand?'

'Yes.'

'Then in the spirit of partnership, if you could just shout out as I have suggested. Say, "I shot him!" or something like that. Maybe a "Hurry!" or two for dramatic effect.'

I clear my throat. 'Help!' I shout. I eye the desk drawer, where Liago's gun is within reach – surely it must be.

'Help!' I scream. 'I've killed him. I shot Mitchell. He's dead. I need your help. Please!'

'Very nicely done, Mr Thane,' he whispers. 'Now we'll just wait...' He stands up and turns his gun to the open door, ready to blast whoever steps through. Outside Liago's study, I hear the sound of the house door opening.

'Jim?' comes a voice from the foyer. Amanda's voice. 'Are you in there?'

With my free hand, I reach to Liago's desk, and I pull open the drawer. The pistol is there. I wrap my fingers around it, and point it at Agent Mitchell. I pull the trigger.

There's a *click* – but no more – just the sound of metal striking metal. No bullet in the chamber. No magazine in the grip.

Mitchell turns to me – his smile gone, his eyes soulless – and points his gun at my face.

There's a *thwip* sound.

Mitchell looks surprised. He stares at me with a questioning look, as if he wants to ask me something that has been on his mind a lot lately.

Then he crumples. He's dead before he hits the ground.

Amanda stands in the doorway, with a gun out, a long cylindrical silencer on the end of the barrel, pointing at the spot where Mitchell just stood.

She studies his body. Then she looks around at the rest of the room, taking in the carnage, with a strange clinical detachment that surprises me.

She sees the hacksaw on the desk. She goes to it, and she brings it to where I sit. She cuts through the tape binding me to the chair.

I try to stand.

I do stand, for exactly one second.

Then something in my leg gives way, and I crumble. Down I go, and my chin slams against the wooden desk drawer, still open, directly under the path of my head, and for the fourth time in one day, I'm out cold.

CHAPTER 52

She wakes me, and this time I know I haven't been out long. Maybe a minute or two. Maybe five. In the slatted window, the sun hasn't moved from its place high in the east. It is still Florida morning.

'Are you OK?' she asks.

I'm lying with my head in her lap, and she's stroking my hair.

'Fine,' I say. Which is not exactly true. My leg throbs. My vision is hazy, as if I am peering at her through an inch of cobwebs. I feel confused, dim, forgetful. My mouth is dry.

'We need to leave here,' she says.

I try to sit up. Pain shoots through my leg, into my back. My jaw aches. I taste blood where I bit my tongue.

I ignore the pain, and scuttle away from her, to put distance between us. 'Who are you?' I ask.

'You know who I am.'

'What's your name? Your real name?'

'My real name?' she says. She thinks about this for some time, as if she long ago forgot what she was once called. Finally, she says, 'Katerina.'

A man groans. Amanda grabs her pistol. We turn to see Dr Liago slumped against the far wall, his eyes fluttering open. 'Help me,' he says, softly.

I struggle to my feet. My head swims. I see a burst of light, and I feel myself losing consciousness. I grab a chair to keep my balance.

I say to her, 'Give me your gun,' and hold out my hand.

She looks at my open palm, considering. She clicks the safety off, and hands me the pistol.

I limp with it to Liago, slinging my weight from one chair to the next, keeping my shattered leg raised above the floor.

'I'm dying,' Liago says.

'Yes,' I say. I lower myself into the chair in front of him. I stick the gun against his chin. 'Tell me what you did to me.'

'Please, call an ambulance.'

'Who the fuck am I?'

'You're Jim Thane—' he starts.

I swing the gun an inch from his head and pull the trigger. The silencer muffles the shot, but the bullet slams into the wall near his head, and the sound of metal striking wood is loud, like the kick of a steel-toed boot beside his face. The wood splinters, and flies into his cheek. A drop of blood wells from the gash, and drips down his jaw. Liago shrinks away from me.

'Tell me what you've done,' I say.

Behind me, Amanda – or Katerina – or whatever her name is – says, 'Jim, we have to leave this place now.'

'Soon,' I say to her, and turn again to Liago. 'Dr Liago—' I begin. I think about it. 'Are you even a doctor?'

'Oh yes,' he says.

'What did you do? In our sessions? Our hypnosis sessions? What did you do to me?'

'I did what I was told.'

'*What* were you told?'

No answer.

'Who told you?'

'He'll kill me if I say.'

'*I'll* kill you, asshole,' I whisper, and I realize for the first time that I mean it. I will kill him. It doesn't matter what he tells me, or doesn't tell me. I will kill him for what he has done.

He shakes his head. 'You still don't understand what's happening to you, do you?'

'Enlighten me.'

He looks from me, to Amanda, and then back to me.

'The folder,' he says. 'Top drawer.' He looks at the filing cabinet across the room.

To Amanda, I say: 'Bring it.'

She hesitates.

'Bring it,' I growl.

She goes to the filing cabinet. She opens the drawer and removes the single green folder that I found long ago, when I was alone in Liago's office. The folder is thick with paper. She hands it to me. Her expression says, *You're not going to like this.*

'Read it,' Liago says. 'Then you'll know.'

I lay the gun in my lap. I open the folder and flip through the pages. Inside are the notes that I saw before – the tight cursive writing, the lines packed with blue ink. It's exactly as I remember – a chronological list of important events from my life:

VP Sales Lantek - Palo Alto 1999 - Met Libby Granville at The Goose (his waitress).

Jim Thane asks Libby to date him four times.

First time (1) "she said 'Go to hell - her voice plain. Pointed finger to show him direction to find hell.

Second time (2) she laughed - idea was hilarious - Very funny, Jimmy! Me and you on a date!'

Third time (3) handing him scotch over the bar. He speaks softly. Wisps of hair in Libby's face. Indecision.

Fourth time (4) runs into her at grocery store at night - express

checkout lane - spying each other's dinners -
SHE SAYS YES.
Party at Bob Parker's loft, Thane gets drunk, makes pass at
Parker's wife when she serves canapés, Libby escorts him home.

Gordon Kramer, St. Regis. Garage. Handcuffs. Parking Area 4C.
Sobers Thane up. Avoids Parking Area 4C whenever he visits St. Regis.

The list goes on and on, a catalogue of facts and trivia and minutiae. For a moment I'm amazed at this level of detail – they know so much about me! – so much about my life! How could they have gleaned it all? It's practically impossible…

Then I feel horror, as understanding comes.

The details in front of me have not been culled *from* my life.

They *are* my life.

I can recall nothing about myself *except* for the details on these pages.

Yes, I *was* the VP of Sales for Lantek. That much is true. But *then* what? I try to think back to those days… but can recall nothing about that company, other than its name, and other than my position there – Sales VP.

What did my office at Lantek look like? Who was my boss? I can't remember his name, or what he looked like.

I try to think back to my courtship of Libby, but I can recall nothing specific about it… nothing except for that single entertaining fact – so often repeated – that I asked Libby out four times, and that she refused me the first three times; and that it was only on the fourth attempt, when we met in the supermarket, that she agreed to have dinner with me.

'I can't make you believe things that you don't want to believe,' Liago is telling me, somewhere in the distance. 'No one can do that. That's not how hypnosis works.'

'Jim,' Amanda says. She sounds anxious. 'We have to leave here.'

I ignore her. To Liago, I say: 'Tell me how hypnosis works, doctor. I'm fascinated.'

373

'You have to *want* to believe things.'

'This is what I *want* to believe? *This?*' I shake the folder in his face. 'That *this* is me? This pack of... lies? That I'm married to a whore? Who's not even my wife? Did we ever get married? I mean... for real?'

'No,' Liago says, quietly. He pauses, considers his next words carefully. 'The real Jim Thane married a woman named Libby. That part is true. Those *are* his stories...'

'The *real* Jim Thane? *I'm* the real Jim Thane!'

'No,' he says, shaking his head. 'No.'

I shout: 'Who the *fuck* am I?'

And I pull the trigger.

The gun goes off, and I hear a crack, and I am extremely interested to see where the bullet strikes.

About a foot to the left of Liago's heart, it turns out, lodging itself into the wall next to him, although this fact is purely the result of happenstance, not aim. It could just as easily have been twelve inches to the right.

'Please,' Liago says, cowering, 'please. Don't hurt me. I only did what I was told. I didn't have a choice. He was going to ruin me. He was going to show those pictures.'

'What pictures?'

He shakes his head.

'What pictures?' I ask again, and I lift the gun to his forehead.

The words tumble from him in an incoherent rush. 'I had patients... addicts... young girls... I didn't mean to do it... just trying to help... he took pictures... I made bad choices... bad choices... I wish I could take them back.'

'Bad choices?' I repeat.

'He tempts you,' Liago whispers. 'You see? That's what he does. He knows what you want, and he gives it to you. Exactly what you want. And when you accept his gifts, he owns your soul.'

'You fucked your teenage patients, doctor. Let's not get metaphysical about it.'

Behind me, Amanda says, 'Jim, we have to leave *now*.'

I lower the barrel of my gun and place it on Liago's chest, pointing the muzzle at his heart. 'Get it out,' I say.

'Get *what* out?'

'All of it. Everything you put into my head. Take it all out. That party in the loft? That time Gordon chained me up in the parking garage? None of it was true, was it?'

'It *was* true. But it happened to...'

'I know,' I say. 'I know. The real Jim Thane. Just get it out. Take it out of my brain. Right now.'

Liago shakes his head. He looks terrified. He whispers, 'I *can't*.'

'Why not?'

'You don't understand.'

'What don't I understand?'

I push myself up from the chair. Pain fills my body. My nerves are on fire. For a moment, all the colour in the world fades – turns transparent – and I feel myself fainting – falling. I grip the top of the chair. 'Tell me,' I say through gritted teeth, 'what I don't understand.'

'He will kill me if I tell you.'

'*Who* will kill you?'

'You know who.'

'*I* will kill you,' I say. 'I will kill you. If you don't tell me what's going on, I will kill you.'

He looks into my face. 'You want the truth?'

'Yes.'

'The truth is...'

His head explodes like a Chinese paper lantern with a cherry bomb inside. One moment it's there; the next moment it's gone.

I'm sprayed by a pink mist of brain and skull and gristle. My ears ring. I look down at my own gun, to see if I fired accidentally.

But it wasn't my gun.

I turn. Amanda is behind me, holding the big pistol that I last saw brandished by Agent Mitchell.

'Why did you do that?' I ask her, even though I know the answer.

'He was suffering,' she says. 'He was in terrible pain. I put him out of his misery.'

She steps towards me. A shaft of sunlight lands on her face, and I study her. The sun is brutal, and now I can see the lines around her eyes, the dark circles beneath them, expertly covered with concealer. Her eyes are beautiful and blank and deep, hiding ancient mysteries.

'That's why you were always so interested in me,' I say. 'Why you were always keeping tabs on me.'

'Jim…' she begins.

'That's why no one killed you in the meth lab. Because it was you. There was no man with long hair, dressed in black. There was just you. You did the killing.' I realize something. I whisper, in horror, 'My God. You took out his eyes.'

She doesn't react. She just looks at me blankly. She lowers her gun.

'Should I even call you Amanda? Or Katerina?' I ask. 'Or should I call you Ghol Gedrosian?'

She is silent.

'Because that's your name, isn't it? Ghol Gedrosian?' I point to Agent Mitchell, crumpled on the floor. 'That's what he was trying to tell me.'

She steps forward. She kneels next to me. She looks into my eyes.

She's close, so close that I can smell her. Beneath the sweat and metallic tang of the crank we smoked hours ago, I detect that sweet floral scent, the scent from that night in the church basement, and from her bedroom. The scent of flowers laid on a grave, the scent of a funeral home. She says: 'I promise that I will explain everything. But we have to leave here now. There's a clean-up crew coming. They're probably already here.'

'A "clean-up crew"?'

She glances out of the window. I follow her gaze. Parked in Liago's driveway is a black Lincoln Town Car. Four men get out, slamming their doors. Their faces are unfamiliar, but their posture and demeanour is not. They are big and muscular and move with the brutal certainty of men following orders from someone more frightening than they. Two of them carry red gasoline cans. They come towards the house.

'They're here,' she says. 'They won't wait. They have orders.'

'Orders from who?'

'You know who.'

'Tell me the truth. Is your name...'

She stops my question, while it's still in the back of my throat, by kissing me. I let her. Her lips are soft, her mouth warm, her tongue gentle.

When she breaks off the kiss she says, 'We have for ever, you know. To get this right.'

The pain in my leg is just a dull presence now, like an old friend that won't leave after a long dinner. 'To get what right?'

'I'll explain everything,' she says. 'I promise. But you have to go.'

'Go where?'

She takes an envelope from her pocket and hands it to me. On the outside is written, 'For Jim Thane.'

I look at it without taking it. 'What is it?'

'Your last assignment.'

'I don't want an assignment,' I say, and push back her hand.

She ignores me. 'There's an address inside. Go there, and they'll fix your leg. There's also a plane ticket. Use it. I'll meet you when you get there. I promise you.'

'No.'

'You can't stay here. You know that, don't you?'

I look around the room. There are six dead bodies. Blood is puddled on the floor, splattered against the leather chairs, across the wood walls.

Outside the window, the big men are splashing gasoline along the base of the house. Just beyond the office door, I hear heavy footsteps in the foyer, stomping on the wooden floor. I smell the gasoline.

She's right, of course. I can't stay here. Not because of the dead bodies, or because of the gasoline being splashed through the house – but because Jimmy Thane is finished. His life is over.

I think about the money missing from Tao Software. The dead Dom Vanderbeek. The house on Sanibel. The hooker named Libby Thane lying on a gurney with her throat cut. Everything points to a man named Jimmy Thane. Everything points to me.

'I know,' I say.

'You can't be Jimmy Thane. Not any more. That's over. But we'll try again.'

'Try *what* again?'

She prises my fingers from the gun, and takes it from me. She lifts my empty palm to her face. She rubs my fingertips on her skin and on her lips. She kisses them. I feel her wet tears on my hand.

I say, with all the anger drained from my voice, all the emotion gone: 'I don't know who you are. I don't know what you want from me.'

'You will,' she says. She wraps my fingers around the envelope and squeezes my hand. 'It's time to go now.'

I stare at her. 'Ghol Gedrosian,' I say, trying out the name, trying to match it to the face that I see in front of me. The face that looks so much older than I remember Amanda ever being. So much wiser. So much stronger.

Yet still beautiful. I've loved her for ever, I realize now. The feeling comes back to me like a breeze on my face. Not memories, exactly. Just a soft feeling. A sense of comfort. The simplest, deepest kind of love.

'It's time to go,' she says again. 'You have a very long trip ahead of you. A very long trip.'

CHAPTER 53

It's a small shack, on a remote island near Orcas.

There's no road to it, no way to reach it from Orcas itself – no way to reach it from the place where the tourists stay – from the ferry, or the bed-and-breakfasts, or the holistic spas, or the art galleries. I have to hire a boat to take me there. It's a tiny skiff with a putt-putt on the back, and the captain is an old man with sunburnt skin and a melanoma shaped like the State of California on his nose.

On the ride over, as we trace the edge of Orcas Island, he explains to me that he also runs fishing tours, and that if I'm interested, I should return to the dock where I found him. He's there every day. I tell him I might just do that. But not today. It's been a long trip, across the country, and I haven't slept in a long time.

He nods. He rambles on about fishing, and the best hour of the day to find halibut and snapper, and the best hour to find him on the dock, and how if I time it right, I might even have the boat to myself without paying for a private tour.

We round a cove, and up ahead we see gigantic houses built against the water, with wide expanses of green lawn running down to the ocean and touching it. The captain grows quiet, and a cloud darkens his face. He explains that a lot of software executives live on this side of the island. He takes them back and forth to town. Most don't even know how to use a boat. Isn't that crazy – he asks – to own a house on an island, but not know how to use a boat?

It *is* crazy, I agree.

'You in the software business?' he asks.

'I was once.'

He grunts in a way that suggests this doesn't please him. But then we pull around the inlet, the motor putting, and we see the metal sign on a pebble-strewn beach, announcing the address that I read to him when I got on the boat. On a bluff above the rocks, he sees the shack, and when he realizes how small and run-down it is, how dilapidated and close to collapse, he becomes amiable again. I'm no different than he is. Not like those fancy software people.

'Never been this far back,' he admits. 'Didn't even know this house existed.'

'Hardly come here myself,' I tell him.

I pay him sixty bucks, twenty more than we agreed, and tell him to keep the change. 'Thanks,' he says. 'You need any help getting up there?'

He glances at my crutches, and then at the rocky bank that I'll have to climb to reach the shack.

'I'm fine,' I say. 'Pumped up on crystal meth; can't feel a thing.'

'Ha!' he laughs.

Minutes later, his boat pulls away, and I'm left standing on a rocky shore, in the middle of the Puget Sound. The air is cold, and smells like salt, and when drops condense on my cheek, they sting like tears.

The shack has electricity, at least. A black wire arcs from a utility pole nearby. I limp up the hill, the rubber feet of my crutches digging into pebbles, crushing shells. The door opens without a key.

I flick the light. The interior of the shack looks like an execution chamber. Wool blankets, black and rough, are taped across the windows, smothering the sunlight. In the middle of the room is a wooden chair. A video camera on a tripod points at it. Strapped to the chair is a corpse.

Most of the skin on his face is gone, and the patches that remain look like old leather, yellow and brittle, stretched tightly over a skull that leers at me. The man in the chair is held in place with black electrical tape on his wrists and ankles. He wears a business suit. His eye sockets are empty. He stares blindly, smiling.

There's a table on the far side, and a small metal wash basin. I close the door of the shack and go to the basin. There's an old metallic mirror above the faucet. I try to avoid looking at my face. Just below the mirror is a wooden shelf upon which a straight-edge razor lies. In the sink is a pile of hair. Dark brown, fading to grey. My own colour.

I limp back to the table. There's an envelope, and an old manual typewriter, and a laptop computer, which is closed. A Post-it note on the back of the computer says: 'Play movie'.

I open the laptop, and it wakes from electronic slumber. In the middle of the screen is a video file, named 'PLAY ME'.

Instead I take out my cellphone. There's one bar of signal strength. I dial a number. A strange woman answers – someone I don't recognize – and I ask her to connect me to Darryl Gaspar. She doesn't ask me who I am, or why I'm calling. She just says, 'Hold, please,' and then the line rings, and my old colleague, Darryl, sounding quite stoned, answers. 'Yo yo yo?' he says.

'Darryl, it's me. Jim Thane.'

His voice drops to a whisper. 'Jim?' He speaks quickly. 'Where are you? There's a hundred cops looking for you. What's going on?'

'I need your help. Can you set up a demo for me – a P-Scan demo?'

'You want to demo our product? *Now?*'

'I'll need to log in remotely. Can you set it up?'

'Sure… but… '

'No questions, Darryl.'

'Yeah, all right,' he says. 'You know how to use RDC?'

'More or less.'

'Write this down.'

I take out a pen. He reads me four numbers, a computer Internet address. I write them on the yellow Post-it.

'You can log in through that IP,' he says. 'What photo do you want to use?'

'I'll email it to you.'

It takes only a few minutes to set up.

I point my cellphone camera at my own face and take a picture. I stare at the photo on the tiny screen. The man I see is tired, and old, and worn. He has sleepy eyes, red-rimmed and bloodshot, and a glaucous complexion. His hair is matted, dirty. He needs a shower.

I email the photo to Darryl. On the laptop, I fire up the Remote Desktop Client program. I type the Internet Protocol address that Darryl gave. Now, on the laptop screen, I can see and control Darryl's computer, as if I am seated in front of it.

What I see on the screen is familiar to me. It's Tao's P-Scan program, except, this time, it's my own photograph – the one I just sent to Darryl – in the corner of the screen, labelled 'Target to Identify'.

I click the icon that says 'START SCAN'.

On screen, my photo fades and transforms into grey and yellow blocks, highlighting my dark and sleepy eyes, my broken nose, the width of my jaw.

The word, 'Scanning…' appears, and then, below it, flashing strings of text: 'DMV: Alabama… DMV: Alaska… DMV: American Samoa… DMV: Arizona…'

At California, the search pauses, and text appears: 'Possible Match', along with a driver's licence photograph. There's no mistaking it; the driver's licence found by P-Scan contains a photograph of me. Except, the name on the licence is: 'Lawson Chatterlee', and it lists an address in Los Angeles that I do not know.

Other driver's licences come up as positive matches, too – one in Delaware, again with my photograph – clearly and certainly me – but this time with the name Tyler Farnsworth beneath; and one in Hawaii, with my photo supposedly belonging to a man named Manuel de Casas.

Other databases are searched, and they turn up a surprising number of 'possible matches'. A search of *New York Legal Journal* shows a photograph of me, leaning over a desk and poring over a folio-bound law journal, with the caption, 'Attorney Stanley Hopewell joins Cravath, Swain & Moore LLP as a partner in their Intellectual Property practice'.

From the *De Moines Register Online* is another photograph of me, this one black-and-white, with the caption, 'Derrick Fruetel is being sought for questioning in the murder of his wife, Jane Fruetel. He is currently at large.'

Another photograph of me, back in Hawaii, dated two years ago. It's from a local newspaper article announcing that 'James Johnson, Child Psychiatrist' has returned to the Big Island from the mainland, and that I have opened a practice specializing in the treatment of teenage drug addiction.

I don't bother waiting for the P-Scan to finish. There will be other photos, too. Other names. Other restarts. I shut the laptop.

I put off doing it for as long as I can.

But at last, I do it anyway, because it's part of the script. The script that I wrote for myself, long ago.

I swing onto my crutches, and cross the tiny cabin, and approach the dead man waiting for me on the chair.

I see a bulge of wallet in his suit pocket.

Gingerly, I reach for it, trying not to touch the corpse. I hold my breath. My fingers brush something hard, and when I look down they are on white pelvic bone, just above his pants waist. Dried stringy muscle is attached to the hip.

I ignore it and dig my fingers into the pocket. I retrieve the wallet, a beautiful crocodile billfold. Inside, in a transparent plastic window, is a California driver's licence. It shows a photograph of a man. The photograph is blond, handsome, thin, with a pronounced bone structure that makes the man look regal and severe. The man looks absolutely nothing like me.

He does look, however, like the man in the chair – or at least like some version of that man – the version that was once alive.

The name on the driver's licence says: 'James Thane'.

I close the billfold, and gently return it to Jimmy Thane's pocket.

Back to the laptop computer. I open it again, and I click on the video file that I left for myself, at the centre of the screen, named 'PLAY ME'.

I don't need to watch for very long. Just a minute or two is enough. The image on the screen suddenly is familiar, burning through a haze of forgotten memory: it was recorded in this shack, by the same camera that stands on the tripod just behind me. It shows the man in the chair being tortured. It shows the horrible things that were done to him. His fingers being chopped, his body being cut.

The screams. The endless screams.

The man standing over him, performing these deeds, has no expression on his face. There is no pleasure. No disgust.

He asks his questions in a cold, unemotional voice, sucking every bit of information from the dying Jimmy Thane – asking him about his wife Libby, and his drowned child, and his ruthless sponsor Gordon, and that time in the parking garage, and what was Libby buying in the supermarket, that night you ran into her and agreed to have dinner?

The man conducting this torture, and asking these questions, is me.

I close the laptop, so that the screaming will stop.

CHAPTER 54

I see her on the beach, sitting cross-legged atop a rock that juts into the water, not far from the shack. She wasn't there when I went inside. She has been waiting for me, somewhere nearby. Or maybe she just arrived.

I swing onto my crutches, and down the lawn, and onto the beach. The rubber feet sink into pebbled sand. When I reach the rock where she sits, I slant the crutches against it, and I pull myself onto the stone beside her. The rock is wet, and mossy, and cold. We sit, next to each other, looking into the Puget Sound. She doesn't turn to me. Doesn't acknowledge that I've come.

'Amanda,' I say. 'Who was that man, in the chair?'

'Oh, him?' she says, with a casualness that horrifies me. She does not turn to me. 'A weak man. A customer. He never could quite pay what he owed.'

'He was Jim Thane?'

'Yes,' she says.

'And the woman I lived with? The woman that was my wife?'

'Libby,' she says dully.

'But her name wasn't Libby.'

'No,' she agrees. 'She worked for you. You promised to help her daughter, if she did a good job.'

'A good job?'

'If she convinced you.'

'She didn't do a very good job,' I say.

'No,' she agrees. 'The wives are always the hardest to get right. Love is so hard to pretend.'

'And those men that lived across the street from us?'

'Dispensable. They were supposed to watch you. To protect you. To keep the plan on track.'

She turns to me, and smiles. Her teeth are little white pebbles, just as I remember them. There is something so foreign about crooked little teeth. Something un-American.

In Russian she says, 'Do you know how many times I've explained this to you?'

In Russian, I answer: 'How many?'

'Oh,' she says. And she looks into the distance, and her lips move slightly, as if she is counting silently to herself. Then, she gives up, and shrugs, and says, 'Too many.'

We continue in the language that, until moments ago, I did not know that I could speak. 'Tell me anyway,' I say. 'That man in the airport. Gordon Kramer – he—'

'—was not Gordon Kramer. There *is* a Gordon Kramer. Jimmy Thane's friend. But that man in the airport, was just… '

'Dispensable.'

'Yes,' she agrees.

And then, thinking perhaps that I need more explanation, she says, 'You loved Jimmy Thane's stories. More than all the others, I think. You loved to hear his stories best. They fascinated you. That he was so weak. Such a disaster. You liked the idea of it. A drug-addict trying to turn around his own life – while trying to turn around a company. It seemed so… poetical.'

'Poetical?'

'You've always been a beautiful, sensitive man.'

'Yes,' I agree.

'Maybe that is the problem. Your true nature comes through. The real Jimmy Thane… he would have accepted the life that you gave him.

He would have taken the money, and accepted the wife. He wouldn't have asked questions. But you… in your heart, you are too decent, you see? Despite Liago, your true nature comes through. You are too smart. Too good. You can't just live, and be stupid, and happy.'

'Oh, I don't know,' I say. 'Maybe that *is* how Jimmy Thane would have acted. He was trying to change. He wanted to be someone better than he was.'

'I wonder,' she says. 'Was it Jimmy Thane? Or was it you?'

I take her hand. 'Katerina, who am I?'

'You know who you are. Why do you always make me say the name?'

Silence. We stare at the ocean. Fog is pressed into a thin band above the horizon. Just beyond, looming through the haze, is a dark mass of land – British Columbia. The sun is behind us, and I can feel it warming my neck, my back, and it makes the water sparkle with pearly iridescence. The world is a beautiful place, I think, if only men didn't foul it with sin.

I say: 'And Cole? That little boy?'

'Yes, the children,' she says, with something like sadness. 'They are the worst part for you. You do them yourself. You remember that now, don't you?'

'Yes.'

'You never ask other men to bear those crimes. Charles Adams's little girl. Jimmy Thane's little boy. Terrible. But you do it.'

'I'm a monster.'

'Yes,' she says, matter-of-factly. 'But you don't want to be any more. And that's what matters. You want forgiveness. You want your sins washed away. It can be done. I know it can. He promises us. It is written, that anyone can be forgiven. Anyone can be reborn. Anyone can start again.'

'Even me?'

The memories come back.

Rushing back, as if a heavy sea lock has rumbled open deep inside my soul, and the cold grey water has come churning back in. I can see them now – the things that Ghol Gedrosian has done. I can remember them.

He has raped women, in front of husbands and children, and then had those children killed to teach the men a lesson.

He has taken eyes and fingers, made grotesqueries of flesh and bone.

He has listened to men scream like babies as he cut them apart to make them speak.

He has walked into quiet suburban houses at night, and lifted sleeping children, and drowned them in tubs of water while their fathers slept.

I can hear the screams now. I can feel those frantic fingers grasping at mine, the hands of the little boys and girls as they struggle for air.

His deeds are vile. Evil. There is no other word for the things he has done.

For the things I have done.

Yet I know in my heart: I had no choice. These things were required of me. Circumstances required them. Circumstances of birth, of contingency, of chance. Who I was. Where I was born. Who I became. None of these were my choices.

It is easy to live without sin in a monastery in the mountains, or in an American suburb with white picket fences and two cars in the garage. Any man can do that. No one should congratulate himself for living that spotless life.

It is harder to live without sin in Chechnya, to be born in a war that drives children to kill their fathers, and husbands to kill their wives.

'Please forgive me,' I say, to no one in particular.

'Would you like to try again?' she asks tenderly. She tilts her head, and looks into my eyes. 'You don't have to, you know. You have a choice. You always have a choice. You can stay who you are. We can go somewhere together. Somewhere far away, where your enemies cannot find us. We have money. We can go to the other side of the world, and live on an island, and walk on the beach, and make love all day, and be together until we die.'

'That sounds lovely,' I admit. I think about it. 'But... '

'I know,' she says. 'You will always remember.'

'I can't live like this. Being this man. I need forgiveness. I need to be reborn.'

'I know.'

'Will we get it right this time?'

She shrugs. 'Maybe. We will see. Whatever happens, I'll be with you. Because I love you.'

'I love you, too.'

She takes my hand, and holds it in hers, and we watch the fog burn off the ocean, and a new day begin.

EPILOGUE

The headmaster didn't want to like the man who arrived that Wednesday morning at ten o'clock. He was late, first of all, by a full hour. Which is disrespectful, the first day you arrive at a new job.

But more importantly, he was a replacement for Steve Tanner, and the headmaster had liked Tanner – still liked him, even after what had happened. He couldn't understand what had made Tanner do the thing that he did. Why would you throw away an entire career over a woman? It wasn't just the fact that it was a woman – although, to be honest, the headmaster tended to be pulled in the other direction by Eros – but, female or otherwise, why would Tanner quit in the middle of the school year, and board an airplane, literally without a day's notice – and send a mysterious email when he landed, about a lover in Chile, and a need to 'follow his heart'? It was impetuous, almost crazy – not at all like the Tanner that the headmaster had known.

And now here was the new teacher, the replacement, sitting across the desk from the headmaster, in the expansive office, overlooking the manicured athletic fields, and beyond them, the grey stone buildings that housed the dorms and the classrooms.

The new teacher was older than the headmaster had expected. Dark hair, a bit of a paunch, sleepy eyes, a limp. A nose that had been broken, a bit askew. Not unpleasant looking. But the man's covering letters, the glowing references he had received from colleagues and superiors – all had made the headmaster expect someone else – someone younger, perhaps – someone more vibrant.

It didn't matter. As long as the man could run a classroom filled with twenty pubescent eighth-graders, and as long as he was available right now, in the middle of the school year, then he would do. His sudden availability – really extraordinary considering the time of year – meant the headmaster would avoid problems. There would be no pushy parents demanding to know why a teacher had quit an expensive private boarding school in the middle of the year. The fact that his replacement happened to teach Religion and Ethics – the exact subject that Tanner had taught – was an extraordinary break. Not that you ever wished disaster upon someone else, but that horrifying fire in the Vermont boarding school, that had killed so many – young and old – at least had had one salutary effect. The new teacher had not been in the dorm when it had happened, and so he was available, precisely when Tanner went AWOL. So lucky were these circumstances – it was as if God himself were controlling the events, making everything perfect...

...but no, that was an impious thought. God does not set fires, and God does not fill vacancies at boarding schools.

But still.

It was lucky. So lucky, that the headmaster had taken the unusual step of hiring the teacher sight unseen, without having met him, based solely on written references. So the headmaster was secretly glad when the man who arrived in his office proved to be acceptable: white, Anglo-Saxon, probably even Christian.

'I'm sorry I'm late,' the new teacher said. 'It's really unforgivable. To be late on the first day of a new job.'

'Yes,' the headmaster agreed, a bit startled that the man had nearly read his mind. 'But I suppose you're not familiar with the area, and the roads up here can be confusing.'

The new teacher inclined his head.

'Well,' the headmaster went on, 'there's no harm. Your first class doesn't start until after lunch. I still have time to show you the campus.'

'I'd like that.'

The headmaster studied the man. There was something about him, a gentle affability. He'd probably do well with the children. The headmaster complimented himself that he was a good judge of people. This man seemed to have a kind quality, something genuine, something that made you trust him.

'I think you'll fit in here,' the headmaster said.

'Thank you. I hope so.'

'And, if things work out,' the headmaster added, feeling suddenly expansive and generous, 'then we can talk about extending your contract into next year.'

The man smiled. 'I would like that. I have a good feeling about this school.'

'No other plans, then?' the headmaster asked. 'No desire to seek greener pastures?'

'Oh, no,' said the man. 'If you want me, I can stay here for a long time.'

The headmaster realized that he had perhaps over-extended himself, practically offering a job to this man without even seeing him teach. More cautiously he said, 'Well, let's see how these first few months go. We can discuss your future later.'

'That's fine,' the man said. 'I'm in no hurry.' He smiled, and added: 'I have all the time in the world.'